I0771282

AFRICA 1941

PHIL WARD

MILITARY PUBLISHERS LLC

This book is a work of fiction. Names, characters, businesses, organizations, places, events and incidents are either a product of the author's imagination or are used fictitiously. Any resemblance to actual persons, living or dead, events or locales is entirely coincidental.

Published by Military Publishers LLC
Distributed by Military Publishers, LLC
Austin, Texas

www.philwardauthor.com

ISBN10 -099681664x
ISBN13 – 978-09968166-4-9

For ordering information or special discounts for bulk purchases, contact
Military Publishers LLC
3616 Far West Blvd., Suite 117, Box 215 Austin, TX 78731

~~

Be the first to get updates and know about upcoming releases.
To be on our notification list, scan the QR below and sign up.

phil@philward.com

The Raiding Forces Series continues all the way to VE Day.

~ ~

DEDICATION

This book is dedicated to
Margret Ruth Ward, my mother.
When her time came she was as brave as a lion.

GETTING THE MOST FROM
THE RAIDING FORCES SERIES

The Raiding Forces WWII Series is written like a continuous WWII special operations campaign. It unfolds raid by raid. Missions are high intensity, rapid tempo of short duration, characterized by surprise, speed and violence of action. Characters rotate based on tasking and operational necessity while command relationships and strategic objectives remain fixed – win the war. Raiding Forces, the unit, is constantly being reconfigured to meet the demands of different theaters and mission profiles as the conflict develops.

These books are designed to be read in sequence with tempo, reach and lethality escalating as the war progresses.

Jump in and hang on. It's a wild ride.

Phil Ward
RLTW

PS: I recommend researching even the minor characters. Many are real people with amazing tales of their own. You may be surprised at some of the famous names that show up in the story from time to time.

RANDAL'S RULES FOR RAIDING

Rule 1: The first rule is – There ain't no rules.

Rule 2: Keep it short and simple.

Rule 3: It never hurts to cheat.

Rule 4: Right man, right job.

Rule 5: Plan missions backwards (know how to get home).

Rule 6: It's good to have a Plan B.

~~Rule 7: Expect the unexpected~~ *INACTIVE*

RANKS, DECORATIONS AND NICKNAMES

RANK PROTOCOL:

The first time a person is named in a chapter or after a chapter break their full rank and name is given. Addressing military personnel by their rank is a mark of respect. At all levels rank is earned and those who have it from a corporal to a four star general are proud of it.

DECORATIONS:

In the British military officers are authorized to put the initials of their decorations after their name. In the Raiding Forces Series the protocol is the first time an officer is introduced in a book the initials of his decorations are listed following his name. After that for the rest of the book they are not.

In the U.S. military officers do not have the same privilege.

NICKNAMES:

In the British military nicknames are endemic. Radio operators are called Sparks, red heads are called Ginger, tall people are called Lofty but sometimes short people are called that too etc.

In the U.S. military there are a lot of nicknames but nothing like the British.

ONGOING OPERATIONS

OPERATION BATTLEAXE.
A series of raids on Rommel's lines of communications in Syria.
Middle East Command's counterattack to retake Tobruk and relieve
the Port of Tobruk

OPERATION BRAIN-DEAD
Special Mission Team to destroy the military communications system

OPERATION BUZZARD PLUCKER
Clandestine operation that employed Lovat Scouts to snipe Luftwaffe
fighter pilots at their airfields in France

OPERATION CRUSADER
Four primary objectives.
1: Raid enemy airfields to keep as many Luftwaffe attack aircraft out
of the fight as possible highest priority is to Ju-52 tri-motors
2: Destroy enemy fuel dumps, installations and supply points.
3: Interdict the secondary tracks that parallel the Via Balbia.
4: Demonstrate in the Tripoli area. Reconnaissance of the beaches
where British Forces can conduct an amphibious tank landing. The
idea is to tie down as many of Rommel's troops as possible defending
against an amphibious attack that may never come

OPERATION LOUNGE LIZARD
Remove German and Italian ships from San Pedro Harbor

OPERATION PIP'S REVENGE (or PATHFINDER)
'Pathfinders' jump in first and mark the DZ for the main party

OPERATION RUTHLESS
Capture a Kriegsmarine air-sea rescue boat in order to steal an Enigma
machine from the Germans.

OPERATION TOMCAT
Conduct a parachute raid on an enemy signals station/lighthouse
complex, capture or kill the enemy personnel in the target area, collect
any equipment or documents of intelligence value, and withdraw by sea.

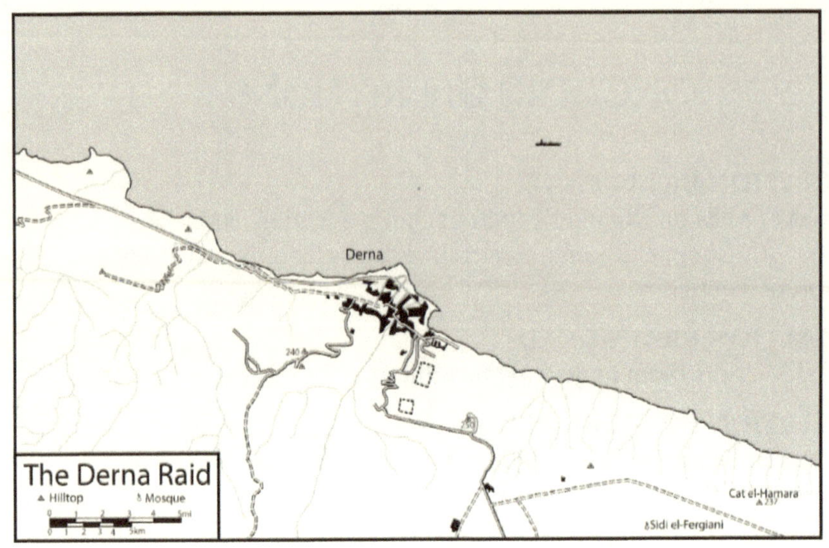

Derna
240 ft
Cat el-Hamara
237
Sidi el-Fergiani
The Derna Raid
Hilltop   Mosque
0 1 2 3 4 5mi
0 1 2 3 4 5km

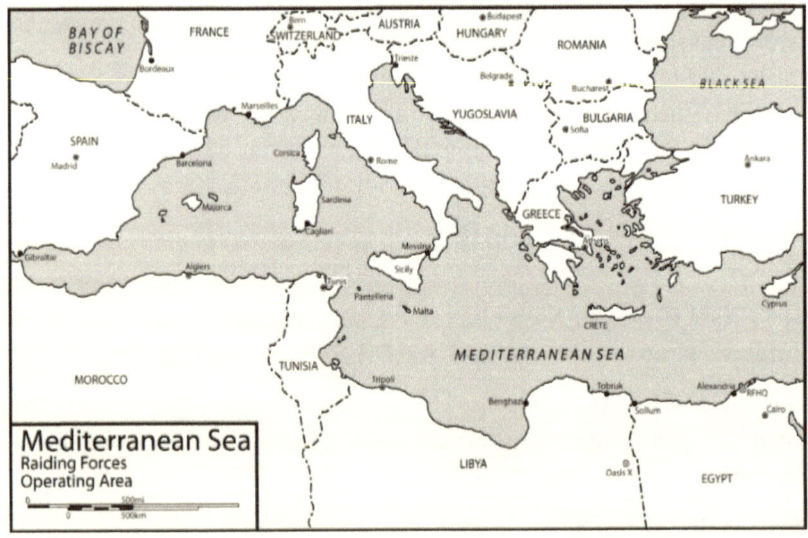

BAY OF BISCAY
FRANCE
Bern
SWITZERLAND
AUSTRIA
Budapest
HUNGARY
ROMANIA
Trieste
Belgrade
Bucharest
BLACK SEA
Bordeaux
Marseilles
ITALY
YUGOSLAVIA
BULGARIA
Sofia
SPAIN
Madrid
Barcelona
Corsica
Rome
Ankara
Majorca
Sardinia
TURKEY
Cagliari
GREECE
Gibraltar
Algiers
Messina
Athens
Sicily
Tunis
Pantelleria
Cyprus
Malta
CRETE
MEDITERRANEAN SEA
MOROCCO
TUNISIA
Tripoli
Benghazi
Tobruk
Alexandria
RFHQ
Sollum
Cairo
LIBYA
Oasis X
EGYPT
Mediterranean Sea
Raiding Forces
Operating Area
0   500mi
0   500km

1

NOT A BLOODY CLUE

LIEUTENANT COLONEL JOHN RANDAL WAS DRIVING DOWN THE Via Balbia, Rommel's main supply route, approximately 900 miles behind the enemy lines in the lead jeep of the remnants of Ranger Patrol. Their location was only approximate because the patrol was enveloped in an eerie white fog. No one, not even the veteran ex-Long Range Desert Patrol (LRDG) navigator who had recently transferred to Raiding Forces and was getting a check ride before being permanently assigned to a patrol, knew exactly where on the map they were at that exact moment.

Besides, the maps of the area were not accurate anyway.

However, Ranger Patrol was not lost.

The Italians had constructed roadhouse rest stops they called casas stratas every fifteen miles along the paved military highway. Sooner or later, the patrol would arrive at the one Lt. Col. Randal was planning to attack. Then everyone would know exactly where they were – or maybe not.

In the event the jeeps had drifted off azimuth as they twisted and turned across the broken ground they crossed before striking the highway and ended up on the wrong side of the rest stop the patrol was aiming at when they made their planned right-hand turn on the Via Balbia, then they would be lost.

Even if that had occurred, Ranger Patrol would eventually arrive at a casa strata and attack, but it would not be the one they had originally planned to hit.

Not that it mattered from a tactical standpoint. One Italian rest stop was as good as another to strafe.

The purpose of the exercise tonight was to spread alarm and despondency deep in the enemy's rear and to rebuild Ranger Patrol's confidence after it had taken heavy losses on its last mission. Material damage inflicted, if any, was secondary.

But raiding the wrong roadhouse would have consequences. Believing you are in one place when, in fact, you are in another does not help you read a topographical map.

Navigating in the desert is always a tricky proposition because terrain features are few and far between. Attempting to navigate in the desert smothered in fog the consistency of cotton candy while disoriented about your start point – you might as well be throwing darts at the map.

Lt. Col. Randal had to keep in mind one simple fact about land navigation: if you do not know where you are on the map, you cannot find where you want to go.

To the uninitiated, a topographical map is the military version of a road map. That is wrong. The only similarity between the two is they are both called maps.

On a road map there are clearly labeled streets that can be looked up in the table of contents. On a military map there are seldom any streets and virtually no labels. There is no table of contents.

Reading a topographical map is as much art as it is skill – psychic ability is a plus. What the map reader looks for are terrain features indicated by contour lines that show elevation. And colors – blue for water and green for vegetation. Sand is white.

For a topographical map to be of any value it's necessary to know your exact location. Military navigators spend an inordinate amount of time poring over their maps trying to figure out where they are.

Once your position is established, then and only then is it possible to decide how to get from where you are to where you want to go.

The trick is to sort out what you know from what you think you know and what you do not know.

Here is what Lt. Col. Randal knew: he was on Planet Earth. He was on the continent of Africa. He was in the country of Libya. And he was in a great big fog bank rolling down a paved road somewhere a long way behind the enemy lines with four gun jeeps armed to the teeth looking for something to shoot.

Driving down Rommel's main supply route in the middle of the night behind enemy lines is not for the faint of heart.

Lt. Col. Randal stuck one of the last of Waldo Treywick's long, thin, custom-rolled cigars between his front teeth.

King was on the pedestal-mounted twin Vickers K .303 machine guns in the back, locked and loaded. The ex-LRDG navigator, Corporal Basil Bunfried, was sitting in the right-hand seat fingering the pistol grip on his pair of machine guns.

Visibility was about six inches. The fog rolling in off the Mediterranean would rival any London fog Lt. Col. Randal had ever seen.

"You OK back there, King?" Lt. Col. Randal asked as he hunched forward, staring over the barrels of his twin Vickers Ks, trying to peer through the mist.

"Affirmative," the Merc said, "except I can't see my front sight, Chief."

Ranger Patrol was running two jeeps light tonight. Ex-2nd Lieutenant Billy Jack Jaxx, Waldo and five other members of the patrol had been captured on its last mission. Captain Pip Pilkington, Desert Patrol's popular demolitions officer, had been killed.

Lt. Col. Randal wanted to get the patrol back out in the field again as quickly as possible to prevent them sitting around Oasis X second-guessing themselves over what went wrong.

Ranger Patrol drove up on a group of trucks pulled off the hardball to the left. It was a convoy that had been attempting to run at night, but the fog had made travel almost impossible. Lt. Col. Randal could not tell how many trucks were in the convoy. Visibility was limited to the vehicles parked closest to the road a few feet away.

Field Marshal Irwin Rommel was attempting to push supplies down the Via Balbia twenty-four hours a day as he was marshaling for his upcoming offensive. He had plenty of everything to send to the front. Over 90 % of Afrika Korps' supplies were arriving in Tripoli from Italy despite the best efforts of the Royal Navy and Royal Air Force to disrupt the Axis air and sea supply lines.

That was the good news for FM Rommel.

The bad news was that after the supplies were unloaded, they sat, piling up on the docks in Tripoli.

FM Rommel had approximately 7,000 trucks. Not enough to transport all the materiel to his fighting troops. Even so, his ground transport burned up 50 to 60% of his total fuel supply hauling freight.

He did not have operational rail lines.

The constant attacks on the only two railroads that serviced Libya and Egypt by Captain "Pyro" Percy Stirling's Railroad Wrecking Crew II had knocked them out of the war.

All along the Via Balbia, Raiding Forces was doing everything it could to reduce FM Rommel's truck count to zero. Every transport damaged or destroyed meant that many more tons of supplies did not reach the fighting men of Afrika Korps.

In the scheme of things, destroying a truck hurt Rommel more than blowing up an airplane. There were 750 or so Luftwaffe and Regia Aeronautica airplanes in Italy and Greece on standby to be flown in to replenish aircraft losses.

A replacement truck had to be shipped to Tripoli by sea. The ship carrying it could be sunk, which meant another truck would have to be dispatched to replace the one that was lost at sea, which had been intended to replace the one Raiding Forces shot up.

Truck transport was Rommel's proverbial horseshoe nail.

The problem Lt. Col. Randal had was that his men wanted to raid airfields. Blowing up an airplane was more glamorous than blowing up a truck.

The instant Lt. Col. Randal recognized the silhouette of a fender through the fog, he opened with his pair of Vickers Ks. King commenced firing crisp bursts, and the ex-LRDG navigator, an experienced operator with more time in the desert than any one in Raiding Forces, was blazing away, taking out his navigational frustrations with his pair of machine guns.

Cpl. Bunfried was not firing short, crisp bursts.

In the gun jeep immediately behind the command jeep, Guns, the ace Royal Navy Patrol Service (RNPS) antiaircraft gunner who had volunteered for duty with Desert Patrol, was working his pedestal-mounted 20mm Oerlikons – *POKKA, POKKA, POKKA* – to deadly effect.

Each gun jeep in the patrol engaged as they came to bear.

Lt. Col. Randal was driving only about five miles per hour. The tactic of a slow motion drive-by was like a naval action – Ranger Patrol "crossing the T."

The 23 Vickers K .303s and the pair of Oerlikon 20mms were putting out a blizzard of tracers at point-blank range. The tracers looked like solid beams of light. Hard to believe the guns were loaded only one tracer every six rounds. The roar of so many massed machine guns was fantastic.

Several enemy trucks started to burn. *KABOOOOOM* – a gas tank exploded, sounding like a 500-pound bomb. The canvas tops on others caught fire. The blaze spread from truck to truck. Ammunition loaded in the beds crackled as it started to cook off.

The belts of ammo on the Ranger Patrol machine guns were loaded tracer, armor piercing and incendiary. The effect on the thin-skinned vehicles was devastating.

The trick was to aim low. That way Ranger Patrol was taking out trucks the gunners could not see due to the limited visibility.

Ranger Patrol had arrived unannounced out of the dark in the middle of the night with bad intent and achieved instant, overwhelming fire superiority.

Surprise was total.

Being so far away from the fighting at Tobruk, none of the enemy truckers ever dreamed they would come under ground attack.

They were in shock.

Most of the drivers were unarmed, having left their weapons in their trucks. Not one of the enemy made any attempt to retrieve them.

No one fought back.

Lt. Col. Randal saw the leading edge of a two-story roadhouse swim into view up ahead in the glow of the machine gun fire and burning trucks. He resisted the impulse to speed up – the urge was almost irresistible. However, the damage his gunners were inflicting was incredible, and he wanted to give them every opportunity to complete the job.

Continuing to fire his pair of Vickers K .303s mounted on a swivel on the hood with one hand while keeping the steering wheel straight by leaning on it with his left forearm, Lt. Col. Randal reached down and picked up his modified Italian Brixia .45mm shoulder-fired mortar. He rested the barrel in the crook of his left elbow. When the jeep rolled up to the building and came level with the front window, he touched off the mortar.

The weapon made a hollow *BLOOOP!*

Glass crashed, white light flashed, and a muffled explosion was instantaneous. Enemy troops inside the building could be heard screaming in panic as Lt. Col. Randal slowly drove by, continuing to fire his machine guns. King and Cpl. Bunfried shifted their fire to the building.

Guns' pair of 20mm Oerlikons were steadily going *POKKA, POKKA, POKKA*. The 20mm was loaded with tracer, armor piercing, incendiary and high explosive (HE). The HE rounds detonated inside the structure, popping like flash bulbs. The combination of incendiary rounds and tracers caught the interior of the building on fire.

Each gun jeep opened on the roadhouse as it slowly rolled past.

Originally, Vickers K .303 machine guns were designed for airplanes. The guns were lightweight, making them perfect to mount on gun jeeps. Their most distinguishing feature was a high cyclic rate of fire – so fast the weapons made a deadly stuttering hissing sound *TSSSSS, TSSSSS, TSSSSS, TSSSSS*. They did not sound like any other machine gun.

The Italian roadhouse was a shambles as Sergeant Ned Pompedous in the last jeep motored by with all guns in action. The building was pockmarked by what looked like a million bullet holes and smoking from the fire burning inside.

A quarter of a mile down the road Lt. Col. Randal pulled over next to a telephone pole.

"King," he ordered, "cut those wires."

As the gunners were reloading their weapons, Lt. Col. Randal held a hasty conference with his vehicle commanders around his command jeep.

"Nothing happened back there loud enough to alert anyone fifteen miles away. Let's keep heading down the road. See what we can develop.

"Tell your gunners I said to aim low – short bursts of six. Conserve your ammo."

Cpl. Bunfried looked sheepish.

King climbed back into the command jeep.

"Prepare to move out," Lt. Col. Randal said. "Let's roll."

The fog showed no signs of thinning. Lt. Col. Randal was driving with the lights on, but they had been modified to look like German "cat's eyes," designed for driving during blackout. The lamps put out only about a third of their normal light. He was not sure whether the cat's eyes helped or hurt tonight. The fog reflected the light back.

After a while Lt. Col. Randal turned them off.

King uncased the .303 Bren light machine gun stored in the back. He racked a round into the chamber then climbed between the front seats to sit on the hood, dangling his legs off the front of the jeep. The Merc rested the butt of the Bren on his thigh.

He gave instructions left or right when the jeep drifted off course or the road turned.

"When you see anything," Lt. Col. Randal said, "jump off on my side, hop in the back as we roll past. I won't fire until you're on board."

"Roger."

They had been driving an hour when a German soldier in a coal scuttle helmet and a great coat stepped out of the fog into the middle of the road, waving a red-lensed flashlight.

Lt. Col. Randal drove straight over him. *WHUUMP! WHUUMP!*

The Merc managed to jerk his legs back and tried to kick at the Nazi a split second before the sentry was ploughed under by the jeep. Even at slow speed it happened fast.

Without warning, King threw the big automatic rifle with the curved magazine mounted on top to his shoulder and emptied it to the right side of the Via Balbia. Then he baled off, waited as the jeep rolled by, and swung into the back.

Cpl. Bunfried opened as soon as the hood was clear. King ditched the Bren and transitioned to his pedestal-mounted Vickers Ks. Lt. Col. Randal swiveled his pair of machine guns as far right as the stop would allow and commenced fire.

He could not see a thing.

Tracers were hitting something solid and ricocheting straight up, disappearing almost immediately in the fog. Could those be armored cars? Tanks?

"What the hell are we shooting at?" Lt. Col. Randal shouted to King, but his question was lost in the thunder of automatic weapons fire.

Hot brass from the Merc's weapon was pelting the front seats.

Funny, Lt. Col. Randal thought to himself as the empties rained down, bouncing off his cut-down Australian slouch hat, never noticed the brass at the first target.

It was not so comical when a casing went down the collar of his sand-green Denison parachute smock. For an instant Lt. Col. Randal thought he had been shot.

The other gun jeeps began firing as they rolled up. Guns' Oerlikon was steadily doing its *POKKA, POKKA, POKKA*. However, some of his 20mm rounds were also ricocheting off, screaming skyward.

And that was not reassuring.

Finally, Lt. Col. Randal made out the shadow of a low-slung tank carrier with a German Mark III tank loaded on the back. Nothing Ranger Patrol carried could defeat a tank, but the tank transporters were nothing more than thin-skinned Mercedes trucks.

They started to catch fire.

A fuel tanker truck exploded, sending a ball of fire mushrooming up into the fog and creating a spooky, otherworldly glow. The light revealed a dozen tank carriers with Mark III tanks mounted on them. The burning fuel truck gave the Ranger Patrol gunners just enough light to aim – and they hammered the tank transporters.

The carriers started to burn, then their gas tanks started to cook off and explode. Mark IIIs chained on the back began to catch fire. Some of the tanks had fuel cans strapped to the sides, and they started to explode, raining liquid fire.

Lt. Col. Randal fired his Brixia 45mm one-handed, which really hurt, but he failed to hit anything.

Ranger Patrol's gunners were engaging at a range of not more than five yards. Raiding Forces trained extensively on the location of the fuel tank on enemy vehicles. That foresight was put to good use now. The tank carriers were going up one by one as tracers and the incendiary rounds homed in on their most vulnerable spot.

The engagement took less than one minute. It seemed to last an hour. Things seemed to be moving in slow motion. Firefights are like that sometimes – time warps.

As Ranger Patrol rolled by, leaving a scene of carnage in its wake, Lt. Col. Randal said, "Good job, King."

"When I first spotted that tank, Chief," King said, "the thought never occurred to me it was sitting on a carrier. My reaction was the Nazis had a new model – a monster."

Lt. Col. Randal said, "I can see how you'd think that."

Ranger Patrol had taken out a full company of German Mark III panzers. The tanks had most likely not all been destroyed, but any surviving machines would have to be returned to Tripoli for a maintenance overhaul to repair the fire damage.

Tank killing was not normally a Raiding Forces' task. They did not have a single weapon capable of destroying one. Knocking these out tonight was a big coup.

Lt. Col. Randal knew from a classified Enemy Order of Battle briefing that Afrika Korps only had 150 Mark III panzers.

Tank carriers were considered strategic targets. The armchair commandos at Middle East Command Headquarters (MEHQ) claimed that if all FM Rommel's tank transporters could be destroyed, the war in the desert would be over.

Being deprived of a dozen of them was going to be a problem for the Desert Fox. Losing 8% of his most modern Mark III Panzers before the battle started – Ranger Patrol was having a good night.

"Know where we are yet, Corporal?" Lt. Col. Randal asked as they continued cruising on down the Via Balbia.

"Not a bloody clue, sir."

2

DR. TREWICK, I PRESUME

"WHAT THE HELL?" LIEUTENANT COLONEL JOHN RANDAL SAID when he opened the package addressed to him.

Inside the box was what appeared to be a pile of fresh camel droppings made out of India rubber.

"MINES, ROAD, CAMOUFLAGE, DEFECATION, CAMEL, FOR THE USE OF," was printed on a card signed "The Great Teddy."

Drop-dead gorgeous Captain the Lady Jane Seaborn, OBE, RM, opened the enclosed envelope. "Teddy says these are experimental explosive devices he helped develop at Station XII for you to mine the Via Balbia, John."

"Station XII?"

"A MOST SECRET Special Operations Executive unit located at Aston House that specializes in developing exotic weapons. Teddy has been working there weekends after class at Eton."

"Right man, right job," Lt. Col. Randal said. "Teddy's magic tricks saved the day at Habbaniya.

"Exploding camel patties might work – fooled me."

"Teddy says," Lady Jane laughed, "that Station XII staff went to the zoo to study camel droppings in order to get them 'anatomically correct.'

"He is working up 'horse apple anti-vehicle mines with mule and donkey to follow.'"

Lt. Col. Randal said, "Ted must not have enough to do at school."

There was another package sitting on the coffee table in the small map board/private briefing area, which was part of Lt. Col. Randal and Lady Jane's suite on the third floor of Raiding Forces' Headquarters (RFHQ).

This one was not as amusing.

The box was wrapped in plain brown paper addressed to Lt. Billy Jack Jaxx. The return address was the Tri-Delta House, University of Texas. The wrapper was covered in fire-engine-red lipstick kisses with a different girl's name signed next to each one. SWAK – sealed with a kiss – or in this case, a lot of them.

What to do?

Ex-Lt. Jaxx was missing in action, believed to be a prisoner of war.

Lt. Col. Randal was not looking forward to breaking the news to the Tri-Delts.

CAPTAIN "GERONIMO" JOE MCKOY SAID, "SO WE'RE SUPPOSED TO sneak up on the Via Balbia, behind enemy lines, in the dark a' night and scatter fake camel chips on the road . . . hide 'em in plain sight?"

"That's the plan," Lieutenant Colonel John Randal said.

"You think these rubber patties pack enough wallop to do much damage, John?"

"I can't ask my demolitions officer – he's KIA," Lt. Col. Randal said. "And 'Pyro' Percy's off in the desert somewhere blowing up Rommel's railroad. But yeah, I think one of Teddy's toys probably contains enough explosive to take out a thin-skinned truck."

"It'll be real entertainin' findin' out," Capt. McKoy said. "That kid Teddy might have the makins' of a genuine genius. The real deal."

Veronica Paige arrived from Cairo.

She said, "Y-Service made a radio intercept of an Italian communiqué confirming the prisoners from Ranger Patrol arrived in the POW camps located at Derna." (The information had actually come from a decrypted message codename ULTRA, but neither Veronica nor Lt. Col. Randal were cleared to know about machines that could break the Axis code.)

"Derna," Lt. Col. Randal said, walking over to the map.

"Mr. Zargo took two jeeps," Veronica said, "and shadowed the enemy unit that caught Lt. Jaxx, Mr. Treywick and the other five men.

"Mr. Zargo notified my MI-9 office he is in the desert outside Derna trying to establish the exact location where the Ranger Patrol prisoners are being held."

Capt. McKoy said, "I'm headin' down to the radio shack right now, John, order my White Patrol refitting at X to saddle up and get started that way. You n' me can work out the details a' how we're gonna break Billy Jack n' the boys outta' the hoosegow while they're on the move.

"I can parachute in and link up with my patrol later once we got us a plan."

"Good idea, Captain," Lt. Col. Randal said, not taking his eyes off the map. "Do it."

Derna was located on the coast almost equidistant between Tobruk and Benghazi. That opened up a number of possibilities.

"Colonel," Veronica said, "would you consider allowing me to relocate MI-9's office to RFHQ permanently?

"Dudley has always wanted MI-9 Escape separate from A-Force. Now he is in prison in Spain.

"Major Stone, my boss – at least on paper, is at Oasis X commanding Desert Patrol. Which leaves me all alone to run the office."

"Jane?" Lt. Randal said, still studying the map.

"Marvelous," Capt. the Lady Jane Seaborn said. "You supervise my Royal Marines when I'm not here, Veronica, and I shall assist you with your Escape work."

"Thank you," Veronica said. "I detest the 'gabardine swine' crowd of GHQ staff officers overflowing Cairo. I do not wish to office at Grey Pillars."

"We can open the stables," Lady Jane said. "Organize the 'Raiding Forces' Hunt.' What fun."

"You said POW *camps*," Lt. Col. Randal said. "What's that mean exactly?"

"There are two prisoner compounds near Derna," Veronica said. "All the information available at present, Colonel."

"Jane," Lt. Col. Randal said, "message Warthog Finley to start steaming toward Derna. Alert Lt. Kidd to have Duck Patrol afloat when he sails. Tell him to stand by for orders. And pull in Randy. We may have need of Hornblower's fast MAS motor torpedo boats."

"Aye, aye, sir."

"Have Sea Squadron's commander cut short his leave and repair to RFHQ."

"Yes, John."

"Get Phantom to contact Mr. Zargo to inquire if he can use Lt. Huxley's assistance. Westcott speaks German like a Bavarian.

"If Mr. Zargo's response is affirmative, notify Terry to figure out some way to get Huxley there."

"Anything else?" Lady Jane asked.

"Butch is on R&R in Cairo," Lt. Col. Randal said.

"Alexandria," Lady Jane said. "Terry advised him flocks of single refugee Greek girls out for a good time had arrived in town."

"Notify him to report to me," Lt. Col. Randal said. "The Headhunter will want in on this."

JAMES "BALDIE" TAYLOR ARRIVED AT RAIDING FORCES' Headquarters. Jim was the senior MI-6, British Secret Intelligence Service (SIS), Special Operations (SO) officer in Middle East Command. Which meant he was in charge of direct action missions and guerrilla warfare for SIS.

Jim's assignment was so secret he used one of the most covert government agencies, Special Operations Executive (SOE) aka "The Ministry of Ungentlemanly Conduct" as his cover.

SOE believed Jim actually did work for it. In fact, his job description was the same at both spy organizations. All SO in Middle East Command flowed through his office.

Jim Taylor was Lieutenant Colonel John Randal's boss – only the Raiding Forces' commander did not know that for a certainty.

He was also Major Sir Terry "Zorro" Stone's boss, in the latter's role as the commanding officer of MI-9 Escape, which made him Veronica Paige's boss, something she was only obliquely aware of.

MI-9 was controlled by SIS, a fact classified MOST SECRET "Need to Know." Virtually no one, even those assigned to Escape, possessed the requisite need.

"Exploding camel chips," Jim said. "Brilliant!"

"General," Lt. Col. Randal said, "what do you know about Derna?"

"A windblown town," Jim said, "located at a point on the coast that juts out into the Mediterranean approximately halfway between Tobruk and Benghazi.

"Why do you ask, Colonel?"

"Veronica Paige has information that Lt. Jaxx and the Ranger Patrol men who were captured are being held in one of two POW compounds there."

"Interesting," Jim said. "I can have my sources provide us everything available on the place – enemy forces stationed in and around it and fixed military installations.

"Derna is a village inhabited by town Arabs who do not belong to any particular tribe. Italians run it."

"Good," Lt. Col. Randal said.

"Remember the tubby, middle-aged Russian," Jim said. "Major Peniakoff? He briefed us when you were first organizing Desert Patrol?"

"Roger."

"'Popski' operates a small spy ring of desert Arabs in the general vicinity of Derna. I shall have him attached to MI-9 straight away.

"He and another British officer, Major Chapman-Andrews, have a radio. They may be able to provide eyes-on intelligence of the POW camps. Zargo probably has someone in the area too."

"Mr. Zargo is there now," Lt. Col. Randal said. "He followed the bad guys who took Billy Jack."

"Colonel," Jim said, "I know you're planning a rescue attempt for Ranger Patrol. But let me remind you, you have been placed on alert for a priority mission to spring Dudley Clarke out of the Spanish prison where he is being held, or in the event that is not feasible . . . eliminate him.

"In addition, your presence has been requested in the United States."

"When did that happen?"

"Jimmy Roosevelt sent a wire to Field Marshal Auchinleck. Seems Capt. Roosevelt, a U.S. Marine Corps Reserve Officer, wrote a paper on Commando-type operations for implementation by the Army and the Marine Corps. His father – the President, as I'm sure you know – has endorsed the concept.

"You, Colonel, have been requested by name to fly over most immediately to brief the interested parties in person.

"The itinerary is for you and Lady Seaborn to fly to Gibraltar where you will be met by one of my operatives. You resolve the Dudley Clarke situation. Then you and Lady Seaborn continue on by air to the United States."

"I'm not going anywhere," Lt. Col. Randal said, "until I get my men back."

"Knew you were going to feel that way, Colonel," Jim said. "Settling the Dudley Clarke problem is a matter of National Security of the highest priority."

Captain "Geronimo" Joe McKoy barged in. "Veronica just got confirmation Billy Jack is bein' held in a transit POW camp outside Derna. No word yet on the rest a' the boys, includin' Waldo."

"Know what I used to do," Jim said, "when the Nazis invaded France, if they caught one of my people and imprisoned them in one of the small metropolises?"

"What might that be?" Lt. Col. Randal said, lighting a cigarette with his old battered U.S. 26th Cavalry Regiment Zippo.

"We walked into the jail and asked for the prisoner to be turned over to us," Jim said.

"Did that work?"

"Every time."

MAJOR SIR TERRY "ZORRO" STONE, KBE, DSO, MC, FLEW IN FROM Oasis X. The Errol Flynn look-alike 2nd Life Guardsman immediately went into conference with Lieutenant Colonel John Randal. They were best friends.

Maj. Stone was not happy.

"I realize Ranger Patrol is a Raiding Forces' asset, old stick," he said. "Nevertheless, White Patrol belongs to me. Either I am in command of the Desert Patrol or I am not."

"Roger that," Lt. Col. Randal said. "Captain McKoy and I got carried away responding to the situation. I should have consulted you first."

"Perfectly understandable," Maj. Stone said, "under the circumstances.

"What is the plan?"

"There is no plan," Lt. Col. Randal said. "Jane and I have to fly to Gibraltar tonight then on to the United States.

"You're going to take charge of the rescue operation."

"Vacation?"

"Hardly," Lt. Col. Randal said. "Here is what we know, Terry.

"Lt. Jaxx is currently being held in a POW camp at Derna, and we have the location. We've not established where Mr. Treywick and the other five Raiders are, but there are two prisoner camps near the town, and it makes sense they're in one of 'em."

"Intel on the installations?" Maj. Stone asked.

"Only that they're transit camps," Lt. Col. Randal said. "With prisoners passing through all the time, it's going to be difficult for the Italians to keep up with who's there and who's not."

"Advantage our side," Maj. Stone said, studying the map, "however small.

"Derna is isolated on the coast – accessible from desert and ocean, even better."

"I've ordered Jeb to report here as well as recalling Butch and Randy from their leave," Lt. Col. Randal said.

"Captain Finley is steaming toward Derna. Lt. Kidd's Duck Patrol is onboard his Landing Craft Tank standing by for orders.

"Jim is developing local intelligence with Veronica assisting. And that's everything you have to work with at this point."

Maj. Stone looked at Lt. Col. Randal as he took a Player's Navy Cut out of his elegant silver cigarette case and tapped it on the cover.

"Quite," he said. "Now, what is the part you are leaving out, old stick?"

THE IMAM RO.63 AIRPLANE CAPTURED AT THE MUD FORT LINED up on the road running past the Italian prisoner of war compound west of Derna. Snow-blond, Vargas Girl look-alike Lieutenant Pamala Plum-Martin, OBE, DFC, RM, set the plane down as light as a feather. She taxied up almost to the front gate.

No one at the POW camp was expecting an airplane.

The door opened. Capt. "Geronimo" Joe McKoy and Lieutenant Colonel John Randal climbed out. Both men were wearing Western-cut business suits, Stetson hats and Ray-Ban sunglasses.

Silver U.S. Marshal Service badges were hanging from the breast pockets on their suit jackets, attached to brown leather credential holders.

Lt. Plum-Martin remained onboard the Ro.63 and kept the motor ticking over.

A *prima capitan* accompanied by two *tenenti* rushed out the gate of the POW compound.

The Italian officers had no idea who was arriving, but whoever it was had to be someone of importance. The Regia Aeronautica did not make a habit of chauffeuring junior officers or minor officials to their destinations in its airplanes.

In fact, this was the first time one had ever landed here.

There was a problem. Neither Lt. Col. Randal nor Capt. McKoy spoke Italian. No one in the reception party spoke English. However, it was immediately clear to the Italians that the visitors were American.

Englishmen did not wear pointy-toed cowboy boots or pearl-gray cowboy hats.

Lt. Col. Randal and Capt. McKoy were escorted to the camp commandant's office straightaway.

The man-in-charge, *Colonnello* Mario Luigi Camarano, wearing shoulder boards sporting the three stars and Italian crown of a full colonel, spoke flawless English. He loved all things American and aspired to emigrate to the U.S. after the war.

"I'm United States Marshal McKoy an' this here is Deputy Marshal Randal," Capt. McKoy said.

"We got a warrant on a man you're holdin' in this here facility. A U.S. citizen goes by the name a' Billy Jack Jaxx. Appreciate it if you'd round him up for us, Colonel.

"Got hisself a date with the United States Federal Court in Columbus, Georgia, for desertin' the United States Army."

Col. Camarano said, "Billy is a deserter?"

"Shot a man in Phenix City, Alabama," Capt. McKoy said. "Jumped bail – didn't care to hang around and stand trial, there being about a dozen witnesses."

Italy was not at war with the United States. The two countries enjoyed warm relations despite the fact the U.S. clearly favored the Allies over the Axis powers. Col. Camarano did not intend to do or say anything that might be interpreted as detrimental to that relationship.

International politics were not something he cared to become embroiled in. Col. Camarano was sitting out the war in a nice safe job. Priority No. 1 was for him to keep it that way. He did not plan to rock the boat.

A U.S. citizen was not the kind of inmate he desired in his camp. Nothing good could come from having a nonbelligerent incarcerated. Even if the man had been serving (or observing, as he claimed) in the British Army.

If anything unfortunate should happen, it would be on his watch. The camp commandant did not want an international incident to put a blot on his record.

The arrival of two federal law enforcement officials from the United States to take the problem off his hands was like a gift from heaven. He picked up the phone on his desk and spoke into it.

"Billy is very colorful," Col. Camarano said putting the phone down. "Everyone likes him. None of my staff had ever heard of a panty raid. He promised to take them on one if they ever came to Texas.

"And hunting for the white-assed deer."

"White tail," Capt. McKoy said.

"I asked Billy how many Rangers were in Africa, the name was stenciled on the little car he was captured in, curious if many Americans were serving with the British Army," Col. Camarano said.

"Can you imagine what Billy told me?"

"No," Capt. McKoy said. "What'd the miscreant have to say?"

"'There are one million'," Col. Camarano quoted. "'All the American Rangers have to be kept behind barbed wire to keep them from striking off on their own to come and kill you bastards.'

"Billy is a Texas Longhorn."

"That's Jaxx right enough," Capt. McKoy said. "Too bad he's goin' to jail at hard labor for the rest a' his natural life."

"Would you possibly have any interest in the American anthropologist who was picked up at the same time as Billy?" Col. Camarano inquired.

"Anthropologist?" Lt. Col. Randal said.

"Dr. Treywick," Col. Camarano said. "Chicago Museum of Natural Sciences.

"The professor was on an expedition for the museum to photograph prehistoric desert cave drawings of aquatic creatures. He had taken the precaution of attaching himself to a passing British patrol traveling in his direction for protection from marauding Arab bandits.

"For his own safety, Dr. Treywick has been temporarily detained in protective custody here until we are able to determine the best course of action to speed him on his journey.

"He is not a prisoner."

"Well, we don't have any papers on the man," Capt. McKoy said, "but I reckon we can give the professor a lift to some place he can start his field trip all over again and hope for better luck next time or catch a plane ride back home to Chicago."

"I would consider it a personal favor," Col. Camarano said. "Dr. Treywick has been a model guest, more than generous with his seemingly unlimited supply of most excellent cigars.

"The doctor enlightened me to the fact that Plato, nor any of the other ancients, ever mentioned the color blue in their writings and that there were no known cave paintings anywhere in the world depicting plant life."

Capt. McKoy said, "I didn't know that."

Col. Camarano spoke into his phone again. Within minutes, ex-Lieutenant Billy Jack Jaxx was escorted into the room, soon followed by Waldo Treywick.

Neither man showed any sign of recognition or surprise at finding Lt. Col. Randal and Capt. McKoy in the camp commandant's office.

Capt. McKoy silently handcuffed ex-Lt. Jaxx.

Lt. Col. Randal said, "Dr. Treywick, I presume."

Col. Camarano pulled a Smith & Wesson N-frame 38/44 from out of the drawer of his desk and handed it to Waldo.

"Thanks, Colonel."

Capt. McKoy asked, "You wouldn't have Jaxx's side arms by chance? Need 'em as evidence for the trial."

Col. Camarano produced the weapons. He stood up to escort the party to the waiting Ro.63.

"Can't help but noticin', Colonel . . . ain't that the Military Cross ribbon you're wearin'?" Capt. McKoy commented as they were walking out to the plane.

"British ain't in the habit a' passin' out MCs in Cracker Jack boxes."

"A vagary of war," Col. Camarano said. "Italy was allied with England against Germany in the last conflagration."

"Don't much care for Nazis," Capt. McKoy said. "Seem kinda' fulla 'emselves."

"Nor do I," said Col. Camarano. "Hook 'em Horns, Billy."

3

SIR WALDO

EX-LIEUTENANT BILLY JACK JAXX SAID, "WE CAME OVER A DUNE and saw six or seven trucks displaying British Army markings all stuck in soft sand. Men in khaki shorts and no shirts were working with shovels to extract them.

"Mr. Treywick and I took our two jeeps and drove over to see if we could be of any assistance.

"Turned out to be a platoon of Italians in captured trucks.

"Rode right up on 'em before we realized our error. Captain Pilkington was killed at point-blank range in the initial exchange of gunfire. Then the bad guys swarmed all over us.

"We didn't stand a chance, sir."

Lieutenant Colonel John Randal said. "You're lucky you got off as light as you did."

"Bad move, sir," ex-Lt. Jaxx said. "Never saw it coming."

"Combat officers get paid to make mistakes," Lt. Col. Randal said. "Just not stupid mistakes.

"Would you say you made a stupid mistake, Lieutenant?"

"I've replayed what happened over and over a million times in my head, sir," ex-Lt. Jaxx said. "I'd probably do the same thing again tomorrow."

"Pip the first man you ever lost?"

"Yes, sir."

"You'll never forget it," Lt. Col. Randal said. "That's the price for wearing a gold bar and crossed infantry rifles on your collar, Jack."

"Have you had a lot of men KIA, sir?"

"More than I'd care to admit to," Lt. Col. Randal said. "When men like us get something wrong, good people die."

"You'll probably never have any confidence in me again, Colonel," ex-Lt. Jaxx said. "I wouldn't blame you if you kicked me out of Raiding Forces and shipped me home."

"Pam," Lt. Col. Randal said.

He was sitting in the right seat of the IMAM Ro.63 airplane she was piloting. Ex-Lt. Jaxx was kneeling on the deck in between the two seats.

Lieutenant Pamala Plum-Martin reached down, retrieved the large aerial map she had tucked in the cargo pocket on the left leg of her tailored flight suit, and handed it to him.

The blond pilot gave ex-Lt. Jaxx a dazzling smile.

Lt. Plum-Martin looked like she should be in a swimsuit on a billboard advertising suntan lotion, not flying a captured Regia Aeronautica plane that had just landed and taken off from an enemy POW camp a hundred miles behind the lines.

Lt. Col. Randal spread out the chart. "Right about here is an Italian roadhouse. The Via Balbia runs approximately a quarter mile inland off the Mediterranean coast along this stretch of the highway. There's a sandy beach seaside.

"Raiding Forces is going to conduct a small-scale combined operation raid to take it out.

"Butch Hoolihan will launch a team from one of the MAS boats to seize the beach behind the roadhouse. Once it's secure, Roy Kidd then lands Duck Patrol ashore in their DUKWs from Warthog Finley's Landing Craft Tank, *King Duck*.

"You, Jack," Lt. Col. Randal said, "are to conduct a night parachute drop with a handpicked stick of eight men to support the attack.

"Pam will be the command pilot flying the Hudson troop transport for the jump. She's also been designated mission air officer. When it comes to airplanes, do what she tells you."

Ex-Lt. Jaxx said, "Wilco."

"Plan to extract your jumpers by sea on the DUKWs or return overland to Oasis X by gun jeep," Lt. Col. Randal said. "We'll let the situation on the ground dictate which option to execute after we take down the roadhouse."

"Yes, sir!

"I can't believe," ex-Lt. Jaxx said, "you're going to trust me with another mission, Colonel."

"Somebody has to do it," Lt. Col. Randal said. "Lady Jane and I are flying out tonight to the States. Probably be gone at least two weeks.

"Be ready to go the minute I return."

"Can do," ex-Lt. Jaxx said. "What about rescuing the remainder of Ranger Patrol, sir?"

"Major Stone, Captain Pelham-Davies, Captain McKoy and Mr. Zargo are on it," Lt. Col. Randal said.

"Mr. Treywick will be working with them as soon as we get back to RFHQ."

"Request permission," ex-Lt. Jaxx said, "to be a part of the rescue team, sir."

"We'll see how it plays out," Lt. Col. Randal said. "You have your orders, Lieutenant."

"Who do I report to, sir," ex-Lt. Jaxx asked, "while you're out of the country?"

"Report?"

"For mission prep, sir."

"Apparently I didn't make myself clear," Lt. Col. Randal said.

"You are the officer in charge of planning the raid. Pencil me in for the jump with your stick.

"Let's get some payback, Jack."

"That's a definite Rodge, sir," ex-Lt. Jaxx said. "Airborne!"

LIEUTENANT PAMALA PLUM-MARTIN SET THE IMAM RO.63 DOWN on the private airstrip next to Raiding Forces' Headquarters on the coast outside of Cairo. There was a small crowd of men and women on hand – everyone present at RFHQ at the time – waiting when she cut the motors. The celebration started the instant the door of the plane opened and a grinning Waldo Treywick stepped out.

Major Sir Terry "Zorro" Stone popped the cork on a magnum of champagne and handed the foaming bottle to a startled ex-Lieutenant Billy Jack Jaxx. He took a drink and handed the heavy green bottle to Captain "Geronimo" Joe McKoy, who then passed it over to Waldo.

Captain the Lady Jane Seaborn kissed Lieutenant Colonel John Randal. Several of her Royal Marines kissed ex-Lt. Jaxx.

A number of men present would have liked to kiss the Vargas Girl look-alike pilot, Lt. Plum-Martin.

Lieutenant Mandy Paige, RM, said, "John, you are *soooo* reckless."

"All we did. . ." Lt. Col. Randal tried to say, but Lady Jane kissed him again.

"The Italians handed Mr. Treywick and Lieutenant Jaxx over," Major Stone said, "as simple as that, old stick?"

Lt. Col. Randal said, "Simple as that."

"Sounded like the single worst idea I had ever heard," Major Stone said. "Never actually expected to see you again."

"Agreed," Lady Jane said, hanging off Lt. Col. Randal's shoulder.

James "Baldie" Taylor said to Veronica Paige, "MI-9 Middle East Command is getting off to a ripping start. Today makes your second successful escape. Congratulations."

"I am ecstatic," Veronica said.

"Raiding Forces has a rule," Jim said. "Right man, right job. They apply it to women too."

"Only wish I knew what I was doing," Veronica said. "So far, MI-9 has simply been making it up as we go along."

"Been a lot of that going around lately," Jim said. "You can count on me trying to provide more support in the future."

"Mr. Treywick," Lady Jane said, "you are wanted in Addis Ababa."

Waldo nearly choked on the bubbly he was chugging out of the bottle. "*Wanted?*"

"A Royal Summons has arrived for you to appear in the Court of His Imperial Majesty Haile Selassie I, King of Kings, Lion of Judah," Lady Jane said.

"Wear your best suit."

Capt. McKoy stood listening to the conversation. He was studying Waldo through the blue smoke of the thin cigar he was smoking, gunfighter casual.

"I'd rather have you fly me straight back to Derna and hand me over to the Italians," Waldo said, "than to visit the place I was held slave for five long years. I ain't never returnin' to Abyssinia, no matter what Lady Seaborn."

"Butch will be there."

"Butch?"

"You, Lt. Hoolihan, and John are to be invested into the Knight's Order of the Imperial Abyssinian Star," Lady Jane said.

"A rare accolade, Mr. Treywick. The Emperor almost never awards honors to foreigners.

"Unfortunately, John shall not be able to be there in person since we will be traveling."

"Well, Lady Seaborn, I ain't gonna be available to make the ceremony myself," Waldo said.

"Send in my regrets."

"What a shame."

"You can explain I need me some serious down time for rest and recuperation due to the strain resultin' from my recent incarceration in that Italian POW camp.

"HIM'll just have to understand my weakened condition."

Lt. Col. Randal said, "I'm sure he will."

As soon as possible, Capt. McKoy discreetly pulled Waldo aside.

"Reckon ole Haile knows about the mule train a' gold you and me hauled out of Abyssinia after Force N stood down?"

"Don't know," Waldo said. "HIM might a' done found out about that. And our duffel bag full a' diamonds, rubies and emeralds you hand-carried to the States, robbed from all them monasteries and religious shrines by the lowlife shifta ras Colonel Randal shot his first day in country.

"The one a-holdin' me hostage."

"Hard to say," Capt. McKoy said. "Anythin's possible. Best maintain a low profile and stay alert. Too bad. You'd a' made a real good knight, Waldo."

"I'm gonna have to pass on bein' a knight, Joe," Waldo said. "Ain't no chance a' me gettin' lured back to Addis Ababa. Not in this lifetime."

"Yeah, that medal deal could be a fool's ploy," Capt. McKoy said. "But you gotta' admit, *Sir Waldo* does have a nice ring to it."

"Not when it's the *late* Sir Waldo."

CAPTAIN THE LADY JANE SEABORN WAS STUCK TO LIEUTENANT Colonel John Randal like glue. Clearly she had been worried about the rescue mission. He could feel her heart pounding like a runaway gun.

Captain Hawthorne Merryweather said, "Congratulations, Colonel. Well done, sir." The Political Warfare Executive officer, who had been attached to Raiding Forces in England for a mission over a year ago, had made a place for himself and stayed on ever since.

"Interested in taking on an off-the-books project, Hawthorne?"

"Absolutely, sir," Capt. Merryweather said.

"Meet me in Jane's suite after the festivities wind down," Lt. Col. Randal said.

"Yes, sir."

As they walked away Lady Jane asked, "What was that about?"

"Tell you later."

Ex-Lieutenant Billy Jack Jaxx was chatting up Lieutenant Mandy Paige and two of Lady Jane's Royal Marines. "There's a package on the coffee table in our suite for you, Billy Jack," Lady Jane said as they walked past. "From the University of Texas."

"I'll be up in a minute," ex-Lt. Jaxx said.

Major Sir Terry "Zorro" Stone was talking to Captain "Geronimo" Joe McKoy and Waldo Treywick.

"Upstairs in half an hour, gentlemen," Lt. Col. Randal said as he and Lady Jane walked by. "Ask Jim to come with you."

Lt. Col. Randal and Lady Jane went inside RFHQ to their third-floor suite where he changed out of the civilian Western-cut suit he had worn to Derna into his exquisitely Pembrooks-cut lightweight khaki drill service tropical uniform (KDS) for the flight to the United States. There were no decorations, only a pair of parachutist wings.

Lady Jane had packed his bags.

She was in the bedroom doing whatever beautiful women do. He had no idea what that was. Lady Jane was very good at entertaining herself.

Lt. Col. Randal was cleaning his 9mm Browning Hi-Power with the smooth, oil-finished, English walnut stocks when King announced, "Jack Cool and Mandy to see you, Chief."

"There's your box, Jack," Lt. Col. Randal said, racking the slide on his pistol when they came in. "Glad I don't have to write those girls an unhappy letter."

"Not half as glad as I am, sir."

When Lt. Mandy saw the bright red lipstick kisses all signed by different Tri-Delta sorority members, she said, "Help me understand, Billy Jack. You are arrested for trying to steal the girl's panties, now they are sending you presents.

"How does that work?"

"Aaahh . . ."

"Take the rest of the afternoon off, Jack," Lt. Col. Randal said, coming to his young Lieutenant's aid.

"You and Mandy hit the pool. Tomorrow, go to work. You've got your marching orders."

"Yes, sir," ex-Lt. Jaxx said. "I'll meet you downstairs, Mandy."

"Use our pool if you like," Lt. Col. Randal said, offering the small private lap pool on the flat-topped roof outside the suite. It had a great view of the ocean and it was very secluded.

"Thanks, John," Lt. Mandy said. "How nice of you."

"Captain Merryweather," King called from the door.

After Lt. Mandy and ex-Lt. Jaxx left, Lt. Col. Randal said, "We're not having this conversation."

"Naturally, sir," Capt. Merryweather said.

"I need a quick and dirty rumor campaign," Lt. Col. Randal said, "targeted against Emperor Haile Selassie."

Captain Merryweather asked, "What's the storyline, sir?"

"The Emperor recently smuggled a mule train load of gold and precious jewels out of the country," Lt. Col. Randal said.

"The treasure is en route to neutral Switzerland where it will be deposited into his personal, privately numbered bank account."

"Any part of that story true, sir?"

"Not one word," Lt. Col. Randal said. "At least as far as Haile Selassie is concerned. But I want his subjects to believe it is."

"Piece of cake," Capt. Merryweather said. "Am I permitted to inquire why we are undertaking this project, sir?"

"It's a private enterprise," Lt. Col. Randal said. "Not sanctioned by any governing authority. Except me."

Capt. Merryweather said. "Meaning completely illegal."

"Affirmative."

"You understand, Colonel, no one short of the Minister of Economic Warfare is authorized to target the head of state of a foreign power for a psywar attack – particularly an ally."

"I do," Lt. Col. Randal said.

"Major Stone and company to see you, Chief," King called from the door.

"No need to ever discuss this venture again," Capt. Merryweather said. "A tale of treachery such as you described shall spread across Abyssinia like wildfire."

Lt. Col. Randal said, "No fingerprints."

"I can do this one in my sleep sir," Capt. Merryweather said. "Love my job."

Lady Jane came out of the bedroom, "King."

The Merc followed her back into the bedroom to retrieve their luggage.

Maj. Stone, Jim, Capt. McKoy and Waldo arrived and took seats in the small briefing area. Lt. Col. Randal faced the group, sitting in a chair which was turned around backward.

"Time is short," Lt. Col. Randal said. "There are a few things we need to go over before I take off.

"Terry, you're in command of Raiding Forces immediately upon conclusion of this meeting.

"Capt. McKoy, take charge of developing the intelligence to establish the location of the Ranger Patrol prisoners – coordinate with Mr. Zargo.

"You'll want to rejoin White Patrol at some point. Squadron Leader Wilcox is away in England, so Pam is our air officer. I've instructed her to have aircraft standing by to air-land or drop you in to White Patrol whenever you're ready.

"Skipper Finley is steaming toward Derna and will take up station offshore. Duck Patrol is on board his LCT," Lt. Col. Randal said. "Warthog's standing by for orders.

"Capt. Pelham-Davies is en route here to assist with mission planning in the event a sea element is needed for the rescue.

"Terry," Lt. Col Randal said, "your job is to develop the situation, plan the concept of the operation and the scheme of maneuver, then message me before you act. If possible I intend to fly back to be a part of the rescue attempt."

"Will do, old stick."

"On a different subject, I've ordered Lt. Jaxx to begin planning for another unrelated mission. A raid on a roadhouse," Lt. Col. Randal said. "The operation is small in scale, but it will have air, sea and ground components. We have never attempted anything like it before.

"Lt. Kidd is en route here to assist Jack. Butch is headed to Addis Ababa to an awards ceremony, then he'll return here to help the two of them.

"Call on any or all of the three, Terry, if and when you need 'em for the prisoner rescue."

"Thanks, John."

"The rescue of Ranger Patrol takes priority over everything – patrols in the field, Lt. Jaxx's mission planning, the acquisition of Admiral Ransom's private navy . . . whatever," Lt. Col. Randal said.

"Is that clear?"

"Clear," Maj. Stone said.

"General," Lt. Col. Randal said, "you have anything you want to add?"

"Not at this time," Jim said.

"Terry?

"Have a nice trip."

4

QUEEN OF SHEBA IN TECHNICOLOR

JAMES "BALDIE" TAYLOR WAS SITTING WITH LIEUTENANT Colonel John Randal and Captain the Lady Jane Seaborn at a table in the VIP Club of the British Overseas Airway Corporation (BOAC) Flying Clipper's departure dock.

Since the Boeing 314 restricted overseas flights to thirty-six passengers, everyone with a ticket was a VIP, and they were all in the club waiting to board.

"When your plane arrives in Gibraltar," Jim said. "You will be met by an agent or agents known to you. At that point you will receive detailed instructions. Follow your orders to the letter, no more no less."

Lt. Col. Randal glanced at Lady Jane. Every time he had been given similar instructions in the past, things had tended to get very exciting very fast shortly thereafter. She was repairing her lipstick and did not appear to be paying attention.

"Spain has a common border with Gibraltar. Access should not be a problem for someone with an American passport," Jim said.

"Resolve the Dudley Clarke situation as quickly as possible then reboard for the flight to the U.S. The Flying Clipper will have developed engine problems until you are back aboard."

King arrived with Rikke Runborg who may or may not have been Marina Lee, the beautiful Norwegian ballet dancer and Russian spy known to have penetrated the Abwehr before the war. Who then, acting as a spy for the Nazis, stole the British battle plans in Norway, causing British Forces to lose the battle that ultimately cost them the Norwegian campaign.

Rikke admitted to dancing in the Russian ballet and being a German intelligence operative. Said she'd never heard of Marina Lee.

The SIS did not believe her. Nor did MI-5 Counterintelligence. They were convinced she was Marina Lee – master spy.

Rocky, as she liked to be called, was presently working for MI-6 and MI-5, making her a triple agent – Russia against Germany, Germany against the U.K., now for the U.K. back against Germany.

Part of the arrangement – actually it was one of Rocky's demands – was that she be seen in public with Lt. Col. Randal at least once a month. He was her benefactor of choice, the idea being that MI-6/MI-5 would not harm or compromise her while she was under his protection.

For obvious reasons, she had no intention of trusting any intelligence agency.

Rocky slipped into a chair next to Lt. Col. Randal; Lady Jane sat on his other side. King continued on to the bar and stood at the far end where he had a good field of vision covering the room.

The arrival of the dancer with hair the color of ice created a certain amount of tension.

She was reputed to have met both Stalin and Hitler. And may have met Field Marshal Rommel, when he was the commander of the *Führerbegleitbrigade*, Hitler's escort battalion that accompanied the Nazi dictator whenever he traveled outside the country.

If that proved to be true, it made Rocky a priceless asset for British intelligence.

Some of the strain was because Rocky had been the lover of Lady Jane's husband after his ship was sunk off Norway and he washed ashore, the sole survivor in the only lifeboat to make it off the ship.

Lt. Col. Randal had inadvertently come in contact with Rocky when he brought the couple out of enemy-occupied France for MI-9.

A photographer taking souvenir photos for travelers appeared at the table. When Lt. Col. Randal attempted to wave him off, Jim stood up.

"By all means, proceed," he said, reaching for his wallet. "Take one of my friends together as a keepsake."

The MI-6 operative had plans for the picture.

The photo of Middle East Command's top Special Forces commander, Lady Jane and the German spy was going to appear in the evening edition of the Cairo newspaper; Jim hoped Spanish Intelligence Service personnel operating under diplomatic cover at the Spanish Embassy would see it.

And that a copy with the photo circled would manage to find its way to Field Marshal Erwin Rommel's desk.

Always the consummate intelligence officer, Jim was playing both the short and long game. He was setting up Lt. Col. Randal's mission to spring Lieutenant Colonel Dudley Clarke out of the Spanish prison where he was being held. At the same time, he would be establishing Rocky's credentials as having insinuated herself into the rarified world of Cairo high society, secret intelligence and military special operations.

Jim believed that if you wanted the opposition to know something, you had to tell them.

"Are you packed?" Lady Jane asked after the flash bulb temporarily blinded the three at the table.

"Flanigan has all my belongings aboard your Rolls Royce," Rocky said.

Lt. Col. Randal looked up.

"Rocky shall be staying at Raiding Forces' Headquarters," Lady Jane explained, "for the time being."

"I see," Lt. Col. Randal said.

He had no clue what was going on. Not that it mattered. However, the thought of Lady Jane and Rocky making a joint decision without his being aware they were even in contact with each other gave him something to think about.

"Rocky does not feel safe in Cairo," Lady Jane said. "Especially after you shot the intruder outside her apartment."

"Well," Lt. Col. Randal said, "he's dead."

"Imperative we ensure Miss Runborg her personal protection," Jim said. "Besides, it does not hurt for the other side to believe their agent has infiltrated Raiding Forces."

Which in fact, she had.

LIEUTENANT COLONEL JOHN RANDAL WALKED OUTSIDE TO THE Rolls Royce. The former slave girls, Rita Hayworth and Lana Turner were sitting in the back. Flanigan was at the wheel.

"Could you give us a moment?" he said to the ex-policeman who had been his bodyguard/driver at RAF Habbaniya during the siege and was now performing those services for Captain the Lady Jane Seaborn.

"I'd like to speak to the girls in private."

"Sir!" Flanigan stepped out of the limousine, leaned against the bonnet and lit a cigarette.

Lt. Col. Randal climbed in the back seat. Rita and Lana were sitting in the front. They turned to face him.

The two girls had recently attended charm school in Alexandria. Lady Jane had wanted them to know which fork to use in polite company. However, they had apparently spent most of their time perfecting eye liner and eye shadow technique.

Queen of Sheba in Technicolor was their favorite new look. Rita and Lana were practitioners of the P-for-Plenty formula.

"Lady Jane and I are flying out shortly for the United States. I have a mission for you while we're gone.

"We're not having this conversation . . . clear?"

There was not going to be any conversation. The girls never spoke to him. It was a pledge they had made during a mystic ceremony they had conducted when treating him after he had been mauled by a giant, man-eating lion in Abyssinia. Rita and Lana were practicing Zar Cult priestesses.

They were also very capable with firearms and knives.

"I want one of you to guard Mandy while we're gone – understood?"

The girls nodded.

"You've met the pretty blond woman, Rocky," Lt. Col. Randal said. "She's a German spy . . . or she used to be. I want one of you watching her every second while we're away too – is that clear?"

The ex-slave girls looked at each other with expressions that could only be interpreted as "Oooooh!"

"Clear?"

Wearing serious expressions, both nodded.

"I'll bring you girls a present from America," Lt. Col. Randal said.

Rita and Lana twittered like canaries. They liked presents.

"When I get back," Lt. Col. Randal said, "I expect you ladies to spend more time with me. Haven't seen you much since you joined the Royal Marines."

He surprised himself when he said it but meant every word. The girls had been his constant companions all the time he was conducting guerrilla operations behind the lines in Abyssinia with Force N.

Lt. Col. Randal liked having them around.

The girls rewarded him with Lady-Jane-class smiles."

"I want a full report on Rocky's movements when we return," Lt. Col. Randal said. "Give it to Lady Jane – she can brief me."

Brandy Seaborn and Lieutenant Penelope "Legs" Honeycutt-Parker, OBE, RM, arrived at the Flying Clipper VIP departure lounge in time to walk Lt. Col. Randal and Lady Jane out to the loading gate.

Travel in the BOAC Flying Clipper was a throwback to the old-world, prewar luxury normally associated with first-class travel on luxury ocean liners reserved for the rich and famous. With only thirty-six passengers onboard, the ratio of flight staff to guests was high.

To rate a berth you had to be wealthy, titled, or a top-tier government official/ high ranking military officer.

Lady Jane qualified in two out of the three categories. Some might argue she was eligible in all three as she was the highest-ranking female officer in the Royal Marines.

The carry-on bags were already in their lounge – there were no seats or compartments on the Flying Clipper, only "lounges." When they arrived, one of the glamorous Clipper Girls was in theirs, the "deluxe suite" snuggled in the tail of the aircraft.

Each lounge was decorated in classic art deco – no two alike. The deluxe suite had thick, pale beige pile carpeting and cream-colored wall soundproofing accented by golden burled walnut paneling. Two plush recliners that made into beds were against the back bulkhead.

There was a small couch that could be put away to make room for a table at mealtime in the event the occupants chose to dine alone.

The Clipper Girl had finished unpacking their bags and was making sure everything was absolutely perfect when Lt. Col. Randal and Lady Jane walked in.

Lady Jane swung her purse up on one of the recliners. The bag was very heavy and clinked when she set it down. If the Clipper Girl noticed, she did not make any comment.

On his first trip on a Flying Clipper, when he and Major Sir Terry "Zorro" Stone had flown to the Gold Coast, Lt. Col. Randal had learned that Clipper Girls do not like weapons in the passenger compartment of their aircraft.

Inside her purse Lady Jane had one of his well-used U.S. Government Model 1911 .38 Supers, his .22 High Standard with its silencer and her engraved Walter PPK 7.65. In their checked luggage was her Colt .38 Super and his spare.

He kept his KDS uniform jacket on until the Clipper Girl departed the lounge. Tucked in a Mexican slide holster on his belt around back, under the lightweight jacket, Lt. Col. Randal was wearing his 9mm Browning P-35.

He was not expecting the plane to be boarded by pirates or hijacked by Brandenburg Commandos, but you could never be sure.

When a sexy voice over the intercom advised passengers to prepare for takeoff, Lt. Col. Randal and Lady Jane took their seats and buckled up.

"All right, John," Lady Jane said, "what mischief were you and Hawthorne cooking up before we departed RFHQ?"

"When we flew out of Addis Ababa," Lt. Col. Randal said, "Captain McKoy and Waldo stayed behind to take care of what they described as 'private business.'"

"I remember," Lady Jane said. "You worried about them for weeks."

"Their *business,*" Lt. Col. Randal said, "consisted of smuggling a mule train load of gold and precious stones out of country to Kenya. Waldo had it stashed away – never mentioned it to me because he knew I'd have used the money to finance the Force N guerrilla campaign."

"Where would Mr. Treywick lay his hands on such a fantastic fortune?" Lady Jane asked, intrigued.

"An archeologist sponsored by the Chicago Museum Waldo was guiding before the war discovered what he believed was King Solomon's lost gold mine."

"Are you making this up?"

"Negative," Lt. Col. Randal said. "Waldo showed me an old Chicago newspaper article describing the expedition. Read like fiction.

"The professor claimed he'd found Solomon's lost gold mine only to be chased off by a shifta warlord. That's when Waldo was captured. He doesn't really think it was King Solomon's, but there was a lot of treasure.

"When Force N flew out of Addis Ababa, Waldo and Captain McKoy went back to the Gheralta Plateau, recovered the loot and spirited it out of Abyssinia."

"Where is it now?" Lady Jane asked.

"The gold is stored in the basement of the U.S. Embassy in Nairobi in sealed crates marked as property of the U.S. Marshals Service," Lt. Col. Randal said. "The jewels are deposited in a bank in Beverly Hills."

"Marvelous," Lady Jane laughed. "Good for them – true action millionaires."

Lt. Col. Randal said, "You nearly gave Waldo a heart attack when you said he was 'wanted' in Addis Ababa."

"Why, John?"

"I'm sure," Lt. Col. Randal said, "Waldo imagines the Emperor was attempting to trick him into returning to Abyssinia with the promise of a medal so he could hold him hostage until Captain McKoy returns the treasure."

"Perhaps," Lady Jane said.

"Was the hush-hush project you and Captain Merryweather were plotting related to their treasure?"

"It was," Lt. Col. Randal said. "We're setting up a black propaganda campaign claiming the Emperor stole a mule train load of gold for deposit in his personal numbered account in an unnamed Swiss bank."

"Whatever for?"

"My idea," Lt. Col. Randal said, "is to force the Emperor to issue a public denial."

"Excellent," Lady Jane said. "If Haile Selassie says no treasure ever existed, Captain McKoy and Waldo are off the hook.

"Unless, of course, the Emperor is unaware of any gold or jewels being smuggled out of the country."

Lt. Col. Randal said, "Why take a chance."

"While on the subject of Abyssinia," Lady Jane said, "have you heard about Orde Wingate?"

"No, what's he up to now?"

"Suicide," Lady Jane said. "More precisely, attempted suicide."

"Wingate tried to kill himself?"

"On his return to Cairo, Colonel Wingate got in a terrible row with the senior staff at MEHQ who want nothing more to do with him. He was reduced to his original rank of Major," Lady Jane said.

"Lady Hermione Ranfurly, who works at Special Operations Executive, told me Wingate came to their office in a huff after the scene at Grey Pillars, only to be informed SOE no longer required his services."

"Fired him?"

"Went straight to his hotel room at the Continental, cut his throat with a razor," Lady Jane said.

"Failed – sent to an institution. He has been declared insane."

"Never knew the man," Lt. Col Randal said. "The newspapers say he's a guerrilla warfare genius."

"No one in our military command authority," Lady Jane said, "seems to share the media's assessment.

"Even Emperor Halle Selassie decided not to include him on his honors list.

"Colonel Boustead, who commanded one of the columns in Gideon Force, went to visit now-Major Wingate in the hospital," Lady Jane said.

"Advised him, 'Next time use a revolver.'"

"That's cold," Lt. Col. Randal said.

"Agreed."

"Jane, you tell great stories."

THE FLYING CLIPPER SPLASHED DOWN AT GIBRALTAR. THERE was not much to see since virtually all the military and civilian installations were buried in a labyrinth of underground tunnels.

The fortress was subject to constant air attack. And Gibraltar was standing by for a ground assault. Invasion by German troops advancing through semi-neutral Nazi-leaning Spain was expected at any moment.

The flying boat was towed in into a giant pen carved out of solid rock, which was also what Gibraltar was called: "the Rock."

The air crew deplaned, and the relief crew for the remainder of the flight to the United States boarded.

Red, the stunning Clipper Girl who was one of Major Sir Terry "Zorro" Stone's girlfriends, appeared at Lieutenant Colonel John Randal and Captain the Lady Jane Seaborn's lounge.

The question of the "agent or agents known to you" was immediately cleared up. Red had worked with Lt. Col. Randal during the siege of RAF Habbaniya. She was also a member of MI-6, the British Secret Intelligence Service.

"Here's the drill," Red said. "John, you are going to deplane and be photographed getting into a command car driven by a known Spanish agent.

"The car will depart the dock area, you will be driven to a location where you will switch into a different auto, wait a discrete amount of time, then drive back here and reboard the Clipper.

"Questions?"

"So," Lt. Col. Randal said, "I don't have to cross into Spanish territory, spring Dudley Clarke out of prison or kill him?"

"Your photo," Red said, "will appear in the Spanish newspapers saying something like, 'Famous British Commando Arrives on the Rock.'"

"That's it?"

"John," Lady Jane laughed, "after you shot up Istanbul, you could not possibly have believed anyone was actually going to allow you to go to Spain for a repeat performance!"

"Mine is not to reason why," Lt. Col. Randal said. "I serve where sent."

"When you get off the plane," Red said, "buckle on your pistol and do not smile for the camera."

"I can do that."

5

GERONIMO!

IT WAS LATE IN THE AFTERNOON. LIEUTENANT COLONEL JOHN Randal was standing aboard a Douglas C-39 flying out of Lawson Army Airfield at Fort Benning, Georgia. He was hooked up in a line of novice paratroopers still in training. Down below was the Chattahoochee River. The stick was waiting for the green light.

This was his fifth jump of the day.

Captain James "Jimmy" Roosevelt, USMCR, had arranged for him to visit the U.S. Army's Provisional Parachute Group commanded by Colonel William "Bill" Lee. Paratroopers were a new component of the U.S. Army consisting of neophyte jumpers. The staff of the new outfit was pretty much making it up as they went along.

No one at Provisional Parachute Group knew about the organization, doctrine, strategy or tactics of Airborne Infantry. There were no governing U.S. Army manuals. The planners were copying the British and even the German method when they could lay their hands on the information.

Nevertheless, Lt. Col. Randal's assessment was that Col. Lee and his staff were doing a pretty good job.

Capt. Roosevelt had hoped the commander of Raiding Forces might be able to share his experience with airborne operations. That did not exactly happen.

No one was very interested.

What did take place was that he was assigned an escort officer, Captain James M. Gavin aka "Slim Jim" or "Jumping Jim," commander of C Company, 503rd Parachute Infantry Battalion. The two had met briefly in the Philippines when they were lieutenants serving in the Islands.

Capt. Gavin arranged a whirlwind tour of the U.S. Army Airborne School, better known as "Jump School," which was modeled on the No. 1 British Parachute Training Establishment. It had swing landing trainers, thirty-four-foot towers to simulate exiting an aircraft, and giant fans that blew towed parachutists to teach them how to recover from a jump in winds. There was a lot of sawdust, men jumping off platforms of various heights practicing parachute landing falls (PLFs) and soldiers in formation double-timing from one training station to another.

And push-ups. A lot of push-ups.

Everywhere Lt. Col. Randal looked, men were on the move.

The main noticeable difference between the British and U.S. schools were the four 250-foot towers at Ft. Benning that dominated the flat Georgia skyline. The towers had been brought to the fort from the 1939 New York World's Fair where they had been a major attraction called "Parachute Jump."

The tall structures proved to be outstanding training devices. Seeing how high the pylons were, a lot of men who had volunteered for service in the paratroops decided on the spot that jumping out of an aircraft-in-flight was a bad decision. Those soldiers went back to their original units, wiser men.

Others found they could do it.

The U.S. Army utilized the T-5 parachute produced by the Reliance Manufacturing Corporation – a reassuring name for a company that made parachutes. The T-5 was a fast-deploying chute, the fastest in the world, but at a price. It delivered a punishing opening shock.

Lt. Col. Randal hated it.

More importantly, the T-5 harness did not have a quick release system. The jumper had to land and then unbuckle the wide canvas harness straps. That could be problematic if the jumper was being dragged by the canopy or if the straps were wet.

The good news was that U.S. Army paratroopers jumped with a reserve parachute. Lt. Col. Randal liked that. British Airborne Forces did not have reserves.

Capt. Gavin said, "Jump School is three weeks long. The first week we separate the men from the boys. In week two we separate the men from the fools. Week three – the fools jump out of a perfectly good airplane."

"There's something to be said for serving in a military outfit where everyone in it admits he's crazy right out front," Lt. Col. Randal said.

At Capt. Roosevelt's behest, before traveling to Ft. Benning, Lt. Col. Randal had met separately with representatives from the U.S. Marine Corps and the U.S. Army. He briefed them about British Combined Operations training, the general table of organization & equipment (TO&E) of a Commando Battalion, Raiding Forces' amphibious small-scale, pinprick raids and parachute operations – at least the parts he could talk about.

Results were mixed. The Marines were receptive to the British Commando concept and were already planning to organize a raiding battalion though they considered the Marine Corps an elite organization and were not much interested in having an 'elite within an elite'.

The Army had no plans for a Commando-type unit.

The Marines were openly dismissive of paratroopers even though the Corps currently had three battalions of Para-Marines in training.

The Army was all for them.

After completing his tour of the Provisional Parachute Group at Ft. Benning, Lt. Col. Randal was scheduled to travel back to Washington, D.C., to meet with Colonel William "Wild Bill" Donovan, a politically connected lawyer who headed the Office for Coordination of Information (OCI).

The United States did not have a national intelligence agency, but it was planning to organize one. Col. Donovan was the leading candidate to run it. He was not on active duty but everyone called him Colonel because he had commanded the "Fighting 69th Regiment" in the last war, earning the Medal of Honor.

Most likely the U.S. Intelligence Agency would be divided into two divisions: secret intelligence (SI) and special operations (SO). Col. Donovan and Capt. Roosevelt wanted to consult with Lt. Col. Randal on how best to quickly involve the U.S. in special operations in the event America entered the war against Germany.

Down below orange smoke could be seen drifting across the drop zone (DZ). This was Lt. Col. Randal's qualifying jump for U.S. Airborne Wings. It was a macho test to do all five in one day. The leading lights at the Provisional Parachute Group wanted to see if he had the right stuff.

Following the jump, Lt. Col. Randal would have his wings pinned on by Captain the Lady Jane Seaborn who was observing today – escorted by the Deputy Post Commander. Then all the Airborne officers would repair to the Ft. Benning officer's club and conduct a ritual known as a "Prop Blast," with Lt. Col. Randal, the honoree, being "blasted."

Prop Blasts are a stag party. No women allowed. Not even strippers – maybe the occasional stripper.

The paratroopers would drink a secret concoction of alcohol called Prop Blast, get drunk, sing *Blood on the Risers,* scream "Geronimo" and jump off tables. Hopefully, no one would be injured too badly.

Lady Jane was less than thrilled at not being invited.

"There's a number of theories," Capt. Gavin said to Lt. Col. Randal as they were standing holding their yellow static lines in their right hands, knees bent, swaying with the buffeting of the aircraft as it thundered toward the DZ, waiting for the green light, "concerning the origin of shouting 'Geronimo' when we jump."

"Been wondering about that," Lt. Col. Randal said over his shoulder.

"One version is the movie *Geronimo* was showing in Columbus the night before Lieutenant Red Ryder's Test Platoon made one of its jumps. Several of the platoon members went to see it. As the story goes, someone dared the lead jumper he was not cool enough to shout 'Geronimo' as he exited," Capt. Gavin said.

"Another is there was a carnival with a shooting exhibition out in front of Infantry Hall the afternoon before the jump. The old silver-haired gunfighter putting on the show was named Joe,' and he could shoot the lights out.

"He observed the jump the next day. I know because I was there. Personally, I believe the Test Platoon guys were shouting at him."

Lt. Col. Randal turned his head toward Capt. Gavin in disbelief, but at that instant the jumpmaster barked, "GO!"

The stick started shuffling forward. When he got to the door, Lt. Col. Randal slammed his snap link at the jumpmaster, turned right, slapped his hands outside against the skin of the Dakota and leapt out into space. Placing his hands on the ends of the reserve chute, feet and knees together, elbows tight against his sides, he tucked his head down on his chest in anticipation of the opening shock he knew, from four previous jump experiences, was coming hard and fast.

He shouted, "GERONIMO!"

The T-5 cracked open with its customary bone-shattering jar. Lt. Col. Randal really hated that parachute. The British Army did not have much gear he preferred to its U.S. counterpart, but the X-chute was one of them. It was a substantially superior parachute to jump.

On the DZ, Captain William P. Yarbrough, S-2 (Intelligence Officer) of the Provisional Parachute Group was waiting when he jogged up to the assembly point.

Lt. Col. Randal had the T-5 parachute packed in a lightweight universal parachute recovery bag. The parachute bag was snapped to the reserve and slung over his head, riding on his back like a pack. The reserve was on his chest in the approved airborne manner. Swinging the parachute to the ground, he returned the salute.

Capt. Yarbrough was a legend in the Provisional Parachute Group, having designed the silver parachutist badge. The captain also designed the jump suit based on a safari-style jacket with pants sporting large cargo side pockets. And he was responsible for having selected the slick, brown, high-topped Corcoran jump boots that U.S. Army paratroopers proudly bloused their pants into so they could show the world they were a superior breed of fighting men.

Promotion came slow in the peacetime U.S. Army – Capt. Yarbrough and Capt. Gavin had been senior to Lt. Col. Randal in the Philippines.

Capt. Yarbrough saluted, "Sir, a message marked 'CONFIDENTIAL' arrived for you. Lady Seaborn read it and had the general drive her to your quarters in order to begin packing for your immediate departure. My instructions are to take you there ASAP."

Lt. Col. Randal opened the brown envelope and read the flimsy.

```
LOCATION OF RP PERSONNEL KNOWN.
PREPOSITIONING OF ELEMENTS FOR
RESCUE. ATTEMPT ONGOING. YOUR
RETURN REQUESTED MOST IMMEDIATE
STONE
```

"Let's go."

In the car, Capt. Gavin said, "Looks like you're not going to make the Prop Blast tonight, sir."

"Maybe next time," Lt. Col. Randal said.

"Too bad, sir," Capt. Yarbrough said regretfully. "Our plan was to get you drunk then pump you for everything you know about airborne operations."

"I'll give you men the short version," Lt. Col. Randal said, "right now."

"We liked our idea better, sir."

Lt. Col. Randal said, "Hate it when a good plan goes south."

The two paratroop captains laughed.

"The purpose of the exercise," Lt. Col. Randal said, "is to get your troopers from the jump aircraft to the ground in one piece, assembled in a tactical formation with all their weapons and equipment ready to move out to the objective and fight as fast as possible. Sounds simple, but it's not.

"Get rid of the T-5 parachute and adopt the British X-type. It opens without any discernible shock. Your paratroopers will like to jump it and it won't rip off their exposed equipment the way the T-5 is going to. On an actual combat jump, each jumper will carry as much ammunition and equipment as he physically can – extra grenades, knives, pistols – you name it. That's important.

"Both the Brits, the Germans and now your Provisional Parachute Group all drop their rifles, submachine guns and other crew-served weapons separately packed in containers, then recover them on the DZ. You don't want to do that.

"In my outfit, Raiding Forces, we break ours down then put the disassembled weapons in canvas jump bags. Then we tie the bag to our left leg with a lowering line. Experiment with that technique – there's no hunting for lost bundles in the dark of night unarmed behind enemy lines.

"Adopt a quick-release system," Lt. Col. Randal said. "Without one, you're going to lose a lot of people on combat jumps trying to unbuckle from their parachute. On actual missions you're going to jump in excessive winds, land in water, people shooting at you . . . whatever."

"Anything else, sir?" Capt. Yarbrough asked.

"About it," Lt. Col. Randal said. "We're experimenting with deploying a team of 'pathfinders' who jump in first and mark the DZ for the main party, but we don't have the tactics perfected yet. Might want to give the idea some thought.

"You men are doing a good job."

"Lt. Billy Jack Jaxx was one of my platoon leaders," Capt. Gavin said as the khaki-colored Chevrolet staff car arrived at the beautiful Ft. Benning officers' club where he had been staying.

"At least he was for one day before shooting the officer prisoner he was escorting."

"Heard the story," Lt. Col. Randal said.

"I handpicked Lt. Jaxx for my company," Capt. Gavin said, "because a buddy of mine who is the Officer-in-Charge of the Leadership Committee over at the Officer's Candidate School told me Jaxx tested out the best score of anyone who had ever come through the course."

"Captain Travis McCloud mentioned that," Lt. Col. Randal said. "You know him?"

"We know McCloud," Capt. Yarbrough said. "Used to be the Airborne Tactics instructor at the Infantry School before he volunteered for service in the American Volunteer Group."

"In that case, Travis can tell you everything you need to know about parachute operations," Lt. Col. Randal said.

"He was my Operations Officer for a night combat jump on a country we were invading – some of the details are classified, but McCloud planned the airborne phase for Raiding Forces and went on it.

"Mail him a list of questions you want answered, or send someone out to Egypt to do a post-mission interview. I'll authorize Travis to discuss the tactical aspects of the operation – make him available to talk to you if that's the way you want to go."

"Might be possible to arrange, sir," Capt. Yarbrough said.

"Better yet, Lt. Jaxx is working up a small-scale airborne raid we intend to execute shortly after I get back," Lt. Col. Randal said. "Come over – go along and observe our mission if you like."

"I'll do my best," Capt. Yarbrough said, "to make *that* happen, Colonel."

"Is it true, sir," Capt. Gavin asked, "you walked into an Italian POW camp a hundred miles behind the lines disguised as a United States Marshal and rescued 'Jack Cool' after he got himself captured?"

"A lot easier in the doing," Lt. Col. Randal said, getting out of the car, "than the telling."

THE FLYING CLIPPER TOOK OFF. LIEUTENANT COLONEL JOHN Randal and Captain the Lady Jane Seaborn were comfortably ensconced in the deluxe suite in the tail of the airplane. Red was on board.

They had not expected to be returning so soon.

Red said, "The Spanish authorities released Dudley Clarke within twenty-four hours after you were photographed on Gibraltar."

"No kidding?"

"Unfortunately, Dudley is under a cloud," Lady Jane said. "Instead of being allowed to return to A-Force he was ordered home to London to explain to the intelligence establishment what he was doing in Spain dressed in drag."

"Could be a tough sell," Lt. Col. Randal said.

"Agreed," Lady Jane said.

"Dudley holds what is known as a 'God High Priority.' He can show up for any flight, any time, anywhere, without reservations. Some passenger will be bumped from the plane to allow him on board," Lady Jane said.

"Strangely, instead of flying home he chose to travel by ship, the *Ariosto*. Possibly he was hoping passions would cool by the time he arrived."

Lt. Col. Randal said, "Can't blame the man."

"The *Ariosto* was sunk," Lady Jane said. "Torpedoed by a U-boat.

"Dudley has gone missing again."

6

COW MARK III

LIEUTENANT COLONEL JOHN RANDAL WAS IN THE DESERT approximately seventy-five miles outside of Derna. Lieutenant Pamala Plum-Martin had flown him there to rendezvous with Captain "Geronimo" Joe McKoy and Mr. Zargo. With them was Major Vladimir Peniakoff aka "Popski," who had established an intelligence network in the area.

Lt. Plum-Martin had landed on a strip of hard sand. The IMAM Ro.63 was parked, tied down under camouflage netting. She was sitting in the shade in a folding canvas chair, filing her nails.

Popski knew where the Ranger Patrol prisoners were being held. Under another camouflage net in a wadi a short distance away they were pointing out the details to Lt. Col. Randal on a map. There were two POW camps at Derna – one was the officers' camp where ex-Lieutenant Billy Jack Jaxx and Waldo Treywick had been held.

The remaining five Ranger Patrol captives were in a different compound, a larger facility reserved for the other ranks.

Maj. Peniakoff said, "Information came to light indicating where the remainder of your Raiding Forces people were incarcerated. I made a personal reconnaissance to verify the report, then sent one of my agents inside to make contact with them.

"Penetrating the camp was simple enough. At night the Arabs sneak in and sell the internees foodstuffs. After the disaster of BATTLEAX, the vast influx of POWs overwhelmed the Italian's ability to adequately safeguard them.

"Italian theory on POW control is simply to put the prisoners in a compound, surround it with a couple of strands of barbed wire with watchtowers spaced every two hundred yards around the perimeter. On a moonless night, the guards in the towers are unable to see each other, much less prevent movement in or out. If a few internees go missing it is of no great consequence.

"What keeps them from all escaping?" Lt. Col. Randal asked.

"The vastness of the desert. They have nowhere to go."

Lt. Col. Randal said, "What's the plan?"

"On the night of the escape," Maj. Peniakoff said, "the men in the camp desiring to get away will exfiltrate through the wire where they will be met by my people and led cross-country to my camp here. We shall not reveal the exact location they will be traveling to. Only the native guides will know.

"In fact, the word will be leaked the rendezvous site is close to Derna."

"Why?"

"The breakout will not be limited to Ranger Patrol personnel," Maj. Peniakoff said. "What we intend to stage is something like you see in your Hollywood movies when someone shouts '*jailbreak*' and all the inmates make a mad dash for it.

"Some escapees will be recaptured or will return to the prison on their own accord when they are unable to keep up on the long, forced march to our rendezvous point.

"The purpose of the exercise is to mislead the Italians when the recaptured evaders are interrogated. Our hope is to have the Blackshirts searching for us nearby Derna.

"I'll have transportation standin' by for everone who makes it this far," Capt. McKoy said. "I'm sure our boys 'll be among the ones who do."

"Any chance," Lt. Col. Randal asked, "for me to conduct a quick recon of the POW camp?"

"I recommend against it, Colonel," Maj. Peniakoff said. "Everything is in place for the operation to proceed. If you should be detected by the Italians or reported by Arab informers it could jeopardize our plans."

"Roger," Lt. Col. Randal said. "Sounds like you men have everything under control. I'll leave you alone to get on with it.

"Capt. McKoy, might I have a word before Pam and I take off?"

As they walked out to the Ro. 63, Lt. Col. Randal said, "Move the escapees out as they trickle in, but don't hang around here waiting for Ranger Patrol people to show up, Captain.

"I'll have Jack Merritt send some of his Sudanese from No. 9 Company to provide additional truck transport. When they arrive, you pull White Patrol out and move back to Oasis X.

"Time for us to get back on offense raiding the Via Balbia."

"What you got up your sleeve, John?"

"The POW compound is only a mile from the coast," Lt. Col. Randal said. "Roy is going to land a couple of his DUKWs on the beach. King and I will infiltrate the camp and lead our people out to the coast while the Italians are distracted by the breakout here in the other direction. Peniakoff's plan is a diversion – he doesn't know that."

"That'll work," Capt. McKoy said.

"Brief Mr. Zargo," Lt. Col. Randal said. "No one else."

"Glad you're back, John."

"PUT THIS IN YOUR POCKET, MR. TREYWICK," LIEUTENANT Colonel John Randal said. The two were in the suite he shared with Captain the Lady Jane Seaborn at Raiding Forces' Headquarters. He handed a custom short-barreled Smith & Wesson N-frame 38/44 to the ex-ivory poacher turned diamond-and-gold smuggler.

"You got me a present?" Waldo said. He had never been the recipient of many gifts.

"From Abercrombie & Fitch," Lt. Col. Randal said. "Outfitted the likes of Teddy Roosevelt, Clark Gable and Ernest Hemingway on their safaris. You never saw so many autographed eight-by-ten glossies of movie stars, generals and politicians as they have on their walls."

"What in the world is this?" Waldo asked in awe, admiring the special-order revolver."

"Fritz Special – same N-frame and 38/44 caliber as your five-inch S and W," Lt. Col. Randal said. "Barrel's chopped to two inches for concealed carry. The hammer's bobbed so it won't snag when you draw from under your shirt or coat; grip's rounded and the front of the trigger guard cut away for quick access and fast shooting. The trigger pull has been tuned to a light three pounds.

"Be careful."

"Nice lookin' piece, Colonel," Waldo said. "Got my name engraved in block letters on the back strap. Don't know how to thank you."

"Not necessary, Mr. Treywick," Lt. Col. Randal said. "Keep it close."

"Don't worry," Waldo said. "Ain't never gonna catch me leavin' home without it.

"Remember all them rules I taught you about huntin' bad cat?"

"I do," Lt. Col. Randal said. "You claimed every one was 'the most important.'"

"Well, the most important rule you need to know 'bout gunfightin," Waldo said, "is have yourself a gun."

Lt. Col. Randal said, "Roger that."

HEARING VOICES ON THE LANDING OUTSIDE, LIEUTENANT Colonel John Randal walked out of his suite on the third floor of Raiding Forces' Headquarters. Lieutenant Pamala Plum-Martin, wearing shorts with her peewee cowboy boots, was sitting on King's security desk outside the door. She and Captain the Lady Jane Seaborn had acquired the boots when they were masquerading as Texas "cowsluts" while undercover doing an advanced reconnaissance of the Portuguese protectorate the island Rio Bonita, prior to OPERATION LOUNGE LIZARD. The Vargas Girl look-alike Royal Marine was talking to the Merc.

"*Ciao*, John," Lt. Plum-Martin said, flashing a beautiful white-toothed smile before sliding off the desk and dancing down the stairs.

She passed Veronica Paige, who was on her way up to see Lady Jane.

Lt. Col. Randal asked, "What was that about?"

"Plum-Martin wants to bomb an Italian roadhouse on the Via Balbia," King said. "She was wondering if it was doable for me to scale one some night to put a light on the roof for her to use as an aiming point – X marks the spot."

"Pam wants to do that?"

"Could work, Chief."

Lt. Col. Randal said, "It might."

LIEUTENANT COLONEL JOHN RANDAL, CAPTAIN THE LADY JANE Seaborn and Veronica Paige were sitting in the spacious living area of the third-floor suite.

Lt. Col. Randal said, "MI-9 Escape is a function of Dudley Clarke's A-Force. Jim Taylor was assigned to supervise the unit. He placed Terry Stone in charge, but you run the day-to-day operation since Terry also commands Desert Squadron of Raiding Forces."

Veronica said, "That is correct."

"Pretty confusing chain-of-command," Lt. Col. Randal said.

In fact, it was more convoluted than he realized.

Lady Jane understood the reason for the complex layering of command of MI-9. She knew Escape was the cover for A-Force. That information was "Need to Know."

However, she did not know what the A-Force mission consisted of – not in its entirety. No one did except Lieutenant Colonel Dudley Clarke. His assignment to "mystify and mislead" ranked second in national security importance to the ULTRA SECRET, the most highly guarded British secret of the war, which was the penetration of the German Enigma encoding machine.

And that was the reason everyone in a position to know had been so worried about Col. Clarke being arrested in Spain. Now he was missing at sea.

Veronica Paige was not aware that MI-9's primary mission was to provide cover for A-Force. Lt. Col. Randal and Veronica were aware that MI-9 did not get much command guidance. It was clear Escape was not high on Col. Clarke's priority list.

No one at GHQ Middle East Command was much interested in MI-9 either. Staff at Grey Pillars had more pressing problems to deal with than POWs.

Lady Jane knew that the British Secret Intelligence Service had big plans for MI-9 in the future, although she did not know what they were. She had a firm directive from SIS to ensure MI-9 was kept running until such time as "C" was ready to put his long-range plan for it into operation.

Lt. Col. Randal liked the mission of rescuing prisoners. He liked Veronica. And Maj. Stone had briefed him that MI-9 would offer up missions for Raiding Forces at some later date. So he was all for advancing the Escape program, unaware of the complexity of the tangled web of intrigue.

Raiding Forces was shot through with SIS operatives – some Lt. Col. Randal knew about and some he did not: James "Baldie" Taylor, Lady Jane, Maj. Stone,

Squadron Leader Paddy Wilcox, Lieutenant Pamala Plum-Martin, Red, Mr. Zargo and Veronica were MI-6 – or would soon be.

"There's an over-age officer," Lt. Col. Randal said to Veronica. "Major Vladimir Peniakoff. Everybody calls him 'Popski.' Used to be in an outfit called the Libyan Arab Force.

"The LAF has been disbanded, so Popski's trying to carve out a job for himself as an intelligence officer. He's with Captain McKoy and Mr. Zargo outside of Derna working on the rescue of our Ranger Patrol people.

"I asked Jim to have Popski attached to MI-9. Done – you're now in possession of a small intelligence network operating in close proximity of two Italian POW camps with the ability to slip operatives inside at will."

"Marvelous," Veronica said.

"Agreed," Lady Jane said, rewarding Lt. Col. Randal with one of her patented heart attack smiles. "Very good, John."

King stuck his head in the door. "Lt. Jaxx would like to see you outside, Chief."

As Lt. Col. Randal was leaving, Lady Jane and Veronica were debating the merits of accepting Jim Taylor's offer to have FANYs assigned to MI-9 or to expand the female Royal Marine detachment to take on its clerical duties.

FANY stood for Field Auxiliary Nursing Yeomanry. Nowadays the girls did not ride horses (at least on official duty) and they were no longer nurses, but some did serve in the field as secret agents for SOE. Others were guerrillas in the French Underground.

It was an elite organization, difficult to join. A photo was required. As were three references. FANYs were known to be high-spirited party girls.

The FANYs had become synonymous with Special Operations Executive. Female agents recruited into SOE who were not already affiliated with a military organization were badged into FANY. The idea was that if they were captured, the women would be protected under the Geneva Convention.

Hope springs eternal.

The Gestapo did not adhere to the Geneva Convention.

Not where it applied to captured female agents.

LIEUTENANT COLONEL JOHN RANDAL FOUND EX-LIEUTENANT Billy Jack Jaxx, Lieutenant Randy "Hornblower" Seaborn, OBE, DSC, RN and Lieutenant Roy Kidd talking to ex-Sergeant Hank Rawlston.

"What are you men up to?" Lt. Col. Randal asked.

"Gun DUKWs, sir," said Lt. Kidd, the leader of Duck Patrol.

"What's a gun DUKW?"

"When them technicians from GMAC was out here," ex-Sgt. Rawlston said, "they told me you could mount a forward-aiming 105 in the back of a DUKW, Colonel."

"A 105?"

"You can fire it out of the DUKW too," ex-Lt. Jaxx said. "That's a gun DUKW, sir."

"No kidding," Lt. Col. Randal said, mentally running through the combination of tactical possibilities that an amphibious cannon offered Raiding Forces.

Lt. Kidd said, "We don't have a 105, sir. But if we did, with an AP round, it would defeat any known armor in the world."

"We're not thinking antitank weapon, sir," ex-Lt. Jaxx said. "What we need is something that'll shoot big holes through a Via Balbia roadhouse."

Lt. Kidd said, "As heavy as a 105 howitzer is, it would probably be difficult to drive off a sandy beach with one aboard a DUKW."

"I suggested the QF 1.5-pounder Mark III COW 37mm, sir," Lt. Seaborn said. "In the last war they were used on motor gunboats."

"Break it down for me," Lt. Col. Randal said. "Slow."

"The 37mm was originally a light antitank weapon, but nowadays it won't penetrate the armor on many tanks, sir," ex-Lt. Jaxx said. "The QF prefix stands for 'quick firing.' The COW 37mm Mark III has a five-round clip."

"Ninety rounds a minute, sir," Lt. Kidd said, "if you load fast."

"What's COW stand for?"

"Coventry Ordnance Works," Lt. Seaborn said. "There are single and multiple-barreled models, sir, but we are interested in the hand-cranked single-barreled Mark III because it only weighs two hundred pounds total – cradle, gun and breech.

"I broached the subject to grandfather, and he said the Royal Navy had experimented with mounting the COW in flying boats. One recently crashed near Alexandria and he made arrangements for Sgt. Rawlston to salvage the gun.

"Admiral Ransom says if it turns out we can use single-barreled 37mm Mark IIIs, he can supply us all we want, sir," Lt. Kidd said. "The Navy has declared the Mark III obsolete."

"Any problem mounting one, Sgt. Rawlston?" Lt. Col. Randal asked.

"Not really, Colonel," ex-Sgt. Rawlston said, chomping on the stub of an unlit cigar. "Come with a pedestal mount. COW Mark III's not real heavy – ain't like lifting a fully-loaded gun jeep in and outta the back of a DUKW with a crane. With a basic load of ammunition, the whole piece an' ordnance only weighs in about the same as two armed and equipped men."

"That's what I wanted to speak to you about, sir," ex-Lt. Jaxx said. "We'd like to try a pedestal-mounted 37mm COW Mark III on a jeep.

"Provide our patrols crazy bad shoot 'em up, sir."

"Yes, it would," Lt. Col. Randal said.

"Good thinking men – keep it up."

TRUCKS STARTED ARRIVING AT RAIDING FORCES' HEADQUARTERS. Workmen. unloaded large squares of something covered by padded quilting. Two men were required to carry each one. Being extremely careful, they manhandled them into one of the large rooms on the second floor.

King showed the way.

"What's going on?" Lieutenant Colonel John Randal asked.

"Those are mirrors, Chief," King said. "Rocky's setting up a dance salon for the Royal Marines."

"Rocky?"

"Lady Seaborn detailed her to integrate ballet exercises into the Marine's daily physical fitness program – do not be found anywhere near the area when those women are working out."

"Why not?"

"Lady Seaborn caught me peeking," King said. "Made me come in and take part in the exercises. Those Marines are insane.

"An expatriate who used to coach the female Polish Olympic gymnastics team comes every morning at zero six hundred to lead the drill. After an hour of torture and yoga we all staggered outside, down to the beach, jumped in the ocean and had to swim around a buoy a half mile out.

"Nearly murdered me," King said.

"Now Lady Seaborn says I have to conduct an unarmed combat class for her women three days a week."

"Thanks for the heads up," Lt. Col. Randal said. "Jane's been suggesting I join in the fun some morning."

"Don't do it, Chief.

7

DRESSED FOR SUCCESS

CAPTAIN JEB PELHAM-DAVIES, COMMANDER OF SEA SQUADRON, was the officer tasked with the rescue of Ranger Patrol. The mission had been assigned to him the minute Lieutenant Colonel John Randal learned the exact location of the five POWs.

The assignment allowed Major Sir Terry "Zorro" Stone to return to Oasis X and resume his duties commanding Desert Patrol.

Raiding Forces was a small, special operations unit spread over a wide area from Cairo to Tripoli operating by gun jeep across the Great Sand Sea out of Oasis X and along the Mediterranean coast from a Landing Craft Tank that transported Duck Patrol's gun jeeps in DUKWs.

Vice Admiral Sir Randolph "Razor" Ransom, VC, KCB, DSO, OBE, DSC, had recently located a tramp Castle Class trawler he was having refitted as a troopship. The idea was to use it as an amphibious base for a Sea Squadron mobile coastal force (MCF). The trawler was going to rove up and down the thousand-mile-long Mediterranean coastline launching pinprick Commando raids against the Via Balbia. He was in the process of hand-picking officers and men to be the crew from the Royal Navy Patrol Service (RNPS) replacement depot.

Lt. Col. Randal and Capt. Pelham-Davies were in the third-floor suite at Raiding Forces' Headquarters studying the map of the Derna area. The mission to rescue the five Ranger Patrol troopers adhered to one of the key principles of the Rules for Raiding: "keep it short and simple." However, no special operation conducted 100 miles behind enemy lines that involved travel to the objective by sea, landing on a hostile shore during the hours of darkness, infiltrating an enemy prison camp, clandestinely bringing out five prisoners and extracting undetected could ever be described as "simple."

King joined the two officers.

"As I understand the plan," Lt. Col. Randal said, "the Headhunter will land with a small party in Goatly dories to secure the beach. On the signal 'all clear,' Roy Kidd will bring in two DUKWs, take up a defensive position, then wait while King and I move overland, infiltrate the POW camp and bring out our men."

"Negative," King said. "Jack Cool and I will be infiltrating the camp."

"Lt. Jaxx?"

"He says it's his responsibility to get the Ranger Patrol men out – they were captured on his watch," King said. "Besides, we have already surveyed the beach and recced the route to the POW compound."

Lt. Col. Randal said, "You've reconned the target – on the ground?"

"Admiral Ransom arranged for a submarine, the HMS *Urge* out of Alexandria headed past Derna on a war patrol to Malta, to drop us off in a rubber raft. Jack and I paddled ashore," King said.

"We hit the beach, concealed the raft in the sand dunes, then conducted a route reconnaissance to the objective. At the compound we were able to covertly inspect the section of the perimeter where the link-up with Ranger Patrol will take place."

Capt. Pelham-Davies said, "King and Billy Jack reported it possible to walk in and out of the POW camp at will, sir."

"Squares with the intel Maj. Peniakoff gave me," Lt. Col. Randal said.

"Once our mission was accomplished," the Merc said, "Jaxx and I exfiltrated back to the beach. Plum-Martin picked us up out at sea in a Walrus."

"Very good, King. You two men showed real initiative," Lt. Col. Randal said.

"Now what am I supposed to do?"

"Be in charge, Chief," King said. "That's what you are good at."

"IS IT TRUE," JAMES "BALDIE" TAYLOR ASKED, "YOU HAD A private meeting with the President in the Oval Office at the White House?"

"If I did, General," Lieutenant Colonel John Randal said, "the subject matter would be classified."

"Understood."

The two were standing on the bridge of the Landing Craft Tank *King Duck* three miles out to sea off the Italian-held town of Derna approximately 100 nautical miles west of Tobruk. It was 0100 hours. There was no moon. The raid to rescue five members of Ranger Patrol being held in the Other Ranks POW camp outside the town was underway. Lieutenant Butch "Headhunter" Hoolihan, DSO, MC, MM, RM, and a five-man party of his Sea Squadron Commandos were boarding their rubber rafts for the trip to the beach as Taylor and Lt. Col. Randall observed.

The plan called for the rubber rafts to be towed to within a quarter mile of the beach by two DUKWs under the command of Lieutenant Roy Kidd. At that point, Lt. Hoolihan's two boats would cast off in order to paddle surreptitiously to the beach. His Commandos would then set up a perimeter.

When the beach was secure, the plan called for Lt. Hoolihan to signal Lt. Kidd to land the two DUKWs. The amphibious GMAC trucks were going to take up a defensive position in the dunes off the beach.

Once on shore, having landed in the DUKWs, ex-Lieutenant Billy Jack Jaxx and King would proceed on foot overland under cover of darkness to the POW camp, bring out the five Raiding Forces' men being held prisoner and lead them back to the beach. Then the DUKWs were to bring the entire party out – rubber rafts, Commandos, liberated POWs, etc. – to the *King Duck*.

Somewhere out in the pitch black, Lieutenant Randy "Hornblower" Seaborn was screening the operation with his two heavily armed MAS boats. The pair of motor gunboats had to be vigilant. Both the Italian and the German navies had aggressive coastal units operating in the Mediterranean.

Squadron Leader Paddy Wilcox, DSO, OBE, MC, DFC, and Lieutenant Pamala Plum-Martin were orbiting overhead in two blacked-out Walruses. Each was armed with a pair of 250-pound bombs, a pair of organic .303 machine guns mounted externally on the fuselage, plus the eight .303 Bren gun nose-mount configuration improvised for night ground strafing in Abyssinia. The massed machine guns represented more forward firepower than any single-engine fighter in the RAF inventory. They would be effective against enemy light motor torpedo boats should any attempt to interfere with the operation.

Captain Jeb Pelham-Davies, DSO, MC, was doing his best to have a plan in place for any contingency. It paid to be vigilant.

The former instructor at Achnacarry was a brilliant squadron commander. He had the distinction of being the only officer in Raiding Forces invited into the unit by the troops when they were going through Commando School.

"Jimmy Roosevelt briefed his boss 'Wild Bill' Donovan about guerrilla warfare based on what he had learned of our Force N operation in Abyssinia," Lt. Col. Randal said.

"Donovan sent a letter to Jimmy's father, President Roosevelt, recommending the U.S. raise an organization like Special Operations Executive to conduct guerrilla warfare."

Jim said. "I knew you were at the White House."

"Jimmy took me over for a quick in and out with his dad," Lt. Col. Randal said.

"We never had this conversation."

"What conversation?"

"Want to hear *who* President Roosevelt asked me about?"

"You know I do," Jim said. "Most definitely."

"Captain McKoy," Lt. Col. Randal said. "The president said he led his cousin Teddy's mare, Little Texas, up San Juan Hill."

"I thought the Cuba story was pure fiction," Jim said, "part of Geronimo Joe's stage résumé – like the bit about his fighting Apaches."

"The President," Lt. Col. Randal said, "called him *'Colonel.'*"

JAMES "BALDIE" TAYLOR SAID, "THE DIVERSION WE PARTICIPATED in when we jumped on Cyprus worked like a charm. Exactly as Dudley Clarke planned."

"What diversion?"

"Failed to mention it at the time, Colonel," Jim said. "The short-lived island vacation when we parachuted on to Cyprus was part of an A-Force deception operation. Dudley was endeavoring to convince the Germans not to invade."

"Used us as bait," Lt. Col. Randal said.

"Not bait," Jim said. "Tricking the opposition into believing we were the advance party of 1 SAS Brigade."

"Sounds like bait to me," Lt. Col. Randal said. "Any word on the whereabouts of our cross-dressing Colonel?"

"After his ship was torpedoed he made it into a lifeboat that was picked up by a Royal Navy ship," Jim said.

"Now Dudley is back on Gibraltar."

"Think Colonel Clarke's seen enough action," Lt. Col. Randal asked, "to last him a while?"

"Lord Gort has instructions to interview Dudley in order to obtain a full explanation. If he passes muster with the governor, the plan is for him to return here to resume his duties at A-Force instead having to travel to England to face the music."

"Looking forward to his story," Lt. Col. Randal said. "Got to be good."

"Forget it," Jim said. "Dudley's been away from his post for three months now. When he returns, no one will ever mention the incident again – ever. Never happened.

"Is that clear?"

"Not exactly," Lt. Col. Randal said. "But then that's Colonel Clarke's specialty – not being clear."

"I admit to being interested to hear Dudley's account myself," Jim said. "Since you were straightforward with me about your visit to the White House, you shall hear it when I do – at least the juicy parts.

"*My* particular talent is ferreting out details people rather I not."

"Like I said," Lt. Col. Randal said, "story has to be good."

LIEUTENANT COLONEL JOHN RANDAL ASKED, "READY TO HAVE me run ashore, Captain Finley?"

"Dory party standing by, Colonel," Acting Provisional Sub-Lieutenant Skipper "Warthog" Finley, OBE, RNPS, rasped in his whiskey-ruined voice.

The commander of the *King Duck* ran his LCT with an iron fist. Countless drills day and night forged the RNPS crew and the Raiding Forces' personnel stationed onboard into a fine-tuned machine. The professionalism of the Captain and the skill level attained by the crew by dint of hard work and intensive training made for a happy, efficient fighting ship.

The night was cool. Lt. Col. Randal was wearing the leather bomber jacket with the fur collar, captured from a downed Italian pilot, a gift from the bandit chieftain Cheap Bribe in Abyssinia. Inside the jacket he had his silenced High Standard .22 in a chest holster. One of his 1911 Colt .38 Supers was buckled around his waist. He carried his 9mm Beretta MAB-38 submachine gun slung over his shoulder in front – barrel down.

Raiding Forces' version of being dressed for success.

Waldo Treywick was waiting on the ramp with two Lifeboat Servicemen. They were standing by with the Goatly dory. When Lt. Col. Randal arrived, he and Waldo climbed aboard and the Lifeboat Servicemen launched the dory.

The ex-ivory poacher produced a couple of his thin cigars and offered one to Lt. Col. Randal. The two men stuck them, unlit, between their teeth. Tonight they were passengers.

Waldo was armed with a sawed-off, humpbacked 12-gauge Browning Model A-5 semi-auto shotgun loaded with 00 buckshot. In addition, he carried his two Smith & Wesson N-frame 38/44 revolvers. One of them, the custom Fritz Special Lt. Col. Randal had brought him, was tucked beneath his left arm in a shoulder holster under his three-quarter-length Denison parachute smock. The full-sized five-inch S&W was buckled around his waist on the outside of the parachute smock.

The mission was intended to be covert. It was hoped not a shot would be fired. However, Lt. Col. Randal and Waldo had experience where the best-laid plans disintegrated into a hail of gunfire. They never took an unnecessary chance.

The dory made steady progress. No one said a word as the Lifeboat Servicemen labored over their oars. The quality of Raiding Forces' small boat work had taken a quantum leap for the better after Captain the Lady Jane Seaborn arranged for the Lifeboat Servicemen to volunteer for the unit back in the dark days when the Commandos were going round in circles and capsizing in the surf trying to learn boat handling at Seaborn House.

After what seemed like a long time, but was in fact only about thirty minutes, a blinking red light appeared off the starboard bow – Morse Code for the letter *R*.

Lt. Col. Randal took out his red filtered flashlight and transmitted the letter *F*.

The Lifeboat Servicemen turned beam on into the light and continued to row. Within minutes the Goatly dory was through the surf and grinding up on the beach. Lt. Col. Randal leaped over the side with a line. Lieutenant Butch "Headhunter" Hoolihan appeared out of the dark to assist, and with Waldo now on the beach, the three pulled the boat up on the sand.

Two of Lt. Hoolihan's men arrived and helped the Lifeboat Servicemen carry the dory to one of the DUKWs and put it in the back.

"The beach is secure, sir," Lt. Hoolihan said. "Lt. Kidd has his DUKWs hull down in the sand dunes up ahead. Lt. Jaxx and King should have arrived at the POW compound by now, made contact with the escapees and be on the way back."

"Good report, Butch," Lt. Col. Randal said.

He and Lt. Hoolihan had a long history together going back to when Lt. Col. Randal had recruited the then-Royal Marine private to stand guard outside the door of his room on the train out of Achnacarry while he was being briefed on OPERATION TOMCAT – Raiding Forces' first parachute raid on enemy-occupied France. That had been over eighteen months ago while the unit was still in Commando training.

Later, the young Royal Marine had been given a commission when he jumped on Abyssinia with Lt. Col. Randal to form Force N. Lt. Hoolihan had proven to be a talented guerrilla leader, and he had Lt. Col. Randal's absolute confidence.

For the last four months the Royal Marine had been operating with Sea Squadron out of Tobruk surrounded by Germans and Italians under constant incoming artillery fire and air strikes during the day and carrying out pinprick commando raids along the Mediterranean coast from Lt. Seaborn's two fast MAS boats by night.

Lt. Hoolihan may have been the most decorated Royal Marine lieutenant in the Corps, though no one in Raiding Forces was counting or paid much attention to medals.

Tonight he was the on-ground commander of the operation to free the Ranger Patrol prisoners.

Lt. Col. Randal knew that Lt. Hoolihan needed a break from combat operations. Unknown to the young Royal Marine, when the mission was concluded, the Headhunter was slated to be assigned to Raiding Forces' Headquarters for a month of token staff duty. He would have plenty of time off to explore the fleshpots of Cairo and Alexandria.

Lt. Hoolihan escorted Lt. Col. Randal and Waldo to the spot where Lieutenant Roy Kidd was sitting in his command DUKW.

"I have a security team a quarter mile off the beach to intercept Jack and King's party when they return, sir," Lt. Kidd said. "It's pretty dark. We don't want them to waste any time looking for us."

"Perfect," Lt. Col. Randal said.

Then they waited. Time seemed to stand still. Waiting was always tedious on a mission . . . standing by for the next thing to happen. Which always had the potential to be bad.

What sounded like 10,000 frogs were croaking in the dunes.

Waldo showed Lt. Kidd the Smith & Wesson Fritz Special Lt. Col. Randal had given him, knowing he was a knowledgeable firearms aficionado with a taste for exotic weapons.

Lt. Kidd said to Lt. Col. Randal, "I'm in the market for another sidearm myself, sir."

"Trading in your Lugers, Roy?"

"Can't keep 'em running, Colonel," Lt. Kidd said. "P-08s are beautiful precision instruments. Unfortunately, salt and sand are more than they can handle.

"Jam from time to time."

Lt. Col. Randal said. "We'll find you a weapon that's more reliable."

"9mm," Lt. Kidd said. "I need something that utilizes the same ammo as the Czech ZK-383 submachine gun I picked up in Persia.

"How about a P-38?"

"A Walther P-38's double-action trigger is too heavy . . ."

All 10,000 frogs stopped croaking at the same time.

There was a rattle of weapons as Lt. Hoolihan's security detail on the beach went on high alert. Tension shot up. Lt. Col. Randal brought up his 9mm Beretta MAB-38 submachine gun, slipped it out of the sling and rested the steel butt on his thigh.

Out in the dark came the command: "HALT."

Followed by the challenge: "Blue?"

"Zebra!"

King led the small column down to the beach through the dunes with ex-Lieutenant Billy Jack Jaxx bringing up the rear.

"We have a good count," King said to Lt. Hoolihan. "Five Ranger Patrol operators, Lt. Jaxx and myself."

The security detail rolled up, silently folding back on the beach.

In the distance, back on the line of march from the direction of the POW camp, a faint boom was heard, followed by a pale turquoise flash of light that flared briefly.

"Camel chip," ex-Lt. Jaxx said. "I left a handful of the camouflaged bangers as a calling card, sir."

"Worked," Lt. Col. Randal said.

"'The Great Teddy' hit a homerun with his camel-dung road poppers," Lt. Kidd said. "Duck Patrol's been scattering them along the Via Balbia every chance we get, sir."

"So has my Sea Squadron troop," Lt. Hoolihan said. "A lot easier and faster to deploy than burying a series of conventional mines in the right-of-way then having to cover them back up and make it look like the road has not been disturbed.

"Teddy's mines will not destroy any vehicle larger than a staff car, but they knock a wheel off and cause serious damage to the undercarriage.

"We need all we can lay our hands on, sir."

"I'll see what I can do," Lt. Col. Randal said.

"You Ranger Patrol men ready to get the hell out of Dodge?"

The rescued Raiders laughed, anxious to quit the beach. All five men were relieved not to have to face the prospect of sitting out the war in a prisoner of war camp. Or of having to escape by trekking through the Great Sand Sea without food or water.

Ranger Patrol's ex-POWs had spent more time in this part of Africa than any of them ever intended.

"Let's do it, Butch."

8

L-DETACHMENT, SPECIAL AIR SERVICES

EX-LIEUTENANT BILLY JACK JAXX WAS IN LIEUTENANT COLONEL John Randal's third-floor suite at Raiding Forces' Headquarters. Jack Cool was briefing Raiding Forces' commander on the small-scale combined operation he had planned. While the presentation was short – only a fragment of a full Operations Order – the information was detailed.

"Situation: There is an Italian roadhouse located at grid coordinates WF493638," ex-Lt. Jaxx said, tapping the map with a pointer. "It is situated on the coast on the edge of a fifty-foot sheer cliff down to a sliver of a shingle beach.

"Mission: Raiding Forces is to conduct a raid on the roadhouse.

"Execution: An eight-man team of paratroopers will drop in the desert two miles south of the target at zero-one-thirty hours. Once on the ground the jumpers will divide into two teams. One will cut the road east of the objective, and the other party will cut the road one-half mile west of the objective, setting up roadblocks to isolate it. Both teams will also mine the hardball.

"While that's taking place, a six-man Sea Squadron party of Commandos will paddle ashore from a MAS boat, scale the cliff behind the roadhouse and silently eliminate any sentries or enemy personnel outside the objective.

"Duck Patrol will proceed by DUKW to another beach a quarter-mile west of the objective that offers access to the Via Balbia not obstructed by a cliff, high embankment or marshy ground, drive to the roadhouse and attack it with its organic weapons.

"While the attack is in progress, the empty DUKWs used to deliver Duck Patrol ashore will withdraw out to sea and proceed west to the location where the Commando party went in, land and stand by.

"Once Duck Patrol carries out its gun-jeep attack, on signal the two roadblock parties will fold in on the objective. Upon arriving at the roadhouse, the Airborne teams will link up with the Commandos, move down the cliff and be extracted by the DUKWs.

"While the withdrawal by sea to the *King Duck* is in progress, Duck Patrol will proceed inland to a rendezvous with one of Mr. Zargo's intelligence operatives, be provided a target list and carry out a two-week raiding patrol. Then it will exfiltrate back to RFHQ through Oasis X.

"Questions, sir?"

"Team leaders?"

"I'll jump in with one of the airborne roadblock parties. Lt. Huxley will command the other. Sgt. Maj. Mikkalis will accompany us. Lt. Seaborn commands the MAS boats. Lt. Hoolihan is cutting short his leave to lead the Commando sentry elimination team. King intends to go in with them, sir. Lt. Kidd has Duck Patrol."

Lt. Col. Randal noted ex-Lt. Jaxx had stacked his operation with the most experienced leaders in Raiding Forces.

Very good – Lt. Col. Randal wanted Raiding Forces to thrive on *leadership*, not command. It was a good plan. Short but not simple.

"Admiral Ransom, General Taylor and Captain McKoy have requested to observe, Colonel."

"Who's the mission commander?"

"You are, sir."

"Nice choice," Lt. Col. Randal said. "What's the part you're not telling me?"

"I'm bootstrapping with Roy when Duck Patrol moves out to pull their patrol, sir."

"Negative," Lt. Col. Randal said, lighting a cigarette with his hard-service U.S. 26th Cavalry Regiment Zippo.

"I want you back here at RFHQ after the raid to rebuild Ranger Patrol."

"Yes, sir."

"Then," Lt. Col. Randal said, "we'll conduct our own patrol."

"Roger that!"

LIEUTENANT COLONEL JOHN RANDAL AND CAPTAIN THE LADY Jane Seaborn were at a table in the back of the Gezira Club restaurant, almost hidden behind a palm. As usual, there was a raucous group of officers at the bar at the other end of the room. Most, but not all, of them were what was now being referred to around Cairo as "gabardine swine" – the well-tailored staff types from Grey Pillars (Middle East Command Headquarters aka MEHQ, GHQ or GHQME) who showed up for work at irregular hours then retired to one of the swanky bars at the best restaurants in Cairo for liquid refreshment.

It was hot in Egypt.

Lt. Col. Randal, distracted by the impending raid, was only half listening to Lady Jane. That did not mean he was not enjoying her company. He always did.

"Something is very wrong with our staff," Lady Jane said.

"Like what?"

"The war in the desert is in a state of stalemate. Everyone knows the Army is building up for a major offensive," Lady Jane said.

"Despite our past failures, GHQ has come to believe the next battle shall be a walkover. British Forces will attack, relieve Tobruk, then drive Rommel and the Italians all the way back to Tripoli straight into the sea. Game over," Lady Jane said.

"There is an atmosphere of extreme overconfidence at Grey Pillars. Officers drift in to work when convenient, put in an hour or two shuffling papers or sticking pins in their wall maps, possibly attend a meeting or a briefing, then it is off to the Long Bar at Shepard's."

"I've heard that."

"Anyone with experience of actually fighting the war in the desert," Lady Jane said, "is baffled. Why the overconfidence?

"What's your boss think?" Lt. Col. Randal asked.

"Field Marshal Auchinleck seems oblivious," Lady Jane said. "Rumors abound the Auk's wife, Jessie, is having an affair with Air Chief Marshal Sir Richard Peirce in India . . . so possibly, he is distracted.

"The attitude at Grey Pillars is dangerous and frightening."

"You're right," Lt. Col. Randal said. "Bad idea holding your enemy – any enemy – in contempt. Learned that one the hard way, Jane. Applies equally to Huk bandits or Nazi storm troopers."

"See that tall, gangly lieutenant at the bar?" Lady Jane asked, "The one with the Grenadier Guards' captain and the slim brunette?

"David Stirling, of the illustrious Scottish Stirling family. His mother is a Lovat – *her* father founded the Lovat Scouts."

"Interesting family tree," Lt. Col. Randal said. The few Scouts serving in Raiding Forces were some of his most valuable assets.

"The other man is Capt. Peter Fleming, Ian's brother," Lady Jane said. "The woman is Lady Hermione Ranfurly. I mentioned her to you. She runs the administrative office of Special Operations Executive. Her husband, a Sherwood Rangers Yeomanry officer, is General O'Connor's aide, or was. Both were captured during OPERATION BATTLEAXE and flown out of Africa to Italy."

"Seem to be enjoying themselves," Lt. Col. Randal said.

"David was an officer in 8 Commando assigned to Layforce, the amphibious raiding brigade Churchill personally ordered dispatched to the Middle East. Field Marshal Auchinleck has disbanded it due to misuse by GHQ. Some of the most elite troops in the Empire frittered away on pointless missions for which they were neither trained nor equipped," Lady Jane said.

"Somehow David laid his hands on a small consignment of parachutes and set about forming his own raiding group. He recruited officers and men from the remnants of Layforce.

"The Commandos tried to teach themselves how to parachute. As a result, two of David's men were killed and he ended up in the hospital temporarily blind and with a badly injured back."

"I can see how that might happen," Lt. Col. Randal said.

"Before going missing in Spain on his unauthorized undercover mission, Dudley Clarke visited David in the infirmary and told him he would back his plan to form a raiding syndicate provided he agreed to name it 'L-Detachment, 1st Special Air Service Brigade.'"

"There is no Special Air Service Brigade," Lt. Col. Randal said.

"It's a myth," Lady Jane laughed, "and you are the mythical SAS commanding officer."

Lt. Col. Randal said, "That's true."

"Things have not gone well for L-Detachment," Lady Jane said. "The troops spend their days in the desert training hard, but no one ever assigns them a mission."

"What Stirling needs," Lt. Col. Randal said, "is for Colonel Clarke to get back here and run interference for him at GHQ."

"Agreed," Lady Jane said. "Dudley has been away for going on three months, leaving David twisting in the breeze. But then, who is to say L-

Detachment is anything more than window dressing for Dudley's long-time obsession with promoting his 1st SAS Brigade deception?"

Lt. Col. Randal said, "That's a possibility."

"Peter is with Special Operations Executive out from London to evaluate the Cairo office's performance but is looking for other employment. He detests the firm. Says everyone in Great Britain refers to SOE as 'Stately 'omes' of England' because of all the country estates it has requisitioned for training schools.

"Peter is also waiting to see Dudley on some hush-hush project when our hero returns from his misadventures abroad," Lady Jane said.

"Could have a long wait," Lt. Col. Randal said.

"SOE Cairo has given Peter the cold shoulder." Lady Jane said. "Totally refuse to cooperate with him. Lady Hermione believes there is something the office wants covered up."

"Like what?"

"Misappropriation of funds, incompetent or corrupt senior management. Perhaps worse," Lady Jane said.

"R.J. has taken an interest," she said, speaking of Brigadier Raymond J. "R.J." Maunsell. The brigadier, as you are aware, is in charge of all things counterintelligence."

"That's not good," Lt. Col. Randal said.

"Hermione is smuggling classified documents out of the office to Peter the way spies do in the movies," Lady Jane giggled, "tucked in her bra."

"Jane," Lt. Col. Randal said, "You tell great stories."

He was immediately rewarded with one of her magnificent drop-dead gorgeous, heart attack smiles. Lt. Col. Randal was convinced constant exposure to them was going to reduce his life expectancy.

It was worth it.

ALL THE KEY OFFICERS OF RAIDING FORCES WITH THE EXCEPTION of the commanders of the patrols in the field on distant missions were arriving at Raiding Forces' Headquarters. Several had assignments in the upcoming raid on the Italian roadhouse. Others were slated to observe one phase of the operation or the other, while the rest were there for a briefing. Every officer and NCO at RFHQ were required to attend.

Lieutenant Colonel John Randal wanted to refocus his troops on the Raiding Forces' mission. During the ramping up of Desert Patrol and Sea Squadron, most, but not all, of his junior officers had lost sight of the main objective: attacking the enemy's lines of communications. Specifically, knocking out Axis thin-skinned truck transport traveling on the only paved highway in Libya and Egypt – the Via Balbia, which ran along the Mediterranean coastline.

Additionally, drawing on past experience with OPERATION BUZZARD PLUCKER, Lt. Col. Randal was planning to expand Raiding Forces' mission to include the killing of enemy pilots – though that was not part of this briefing. Having been wounded himself by an Italian Macchi fighter and spending a lot of long, hot days on desert operations hiding under camouflage netting from enemy air (the biggest threat to a gun jeep patrol), he was ready for some payback.

This was the first time in over six months many of these officers had been in the same room together. Raiding Forces was spread out over a wide operating area.

Lt. Col. Randal was the first person in the Tactical Operations Center's briefing room. When he briefed, he liked to be there as his people arrived – unlike most commanders who generally preferred to arrive late and make a showy entrance. He wanted his people to realize he respected their valuable time and also signal that what was about to take place was important.

Today's briefing was informal. Attendees were authorized to bring in soft drinks and smoke. That did not happen often.

The purpose of today's exercise was to direct his key leaders to focus on the primary mission – thin-skinned trucks traveling the Via Balbia – and not become sidetracked with targets of lesser strategic value.

Lt. Col. Randal was well pleased with his people. Not only were his officers thinking offensively, they were coming up with innovative ways to act offensively on their own initiative.

Major Sir Terry "Zorro" Stone had Desert Patrol running flawlessly.

Vice Admiral Sir Randolph "Razor" Ransom was putting together a Raiding Forces' Mobile Coastal Force (MCF) consisting of a troop transport ship, a Landing Craft Tank, a pair of MAS boats, a number of Landing Craft Vehicle Personnel and a half-dozen DUKWs able to cruise up and down the Mediterranean to drop off raiding parties from Sea Squadron.

Captain "Geronimo" Joe McKoy was developing tactics to better utilize the Lovat Scouts to plink enemy vehicles traveling the Via Balbia from long distance with scoped .55 Boys Anti-Tank Rifles.

Mr. Zargo and his team of intelligence operatives were providing priceless information on point-type targets to be raided.

Acting Provisional Sub-Lieutenant Skipper "Warthog" Finley had mastered the art of landing DUKWs on a distant hostile beach with a scratch crew of Royal Navy Patrol Service sailors utilizing a ship rejected by the Royal Navy.

Lieutenant Pamala Plum-Martin and King were conspiring to develop techniques which would allow her to fly under cover of darkness and bomb Italian roadhouses along the Via Balbia with pinpoint accuracy.

Lieutenant Roy Kidd had started with a blank page and developed doctrine, tactics, and methods for DUKW offensive raiding.

Ex-Lieutenant Billy Jack Jaxx had planned a school solution quality raid on an Italian roadhouse that combined air, sea and land elements.

Each of the gun jeep patrol leaders had conquered the challenge of long-range mobile desert operations in a hostile environment.

Veronica Paige was organizing MI-9 Escape and had helped plan three successful missions.

Brandy Seaborn and Lieutenant Penelope "Legs" Honeycutt-Parker were pursuing the will-of-the-wisp Nazi desert operative, Count Lazzlo Almasy.

The list went on and on.

Raiding Forces was conducting tactical missions it generated itself while standing by, available for strategic operations brought to it by outside agencies. And with every patrol, every raid, every operation, they gained experience – making the Raiders and support staff better and better at their jobs.

As the designated personnel entered the briefing room, they were clearly enjoying catching up with each other on what had been happening on missions scattered all over Middle East Command. Most were making plans for leave in Cairo or Alexandria in the next few days.

They were a band of professionals, men and women. Mutual respect was thick on the ground.

When everyone was present, Maj. Stone ordered, "Take seats."

"In the spirit of our Rules for Raiding," Lt. Col. Randal said. "I'll keep this 'short and simple.'

"Raiding Forces' stated mission is to damage or destroy enemy truck transport when and where we can find it, but generally along the coastal highway – the Via Balbia.

"Lately we have lost sight of our primary objective – preferring instead to shoot up enemy airfields, raid isolated installations and blow things up. Starting right now we are going back to basics.

"Is that clear?"

"CLEAR, SIR!" the room chorused.

"That's the bad news," Lt. Col. Randal said.

The room rocked with laughter. Everyone knew killing trucks was not as glamorous as racing down an airstrip in their jeeps in the dark of night blasting parked airplanes at point-blank range with massed machine guns. They also knew what their main mission had always been: taking out enemy transport.

"Lady Jane," Lt. Col. Randal said, "give 'em the good news."

Captain the Lady Jane Seaborn came up to the front of the assembled group while Lt. Col. Randal stepped off to the side, watching his people in the audience like a hawk.

"Field Marshal Auchinleck has been giving thought to Raiding Forces' operations," Lady Jane said. "He asked me to emphasize to you how vitally important our assignment is . . . strategic.

"And, he has wanted to find a way to demonstrate the value of what you are accomplishing."

The room grew quiet. Everyone present held Lady Jane in the highest regard. She was their patron, having adopted the unit as her personal project in its infancy and sticking with it over time even when other opportunities at higher levels of service presented themselves.

Lady Jane flipped the cover off a chart on a three-legged stand.

"When a patrol destroys or damages a total of one hundred German or Italian trucks, the patrol leader will receive the Military Cross. His patrol sergeant and the other NCOs in the patrol will be awarded the Military Medal and every man in the patrol will receive a Mention in Dispatches.

"Destroy or damage three hundred trucks and, as Capt. McKoy says, 'the price of poker goes up.' The patrol leader will be awarded a Distinguished Service Order, NCOs a Distinguished Service Medal and troops, the Military Medal," Lady Jane said.

"I have assigned one of my Marines to be Awards Officer – the number of kills will be based on confirmation by Y-Service radio intercepts or by RAF aerial reconnaissance. No distinction will be made – strafing with guns or blowing up an enemy truck with a mine. That way Sea Squadron won't be left out.

"We have good intelligence on the enemy vehicle losses, when and where they occur – that is classified MOST SECRET, by the way. Do not discuss confirmation of kill details with anyone not in this room."

"Is that clear?" Lt. Col. Randal said from where he was standing.

It was not really a question.

"CLEAR SIR!"

"We shall develop a point system where some trucks are more valuable than others. For example – fuel transports, tank recovery vehicles or tank carriers rank higher than cargo trucks," Lady Jane said.

"In this way, each of you and the troops you command shall be recognized for your achievements.

"We do not place undue emphasis on medals in Raiding Forces. That said, if anyone is going to be decorated in Middle East Command, I intend for it to be you."

Everyone in the room jumped to their feet, cheering and clapping, when Lady Jane sat down. Being recognized for performance was something to be appreciated. Knowing their best interests were being looked after while they were away in some distant location engaged in fighting their own private war was a real morale booster.

"Last thing," Lt. Col. Randal said, back in front of the group.

"I'm putting enemy aviators on our priority target list. Squadron Leader Wilcox has informed me the bad guys can build an airplane in a matter of days. He claims it takes two years to train and get a pilot fully combat capable.

"I've instructed Mr. Zargo to begin gathering actionable intelligence on the location Axis fliers are housed, bars they frequent, any place they congregate. Raiding Forces will go after 'em.

"Starting today, it's war on pilots."

As the crowd began filing out of the room, ex-Lt. Jaxx said, "I don't know how you do it, Colonel."

"Do what?"

"Hang out with Lady Jane as much as you do," ex-Lt. Jaxx said. "When she starts talking, I stop breathing."

"Yeah," Lt. Col. Randal said. "That's a problem."

"RANDY, THERE'S NO GOOD WAY TO DO THIS," LIEUTENANT Colonel John Randal said. "Commodore Seaborn was involved in the Royal Navy operation to hunt down and sink the *Bismarck*. They got her.

"Unfortunately, your father's cruiser was lost in the action. Survivors report seeing him go down with the ship.

"Inform your mother," Lt. Col. Randal said, "before someone else does."

"Straight away, sir," Lieutenant Randy "Hornblower" Seaborn said, completely stoic. "Father sacrificed his life for King and Empire in the best tradition of the service – not that it feels like as much consolation as one might expect."

"At times like this, Randy, people say really silly things," Lt. Col. Randal said. "I'm going to try hard not to."

"I can fully appreciate that, Colonel," Lt. Seaborn said. "I intend to adopt the same policy."

"Speak to Jane," Lt. Col. Randal said, "She's in the bedroom crying her eyes out."

9

LAID BACK AS A SNAKE

CAPTAIN THE LADY JANE SEABORN, LIEUTENANT PENELOPE "Legs" Honeycutt-Parker, Lieutenant Mandy Paige and Brandy Seaborn were having cocktails on the deck out by the private pool belonging to the third-floor suite occupied by Lieutenant Colonel John Randal and Lady Jane. It was a beautiful night. Stars were sparkling like diamonds in the Egyptian sky.

They were there to console Brandy over the loss of her husband, Commodore Richard "Dickey the Pirate" Seaborn, VC, OBE. The happy girl was not quite so happy, but she was doing a surprisingly good job of keeping a stiff upper lip, as was expected of her class – the Six Hundred. The women of those powerful families who controlled England through their great wealth, social standing and political connections were expected to show no emotion except happiness.

Since marriages in the Six Hundred were virtually all arranged, that element played into the equation when there was a death of a spouse in a military family. Particularly in the case of a Royal Navy couple who spent very little of their married life together, the husband being away at sea most of the time.

That did not mean Brandy had not loved her husband. She had, but she had not been in love with him, which is a different matter entirely.

Brandy gave every indication of being determined to "press on" as was expected of her. What choice was there?

None.

Somehow the conversation turned to Lt. Col. Randal. No one actually wanted to dwell on the subject at hand, there being nothing they could do about it.

"All the emotions of a rock," Brandy said.

"Billy Jack says John is about as laid back as a snake," Lt. Mandy said.

"Personally, I find the man fascinating," Lt. Honeycutt-Parker drawled. "One never knows what John Randal will do next."

Lady Jane said, "He makes my heart beat fast."

LIEUTENANT COLONEL JOHN RANDAL WAS STANDING ON THE bridge of the *King Duck*. It was steaming parallel to the Mediterranean Coast fifteen miles out to sea toward a release point three miles offshore, seventy-six nautical miles past Tobruk, deep behind German and Italian lines. The raid planned by ex-Lieutenant Billy Jack Jaxx and christened OPERATION PIP'S REVENGE was in motion.

Vice Admiral Sir Randolph "Razor" Ransom was standing next to him. The Royal Navy Deputy Director of Operations (Irregular) was along tonight as an observer, this operation being about as irregular as it gets in the Navy.

"Colonel," VAdm. Ransom asked, "do you happen to remember Lieutenant Commander Milner-Gibson?"

"The navigator on the first Commando raid when Dudley Clarke got wounded?" Lt. Col. Randal said. "Landed ashore in enemy-occupied France on reconnaissance eleven times prior to the mission?"

"Correct, that is the man," VAdm. Ransom said. "Moved on to be the first lieutenant of the *Fidelity,* a Q-ship."

"Q-ship?"

"An idea from the last war. A specially fitted, heavily armed ship that masquerades as an unarmed freighter. The concept is to invite attack from a U-boat or one of the Nazi surface raiders by pretending to be a helpless victim.

"In addition to cannon and torpedoes concealed on Milner-Gibson's ship were two Kingfisher spotter planes, a forty-five-foot motor gunboat and a troop of Royal Marines. The plan was for *Fidelity* to lure an attacker in close then sink, or better still, board and capture her."

"The Commander's a fire-eater," Lt. Col. Randal said.

"*Fidelity* was sunk with the loss of four hundred and six men," VAdm. Ransom said, "including Milner-Gibson and all the Marines. This causes me to have second thoughts about posting two troops of Sea Squadron Raiders on board a single trawler. It will be subject to air and sea attack as it cruises up and down the Mediterranean dispatching raiding parties ashore.

"Risk losing all of them, Colonel."

"Maybe we should only station one troop aboard the trawler," Lt. Col. Randal said. "Split the other troop between Randy's two MAS boats?"

"A worthy thought," VAdm. Ransom said. "Raiding Forces is a national treasure. Our men are peerless assets – we must treat them as such."

"Make sure," Lt. Col. Randal said, "you don't let anyone hear you say that, sir."

"Quite right," VAdm. Ransom said. "Strictly Need to Know, what! The troops do not have the need – nevertheless, it is true."

"Roger that," Lt. Col. Randal said.

Acting Provisional Sub-Lieutenant Skipper "Warthog" Finley walked by.

"Admiral," he said, "have you named a captain for your Sea Squadron trawler?"

"Not as of yet," VAdm. Ransom said. "Are you applying for the position?"

"Negative," Skipper Finley said. "But I can recommend the man for the job. Been planning to speak to you about him first chance I got."

"By all means," VAdm. Ransom said. "Randy and I had no luck finding a suitable ship's captain when we were on our recruiting trip to the Royal Navy Patrol Service Replacement Depot.

"What a circus," VAdm. Ransom said. "When we arrived, the two sentries posted at the front gate saluted us with cigarettes dangling out of their lips.

"As we departed the same two lads were jabbing at each other with bayonets, play-fighting," VAdm. Ransom said.

"Who is this officer you have in mind, Skipper Finley?"

"Mud Cat Ray," Skipper Finley said, jamming the blunt stub of a cigar in his jaw. "Former tugboat captain on the African Gold Coast."

"Tough as nails," Lt. Col. Randal said. "Good in a tight spot."

"When and where can I arrange an interview?" VAdm. Ransom asked.

"Most anytime, Admiral," Skipper Finley said. "Mud Cat's incarcerated in the Cairo jail.

"Killed a man."

THE LANDING CRAFT TANK WAS RUNNING PARALLEL TO THE coast. Acting Provisional Sub-Lieutenant Skipper "Warthog" Finley ordered a change in course. The big, ungainly craft made an abrupt turn and headed straight toward land.

When it was three miles offshore, Skipper Finley hove to. Lieutenant Colonel John Randal and Vice Admiral Sir Randolph "Razor" Ransom left the bridge and made their way to the bow of the ship. They climbed into the DUKW at the head of the queue of Duck Patrol DUKWs lined up ready to disembark.

Their beach was further up the coast.

VAdm. Ransom climbed in behind the wheel of the DUKW while the RNPS coxswain moved over into the passenger seat. The plan was for a single DUKW to make the run to shore carrying a gun jeep accompanied by a second DUKW with a crane mounted.

Once on the beach the crane would lift out the gun jeep and it would be on its way inland. Then the two amphibious trucks would drive back into the sea, return to the LCT, be recovered and Skipper Finley would come about and sail back out to the fifteen-mile mark. The *King Duck* would continue on up the coastline toward the next release point.

After reviewing ex-Lieutenant Billy Jack Jaxx's plan, Lt. Col. Randal had made one addition – a PATHFINDER element to mark the drop zone for OPERATION PIP'S REVENGE. He was planning to drive inland, slip across the Via Balbia then proceed to Lt. Jaxx's drop zone two miles out in the desert, directly opposite the Italian roadhouse targeted for tonight's raid.

On the DZ, Lt. Col. Randal and his scratch Pathfinder Team would put out railroad flares to illuminate it for Lieutenant Pamala Plum-Martin piloting the Hudson jump aircraft. Experience had taught that having the DZ marked greatly improved the accuracy of a drop.

One of Raiding Forces' Rules for Raiding was 'It Never Hurts to Cheat.' Pathfinders going in first to light the drop zone with flares was as close to cheating as it gets on a combat parachute jump.

Raiding Forces had learned quite a lot by trial and error over the last two years. There was still much to understand about small-scale unconventional warfare. And that was what tonight's combined operation was all about – another of Lt. Col. Randal's live-fire training exercises against a real target.

Relying on a single gun jeep to carry the Pathfinder Team, which consisted of Lt. Col. Randal, VAdm. Ransom, James "Baldie" Taylor, Capt. "Geronimo" Joe McKoy and Waldo Treywick, violated Raiding Forces' principle that jeeps always travel in pairs. Because the distance from the beach to tonight's DZ and from the DZ to the objective was short and because stealth was vital, the decision had been made to violate that dictum.

The senior officers making up the Pathfinder Team – the Royal Navy Deputy Director of Operations (Irregular), the senior MI-6 Secret Intelligence Service officer (Special Operations) in the Middle East Command and the commander of Strategic Raiding Forces knew to a man they were not supposed to be going behind enemy lines in one small element. To do so was a violation of military doctrine forbidding high-ranking commanders being concentrated in one spot during a combat operation to avoid the risk of them being killed or captured en masse.

The idea that they would go behind enemy lines in advance of the raiding troops was pure military sacrilege. However, Raiding Forces' Rules for Raiding did stipulate: The First Rule is There Ain't No Rules.

Who was going to tell them no?

"Ready, Colonel?" VAdm. Ransom said over his shoulder to Lt. Col. Randal sitting in the driver's seat of the gun jeep in the back of the DUKW behind him.

"When you are, sir."

It is no small thing to be invading enemy territory seventy-five miles or so behind their front line in a single gun jeep. Lt. Col. Randal glanced at the lime green hands of his Rolex – a gift from Lady Jane. Zero one hundred hours on the nose.

Ninety minutes to reach shore, unload the gun jeep, drive inland and set out the flares. Lt. Col. Randal was clicked on, very aware but relaxed . . . almost detached. At this point in the mission he was a passenger spectator watching events unfold.

Anticipation was building.

The ramp of the LCT went down. VAdm. Ransom eased out the clutch of the DUKW and it began to roll into the sea. No matter how many times he had done it before, riding in a two-and-a-half-ton truck while it was intentionally being driven overboard always seemed like suicide to Lt. Col. Randal.

Tonight was no different.

The sea was calm. However, the Mediterranean could be deceptive. One minute the sea was glassy still and the next a gale sprang up, seemingly out of nowhere, raged and then blew itself out quickly. A lot of bad things could happen to a small craft in the short time the tempest was taking place.

VAdm. Ransom set course, and the little two-DUKW convoy puttered toward the beach, bobbing, weaving and swaying.

Waldo leaned over from the back of the jeep and offered Lt. Col. Randal one of his custom-rolled cigars.

He took the thin cigar, stuck it between his front teeth, then sprawled back in the driver's seat resting one arm on the steering wheel of the jeep and gazing into the darkness, waiting for his first glimpse of the shore.

Finally the beach swam into view. The DUKW undulated through the surf, which was mild. VAdm. Ransom smoothly shifted into wheel drive. The two DUKWs drove up off the beach. Lt. Col. Randal and the other men in the jeep bailed out. The crane truck pulled up.

RNPS personnel scrambled off the crane DUKW and swarmed over the gun jeep, preparing it to be lifted out. The faster the sailors had the jeep offloaded, the quicker they could be on their way back to the *King Duck* and on the way to their next beach.

The sailors were working robotically like a precision drill team, no one having to pause and reflect on what to do next. Skipper Finley had trained his men well. Hours and hours of mind-numbing repetition had been necessary for the RNPS men to achieve the level of skill they demonstrated tonight.

The performance was not lost on Lt. Col. Randal.

Within minutes the gun jeep was sitting on the beach. Lt. Col. Randal and the rest of the Pathfinder Team climbed back in and drove toward the Via Balbia 400 yards off the beach. Everything was proceeding according to plan.

When the jeep had traveled approximately 300 yards, Lt. Col. Randal brought it to a stop. Waldo dismounted and disappeared into the night ahead. Time seemed to stand still.

Waldo reappeared by the driver's side of the jeep. "Road's straight ahead 'bout a hunert yards. No traffic."

"Hop in," Lt. Col. Randal said.

There are several techniques for making a road crossing in enemy territory. Tonight with just one jeep, Lt. Col. Randal elected to take the Via Balbia in a rush. That way the Pathfinder Team would be in and out of the danger area fast. If an enemy did happen to be watching from a distance, he might think the jeep was nothing more than a camel or maybe a shadow caused by a cloud passing over the moon.

This far behind the lines, no sentry would be expecting a single enemy vehicle at night.

The jeep bounced when it hit the pavement then again when it left the road and plunged into the shrub brush on the far side. Lt. Col. Randal fought the wheel – he had a lot of practice driving off-road at night.

VAdm. Ransom and Jim Taylor both had their compasses out, helping to keep him on azimuth. Slow is fast at night driving on unknown ground. The good news, as far as navigation, was that tonight they did not have to hit a pinpoint target. All the Pathfinder Team needed to find was an open space that would make an acceptable DZ – with no brush, intermittent streams or wadis.

The jeep had traveled approximately a mile and a half. Lt. Col. Randal was keeping an eye on the odometer when he noticed a yellow glow straight ahead in the distance.

"On azimuth," Capt. McKoy said, looking at the luminous dial on his compass then up at the light.

"Dead on the gun target line," VAdm. Ransom said.

The gleam was about a half mile ahead. At the exact spot designated as ex-Lt. Jaxx's drop zone. That was not good.

Lt. Col. Randal drove halfway, brought the jeep to a stop and turned the engine off. He rested both arms over the steering wheel and stared hard at the flickering light, which was most likely a campfire.

No one in the gun jeep said a word.

"Captain," Lt. Col. Randal said, "let's take a walk."

"Sounds like a plan," Capt. McKoy said.

"Admiral, take the wheel. You hear gunshots, drive up fast to support us with the Vickers Ks. Otherwise, wait ten minutes then ease in slow – we might be prisoners by then. If that's the case, shoot everyone standing, we'll hit the deck.

"Questions?"

"None I care to ask," VAdm. Ransom said.

With Capt. McKoy leading, they circled until the breeze was blowing gently in their face, then moved off through the desert toward the glow. The ex-Arizona Ranger was a ghost floating across the ground. He had spent a lifetime sneaking up on people who did not want to be snuck up on.

Lt. Col. Randal remembered the story about him quitting the Arizona Rangers to spend two years in Mexico tracking down and killing the men who had murdered one of his friends.

The advance to the light was like an out-of-body experience, something that happened to Lt. Col. Randal even on training missions. He was clicked on, very, very aware. The night, while dark, was in Technicolor. He felt the sensation of being elevated – looking down watching the two of them moving up on what was now clearly a campfire with several robed figures around it.

Lt. Col. Randal did not believe in ghosts, the paranormal or superpowers, but he experienced extrasensory perception on a regular basis. Enough so that he counted on it. And he knew Capt. McKoy did too.

"I make it six men," Capt. McKoy whispered. "Got their camels hobbled, grazin', so there's probly not a guard with 'em."

The odds against a group of nomads being camped on the exact spot ex-Lt. Jaxx had selected as a DZ was beyond calculation. Another of the Rules for Raiding was "Expect the Unexpected."

This development was a classic example.

The group of Arab men around the campfire was unaligned, meaning they did not belong to any tribe. Lt. Col. Randal had experience with desert scum like them before at RAF Habbaniya. Free-roving criminal scavengers. Many of the Arab tribes, the Italians, and now the Germans shot them on sight.

"Lady Luck," Capt. McKoy said, "does make life interestin'."

"I believe in making my own luck," Lt. Col. Randal said, slinging his 9mm Beretta MAB-38 submachine gun over his shoulder so the ventilated barrel hung down right to left across the back of his sand-green parachute smock.

"Well," Capt. McKoy said, doing the same with his submachine gun, "there's that too."

The two men stepped into the circle of light created by the fire, silenced .22 High Standard Military Model D pistols in hand. If any of the bandits had been assigned guard duty, he had fallen asleep. However, survival was second nature to professional brigands who had no allies and were hated by everyone.

An ancient brass tack-studded 8mm Lebel rifle with a tassel dangling off the forearm came up from one pile of robes and blankets. Lt. Col. Randal shot the owner in the forehead. Then he shot the man who jumped up next to him twice in the face.

Capt. McKoy was working on the men to the far left of the fire with his silenced pistol, taking his time in a hurry. Men were coming to their feet shouting, grabbing for their rifles. The nomads were vultures who would kill without compassion. Murdering unsuspecting or helpless victims was their style – not gunfighting.

The Arab on the far left went down with a pair of .22 rounds just to the left of the bridge of his nose. Capt. McKoy was aiming center of mass for headshots.

The one next to him made it to his feet holding a three-foot-long sword before he caught two of Capt. McKoy's bullets in his right eye. So much for sword fighting one of the world's best pistol shots.

Lt. Col. Randal shot any man who stirred. Movement attracted his eye, and he had phenomenal peripheral vision. He was using double-taps, two rounds per target. Like Capt. McKoy, going for headshots.

His next two targets were a pair of bandits who were up and running away in a single bound. Four rasps that sounded like matches being struck knocked them flat. Shot in the back of the head.

The last man to come up on his knees caught bullets from both Lt. Col. Randal and Capt. McKoy who were firing fast but calling their shots.

From start to finish, the fight lasted less than five seconds.

"Miscounted," Lt. Col. Randal said as he and Capt. McKoy were changing magazines.

"Turned out to be seven of 'em."

Capt. McKoy said, "I never was good at math."

10

DEAD MEN TELL NO TALES

JAMES "BALDIE" TAYLOR SAID, "WE COULD HAVE MOVED OFF A half mile in either direction, Colonel, selected another flat stretch of desert out of a million square miles of sand and placed out our flares. Saved you the gunplay. These fools would have slept right through and never known about ex-Lieutenant Billy Jack Jaxx's drop."

He was surveying the carnage.

"Dead men," Vice Admiral Sir Randolph "Razor" Ransom said, "tell no tales."

"Ain't one a' Raidin' Forces' reglar rules," Captain "Geronimo" Joe McKoy said, "but it's a good un.

"Maybe we oughta' make it a ancillary fallback – sorta the way we do 'Don't Forget Nothin.' What say you, John?"

"I say let sleeping dogs lie," Lieutenant Colonel John Randal said, sliding his .22 High Standard Military Model D back into his chest holster. "But if they wake up, shoot 'em."

"Why take a chance?" Waldo Treywick said. "That oughta' be one a' your rules."

"On second thought," Jim said, "good point."

THE *KING DUCK* MOVED ON TO ITS NEXT POINT OF DISEMBARKATION. Three miles directly opposite the target of OPERATION PIP'S REVENGE – an Italian roadhouse on the Via Balbia – the ship hove to. Acting Provisional Sub-Lieutenant Skipper "Warthog" Finley ordered the Landing Craft Vehicle Personnel (LCVP) to launch.

This was the first time the "Higgins" boat had been used on a Sea Squadron raid. The LCVP was mounted on the *King Duck* and could be lowered over the side by a pair of davits. On board were Lieutenant Butch "Headhunter" Hoolihan, King and four Raiders plus the RNPS crew consisting of a coxswain, engineer and bowman. They were a little anxious about being lifted over the side.

Skipper Finley was overseeing the launch personally. A high degree of seamanship was essential to accomplish the task without any mishap. There were a lot of things that could go wrong. The *King Duck's* sailors had been drilled, and drilled, and drilled until they could perform the complicated maneuver blindfolded.

The LCVP was going to make the three-mile run into a narrow shingle beach below a fifty-foot cliff located directly behind the roadhouse, land, and discharge its passengers. Then it was to wait off the beach while Lt. Hoolihan's party scaled the cliff and silently eliminated any sentries or other enemy personnel outside the building.

Capable of transporting thirty-six Commandos armed and equipped ready to fight, the LCVP was virtually empty on the way to the beach. Following completion of the raid, it would be returning to the *King Duck* with Lt. Hoolihan's Sea Squadron Commandos, ex-Lieutenant Billy Jack Jaxx and Lieutenant Westcott Huxley's paratroopers, and Lieutenant Colonel John Randal's Pathfinder Team on board.

The instant the LCVP was over the side, in the water and on its way toward the beach, Skipper Finley ordered the *King Duck* to get underway. The LCT was setting sail up the coast for its third beach of the night.

The plan called for Skipper Finley to cruise up the coast approximately two miles until the *King Duck* came opposite a landing point where there were no cliffs. Lieutenant Roy Kidd's Duck Patrol would launch in DUKWs, again at the usual distance of three miles offshore. Once on the beach, the amphibious trucks would unload the gun jeeps and then immediately return to the LCT while Lt. Kidd continued on with his mission – driving down the Via Balbia to the roadhouse and initiating the attack on the objective.

As soon as the DUKWs were recovered, the *King Duck* would come about and steam back down the coastline opposite the Italian roadhouse. The LCT would take up station to recover the LCVPs with Lt. Hoolihan, ex-Lt. Jaxx, Lt. Huxley and Lt. Col. Randal's men on board following the completion of the raid.

Skipper Finley was commanding a ship of war capable of launching LCVPs or DUKWs loaded with Commandos and/or gun jeeps. It was a ship that no one else wanted any part of because the LCT Mark I was such an unstable tub.

He had ordered depth charge rails jury-rigged on the stern in the event the *King Duck* encountered an enemy submarine.

Whenever the LCT was underway there was an RNPS operator/technician on duty in the ASDIC room manning a device pinging the depths of the Mediterranean in hopes of hearing an echo indicating an enemy submarine. The tiny, pitch-black ASDIC shack was located adjacent to the captain's cabin, making it convenient for Skipper Finley to drop in at all hours to check on the never-ending quest to make contact.

To date, no joy but he had no intention of giving up. There be subs out there somewhere – only a matter of time and perseverance until they ran across one.

The biggest threat to the *King Duck* was from enemy air. Skipper Finley had scrounged some captured Italian 20mm and 40mm Breda fast firers and mounted them all over the LCT. All the jeeps and DUKWs had multiple twin .303 Vickers Ks, making the *King Duck* a virtual flak ship with a forest of machine gun barrels pointed skyward.

The ex-Gold Coast tugboat captain was living the life of a modern-day pirate, roving up and down the Mediterranean coast, striking the enemy at will then disappearing in the night.

Skipper Finley reveled in every aspect of commanding Sea Squadron's attack ship. He had even begun to consider curtailing his legendary drinking sprees when on liberty ashore because he did not want to miss any action while sitting in jail for breaking up a bar or two. Cut back on the binges, that is – not give them up.

He *was* a two-fisted sailor man with a reputation to maintain.

Skipper Finley had overheard Vice Admiral Sir Randolph "Razor" Ransom mention to Lt. Col. Randal that a certain Q-ship had a pair of Kingfisher amphibious airplanes stationed on board. He was not sure what a Kingfisher was exactly, but he was planning to explore obtaining one for the *King Duck*.

Skipper Finley was able to conjure up of a lot of possibilities if he could lay hands on his own private airplane.

THE ROYAL NAVY PATROL SERVICE COXSWAIN BROUGHT THE LCVP in as close to the beach as possible. King was the first man over the side running through the surf to the narrow, hard shingle beach below the cliff. He had a rope coiled across his chest. Lieutenant Butch "Headhunter" Hoolihan was right behind him in a knit cap with his face blackened, carrying his .45 Thompson submachine gun at the high port, followed by the other four Sea Squadron Commandos on his team.

Their first challenge was to scale the cliff. In preparation for the mission, King had asked Captain the Lady Jane Seaborn to acquire a pair of Italian M91/38 bayonets from the stock of captured enemy equipment stored in ordnance sheds outside Cairo.

The bayonets were very well made and, in keeping with Italian military tradition, looked almost exactly like the short swords carried by Roman Legionnaires. He had ex-Sergeant Hank Rawlston grind down the blades to six inches and taper the tip to a semi-stiletto point.

Then King wrapped the wooden handles in soft parachute cord, leaving a lanyard loop on the end.

When the Merc arrived at the bottom of the cliff, he reached up on his harness where he had the two shortened M91/38s attached, pulled them out, one in each hand with the lanyard loop over his wrists. Without pausing, King stabbed them into the chalk face of the cliff and went up, hand over hand, using the modified bayonets as hand-holds.

King, who was not wearing face camouflage or a hat, reached the top in no time. The M91/38 bayonets went back in their scabbards, and he drew his Fairbairn Fighting Knife. He was standing within a few feet of the back of the roadhouse. A quick check confirmed no one was aware of his arrival.

After tying the rope off on one of the support beams of the porch outside the back door, he tossed it down the cliff for the Commandos to use to make their way to the top.

Lt. Hoolihan was first up. Moving like a well-choreographed drill team, the Sea Squadron Raiders silently secured both sides of the building, taking up firing positions. Then King walked around to the front. There were five trucks parked in the gravel lot. No one was on guard duty.

The glow of a cigarette led King to one insomniac leaning against a captured British Studebaker truck – originally obtained from the U.S. through Lend-Lease. The smoker noticed King and acknowledged his presence with a casual wave of his cigarette.

The Merc walked straight up to the Italian soldier and plunged the double-edged Fairbairn blade into his heart. One of the Commandos broke cover and left his position to help King drag the enemy soldier to the cliff edge and toss him over.

Lt. Hoolihan signaled his men to place the packs of explosives each Raider was carrying against the back wall of the roadhouse. Acting in concert, they ignited the time pencils, setting them for two hours – well after the raid would be over.

Raiding Forces' Rules: It's good to have a Plan B. In the event the raid never came off for any reason the Italian roadhouse was still in for a nasty surprise.

Then Lt. Hoolihan's entire party shinnied back down the rope to the beach below to secure it until after the assault. At that point Lt. Col. Randal's Pathfinder Team accompanied by ex-Lieutenant Billy Jack Jaxx and Lieutenant Westcott Huxley's Roadblock Teams A and B would come down to be extracted to the *King Duck*.

No one wanted to be standing topside when Lt. Kidd's Duck Patrol rolled up and machine-gunned the place. Particularly not now that it was armed with a 37mm cannon.

THE *KING DUCK* HOVE TO THREE MILES OFF THE EGYPTIAN COAST opposite the beach Lieutenant Roy Kidd had selected for Duck Patrol to land on tonight. The ramp came down, and the four gun jeeps riding in the back of their DUKWs and the two crane DUKWs trundled down the ramp and splashed into the Mediterranean.

Lt. Kidd was sitting in the driver's seat of the gun jeep parked in the back of the lead DUKW. Riding shotgun was Sea Squadron commander Captain Jeb Pelham-Davies. In the back was ex-Sergeant Hank Rawlston manning Duck Patrol's (meaning Lt. Kidd's) newest toy – a 37mm COW automatic cannon with a five-round magazine firing 1.5-pound shells.

There were a lot of straphangers along tonight on OPERATION PIP'S REVENGE – Major Sir Terry "Zorro" Stone was in the back of Lt. Kidd's jeep acting as ex-Sgt. Rawlston's assistant gunner – ostensibly to evaluate the 37mm COW's performance for adoption by the rest of Desert Patrol.

Ex-Sgt. Rawlston claimed to have been an "old pack seventy-five man" before transferring to Ordnance. He had cooked up the idea of mounting the COW on a gun jeep. The original idea had been to mount the 37mm fast-firer on a DUKW. After torching off the gun shield, he realized it would work fine on a jeep.

Now ex-Sgt. Rawlston was trying to find a bigger cannon to mount on one of the amphibious trucks – a DUKW could carry up to a 105mm howitzer.

The convoy snaked its way the three miles to the beach. The RNPS coxswain driving Lt. Kidd's DUKW pulled up on the beach, and the process of unloading the gun jeep began immediately.

Within minutes the four jeeps of Duck Patrol were lifted out of the back and sitting on the ground. The DUKWs performed an about-face and waddled into the water heading back to the *King Duck*.

Half a mile inland, the Via Balbia paralleled the coastline. Without fanfare, Lt. Kidd led his patrol toward the hard-topped road. Duck Patrol was right on schedule.

As soon as the six DUKWs had been recovered aboard the LCT, Acting Provisional Sub-Lieutenant Skipper "Warthog" Finley gave the order to steam back toward the roadhouse. When the *King Duck* arrived, it hove to three miles offshore and took up station.

The LCT had put in a busy night. Now all hands could stand by, take a breather and await developments. The *King Duck's* initial part of the operation had come off like clockwork.

Skipper Finley and his crew made a complex mission seem easy. That was an illusion. Hard work and repetitious drilling had paid big dividends. He wore a stopwatch on a leather cord around his neck tucked into his shirt pocket, but it was usually in his hand, timing every task the crew performed – real or training.

"Well done, men," Skipper Finley called from the bridge. "Keep it up."

No one on board could remember him saying that before – the "well done" part.

"Keep it up," was standard fare. Along with, "Do again."

"STAND UP AND HOOK UP!" EX-LIEUTENANT BILLY JACK JAXX ordered.

Somehow he managed to convey the impression to the paratroops on board that he was having fun – Jack Cool.

Every eye was locked on him.

The Hudson was hurtling through the Egyptian sky. In the cockpit Squadron Leader Paddy Wilcox, who had arrived back from England in time for tonight's mission, was flying with his trademark black eye patch flipped up, using both eyes. Lieutenant Pamala Plum-Martin was his co-pilot.

"CHECK STATIC LINE."

The ten jumpers on board all rattled their snap hooks back and forth on the steel cable running down the roof of the cabin to make sure the hooks were locked and would run freely down the cable.

"CHECK EQUIPMENT."

Up in the cockpit the pilots were searching the horizon for the flares Lieutenant Colonel John Randal's Pathfinder Team would be putting out to mark the DZ.

The Hudson had flown a circuitous route that looped wide out over the Great Sand Sea to avoid the possibility of encountering enemy night fighters even though neither the Regia Aeronautica nor the Luftwaffe currently had night fighter capability in Africa. Then it had turned toward the Mediterranean, flying until the sea was in sight before banking hard left and running parallel to the Via Balbia, visible out their right window.

At that point, ten minutes out, Lt. Plum-Martin switched on the red light mounted above the door for ex-Lt. Jaxx. He and the loadmaster opened the jump door in the tail of the plane. Immediately the wind started howling like a banshee.

Four minutes later ex-Lt. Jaxx gave the six-minute warning signaling the beginning of his series of jump commands.

"SOUND OFF FOR EQUIPMENT CHECK."

On the DZ, Lt. Col. Randal ignited a red parachute flare signaling the rest of the Pathfinders to light off their flares. In seconds all the flares were glowing bright, forming a red arrow pointing in the direction of flight of the troop-carrying Hudson.

Sqn. Ldr. Wilcox made a slight correction to the Hudson's flight path to line up directly on the flaming arrow.

Ex-Lt. Jaxx locked his fingers on the interior edges of the door up high over his head and his boots were wedged on each side spread-eagled. He arched his body outside the Hudson hanging on with his fingertips. Up ahead he could see the flares on the DZ.

Ex-Lt. Jaxx swung back inside the aircraft. "ONE MINUTE. IS EVERYBODY HAPPY?"

At least one trooper lied when he yelled, "Hell yes!"

Captain William P. Yarbrough, U.S. Army Airborne Command, recently arrived to observe the operation, was one of several straphangers onboard the

Hudson tonight. He was having grave second thoughts about jumping from an aircraft in flight without the benefit of a reserve parachute.

"Ex-Lt. Jaxx shouted. "CLOSE ON THE DOOR."

CAPTAIN "GERONIMO" JOE MCKOY STROLLED UP TO LIEUTENANT Colonel John Randal, who was standing next to the burning red flare at the tip of the arrow marking the DZ.

"I been doing some cogitatin' on how to get the Lovat Scouts more involved shootin' up trucks," Capt. McKoy said, "like you ordered me to, John."

"Come up with anything, Captain?"

"The distances out here in the desert is a little too long for the Scouts seven by fifty-sevens," Capt. McKoy said. "Need 'em goin' with the scoped .55 Boys Anti-Tank rifles from max range backed way off the road – at least a mile."

"Makes sense," Lt. Col. Randal said. "The LRDG position some of their Road Watch reconnaissance hides three miles out from the hardball to keep from being discovered. They use telescopes borrowed from the astronomy department of the University of Cairo to spot with.

"What's your plan?"

"We need us a Lovat Scout Patrol," Capt. McKoy said. "Dedicated truck killers. Make it a light patrol – four jeeps with a scoped .55 Boys and a range finder on each one. All they do is sneak, peak and plink thin-skinned vehicles along the Via Balbia."

"We don't have enough Scouts," Lt. Col. Randal said. "Lord Lovat banned me from recruiting any more from the regiment – touchy about losing his best men."

"Munroe's cousin was in that Layforce outfit, got itself disbanded," Capt. McKoy said. "Claims six or eight Scouts who joined the Commandos came out here to Egypt with it. He thinks they'll volunteer for Raidin' Forces. If we can track 'em down from wherever it is they got their selves transferred to."

"Make it top priority," Lt. Col. Randal said. "Lady Jane should be able arrange transfers."

"Got to find the right man to lead the patrol," Capt. McKoy said. "Ain't no Lovat Scout officers available. We need us a specialist."

"Leave that to me," Lt. Col. Randal said. "You enlist those Scouts."

WALDO WALKED UP TO WHERE LIEUTENANT COLONEL JOHN Randal and Captain "Geronimo" Joe McKoy were standing. Literature on railroad flares advised they could be expected to burn from ten minutes to an hour, which was a wide variance. Raiding Forces' tests indicated most lasted at least forty minutes.

"Here it comes."

In the distance they could hear the sound of an approaching aircraft. The Hudson would be dropping the paratroopers from one thousand feet tonight. Normally they jumped from half that height, but no one would be shooting at them and the extra height would cut down on the likelihood of jump injuries.

James "Baldie" Taylor and Vice Admiral Sir Randolph "Razor" Ransom stepped out of the dark. The Hudson appeared, flying straight and slow. Parachutes started spilling out as it came on over.

The jumpers looked like swimming octopuses as their parachutes were deployed automatically by the static lines, then the canopies cracked open and the men began dangling down, drifting straight to where Lt. Col. Randal was standing with the group of Pathfinders.

The paratroopers jumped in a tight cluster that was clearly visible, but they were lost from sight when the parachutes drifted below the horizon as the men came in to land.

The first to arrive at the assembly point was Captain Roy "Mad Dog" Reupart – Raiding Forces' Training Officer, followed by ex-Captain Travis McCloud. Then Captain Hawthorne Merryweather came limping up.

There were a *lot* of straphangers along tonight.

"Landed on a bloody camel," Capt. Merryweather said. "Dashed unpleasant . . . for the both of us."

Waldo said, "Maybe we shoulda rounded 'em up."

Lt. Col. Randal said, "Why didn't you think of that?

"Fall in with us, Capt. Merryweather. We'll give you a ride. What are you doing here anyway?"

"Psychological warfare phase of PIP'S REVENGE, sir. 'The Great Teddy' shipped me some exploding sabotage bullets from England. I intend to leave a few of them behind as a nasty surprise for the opposition."

"Exploding bullets?"

"German 7.92 mm," Capt. Merryweather said. "Salted with 1.2 grams of plastique. Kill the shooter and wound anyone standing nearby the instant the firing pin strikes the cap.

"Your lad Teddy is a right genius."

"Touch one off, *KABOOOM!*" Capt. McKoy said. "That's downright diabolical."

"Gettin' me a headache," Waldo said, "thinkin' about it."

"That is the idea," Capt. Merryweather said.

Captain William P. Yarbrough jogged up.

"Good jump?" Lt. Col. Randal asked.

"Started out a little anxious about the lack of a reserve," Capt. Yarbrough said. "Lt. Jaxx is such a confidence-building jumpmaster, I quit worrying."

"*Lt. Jaxx* was the jumpmaster?"

"Yes, sir," Capt. Yarbrough said. "Now I understand why he rated so high with the Infantry School's Leadership Committee . . . outstanding!"

"Did Billy Jack mention to you tonight was only his seventh parachute jump? He's not jumpmaster-qualified," Lt. Col. Randal said.

"Did a hell of a job," Capt. Yarbrough said.

11

YOUR OWN CHOSEN SPEED

EX-LIEUTENANT BILLY JACK JAXX ARRIVED LAST AT THE assembly point. He was the first to jump, making him the farthest away when he came in to execute his parachute landing fall. Jumping No. 1 put him in position to roll up the stick once he landed.

"All present and accounted for, sir."

"Good work," Lieutenant Colonel John Randal said. "Slight change of plans. Captain Merryweather and Captain Yarbrough will be traveling with me to the objective."

Ex-Lt. Jaxx conferred briefly with Lieutenant Westcott Huxley. In order to rebalance the two Roadblock Teams due to this last-minute personnel adjustment, Captain Mike "Mad Dog" Reupart was shifted from Lt. Huxley to ex-Lt. Jaxx's team.

"Move out Road Block teams," Lt. Col. Randal ordered. "Rally on the objective immediately when you see my two green flares."

He was merely repeating the instructions issued in the Command & Signal paragraph of the Operations Order, redundancy being a good thing in high-stress situations.

Lt. Col. Randal glanced at the luminous lime-green hands on his Rolex. The Concept of the Operation called for him to allow the two teams a twenty-minute head start to reach the Via Balbia and seal the objective from both directions before the Pathfinder Party moved to contact at the roadhouse.

Everyone standing by on the drop zone was impatient to get going. Ex-Lt. Jaxx and Lt. Huxley trotted out on the double, leading their teams on different compass headings through the desert toward their assigned roadblock positions. Unless a column of enemy tanks rolled up, which was highly unlikely, once the two teams were in place and the road mined, the Italian roadhouse would be completely sealed off from any outside reinforcement.

There were no known German or Italian military units stationed in the area. However, it was a common practice for convoys or vehicles driving alone or in twos or threes to travel the Via Balbia at night in order to avoid attack from the RAF fighter-bombers.

Trucks might drive up any time – the reason for the roadblock teams.

Tonight's raid was a Combined Operations exercise against an actual enemy target. The idea was to have air, sea and ground elements all working in concert deep behind enemy lines. By no stretch of the imagination was it simple to accomplish; the Scheme of Maneuver was extremely complicated

While the objective was a handpicked "soft" target, Lt. Col. Randal knew there were no sure things. Anything could happen. The immediate priority was to ensure the operation went strictly according to plan by precision execution.

So far, so good – almost – there was the matter of nomad brigands choosing to camp at the DZ. Captain Hawthorne Merryweather *had* parachuted onto one of their camels. No way to plan for things like that – Raiding Forces' Rules: Expect the Unexpected. One thing for sure – things never went according to plan.

"Let's roll," Lt. Col. Randal said.

EX-LIEUTENANT BILLY JACK JAXX AND LIEUTENANT WESCOTT Huxley had identical tasks. They would be a quarter-mile out cutting the Via Balbia on both sides of the roadhouse to seal it off while the attack took place. On the signal of two green flares fired from Lieutenant Colonel John Randal's flare pistol, the two Road Block teams (RB Team A – ex-Lt. Jaxx – and RB Team B – Lt. Huxley) would fall back to the extraction rally point (ERP), which would be marked by the Colonel's jeep with the lights on.

Both Roadblock Team A and B had reached the black-topped road by the time the Pathfinder Team moved out from the DZ.

Lieutenant Roy Kidd was sitting in his command jeep in Duck Patrol's objective rally point (ORP) – the last rally point before the target. He had heard the Hudson fly past but was not able to see any of the parachutists in the night sky. When the sound of the plane disappeared into the dark, Lt. Kidd checked his watch and began timing.

His orders were to wait thirty minutes after hearing the flyby then drive up on the Via Balbia, advance along the blacktop to the roadhouse and commence the attack.

The thirty minutes seemed like thirty hours. Time stood still. Lt. Kidd was no stranger to the feeling – hunting man-eating leopards at night, waiting for the cat to come try to gobble you, had a way of making time go slow. Even so, he checked to see if his watch was still working.

It was.

"Stand to your gun, Sgt. Rawlston," Lt. Kidd said. "Here we go!"

The jeep pulled up on the hardball, followed by the other three gun jeeps in Duck Patrol. Lt. Kidd's jeep had the COW 37mm mounted on a pedestal in the back while the other three jeeps all had a twin .303 Vickers K on a pedestal mount – all four jeeps had two pair of forward-firing Vickers Ks mounted on the hood.

Duck Patrol was a light patrol, but it packed a lot of firepower.

Lt. Kidd rolled along at a good clip, keeping an eye out not only for the roadhouse but also for Lt. Col. Randal's jeep that would be parked in the desert 400 yards or so off to the right of the building on the far side of the road. He spotted the jeeps and saw the five enemy trucks parked next to the roadhouse.

The Rules of Engagement called for ex-Sergeant Hank Rawlston on the 37mm COW to ignore the thin-skinned vehicles and the gas storage tanks in order to concentrate on the roadhouse. The three gun jeeps following the COW jeep were not to engage until Lt. Kidd commenced firing with his pair of Vickers Ks.

Making an estimate of the situation on the roll, Lt. Kidd decided to hold off on shooting up the trucks until ex-Sgt. Rawlston had an absolutely clear field of fire.

"Open when you come to bear, Sergeant."

The roadhouse was the standard-issue, two-story Italian hostel constructed out of poured concrete made of desert sand. It had a wind-battered, lonely *Beau Geste* look to it. Typically the downstairs was a mess hall with sleeping quarters for the men. Officers and NCOs slept upstairs.

There were fuel storage tanks alongside and gas pumps for the trucks. And the standard Italian Eagle road marker found at every rest stop was planted at the road.

No two roadhouses were built exactly alike, but were all basically the same – a cross between a Foreign Legion fort and a Route 66 motel.

BOOMPA-BOOMPA-BOOMPA . . . the 37mm COW opened on the building, making concrete fly. The first two rounds were armor-piercing (AP) to punch a hole in the building. They were quickly followed up with three rounds of HE that slammed in and detonated inside.

Then Major Sir Terry "Zorro" Stone, serving as Ex-Sgt. Rawlston's assistant gunner, quickly slammed in a fresh five-round magazine.

With the first *BOOMPA,* Lt. Kidd opened on the five trucks with his pair of .303 Vickers K machine guns. The instant he fired, the other three jeeps in his patrol engaged with all their machine guns, shredding the trucks. Then – as one – the gunners shifted their massed fires to the fuel storage tanks, which burst into flames lighting up the night. Finally, all guns turned their attention to the roadhouse.

The strange-sounding stuttering hissing of the fast-firing Vickers Ks sounded like a sudden hailstorm on a tin roof.

From the far side of the road, Lt. Col. Randal's six machine guns opened. That made a total of twenty-one .303 machine guns and one 37mm antitank gun pounding the roadhouse from point-blank range. The firepower concentrated on the roadhouse was awe-inspiring – there was the illusion the walls were swallowing the tracers. Rounds hit the building and disappeared.

Some glanced off, ricocheting skyward.

Any man not on a twin .303 Vickers K was firing either one of the Bren guns captured on OPERATION BRAIN DEAD or the submachine gun of choice. Lt. Col. Randal was launching high-explosive 45mm mortar shells from his modified shoulder-fired Italian Brixia mortar at the doors and windows as fast as he could reload it.

He got off eight rounds.

After ninety seconds or so, Lt. Col. Randal fired two green signal rockets from his AN-M8 Molina flare pistol, recalling the two Road Block teams.

"Check fire," Lt. Col. Randal ordered.

The roadhouse was in a shambles. The 37mm rounds had hammered it. Everyone inside was dead, injured or lacking an interest in fighting back.

Lt. Col. Randal stepped out of his jeep and walked over to Duck Patrol to have a word with Lt. Kidd.

The two Road Block teams arrived, double-timing down the middle of the Via Balbia from both directions.

"Roy," Lt. Col. Randal said, "pull your gear out of the jeep. You're going back to RFHQ.

"I need you to form a Lovat Scout Patrol to specialize in plinking trucks. Independent command. Operate on your own. Come and go as you please. Capt. McKoy will explain."

"Yes, sir," Lt. Kidd said. "Who's going to take Duck Patrol back to Oasis X?"

"I am," Lt. Col. Randal said.

Captain "Geronimo" Joe McKoy, Vice Admiral Sir Randolph "Razor" Ransom, Waldo Treywick and James "Baldie" Taylor walked up. They were ready to move to the cliff to go down the rope to the beach for extraction back to the *King Duck*.

"General," Lt. Col. Randal said, "when you get down to the beach, would you inform King I'm assuming command of Duck Patrol and require his presence?"

"Do it right now."

"Capt. McKoy," Lt. Col. Randal said. "Roy's going back to RFHQ with you. You two men get the Lovat Scout Patrol organized."

"Real good choice, John," Capt. McKoy said. "Right man, right job. Roy's the man – a hunter."

Waldo said, "I'll be comin' with you, Colonel. But we may starve to death without GG along to cook."

"Billy Jack," Lt. Col. Randal said, "turn your team over to Lt. Huxley. You're my assistant patrol leader."

"Yes, sir!"

King came around from the back of the roadhouse – having scaled the cliff for the second time that night.

"Those 37mm AP rounds sliced completely through the roadhouse, Chief. Screamed over our heads out to sea. Hope none of them hit the *King Duck*."

"Throw your gear in my jeep, King," Lt. Col. Randal said. "I'm taking Duck Patrol back to X. We're moving out in zero five."

There was a lot of activity on the objective. Raiders were performing their individual assigned tasks for wrapping up the raid. Men moved with a purpose. Everyone knew exactly what he was doing.

Lt. Huxley, in charge of the combined RB teams, was searching the roadhouse for anything of possible intelligence value. He came out and reported.

"Eleven dead inside, suh. At least that many wounded – 37mm HE is deuced effective at point-blank wange.

"Nothing much of weal intwest found. A few handguns, one submachine gun . . . weal mess in thewe, Colonel."

"Change of plans, Lieutenant," Lt. Col. Randal said. "Take charge of rear security. Capt. Pelham-Davies is already on the beach supervising the extraction.

"Maj. Stone is assuming command of the remainder of the operation, report to him."

"Suh!"

From start to finish, the assault phase of the raid had lasted less than ten minutes. Raiding Forces had no casualties other than their political warfare officer who had banged himself up slightly on the jump.

Exactly how special operations are supposed to work – *hard intel, detailed planning, point-type target, executed with extreme violence under cover of darkness utilizing the element of surprise, hit and run,* Lt. Col. Randal thought as he climbed behind the wheel of his jeep. Waldo was in the right seat and King in the back on the 37mm COW.

Duck Patrol was about to disappear into the Great Sand Sea.

All the intelligence gathering, reconnaissance, planning, briefings, rehearsals, prepositioning, steaming, beach landings, flying, parachuting, cliff climbing, etc., had all been done to place the assault element of OPERATION PIP'S REVENGE against the target for less than two minutes of actual fighting.

"SO," LIEUTENANT COLONEL JOHN RANDAL SAID, "WHAT DID YOU learn last night, Jack?"

The two men were sitting in a wadi under camouflage netting. The blow-up decoy jeeps and all the machine guns from Duck Patrol were under netting in another Laying Up Position (LUP) about 200 yards away, per Desert Patrol standard operating procedure (SOP).

Duck Patrol had traveled hard in the remaining hours before sunrise and had managed to move nearly twenty miles into the Great Sand Sea before stopping to set up. The Regia Aeronautica and Luftwaffe would be out in force at first light looking for the British troops that had carried out the raid.

Waldo Treywick and King were cleaning their weapons as they listened in on the conversation.

"Where would you like me to start, sir?"

"Why not begin at the top with you planning the operation," Lt. Col. Randal said, lighting one of Waldo's thin cigars with his battered U.S. 26th Cavalry Regiment Zippo.

"Which, by the way, was very well done, stud."

"I had all the help in the world, sir," ex-Lt. Jaxx said. "Hornblower and Warthog handled the Navy stuff to include the DUKW tactics. Admiral Ransom helped too. Capt. McCloud and Capt. Yarbrough signed off on the jump phase. Pam prepared the air plan. Roy and I worked out the Actions on the Objective.

"The hardest part," ex-Lt. Jaxx said, "since everybody in Raiding Forces wanted in on the raid, was finding a place for all of 'em."

"What did you learn?"

"It's complicated," ex-Lt. Jaxx said. "You want my opinion or the approved school solution, sir?

"The truth," Lt. Col. Randal said. "Unvarnished."

"We used ships, LCVPs, DUKWs, planes, gun jeeps and paratroopers," ex-Lt. Jaxx said, "to accomplish a mission that could have been carried out by a single Desert Patrol unit operating out of Oasis X, sir, or a Sea Squadron Commando raid launched from the MAS boats or the *King Duck.*

"The idea was to carry out a Combined Operations live-fire training exercise against a hard target to see if we could do it. We did, but I'm not sure we should attempt it again unless we are going after something of high value."

"You're a Ft. Benning Airborne Command-trained paratrooper," Lt. Col. Randal said. "What did you draw from using parachutists on the raid?"

"I'm a believer in the concept of aerial envelopment, sir," ex-Lt. Jaxx said. "The idea being to either insert a small team for a specific mission or to lay down a carpet of Airborne Infantry on a distant target fast.

"But it seems to me, once a paratrooper jumps out of an airplane in a desert environment – unless he can link up with some sort of transport immediately – he's a dead man walking."

"You got that right, Billy Jack," Waldo said.

"King?"

"I concur, Chief."

"That's what I think too," Lt. Col. Randal said.

Raiding Forces' Rules: Keep it Short and Simple. OPERATION PIP'S REVENGE had been short. It had not been simple.

"Now we know," Lt. Col. Randal said. "Mission accomplished Raiding Forces can do a complex Combined Operation. We're never going to do another one unless we have to."

The Phantom radio operator ducked under the netting. "Sir, a FROGSPAWN prefix message for you."

Ex-Lt. Jaxx asked, "Colonel, what does a FROGSPAWN prefix mean?"

"Doesn't mean anything," Lt. Col. Randal said. "Lady Jane made up a story about how she used it to secure an extra railway car for Raiding Forces when we were going on leave after completing jump school.

"Claimed you could whisper *FROGSPAWN* in some official's ear and then they'd do whatever you asked, believing you had some super-secret top priority they had to honor – without knowing what that was and no way to confirm or deny it."

"Does it ever work?"

"Like magic," Lt. Col. Randal said. "Only it turned out Jane owned the railcar. She made up the secret code word story. Jane has a sense of humor – have to watch yourself with her."

"That's pretty funny, sir," ex-Lt. Jaxx said. "I'll try it sometime."

"Nowadays when FROGSPAWN is used in connection with Raiding Forces, it means drop whatever you're doing, comply forthwith most immediate right now no questions asked."

"I'll keep what you said about Lady Jane's sense of humor in mind," ex-Lt. Jaxx said. "I've heard you've had experience with good-looking women, sir. Is it true Miss UCLA was your student teacher in high school?"

"She was," Lt. Col. Randal said, glancing at the flimsy. "English Lit."

"How did that work out, sir?"

"Nearly flunked English Literature."

"One a' these days, Billy Jack," Waldo said, "get me to tell ya the story 'bout how Miss UCLA was responsible for us fightin' a battle in Abyssinia based on her homework assignment . . . *The Man Who Would Be King*."

"I've read that book," ex-Lt. Jaxx said. "Rudyard Kipling."

"Been meanin' to get me a copy ever since that fight," Waldo said. "Ain't never read it."

"Life imitating art," King said. "I would be interested to hear your story too, Waldo."

Ex-Lt. Jaxx said, "I'd settle for a swimsuit shot of Miss UCLA."

Lt. Col. Randal read:

```
MOVE AT YOUR OWN CHOSEN SPEED
NEAREST LOCATION FOR AIR EXTRACTION.
RANDAL AND JAXX THIS NIGHT SEND COORDINATES.
EXPEDITE J.
```

"MOVE AT YOUR OWN CHOSEN SPEED," WALDO TREYWICK SAID, "but haul ass."

Duck Patrol was sitting on a hard stretch of ground with flares out waiting for a twin-engine Anson to land and pick up Lieutenant Colonel John Randal and ex-Lieutenant Billy Jack Jaxx. The troops who were used to living aboard the *King Duck* and carrying out short, quick amphibious coastal raids were now jokingly referring to themselves as Desert Ducks. They had covered a lot of ground in the last forty-eight hours.

And Duck Patrol had taken a risk.

There was no way to make it across the Great Sand Sea in time to be in position for a night extraction by one of Raiding Forces' Special Operations aircraft. So the patrol buttonhooked and drove back in the direction of the Via Balbia to where it could find "good going" – the term commonly used in Middle East Command to mean solid ground.

As soon as the pickup was completed, Waldo was to take charge of the patrol and make a beeline for Oasis X. If all went according to plan he could make it in under three days.

"Colonel," ex-Lt. Jaxx said as they waited for the plane to arrive. "I've been wondering. Why didn't you fire me after I got Pip killed?"

"That's easy, Jack. There's no such thing as a bad soldier," Lt. Col. Randal said, sticking one of Waldo's thin cigars between his teeth. "Only bad officers."

"There's really not any bad officers in Raiding Forces, only bad commanders. It's the commander's job to get rid of any officers who don't measure up to standard."

"Yes, sir. But why didn't you fire me?"

"My officers can make a mistake," Lt. Col. Randal explained. "They can't make bad decisions, violate security or compromise the safety of their troops unless the mission demands it – bad idea to get my men killed or injured foolishly.

"You didn't do any of those things."

"Pip's dead," ex-Lt. Jaxx said, "and I got about a third of Ranger Patrol captured."

"You had one thing in your favor," Lt. Col. Randal said. "Mr. Treywick was in your jeep. If those Italians fooled him, they would have fooled anybody."

"No shirts, khaki shorts, working hard with shovels," Waldo said. "Chevrolet and Ford 30 CWT trucks. I thought they was LRDG."

"Guerrilla war," Lt. Col. Randal said, "is an art, not a science. When things go south, learn from it and drive on.

"Got that, Jack?"

"Loud and clear, sir."

The Anson came in and touched down. In accordance with SOP on desert flights, all Raiding Forces' planes traveled in pairs, a second Anson circled overhead while Lt. Col. Randal and ex-Lt. Jaxx boarded.

Lieutenant Pamala Plum-Martin flashed her standard-issue stunning white-toothed smile over her shoulder from the pilot's seat.

"Next stop, Cairo. You two have an important event tomorrow night.

"Billy Jack is getting a medal."

LIEUTENANT COLONEL JOHN RANDAL WAS CLEANING HIS PISTOLS as he sat in the living room of the suite he and Captain the Lady Jane Seaborn shared on the third floor of RFHQ. Lady Jane and Rikke Runborg, aka Rocky, were in the master bedroom doing each other's makeup for the investiture ceremony for ex-Lieutenant Billy Jack Jaxx, which would begin in about an hour. The two women were clearly having fun. A lot of laughter could be heard coming from the room even though the door was closed.

Seemed odd to Lt. Col. Randal. Rocky was the former lover of Lady Jane's estranged husband Commander Mallory Seaborn, RN. However, the Seaborns had not been estranged at the time.

The family history did not seem to offer much basis for a friendly relationship between the two women.

To be fair, Rocky had not known Lady Jane even existed during the affair. Cdr. Seaborn pleaded amnesia later, but there was some doubt if that was true. He was currently marooned on a tiny windswept island in the semi-arctic Shetland Islands commanding a Royal Navy Depot; Cdr. Seaborn was still under a cloud for having been the sole survivor when the destroyer he commanded was sunk.

The door to the bedroom opened and Rocky came out laughing with one of Lady Jane's evening dresses draped over her arm. The former dancer in the Russian Ballet seemed to ripple when she walked, which had a deadly effect on men.

Rocky was a Russian spy, a German spy – or both – now working for British intelligence. It was possible she was being played back against the Allies by the Nazis, which would make her a quadruple agent. No one knew for sure.

"See you soon, Colonel."

"Rocky," Lt. Col. Randal said, looking up from the Colt .38 Super he was cleaning, "why don't you call me John like everyone else?"

"I will," Rocky said, rippling out the door. "Thank you, John."

"Will you zip me please?" Lady Jane called from the bedroom.

Lady Jane was fastening her diamond ear studs as he zipped up the skin-tight black sheath of the simple style she favored. Lt. Col. Randal asked, "When did you and Rocky become girlfriends?"

"She is very likeable," Lady Jane said.

"True."

"After you shot the man attempting to break into her apartment," Lady Jane said, "Rocky no longer felt safe in Cairo. RFHQ has plenty of bedrooms . . . some say the reason for so many is because King Farouk staged his orgies here."

"I see," Lt. Col. Randal said, thinking there was more to this than she was telling.

"John, the woman has no money, no country, and now she is working for our side," Lady Jane said. "We have to take care of Rocky.

"Besides, you *are* her patron."

THE INVESTITURE CEREMONY WAS HELD IN THE PLUSH, TINY Master's dining room on the third floor as opposed to the opulent, large formal dining room on the first floor. Field Marshal Sir Claude Auchinleck arrived accompanied by his aide. He was seated next to Rikke Runborg. Next to her was Lieutenant Colonel John Randal and Captain the Lady Jane Seaborn. Ex-Lieutenant Billy Jack Jaxx was on his left.

FM Auchinleck asked, "Miss Runborg, have we met before?"

"I believe not," Rocky said with a sparkling smile.

She may or may not have been lying considering Rocky was suspected of being Marina Lee – the Nazi spy who had stolen his battle plan in Norway by infiltrating his headquarters, using the not-so-original ploy of sleeping with one of his senior staff officers to gain access.

They were all sitting on the same side of the dinner table, which Lt. Col. Randal thought was an unusual seating arrangement.

James "Baldie" Taylor was present, as was Brigadier Raymond J. "R.J." Maunsell, and Lieutenant Commander Ian Fleming, RN, who had flown in from England. The three intelligence officers stood off to one side and observed the proceedings.

An official Army Press Corps photographer was there to record the ceremony.

On signal from Brig. Maunsell, FM Auchinleck stood up. Ex-Lt. Jaxx rose and was presented the Military Cross. The citation, read aloud by the Field Marshal's military aide, said "For Service to the Crown."

The photographer took the obligatory stiffly posed official shots. Then the Field Marshal and ex-Lt. Jaxx resumed their seats. The formal proceedings were concluded.

At that point, the photographer kicked into high gear, clicking away like a madman, flashbulbs popping.

Most of the shots were of FM Auchinleck, Rocky and Lt. Col. Randal.

Lady Jane and ex-Lt. Jaxx were virtually ignored.

Lt. Col. Randal clicked on. He was not sure why. Nothing happened – but something must have.

Then it was over.

As they were walking down the hall, ex-Lt. Jaxx asked, "Sir, do you have any idea why I got this medal?"

Lt. Col. Randal said, "Don't have a clue."

"The Military Cross," Lady Jane said, "can only be awarded for valor."

"There you go," Lt. Col. Randal said. "You're a hero, Jack."

Ex-Lt. Jaxx said, "What a joke."

12

SPY VS. SPY

LIEUTENANT COLONEL JOHN RANDAL WAS SITTING IN A WINGBACK chair in the living room of the suite he shared with Captain the Lady Jane Seaborn, looking at a copy of the morning edition of the Cairo newspaper. King had delivered the newspaper to him as soon as it had arrived at RFHQ. He had been staring at the paper for a full five minutes without making it past the first page.

There was a photo of Field Marshal Claude Auchinleck, Rikke Runborg, Lady Jane and himself above the fold. The cutline said, "Field Marshal Auchinleck at a private dinner party with an unidentified female companion, his senior Special Forces Commander, Lieutenant Colonel Randal, who has been called 'the most dangerous man in Middle East Command' and Lady Jane Seaborn."

And that was it. There was no accompanying story. No mention of ex-Lieutenant Billy Jack Jaxx's Military Cross.

In fact, ex-Lt. Jaxx had been cropped out of the shot.

Nothing subtle here, Lt. Col. Randal thought.

Brigadier Raymond J. Maunsell was validating Rocky's credentials with her German spymasters in Berlin. The photo proved beyond any shadow of a doubt that Rocky had insinuated herself into the inner circle of the British High Command in the Middle East.

They say a picture is worth a thousand words. This one was. Lt. Col. Randal guessed the photo had been planted in newspapers all over the world, which meant it was in the hands of German intelligence this very morning.

The Abwehr had to be ecstatic. Rocky had accomplished her mission.

She was in.

KING SAID, "LT. KIDD, CHIEF."

"How's your Lovat Scout recruiting going, Roy?"

"Done, sir," Lieutenant Roy Kidd said. "All eight Scouts from Layforce volunteered. Lady Seaborn had them here same day."

"That's good," Lt. Col. Randal said. "Lovat Scouts are worth their weight in gold. We just haven't figured out a way to exploit their maximum capability in the desert."

"I believe we will, Colonel," Lt. Kidd said. "Billy Jack and I have been talking about the Boys .55 rifle. The way it's rigged now with the No. 32 scope-mounted centerline on the receiver, you have to fire the weapon single-shot.

"Jack said his grandfather mounted a Weaver 4X scope on a Winchester Model 94 lever action 30–30 carbine – what they call a 'saddle gun.' Model 94s eject their spent cartridges out the top, so the Sheriff used an offset side mount.

"If we do that with a Boys .55, sir, we can use the top-mounted magazine, and it's a repeater again the way it was designed. Sgt. Rawlston has his men machining the mounts, sir," Lt. Kidd said.

"Pretty slick," Lt. Col. Randal said.

"Fenwick and Ferguson elected to stay with Ranger Patrol, sir. That's fine by me. I only need three teams of snipers – six of the new Scouts."

"How about the rest of your personnel?" Lt. Col. Randal asked.

"You authorized four gun jeeps for my patrol – three armed with Boys .55s and one Phantom radio jeep which I'm going to use as my command vehicle. It'll also have a Boys on board I intend to shoot, sir."

"We have the three Phantom troopers; Mad Dog has three AVG drivers lined up for me plus an ex-LRDG navigator. My batman, Pan, will be coming along and I'll be driving the command jeep," Lt. Kidd said.

"Scout Patrol is ready to take the field. I'd like to get going if that's all right with you, sir."

"Move out when ready," Lt. Col. Randal said.

"You sure it was OK with you to give up Duck Patrol, Roy?"

"I picked up a lot of experience operating off the *King Duck,* sir," Lt. Kidd said. "But the LCT is a monster in any weather. Capt. Finley loves it, the rougher the better – me personally, not so much.

"I'll be glad to be back on dry land again, sir."

"Scout Patrol's a Raiding Forces' asset," Lt. Col. Randal said. "That means you work for me but coordinate through Maj. Stone. Clear the AO you're planning to operate in with Desert Patrol; they'll coordinate with Mr. Zargo and the LRDG.

"Develop your own tactics. I'll want to accompany Scout Patrol from time to time. See what you work up."

"Yes, sir."

"Here's something for you, Roy," Lt. Col. Randal said, pulling out a web belt with a flap holster. "Polish Vis 9mm – some call it a Radom. Traded Veronica Paige a pearl-handled Beretta 7.65 pocket pistol I took off a senior Regia Aeronautica officer in Abyssinia for it."

Lt. Kidd said, "Nice weapon, sir."

"Heard you say you were looking for a different 9mm handgun," Lt. Col. Randal said. "Give this one a try. If you don't like it we'll find something else."

"I saw these Polish Vis pistols at RAF Habbaniya, sir," Lt. Kidd said.

"Basically appears to be a John Browning design 9mm on a 1911 frame, no grip safety. Should keep right on ticking no matter what," Lt. Kidd said, examining the pistol.

"Has a good feel, sir."

"Hope you like it."

"My Lugers turned out to be finicky . . . beautiful though."

"Function," Lt. Col. Randal said, "is beauty."

Ex-Lieutenant Billy Jack Jaxx walked in.

"If I were you, Colonel, I'd never let Lady Jane hear me say that."

Jack Cool.

"ADMIRAL RANSOM, GENERAL TAYLOR AND LIEUTENANT Commander Fleming to see you, Chief," King said.

Lieutenant Colonel John Randal looked up from the patrol reports he was reading. Field Marshal Claude Auchinleck's plan to award Raiding Forces decorations for performance had worked to immediate effect on Desert Patrol.

Gun jeeps were going after thin-skinned Axis transport on the Via Balbia with a vengeance. Claims of enemy trucks damaged and destroyed had skyrocketed. Legend had it Napoleon declared he could conquer the world as long as factories kept churning out enough ribbon to make medals for his marshals. Maybe not, but the plan was sure working to motivate Raiding Forces' patrol leaders to target enemy trucks.

The three visitors came in and sat down. This was no social call.

"We are not here," Lt. Cdr. Fleming said. "We are not having this conversation."

Lt. Col. Randal leaned back in the wing-backed chair, stuck one of Waldo's cigars between his front teeth and lit it with his U.S. 26th Cavalry Regiment Zippo.

"Do not ask questions, Colonel," Lt. Cdr. Fleming said. "If I respond and inadvertently reveal information not intended for this briefing – the one not taking place, you will never be allowed to take the field on active combat operations for the rest of the war.

"'Why not?' you ask. Because you might be captured and interrogated. We could not run the risk."

"Guess taking notes is totally out of the question," Lt. Col. Randal said.

All the spy vs. spy stuff was beginning to wear thin. He was a soldier, not an intelligence operative.

James "Baldie" Taylor gave him a look.

Allowing himself a small smile, Vice Admiral Sir Randolph "Razor" Ransom said, "What we are about to reveal to you, Colonel, is the most important secret of the war. You will not discuss anything said here with anyone not sitting in this room. Not ever under any circumstances.

"Do you understand?"

"I do, sir."

"The Nazis," Lt. Cdr. Fleming said, "have an encoding machine. Breaking the code it creates is Allied priority number one. Also priority number two, three, four . . . you get the idea.

"The odds against us cracking the German code are staggering, roughly equal to winning the National Lottery once a day every day for one hundred years.

"The best estimate is each enemy message, and there are thousands of messages intercepted every day, contains 10.5 quadrillion combinations of possible solutions. What that translates into is if one thousand cryptanalysts worked seven days a week twenty-four hours per day it would take 1.8 billion years to test them all."

"Our only hope of winning this war," VAdm. Ransom said, "is to penetrate the encoding machine, learn the Nazi's intentions and act accordingly."

"In that case, sir," Lt. Col. Randal said, "it never hurts to cheat."

"Told you he was going to get it," Jim said. "That's one of Raiding Forces' Rules – my personal favorite."

"Lt. Jaxx's Military Cross," Lt. Cdr. Fleming said, "was awarded for capturing the encoding equipment and documents at the German weather station he attacked on a desert patrol a short while back. No way possible to reveal the specific details of the action in the declaration at the investiture ceremony. Would have given the game away if we had.

"That said, Intelligence does wish word to quietly get around our Special Forces units that capturing enemy signals information shall be rewarded."

"In the future," VAdm. Ransom said, "the idea is to plan Raiding Forces' raids on certain targets such as small ships or isolated German weather stations like the one Lt. Jaxx took down where there might be encryption devices, code books, etc., to be found. Booty our code breakers can use, as you say, 'to cheat.'"

Jim said, "We will have to conduct a small amount of specialized training for Raiding Forces. Our men will need to understand what it is they are looking for – but not why."

Lt. Cdr. Fleming said, "The operation is going to be codenamed Golden Fleece – the name is classified *above* MOST SECRET. You are the only individual in Raiding Forces with the 'Need to Know' the meaning.

"The troops involved in Golden Fleece will be codenamed Red Indians, and that is how you will refer to the missions: Red Indian raids.

"The bottom line is we could tie up the best brains in all England for 1.8 billion years trying to break the German code," Lt. Cdr. Fleming said.

"Or you can pinch the key for us."

Lt. Col. Randal said, "Love to."

CAPTAIN THE LADY JANE SEABORN AND LIEUTENANT COLONEL John Randal were sitting in the living room of their suite. Lady Jane was telling him a story. He was paying close attention.

"The wives and girlfriends of Raiding Forces," Lady Jane said, "are patriotic to a fault.

"Unfortunately, when our women gossip with their girlfriends they do not have tales of derring-do performed by their men to share. Operational security prohibits our Raiders from mentioning unit tactics, enemy action or friendly troop movements when they write home.

"'Loose lips sink ships.'"

"Uh-oh," Lt. Col. Randal said.

He was highly sensitive to anything that might affect the morale of his troops.

"Our Raiders' wives and girlfriends have been writing letters to their loved ones saying they are disappointed we are not doing more for the war effort," Lady Jane said.

"And how do you know that?"

"My Marines censor all mail – incoming and outgoing," Lady Jane said.

"Our lads have a tendency to downplay the danger they face to keep their women from worrying. The result is letters back to England making service in Raiding Forces sound like an extended Boy Scout camping trip – lots of sun, sand, great tans, boring."

Lt. Col. Randal said, "We've got a problem."

"Agreed," Lady Jane said.

"Naturally, I did not want to bother you, John. Something had to be done – not to forget your new policy, 'bring me a problem, bring me the solution.'"

Lt. Col. Randal said, "Never meant it to apply to you, Jane."

"The solution," Lady Jane said, rewarding him a magnificent smile, "was to instruct my Royal Marines stationed at Seaborn House to visit the wife or girlfriend of every single Raider stationed in Middle East Command.

"My Marines explained to each one privately their husbands or boyfriends were performing vital classified missions. The ladies were advised to say their loved ones were behind enemy lines engaged in classified national level strategic operations subject to the Official Secrets Act.

"The women were warned they *could* tell their girlfriends the details but then they would have to kill them," Lady Jane said.

"And they were authorized to say exactly that if pressed."

"Oh, that's good," Lt. Col. Randal said. "Outstanding."

"Thank you, John."

"Are you reading *my* mail too?"

"Absolutely," Lady Jane said.

LIEUTENANT MANDY PAIGE SAUNTERED IN WEARING A SUPER short pair of cut-off blue jeans and peewee cowboy boots like the ones Captain the Lady Jane Seaborn and Lieutenant Pamala Plum-Martin wore from time to time. Cowboy boots had been part of the undercover costume the girls sported posing as "urban cowsluts" while spying out the port at Rio Bonita prior to OPERATION LOUNGE LIZARD – before Raiding Forces sailed in and cut out three enemy ships berthed in the neutral Portuguese Protectorate.

Lady Jane had boots made for Mandy locally using hers as a pattern – in Cairo you could get anything for a price.

Except for blue jeans.

"Cut-offs," Lieutenant Colonel John Randal said. "I haven't seen any of those since I left home six years ago."

"Billy Jack showed me a photo of the Tri-Delta girls at the University of Texas wearing cut-off jeans," Lt. Mandy said. "Pam and I wanted some."

"We were unable to buy jeans in Cairo," Lt. Mandy said. "So, Billy Jack wrote the Tri-Delts."

"The sorority sent us Levis to cut off. Those Texas girls do not seem to be very mad at Billy Jack."

"No, they don't."

"You wanted to see me, John?"

"There's a man named Mud Cat Ray. A former tugboat skipper on the Gold Coast," Lt. Col. Randal said. "He's in jail on a murder charge.

"I want him out, Mandy."

"No problem," Lt. Mandy said. "The fine for killing a native is $60."

"Are you kidding?"

"If the man he murdered was a British subject, Sammy Sansom will spring him for us for free," Mandy said.

"Sammy has been promoted to major with the new title Chief Field Security Officer Cairo – king of the Cairo underworld."

"Get it done," Lt. Col. Randal said. "Admiral Ransom has a job for him. Besides, the Skipper's a personal friend of mine."

"Mud Cat . . . you sure know a lot of colorful characters," Lt. Mandy said.

"Likewise," Lt. Col. Randal said.

"I know you, John."

"Have you seen Rita and Lana?" Lt. Col. Randal asked. "I need to talk to them."

"The girls are working undercover for Sammy – nights," Lt. Mandy said.

"Dancing at the Kit-Kat Club."

"HEADHUNTER HOOLIHAN TO SEE YOU, CHIEF," KING SAID.

"Lieutenant Hoolihan reports, sir," the Royal Marine said, doing it by the book.

"Sit down, Butch," Lieutenant Colonel John Randal said. "How's operating off Randy's high-speed MAS boats working out now that you can use the LCT to extend your range up the coast?"

"Quite well, sir," Lieutenant Butch "Headhunter" Hoolihan said.

He and Lt. Col. Randal had a long history serving together going back to before Raiding Forces' first parachute raid on the French Coast. The two trusted each other implicitly.

"Sure beats trying to run missions out of Tobruk – hated that place."

"I can see how you would," Lt. Col. Randal said.

"I am looking forward to Admiral Ransom getting his trawler put to sea sir. We can raid all the way up the coastline to Tripoli once it goes operational."

"Mud Cat Ray's in line to be the captain," Lt. Col. Randal said, "provided we can spring him out of jail. Mandy's on it."

"Getting the old Gold Coast tugboat firm back together," Lt. Hoolihan said. "I will sail with Mud Cat any time, anywhere, sir."

"That's what I wanted to talk to you about, Butch," Lt. Col. Randal said.

"I've pulled Roy off Duck Patrol. He's forming a new patrol made up primarily of Lovat Scouts. The idea is to snipe trucks traveling the Via Balbia from extreme long range."

"Sounds like a plan, sir," Lt. Hoolihan said. "Roy is the perfect choice for the job."

"Would you be interested in taking over Duck Patrol?" Lt. Col. Randal asked. "I need a good amphibious man used to operating independently."

"No, sir. Not if I have a choice," Lt. Hoolihan said. "Once the Admiral completes the trawler's refit and we go operational, my troop will be out virtually every night executing pure Commando pinprick raids somewhere on the coast – mining the road and shooting up roadhouses.

"We are not able to do that with the *King Duck* like we initially thought we could. As it turns out, the LCT is not able to raise enough speed to return to safety before sunrise," Lt. Hoolihan said.

"The Admiral is making arrangements for Sea Squadron to launch raids off submarines. Now that will really be something."

"Submarines, huh?" Lt. Col. Randal said.

"Happy to take over Duck Patrol temporarily until the trawler is ready, Colonel."

"May take you up on that, Butch," Lt. Col. Randal said. "You were my first choice for the job. I don't have a second."

He had wanted Lt. Hoolihan to take over from Lt. Kidd. Duck Patrol was a unique team. It required a special kind of leader.

However, Lt. Col. Randal had a long-standing policy of allowing his Raiders to serve in the position of their choice whenever possible – instead of blindly assigning them a slot with no more thought than filling the immediate need of the service – the way it usually works in the military.

"Don't repeat me on this, sir," Lt. Hoolihan said. "I can't get off that LCT fast enough. In the slightest breeze the *King Duck* goes wild. The ship pitches like a bucking bronco determined to throw everyone and every bit of equipment over the side."

"So I've heard."

LIEUTENANT PAMALA PLUM-MARTIN AND EX-LIEUTENANT BILLY Jack Jaxx arrived.

"Shut the door behind you, King," Lieutenant Colonel John Randal ordered. "I want you in on this."

"Let me go find Flanigan, Chief," King said. "Scheduled to relieve me in a few minutes anyway. Be right back."

While they waited for King to return, Lt. Col. Randal said, "Pam, you've never explained why you gave up your intelligence work to take up flying full time."

"Well, John, after you shot up the Palace Hotel in Istanbul," Lt. Plum-Martin said, "my cover was blown. I was made by every intelligence organization worldwide."

"Yeah," Lt. Col. Randal said, "I can see how you would be."

"Shot up a hotel," ex-Lt. Jaxx said. "Anybody killed?"

"Oh, yes," Lt. Plum-Martin said. "John was found in a hotel room with a dead Nazi Brandenburger Commando and a naked SS female agent . . . also deceased.

"Shot them both."

"Wow!" ex-Lt. Jaxx said.

"Tell you the story sometime, Billy Jack," Lt. Plum-Martin said. "At least the good parts."

"Not my fault," Lt. Col. Randal said.

"Quite all right, John," Lt. Plum-Martin said. "Flying Special Operations missions is my true love."

When King returned, Lt. Col. Randal asked, "Pam, do you remember before we organized OPERATION BUZZARD PLUCKER Squadron Leader Wilcox told us it only took a matter of days to build an airplane but it took two years to get a combat pilot fully qualified?"

"I do, John," the Vargas Girl look-alike Royal Marine said. "Paddy said the Germans had not ramped up their flight schools to train an adequate number of replacement pilots to make up for the losses they will incur in sustained air combat.

"He said the Luftwaffe intends to fight the war with the aviators it has operational now."

"Right," Lt. Randal said.

"Lack of a replacement pilot pipeline will prove awkward for the Nazis absolutely," Lt. Plum-Martin said. "Difficult to believe the Luftwaffe could be that stupid."

"Paddy's estimate of the situation was the reason we launched OPERATION BUZZARD PLUCKER," Lt. Col. Randal said. "Sending in Lovat Scouts teams to snipe German pilots at their landing grounds in enemy-occupied France."

"Wish I had been on flying status," Lt. Plum-Martin said. "Fabulous missions."

"Having invaded Russia now," Lt. Col. Randal said, "the strain on German pilots can only get worse.

"Pam, you were talking to King about an idea to bomb places German and Italian pilots congregate – make that happen.

"Fantastic."

"King, coordinate with Mr. Zargo. Our first task is to develop a target list."

"With pleasure, Chief."

"Billy Jack, you work with the three of them. Report to me," Lt. Col. Randal said. "It's open season on enemy pilots."

"Yes, sir," ex-Lt. Jaxx said. "No bag limit."

"You heard me tell the patrol leaders to go after pilots, but let's keep what we're doing between the three of us for the time being," Lt. Col. Randal said.

"Our own freelance operation."

BRIGADIER RAYMOND J. MAUNSELL ARRIVED AT RAIDING Forces' Headquarters at 2100 hours. Major A. W. "Sammy" Sansom and a man in a cheap suit were with him. The stranger looked like a seedy spy in a movie, and that is exactly what he was – a seedy spy.

Lieutenant Colonel John Randal and Rikke Runborg were waiting for them. The man in the cheap suit appeared nervous but perked up when he saw Rocky. Did they know each other?

No introductions were made except for a brief "This is Colonel Randal" from Brig. Maunsell.

Rocky and the man spoke to each other in German.

James "Baldie" Taylor came downstairs and joined the group.

One of the Royal Marines reported to Lt. Col. Randal, "The Squadron Leader is ready for takeoff, sir."

Lt. Col. Randal helped the man in the cheap suit into an X-type parachute. Then he gave him a thorough jumpmaster inspection, making sure the straps were tight.

Then the group went outside where King had a caravan of jeeps waiting to drive them to the Raiding Forces' private airstrip a short distance away.

The Hudson was ticking over when the party arrived. Everyone except Brig. Maunsell and Rocky immediately boarded the aircraft. As soon as they were on the plane, Squadron Leader Paddy Wilcox and Lieutenant Pamala-Plum Martin began to taxi for takeoff.

When the Hudson was airborne, Maj. Sansom, Jim and Lt. Col. Randal moved a short distance away to the tail of the aircraft to have a private conversation.

King sat with the man in the cheap suit.

Jim said, "We are going to drop our 'Joe,' as we call an agent going on a mission whose name everyone does not need to know, at a certain location in German-held territory. The drop zone will be marked because the Abwehr is expecting him."

"We're dropping our agent to the Nazis?"

"That's right, Colonel," Maj. Sansom said. "He's a German plant. Turned himself in to SIME and volunteered to work for us as a double agent. We do not believe he is telling the truth.

"What we are undertaking tonight is planting some 'chicken feed' for A Force."

"Chicken feed?"

"Intelligence information that is true but of no real value to the enemy," Jim said. "All rubbish except for one golden nugget. Our Joe is carrying documents that will absolutely confirm Rocky has infiltrated the inner circle of British High Command in the Middle East and has access to military secrets."

"I see," Lt. Col. Randal said. Which meant he did not have a clue what was going on.

"The reason we are using you as the dispatcher tonight is because the Joe knows who you are. May give him added confidence," Jim said.

"Your reputation has preceded you, Colonel."

The red light came on.

"Ten minutes," Lt. Col. Randal said loud enough for the Joe to hear.

Tonight they would be dropping from one thousand feet. Lt. Col. Randal hooked the Joe's snap link to the steel cable, gave it a jerk to make sure it was seated, poked the steel safety pin in the hole, then bent it down to lock it.

Lt. Col. Randal took the Joe's hat and tucked it inside his suit jacket above the briefcase strapped to his chest.

Then, waiting until the last minute because the Joe was clearly an apprehensive jumper, he opened the door of the Hudson. Lt. Col. Randal gripped both sides of the frame with the tips of his fingertips and arched outside looking ahead for the drop zone. Since they were flying over a featureless desert, he did not have any checkpoints. The DZ was supposed to be marked with a burning letter *T*.

The wind whipped his face and rattled his khaki bush jacket violently. Up ahead he could see a light on the ground.

Lt. Col. Randal moved the Joe up toward the door but not standing in it yet. King moved in behind the jumper to assist if necessary.

"Remember, keep your feet and knees together when you land," he shouted in the Joe's ear.

The man nodded, looking like a scared rabbit.

A quick check back out the door confirmed the burning light to be the letter *T*.

The Hudson was thundering toward the DZ. Lt. Col. Randal moved his jumper into the door. The man was too afraid to reach out and slap the sides of the fuselage with both hands in the approved manner.

The Joe was going to need help. When the green light flashed on, Lt. Col. Randal shoved him out the door without any warning – not having a jump refusal on his watch.

In an instant the man was gone.

As the Hudson banked into a hard right turn, Sqn. Ldr. Wilcox pushed the throttles forward to pick up speed. Lt. Col. Randal began to haul in the yellow static line.

Snapped in half.

Maj. Sansom said, "The opposition is going to have a warm body – chicken feed and no way to pump their man for information we might not want them to know."

"You sabotaged the chute?"

"Yes, we did," Jim said.

"The Germans will find out," Lt. Col. Randal said.

"We know," Maj. Sansom said. "So we told them we did it."

"You *told* the Nazis?'

"Never make the other side work very hard," Jim said, "to figure out something you want them to know.

"Besides, telling the Germans 'who done it' was the masterstroke A-Force needed to convince the Abwehr that Rocky is working in their best interests – smoke and mirrors."

"Smoked him," Lt. Col. Randal said. "How'd you get the word to the other side?"

"Sammy slipped a message inside the Joe's briefcase while you were conducting his jumpmaster inspection at RFHQ. It informed the Abwehr that Rocky had requested MI-5 to disable the Joe's parachute. She said he was dangerous and might expose her as a spy: 'the fool likes to spend all his time at the Kit-Kat Club, drinks in excess and talks too much to the dancers.'

"Germans are probably reading it right about now."

"Have to play high," Major Sansom said, "to win high."

"Rocky knew tonight was going to happen?"

"Wrote the note," Jim said.

"That's cold," Lt. Col. Randal said.

13

FANCY SHOOTING

LIEUTENANT COLONEL JOHN RANDAL WAS PACKING HIS GEAR preparing to depart Raiding Forces' Headquarters for Oasis X with Ranger Patrol. He traveled light, not carrying much: a hard-used canvas shaving kit (though, to conserve water, no one shaved while in the desert), canteen, eating utensils, wooden-handled Swiss Army knife (a gift from Captain the Lady Jane Seaborn), military-issue lensatic compass (both the compass and knife were worn on lanyards in the breast pockets of his faded khaki bush jacket), one change of clothes, a pair of yellow leather gloves and his Zeiss binoculars – captured from a Panzer Leader at Pas-de-Calais.

And his personal weapons: 9mm Beretta MAB-38 submachine gun, a pair of 1911 Colt Government Model .38 Supers, 9mm Browning P-35 High-Power, .22 High Standard Military Model D with silencer and Fairbairn Fighting Knife – one of the first 500 made by the sword-making firm Wilkinson Sword Ltd.

"Frank Polanski to see you, Chief," King called from the door.

"I've pulled Roy Kidd off Duck Patrol to form another patrol," Lt. Col. Randal said. "I need a replacement for him with amphibious experience. You interested in the job? A commission goes with it."

"Negative," Frank said. "I'm happy to stay assistant patrol leader, Colonel. Looking forward to manning the COW 37mm, maybe mount something bigger on one of the DUKWs . . . they can handle up to a one-o-five."

"So everyone keeps telling me," Lt. Col. Randal said.

"I kind of like the idea of rolling up under cover of darkness," Frank said, "pounding one of those roadhouses into dust point blank, spreading a few camel chip mines on the road, then disappearing back out to sea."

"You know, Frank," Lt. Col. Randal said zipping up the lightweight parachute container he used instead of a duffel bag, "when the U.S. finally comes in the war there's a good possibility the Marines are going to offer you a commission. Your chances will be better if you've been serving as an officer in the British Commandos."

"Ain't planning on re-enlisting in the Marines," Frank said. "My idea is to stay right here in Raiding Forces for the duration. I'm a heavy weapons man, Colonel.

"I ain't officer material."

KING SAID, "I PUT YOUR BRIXIA 45MM BLOOPER IN THE JEEP, Chief. Want me to take your bag down?"

"I'll get it, King," Lieutenant Colonel John Randal said.

"Better let me," King said. "Brandy Seaborn is on the way up."

"You stay on the door," Lt. Col. Randal ordered. "After Brandy gets here, don't let anyone in."

"Understood."

Brandy Seaborn arrived as beautiful as ever, but her fabulous golden-girl smile was absent. She was a brand-new war widow. No one knew what to say on the subject that would not end up making her feel worse.

Lt. Col. Randal had no idea. He felt guilty about her husband being killed. Commodore Seaborn had a nice safe job routing convoys at the Admiralty before Raiding Forces requested him by name to command the naval element of OPERATION LOUNGE LIZARD, the raid on Rio Bonita.

Seeing a happy girl sad was definitely not good.

"My father asked me to speak to you, John," Brandy said.

Lt. Col. Randal said, "Why doesn't he do it himself?"

"Father does not want to put you on the spot," Brandy said, "in case you care to decline his request."

"That bad, huh?"

"No," Brandy laughed, beginning to get some of her old sense of humor back. She felt comfortable around Lt. Col. Randal. The two were close. And had been from the night they met at the promotion party for her son, Lieutenant Randy "Hornblower" Seaborn.

"The Admiral only wants to inquire if you would be willing to allow him to set up shop for Navy Irregular Operations here at RFHQ," Brandy said.

"Not a problem," Lt. Col. Randal said. "Tell the Razor to get with Jane. She'll find him a good spot."

"Father shall be delighted," Brandy said. "He is quite enjoying his role as the Empire's chief buccaneer."

"Brandy," Lt. Col. Randal said, not sure how to put what he wanted to say and not wanting to get it wrong.

"You'll probably return to England for the Commodore's funeral. I'd like you to come back here after it's over. Move into RFHQ . . . you and Parker pick yourself out a couple of the master bedrooms."

"Traveling home is not on," Brandy said. "Richard went down with his ship. No need for a funeral. The family is spread out all over the globe on active service. We shall have to put off a memorial until after the war."

"In that case, I'll feel better knowing you're living here where we've got good security," Lt. Col. Randal said.

"Stage your search for Count Almasy from Raiding Forces' operations room or set up one of your own."

"I accept," Brandy said. "Thank you."

No one had worried about her since she had been married at seventeen, or at least no one had let her know if they were. In the Six Hundred, particularly in Navy families, the women were expected to spend extended periods of time when their men were away at sea. Keep calm and carry on.

"Really sorry, Brandy."

"I know," Brandy said. "So am I."

"KING," LIEUTENANT COLONEL JOHN RANDAL ORDERED, "GO FIND Sergeant Major Mikkalis and Mad Dog. Have them report to me at my command jeep prior to Ranger Patrol pulling out."

"On the way, Chief."

Captain the Lady Jane Seaborn walked him out to Ranger Patrol's little column of six gun jeeps.

Sergeant Ned Pompedous reported, "All jeeps prepared to move out, sir."

"Let's do a quick walk around, Sergeant," Lt. Col. Randal said.

With the exception of the American Volunteer Group (AVG) men and Guns, the Royal Naval Patrol service 20mm ace, everyone in Ranger Patrol had been with Lt. Col. Randal for a long time.

Sgt. Pompedous had served with him since Pas-de-Calais in Swamp Fox Force. Lovat Scouts Fenwick and Ferguson were recruited for OPERATION BUZZARD PLUCKER out of Seaborn House then served with him in Force N. The Phantom radio team and GG, the Italian captured in Abyssinia who had attended college in the U.S. and wanted to open a restaurant in America after the war, had been with his command party.

Waldo Treywick had been with Lt. Col. Randal from the day he had parachuted into Abyssinia to raise a guerrilla army.

The minute Lt. Col. Randal began his inspection, he relaxed. He enjoyed being around his troops. There was nothing he liked better than leading gun jeep patrols.

While Lt. Col. Randal was not crazy about the desert environment, the wide open terrain and millions of miles of desolation to strike out of then retreat back into and get lost made it the perfect place to conduct high-speed, pinprick guerrilla operations.

Hit, run and vanish.

Lt. Col. Randal was looking forward to the patrol. He always thought better on the move. Once the jeeps rolled out, his mind would be focused on the moment, constantly processing everything going on around him. Always planning his next move.

For a cavalry officer like he was, it did not get any better than that.

The inspection did not take long but Lt. Col. Randal did not rush it. He stopped at each gun jeep and joked with the crew as they were checking all the million details that needed to be checked, rechecked and re-rechecked prior to taking the field. The Raiders were fanatical about their jeeps. They traveled, maintained, slept next to and fought out of them.

Ranger Patrol was a tight-knit team. Everyone was a professional. The troops considered themselves a cut above the rest – "the Colonel's men."

Arriving back at his command jeep, Lt. Col. Randal found James "Baldie" Taylor stowing his gear in the back.

"I would like to ride out to X with you, Colonel," Jim said. "Lt. Jaxx and King said they would not be going. OK if I take the wheel for practice desert driving?"

"You bet," Lt. Col. Randal said.

Captain "Geronimo" Joe McKoy strolled up. "I'm your machine gunner this trip out to Oasis X, John. Then I'll link up with my White Patrol boys. My tack's already onboard."

"Good."

Captain Mike "Mad Dog" Reupart and Sergeant Major Mike "March or Die" Mikkalis, DSM, MM, arrived at the command jeep.

"Raiding Forces has an officer problem," Lt. Col. Randal said. "Roy is off the *King Duck* raising a new patrol. I don't have a replacement for him.

"Take command of Duck Patrol, Sergeant Major. At least until we find a qualified officer or you decide you want the job permanently."

"I can work with Warthog and Frank, sir," Sgt. Maj. Mikkalis said.

"Mad Dog," Lt. Col. Randal said, "Raiding Forces has been tasked with taking over parachute training for L Detachment, Special Air Service. Link up with Lieutenant Jock Lewis. He's their training officer. They only have four officers and fourteen men currently, but the word is they're about to expand."

"Yes, sir."

"They've been trying to teach themselves how to jump out of airplanes," Lt. Col. Randal said. "Two men have been killed already and who knows how many injured. Take charge and get 'em parachute qualified.

Capt. Reupart said. "I shall start sorting out the SAS parachuting program this afternoon, sir."

"While you're at it," Lt. Col. Randal said, "be advised Field Marshal Auchinleck wants to set up a Middle East Command Parachute Training School. He asked me to find someone to run it."

"Colonel," Capt. Reupart said, "I have no interest whatsoever in being transferred out of Raiding Forces, sir."

"You won't be," Lt. Col. Randal said. "The school's a Raiding Forces' task. When one of our people is injured we'll let him whip himself back into shape training paratroopers. Once you have everything up and running, we can find someone to step in to take command."

"I like the sound of that much better, sir."

"Running the school," Lt. Col. Randal said, "puts us in the perfect position to cherry-pick recruits from the students."

"That it does," Capt. Reupart said. "Very good point, sir."

"Don't worry, Mad Dog," Lt. Col. Randal said. "I'm not letting anyone steal you. You're one of the most valuable assets Raiding Forces has."

Captain Hawthorne Merryweather appeared, lugging his gear. "Care if I join you, sir?"

"Why should I mind? Everyone else is going," Lt. Col. Randal said.

"Waldo has a spare seat. Ride with him."

Lady Jane's green eyes were glistening. She put her cheek against his and whispered, "Be safe, John."

The loss of Brandy's husband had rattled her. A number of Lady Jane's other family members had died suddenly – parents, brother, husband.

Her husband had only been temporarily declared dead.

He had turned up very much alive in enemy-occupied France having a red hot affair with Rikke Runborg, aka Rocky. When rescued, he claimed amnesia. All interested parties agreed his story was a "dashed good try." Unfortunately for him, it did not fly with Lady Jane, the Royal Navy, British Intelligence or even Rocky.

"I'll be back," Lt. Col. Randal said.

"Don't go anywhere without King, Flanigan, Rita or Lana with you at all times until I return – if you can get the girls to squeeze in time to be your bodyguards when they're not dancing at the Kit-Kat.

"That's an order."

"Aye aye, sir," Lady Jane said.

Watching the exchange, ex-Lieutenant Billy Jack Jaxx said to King, "You reckon he nicks himself?"

"What?"

"Lady Jane's cheekbones are sharp enough to cut glass," ex-Lt. Jaxx said. "Wonder if the Colonel ever cuts himself on 'em when they're making out . . . ever had to patch him up?"

The Merc said, "Those details are classified."

Lt. Col. Randal stuck his finger in the air and made a circle – the signal to crank it up. All six jeeps roared to life.

"Let's roll, General," he said to Jim.

The little convoy snaked its way out of Raiding Forces' Headquarters. Everyone not on duty turned out to see them off and those who were on duty went to a window. A patrol departing on a mission was always an event everyone liked to watch.

No matter how many times people had seen the sight – troops moving out headed in harm's way it was always a thrill. There was no guarantee all the men in Ranger Patrol would be coming back.

Godspeed.

"THERE'S A BIG BUILD-UP GOIN' ON," CAPTAIN "GERONIMO" JOE McKoy said. "Just a matter a' time now before we attack."

"Rommel's marshaling Afrika Korps for an offensive too," James "Baldie" Taylor said. "We are in a race to see who jumps off first.

"Quite a bit of loose talk in the bars. The MEHQ armchair Commandos do not have the first idea of security. Something has gone wrong with the mental attitude of the officers in Middle East Command."

"Jane mentioned that," Lieutenant Colonel John Randal said. "She said Auchinleck's staff is counting on an easy victory."

"Not only the staff," Jim said. "Every unit you visit it is the same story: 'The men are in good heart' . . . or so their officers claim."

Ranger Patrol was driving south up the road to Cairo. Traffic was heavier than usual. There were supply dumps of all kinds under camouflage netting off in the distance dotting both sides of the hardball. Military equipment, cannon, vehicles, fuel, etc., in vast quantities courtesy of the United States Lend-Lease Program. The supply points seemed to have sprung up overnight.

"I doubt them boys is in all that good a' heart," Capt. McKoy said. "If they are, it's on account a' ignorance is bliss."

"Roger that," Lt. Col. Randal said.

"The overconfidence at GHQ has been contagious," Jim said. "All our people *are* anticipating a walkover, due in no small part to the massive amount of supplies arriving from England and the United States. Military stores of all classes are pouring in. Middle East Command will have over thirty thousand vehicles before long."

"After the Civil War, Confederate General George Pickett got hisself asked by a reporter why his charge at Gettysburg failed," Capt. McKoy said.

"You know what 'ole Pickett says? 'I always thought the Yankees had something to do with it.'"

"The same sentiment would apply to what the Germans did to us in Norway, France, Greece, Crete and here in OPERATION BATTLEAXE," Jim said. "What could we possibly have to be confident about?"

"Holdin' your enemy in contempt or believin' in your battle plan too much," Capt. McKoy said. "Bad medicine."

Outside of Cairo, Ranger Patrol ran into a traffic jam that consisted almost entirely of khaki-painted U.S.-manufactured trucks. It was quite a sight. Further up, the traffic on the Cairo to Alexander road was bumper to bumper.

"Don't take a military genius," Capt. McKoy said, "to see we're goin' over to offense right quick."

"Field Marshal Auchinleck has reorganized, the Western Desert Force is now styled XIII Corps," Jim said, "along with XXX Corps, it's part of the new Eighth Army under General Cunningham of Abyssinian fame."

"Good man," Lt. Col. Randal said.

Ranger Patrol finally made it through Cairo, past Heliopolis Airfield, then past Mena House Hotel – where Lady Jane kept a suite with a view of the Great Pyramids – and drove out into the desert. The plan was to drive to Oasis X, which they would reach late tomorrow.

The patrol pulled off the road and mounted their machine guns. Lt. Col. Randal had not wanted people in Cairo to observe all the firepower packed on the jeeps.

Once the patrol reached X, Capt. McKoy intended to link up with his White Patrol and take the field. Jim was planning to meet in person with Mr. Zargo for a briefing on intelligence his operatives might have picked up that could give an indication of the German and Italian intentions for their winter offensive. Major Sir Terry "Zorro" Stone would be waiting when Ranger Patrol arrived to provide Lt. Col. Randal with a target list for Ranger Patrol.

No one was expecting trouble at this point in the trip, barely outside the city limits of Cairo. Lt. Col. Randal was enjoying the ride. They had yet to reach the escarpment. Ranger Patrol would be crossing the Great Sand Sea at the saddle, the narrowest point.

Until then the patrol was a pleasure trip.

So it was a shock when Lt. Col. Randal spotted the turrets of three Italian Autoblinda 40 (AB 40) armored cars – hull down – approximately a half mile ahead. As far as he was aware, the Italian Army had never sent reconnaissance patrols this close to Cairo.

Because he had fought them in Abyssinia, Lt. Col. Randal knew that the AB 40 was armed with a pair of turret-mounted Breda 8mm machine guns and one that was rear-facing. It carried a crew of four. The armor on the AB 40 was so thin the Italians commonly referred it to as a "scout car" instead of an armored car.

"Go straight at 'em, General," Lt. Col. Randal ordered, "pedal to the metal."

"Get the Boys .55 mounted, Captain."

"I'm doing it, John."

Lt. Col. Randal signaled Ranger Patrol to come on line. He needed to get Guns' 20mm Oerlikon into position to engage. It was the only automatic weapon the patrol had capable of penetrating the AB 40's armor, thin as it was.

Every Ranger Patrol gun jeep carried a Boys 55 Anti-Tank (AT) rifle stowed onboard. While it was death on thin-skinned vehicles, the Boys could not defeat any known armor *except* that found on Italian armored cars. A Boys .55 caliber AP round was able to punch straight through the side of the AB 40's turret.

The AT rifles were five-shot, magazine-fed, manually operated, bolt–action, slow–firing, making it virtually impossible to shoot them accurately enough to obtain hits out of a bouncing jeep driving cross-country at speed.

The twin Vickers Ks on the pedestal mount in the back of the jeeps were going to have to be changed out for the Boys AT rifles. Switching out weapons in a gun jeep charging hell for leather at an enemy patrol was not a simple task.

Ranger Patrol was in a life-and-death race to get its heavy weapons into action. The Italians had the advantage of position and firepower – six 8mm Breda machine guns aimed straight at them. And while the AB 40's armor was not impressive, the gun jeeps did not have any armor at all.

Then the Italians made a mistake. Instead of standing and fighting, the scout cars made a run for it.

Captain McKoy got off the first round. He was a marksman of renown – a trick shot artist. His .55 caliber AP round struck the lead Italian scout car a little low at five o'clock in the middle of the turret.

The round penetrated the armor only to be trapped inside. The big homogenous steel bullet – approximately the size of a cigar – whizzed round and round inside the turret like a buzz saw. The Blackshirt crew, except for the rear gunner, was killed instantly.

The AB 40 dove off the edge of a shallow wadi, flipped over, crashed on its side and lay there helpless with its wheels spinning.

Both rear gunners in the two remaining Italian scout cars opened. Possibly dispirited by the sight of their patrol mate lying on its side in the wadi, the unnerved Italians loosed off long bursts, but they fired high. The 8mm rounds cracking over Ranger Patrol made an ugly sound – like a metal tape measure being rattled. Every single rattle sounded like a firecracker snapping.

Guns loosed off a short burst of 20mm. His first rounds were high as well. The tracers streaked over the top of the second scout car now in the lead. In a heartbeat the RNPS sailor adjusted his aiming point and fired another quick burst. *POCKA, POCKA, POCKA.*

Hits sparkled on the scout car. At once Guns fired another burst, obtaining more hits. The AB 40 started to burn.

Captain McKoy transitioned his fire to the third scout car. By now the other four Boys gunners in Ranger Patrol were engaging. The last remaining enemy scout car seemed to have a charmed life, racing through a hailstorm of heavy weapons fire.

The jeeps were faster than the scout cars. Lt. Col. Randal's command jeep closed to within 350 yards. So far he had been a spectator because the maximum effective range of the 45 mm Brixia was only 400 yards. Now he raised the shoulder-fired mortar and touched one off, aiming high using Kentucky windage because the short, fat barrel did not have any sights.

Shooting the stubby little converted mortar was a lot like shooting a Red Ryder BB gun except the kick was equal to a 12-gauge shotgun. Like a BB gun, the Brixia was fired with both eyes open, and it was possible to watch the 45mm round in flight just like a BB, only it was the size of an ostrich egg.

Unlike a BB, when the 45mm round hit something, it exploded.

Lt. Col. Randal followed the fat mortar round heads up with both eyes open while his hands automatically loaded another one into the chamber. The shell flew in a high arc. Miraculously, it disappeared down the open hatch – no one drove buttoned up in the desert.

The 45mm mortar's instantaneous detonation was followed by a spectacular secondary explosion that sent a white flame skyward out the open turret and a small black smoke ring fifty feet in the air. Pieces of metal flew off the fatally damaged scout car.

A one in a million shot.

Jim slammed on the brakes. Now was the time to exercise caution in case there was a gunner left alive in any of the three enemy vehicles who still wanted to fight.

Capt. McKoy leaned on the stock of the smoking pedestal-mounted Boys .55 AT rifle watching the AB 40 shake and belch flame as the ammunition inside cooked off.

"Now that's what I call some fancy shootin', John."

"Luck," Lt. Col. Randal said. "You saved the day, Captain."

"Fools," Jim said. "If the AB 40s had stayed hull down and fought it out, the odds were all in their favor. They had the element of surprise, terrain and at least initially, fire superiority."

"That's a fact," Lt. Col. Randal said.

Jim asked, "How long do you estimate the fight lasted?"

"About twenty seconds," Capt. McKoy said, "start to finish."

"Seemed longer," Jim said.

Lt. Col. Randal would have guessed twenty minutes. Everything had seemed like it was going in slow motion. A sensation that was not unknown to him in dangerous encounters.

While Capt. McKoy and Jim took four men to inspect the three AB 40s, Lt. Col. Randal went around to each gun jeep to see if everyone was alright. With six machine guns firing at close range, there should have been damage.

And there was.

Waldo was inspecting the front of his gun jeep. The radiator had half a dozen bullet holes in it. Two feet higher and the crew would have taken casualties.

"Killed my jeep," Waldo said.

Lt. Col. Randal went to the Phantom jeep. "Radio RFHQ we'll be returning to Mena House with a shot-up jeep. Have Sergeant Rawlston meet us there with a recovery vehicle and a replacement gun jeep.

"Inform Oasis X we'll be running a day late."

Capt. McKoy walked up, "We got us three prisoners, John. One of 'em's an officer. Looks like a field marshal all the gold braid but he's only a lootenant."

Jim ordered the senior Phantom operator, "Notify RFHQ to arrange for an interrogation team to meet us also."

He said to Lt. Col. Randal, "We need to ascertain what the Italians were doing this far behind our lines. Might have been more to it than simple reconnaissance. Possibly dropping off or picking up an enemy agent."

"Seems like," Lt. Col. Randal said, "there's a spy hiding behind every potted plant these days."

"That is true."

A tow chain was attached to Waldo's jeep and hooked up to the command jeep. Ranger Patrol turned around and headed back in the direction of Cairo. Destination Mena House Hotel.

"Barely made it out of sight of the pyramids," Lt. Col. Randal said.

"Shortest patrol I've ever been on."

LIEUTENANT COLONEL JOHN RANDAL, LIEUTENANT MANDY Paige and ex-Lieutenant Billy Jack Jaxx were strolling down the sidewalk in Cairo in front of the Gezira Club. They were planning to meet Captain the Lady Jane Seaborn for dinner. Ranger Patrol would be pulling out for Oasis X at sunrise.

Lt. Col. Randal had decided to take Lady Jane to their favorite restaurant and invited ex-Lt. Jaxx and Lt. Mandy along.

"Security in Cairo is shocking," Mandy said. "Sammy dressed two of his Field Security Policeman in full Nazi SS uniforms, SS Runes, deaths head badges, the whole works and had them go around town to bars.

"No one even noticed – or if they did never reported them. He gave it up as a lost cause after two days."

The city was teeming with people out for the evening as the temperature cooled off. An Egyptian gentleman in an off-white suit approached them from out of the crowd.

"May I trouble you for a light, sir?" the man requested, holding up a cigarette.

Lt. Col. Randal produced his old U.S. 26th Cavalry Zippo, rolled the wheel with his thumb, producing a flame, and held it out for the man. The Egyptian bent to get the light but his eyes traveled up, not down at the cigarette.

Lt. Col. Randal clicked on, but he had no idea why.

The man turned away.

"Stop him, John," Lt. Mandy said. "He was staring at the U.S. Parachute Wings Billy Jack pinned to the front of your hat band – the man's a spy."

"HALT!" ex-Lt. Jaxx commanded, reaching for the 1911 model Colt .38 Super at his waist.

Lt. Col. Randal began to draw his sidearm.

The man broke into a run trying to lose himself in the crowd. But this was Cairo, and people knew to draw back when something like this was taking place.

Lt. Mandy's Saur 7.65 pistol was out of her shoulder bag, up extended in both hands. *BANG!*

Not only was she fast, she was also accurate. Mandy scored a direct hit.

The suspect flinched, reached behind himself for the left cheek of his buttocks with one hand and hunched over. He took three more limping steps then collapsed to the ground writhing in pain, more frightened than injured.

The crowd gathered around watching the drama. Shootings occurred on a fairly regular basis in Cairo.

A police car arrived within minutes, summoned by the Gezira Club's doorman. Major Sammy Sansom stepped out with two of his officers.

The security policemen bundled the wounded man into their car, being none too gentle.

"You shoot this miscreant, Colonel?" Maj. Sansom asked.

Lt. Col. Randal said, "Mandy tagged him."

"Good for you," Maj. Sansom said. "This individual is known to us."

After the police departed, Lt. Col. Randal said, "When did you turn into a gunfighter?"

"Captain McKoy told me the quickest draw is one when you start with your pistol already in your hand," Lt. Mandy said. "You taught me to place my hand on my weapon the instant I sensed danger.

"That's all I did, John."

"Not everybody," Lt. Col. Randal said, "could have done it."

"Texas Heart Shot," ex-Lt. Jaxx said. "Dead in the ass."

Jack Cool.

14

GUNFIGHT AT THE BLUE DUCK REDUX

SOMETIMES LIEUTENANT COLONEL JOHN RANDAL DREAMED about Oasis X. The pure white stone condominium-like structures carved into the side of the escarpment beside the crystal clear river that cascaded down the cliff before traveling underground a mile deep in the lush valley seemed like a fantasy out of a fairy tale.

Ranger Patrol pulled in just after dark.

"Sergeant Pompedous," Lt. Col. Randal ordered, stepping out of his command jeep as he retrieved his weapons and the parachute bag he used to carry his personal gear, "take charge of the patrol. Get the jeeps serviced. We're moving out again first thing in the morning."

"Sir!"

"Have the fitters pull a pre-mission inspection on my command jeep," Lt. Col. Randal said.

"Supervise it myself, Colonel."

"Patrol Briefing at zero-five-thirty."

"Yes, sir."

Lt. Col. Randal, Captain "Geronimo" Joe McKoy and James 'Baldie' Taylor walked up the steep, narrow, winding cobblestone street that had been built by the Romans when a company of Legionnaires had occupied the oasis and been abandoned there when Rome fell. Candles lined the path. They could be seen in the windows and on the patios of the residences of the wealthier denizens. The candles added to the magical effect.

Oasis X was not on blackout. Several attempts had been made to enforce one. The locals refused to comply. The average Xaradian's world view ended at the perimeter of the oasis – they were not at war with anyone.

Finally it was decided to give up trying to enforce a blackout as a lost cause.

Not that it mattered. There was almost no chance an enemy aircraft would be this far out in the Great Sand Sea at night. Navigation was tricky, and there were no military targets worth the risk of a plane going down in the desert – certain death for the crew.

James "Baldie" Taylor and Capt. McKoy peeled off and repaired to the rooms that served as the transit officer quarters.

When Lt. Col. Randal arrived at his room, he found Captain the Lady Jane Seaborn, Lieutenant Pamala Plum-Martin, Lieutenant Mandy Paige, ex-Lt. Jaxx, Mr. Zargo and King sitting out on the deck enjoying the view.

With the exception of Mr. Zargo, he had not expected them to be there.

"We flew out," Lady Jane said. "Mandy has to be here when Mr. Zargo leaves the oasis to keep an eye on internal security. I simply wanted to come along to see you off."

"King and I are here to coordinate Pam's project with Mr. Zargo," ex-Lt. Jaxx said. "He knew of a good target right off."

So much for keeping the plan to go after enemy pilots limited. Mr. Zargo had to know about it to supply the intelligence. Lady Jane, well, she was a part of everything. Somehow Lt. Mandy managed to worm her way into every project Raiding Forces was involved in – or at least tried to.

"Mandy," Lt. Col. Randal said, "this is a classified operation. Do not discuss it with anyone not in this room."

"Absolutely," Lt. Mandy said. "My lips are sealed."

"Well no one else's are," Lt. Col. Randal said.

Lt. Plum-Martin and ex-Lt. Jaxx looked uncomfortable.

"Impossible to keep Mandy out of the loop, Chief," King said. "She has a sixth sense . . . like telepathy."

"Tell me about the target," Lt. Col. Randal said.

Mr. Zargo said, "There is a small Luftwaffe landing ground approximately one hundred miles this side of Tripoli located ten miles from the coast. The base is completely isolated. Regia Aeronautica ground personnel provide security.

"Three squadrons operate off the field, two flying Stuka Ju-87s and one of Me-l09s. The fighters have only recently arrived.

"Entertainment is limited. The pilots are bored. They congregate at night in their officer's mess and drink themselves blind."

"Exactly what we're looking for," Lt. Col. Randal said. "Bored, drunk German pilots all in one place guarded by Italian security."

"The officer's club is only a one-story building," Lt. Plum-Martin said. "My idea of putting a beacon on the roof for me to use as a bombing target does not seem practical."

"I've developed the outline of a plan, sir," ex-Lt. Jaxx said.

"Run it down, Jack," Lt. Col. Randal said.

"On command, Captain Finley will start steaming up the coast. Duck Patrol lands ashore and drives inland to a point five miles from the landing ground. We parachute in and link up with Sergeant Major Mikkalis. Together we make an approach march to the objective and establish an Objective Rally Point. Duck Patrol makes a gun jeep attack on the Ju-87s and Me-109s parked on the airstrip while we infiltrate the built-up area, locate the officer's club, place explosives around the building, then toss a couple of hand grenades in the window," ex-Lt. Jaxx said.

"Both parties withdraw from the landing ground, link back up at the ORP, drive to the coast, board the DUWKs, motor out to the King Duck and sail away home."

Lt. Col. Randal took a look at the map ex-Lt. Jaxx had rolled out.

"Why not get Pam to fly us up there?" Lt. Col. Randal said, "You and I walk in the O club and shoot 'em."

Rules for Raiding: Keep it Short and Simple.

"King can come if he wants."

"What took you so long to arrive at that plan, John?"

Lady Jane did not sound amused.

"Like your style, Colonel," ex-Lt. Jaxx said.

"Deal me in, Chief," the Merc said.

Lt. Mandy said, "Damn!"

LIEUTENANT COLONEL JOHN RANDAL WAS SITTING OUT ON THE white stone deck watching the sunrise and eating breakfast with Rita and Lana. The girls had returned to their primary assignment as bodyguards.

Captain the Lady Jane Seaborn and Lieutenant Mandy Paige were taking an early morning horseback ride in the desert.

"So," Lt. Col. Randal said. "How did you ladies like being strippers?"

Which was not technically correct. The two were belly dancers – they started out practically naked. There was no stripping to it.

The girls twittered like canaries but, as usual, they refused to talk to him.

Waldo Treywick arrived.

"You wanted to see me, Colonel?"

"Billy Jack and I will be away for a few days," Lt. Col. Randal said. "That's the reason we postponed the patrol briefing this morning.

"Need you to take temporary command of Ranger Patrol, Mr. Treywick. Until I can link up with you later."

"I ain't never led a gun jeep patrol," Waldo said. "Ain't there some officer you can get?"

Lt. Col. Randal said. "We don't have any other officers."

"Need to get us some then."

"Mr. Zargo will brief you on your target area. Stay away from the Via Balbia until I show up," Lt. Col. Randal said. "Hit the targets on the list you feel OK about. Who knows, you may like being a patrol leader."

"I'm a reconnaissance man," Waldo said. "Always favored operatin' on my own or maybe with a partner – that's all I ever done. Don't expect much outta' me bein' a leader a' men."

"Try not to get captured again," Lt. Col. Randal said, *"Doctor* Treywick."

"Seriously, Colonel," Waldo said, "I ain't sure havin' me lead a fightin' patrol is such a good idea."

"You may surprise yourself."

Major Sir Terry "Zorro" Stone walked out on the deck as Waldo was leaving. Rita and Lana twittered again. Normally the girls were ambivalent to men, but they thought Maj. Stone looked like the movie star Errol Flynn.

The girls loved Errol Flynn movies.

"Ladies," Maj. Stone said, "expect me front-row center for your next performance at the Kit-Kat Club."

"Don't encourage them," Lt. Col. Randal said.

Changing the subject, he said, "You've really got Desert Patrol whipped into shape since the reorganization. Nice job, Terry."

"Taylor Corrigan and Jack Black do all the actual work," Maj. Stone said. "I spend most of my time riding with one or another of the patrols.

"Clive Adair is superb as the Mayor of X. You did us a valuable service the day you recruited his Phantom N Squadron for Raiding Forces."

"Jane secured another consignment of jeeps," Lt. Col. Randal said. "Nobody's discovered how useful they are yet – that won't last forever.

"I want to organize more patrols while we still have the opportunity. Problem is we don't have qualified officers to lead them or any backups."

"Lt. Llewellyn is ready for a command," Maj. Stone said. "He can take a new patrol for the Wing.

"My cousin can be commissioned. One does not describe the Lancelot Lancers as a family regiment without justification. He graduated Eton, but at the start of the war it was fashionable in the fast set to enlist as gentlemen privates."

"Your call," Lt. Col. Randal said.

"Sergeant Major Mikkalis has taken over Duck Patrol. My guess is he's going to keep it for a while then want to go back to doing what he's been doing.

"We don't have a single spare amphibious-trained officer to take his place unless we dragoon one of yours."

"I shall go to work on the officer problem straight away," Maj. Stone said. "Hang out at the Long Bar long enough, you eventually meet every officer you ever served with. I should be able to recruit the type we require with desert experience – preferably from one or another of the armored car regiments.

"Good," Lt. Col. Randal said.

"I want Lionel Chatterhorn to make a security review of RFHQ when he comes in from patrol. We need an upgrade," Lt. Col. Randal said. "Several classified operations have moved into the compound recently."

"Red Patrol is due back next week." Maj. Stone said. "I shall have Lionel fly down as soon as he arrives.

"On a more personal note – how is Rocky? I tried my best but she gave me the cold shoulder," Maj. Stone said. "Possibly you can put in a good word, old stick."

"Rocky's staying at RFHQ," Lt. Col. Randal said. "She and Jane are best friends now."

"No great surprise," Maj. Stone said, tapping a Player's on his exquisitely engraved sterling silver cigarette case. "The two have quite a bit in common."

"Like what?"

"Same taste in men."

CAPTAIN "GERONIMO" JOE MCKOY WALKED OUT ON THE DECK with a steaming cup of coffee in hand. He liked his hot and black. The ex-Arizona Ranger was known to drink boiling coffee in the middle of the day while crossing the Great Sand Sea in 120-degree heat.

He claimed it kept him cool – a cowboy trick.

"Ladies," he said to Rita and Lana, "enjoyed your act the other night. May have a future on the stage. Right nice a' you to drop by my table."

The girls twittered but did not say anything. Not only would they not speak to Lieutenant Colonel John Randal, they would not talk in front of him out of politeness.

"*You* were at the Kit-Kat Club?"

"John, I may be over the hill," Capt. McKoy said, "but I ain't dead yet.

"Ought to check it out. Right good show – drums a-beatin', swords swingin'…

Col. Randal said, "I've already seen their Zār priestess routine."

"I heard something about you being banned from the club," Capt. McKoy said. "Rumor is you shot the feature dancer. Now why would you go and do a thing like that?"

Hoping to change the topic, Lt. Col. Randal said, "Scout Patrol is ready to depart. Let's go see Roy off."

They walked down the winding street to where Scout Patrol was preparing to move out; the girls tagged along, not wanting to miss anything. Capt. McKoy said, "Word is Rita and Lana managed to bust 'emselves an enemy agent who liked to hang out at the Kit-Kat and shoot off his mouth to the dancers.

"Same operative you dropped back to the bad guys in some kinda spy vs. spy double-game."

Lt. Col. Randal said, "I dropped him all right."

Scout Patrol was lined up ready to roll out when Lt. Col. Randal and Capt. McKoy arrived. As usual, when a patrol was departing the oasis, everyone turned out to see it off. A small crowd had gathered.

"Let me show you something, sir," Lieutenant Roy Kidd said. He pointed to a strange, cylindrical piece of equipment that looked like something out of a science fiction movie when the operator put it up to his eyes.

"FT 37 No2 MK VII range finder.

"Once we reach our AO, sir," Lt. Kidd said, "the plan is to break down into two jeep elements. My command jeep, which is also the Phantom radio vehicle, will be a floater.

"We approach the Via Balbia under cover of darkness and set up hide positions a mile off the road spread out five miles or so apart with the Boys .55s mounted on General Purpose tripods under a camouflage net.

"Our range finders can pinpoint the exact distance. That allows us to stay as far out as possible within the maximum effective range of the Boys .55s. That's important because it gives us a head start to make a run for it in the event one of our sniper teams ever gets spotted and chased, sir."

"It sure is," Lt. Col. Randal said.

"Raiding Rules: It's Good to Have a Plan B."

We've also worked out .55 caliber drop tables for every one hundred yards up to a mile, sir," Lt. Kidd said. "With the GP tripods, all we have to do is dial in the correct elevation adjustment for the range we've acquired from the MK VIIs.

"With a target the size of a truck's engine block, one-shot kills are virtually assured, sir."

"On moving targets?"

"Before sunrise," Lt. Kidd said, "we'll seed the road with a few of 'The Great Teddy's' camel chip mines. Should give us stationary trucks, sir."

"Very good, Roy." Lt. Col. Randal said. "Go easy this first trip. May take a while to work out your tactics.

"I'm expecting big things out of Scout Patrol."

Lt. Kidd was an enigma. Even though he was a badged member of Raiding Forces, he did not mix much. And he was the most independent officer in a group that prided itself on being independent.

That said, he was not a loner.

Girls were attracted to Lt. Kidd. However, he did not pursue them every waking minute in his spare time the way most of the other young Raiding Forces' officers did.

Troops would follow him anywhere.

"Where can I get me some a' these range finder gadgets, Roy?" Capt. McKoy asked. "Definitely want 'em for my White Patrol."

"There's several at RFHQ," Lt. Kidd said. "The MK VII has been declared surplus. No one wants them anymore. We can have all we want.

"Works fine for what we need it for, Captain."

"That's all that counts," Capt. McKoy said.

After Scout Patrol rolled out, up and over the escarpment, Lt. Col. Randal pulled Jim, Maj. Stone, Mr. Zargo and ex-Lieutenant Billy Jack Jaxx aside.

Lt. Col. Randal said, "Don't ask me questions about what I'm about to tell you because I don't have answers.

"Billy Jack's Military Cross was awarded for the signals intelligence he obtained at the German weather station he raided out of the Mud Fort.

"Terry, I want you to quietly let the word get around – capturing signals operators, equipment, codebooks, etc. will be rewarded."

"Straightaway."

"Sometimes in the future, specialized training will be conducted for our patrol leaders on what specifically to look for," Lt. Col. Randal said.

"Mr. Zargo, direct your men to start collecting information on the location of other Nazi weather stations we can raid – be discreet."

"Immediately, Colonel."

"Starting right now we're launching a Weather War. The fact Raiding Forces is concentrating on weather stations is classified MOST SECRET – Need to Know. I'm the sole decision maker on who has the need.

"I want that perfectly clear."

The four men nodded or muttered, "Clear."

Lt. Col. Randal said, "When Mr. Zargo's team identifies a weather station target, it becomes a 'Red Indian' – the code word itself is classified.

"Terry, inform your Wing and Regiment commanders to be advised when they receive a Red Indian alert order they're to drop everything and execute it immediately.

"In the event I'm away at the time a Red Indian target comes up, Billy Jack will survey the target, develop a plan and he may lead the raid if I can't return in time. At that point we will be working for the general.

"Is that clear?"

Maj. Stone said, "Crystal."

"Sir," ex-Lt. Jaxx said, "won't most weather stations be a long way out, isolated deep in the remote parts of the Sand Sea?"

Raiding Forces primarily operated in the narrow strip of hard ground that was over a thousand miles long but only about fifty miles wide, running from the edge of the Great Sand Sea to the bank of the Mediterranean from Tobruk to Tripoli – an AO of 50,000-plus square miles that the Raiders considered their private hunting preserve.

Desert Patrol roved up and down the edge of the Great Sand Sea, struck out of the soft sand then retreated back into it because the Germans refused to go there and the Italians rarely did.

Raiding Forces did not, as a normal practice, make long desert treks to distant objectives across the Great Sand Sea the way the Long Range Desert Patrol did. Deep desert was the LRDG's domain.

"Jack's right, General," Lt. Col. Randal said. "Once we have a Red Indian target we'll want to hit it fast. That might mean dropping a team by parachute and having to depend on the nearest LRDG patrol to extract it."

"I can have General Davy at GHQ coordinate with Colonel Pendergrass," Jim said. "Have him put the LRDG on notice if/when they receive a code word Red Indian message it takes priority.

"Not necessary for Pendergrass to know the details of our mission."

"Alice through the looking glass," Maj. Stone said.

Lt. Col. Randal said, "We're not hunting for giant white rabbits."

LIEUTENANT COLONEL JOHN RANDAL FINISHED PACKING HIS parachute bag. He slid his Brixia 45mm shoulder-fired mortar into the canvas gun case ex-Lieutenant Billy Jack Jaxx had made for him in Cairo. The case was lightweight and had a flap over the butt of the stubby weapon that kept sand out but was not tied down so the weapon could be drawn quickly. It also had a shoulder strap.

A pouch was stitched to the case that held five 45mm rounds.

There was another case for his Beretta MAB-38 9mm submachine gun.

Drop-dead gorgeous Captain the Lady Jane Seaborn was reclining on a love seat in their bedroom watching him make his preparations. She looked like a supermodel.

"Do try not to do anything foolish, John. I would not wish this mission to be the 'Gunfight at the Blue Duck' redux."

"Tell you what," Lt. Col. Randal said, thinking Lady Jane was even more beautiful when she was worried.

"We're flying out in a few minutes. Pam is going to land under cover of darkness, park the two Ansons and we'll link up with Huxley's Blue Patrol. Jack, King and I are going to carry out our raid then fly back here by sunrise.

"I have orders to continue on to Cairo as soon as Pam refuels. Why don't you make dinner reservations tomorrow evening at the Gezira Club – just the two of us?"

"Fabulous," Lady Jane said, "Make sure you do not stand me up."

"Nobody," Lt. Col. Randal said, "could be that crazy."

Lieutenant Mandy Paige walked out to the airstrip with Lt. Col. Randal and Lady Jane. The Anson was ticking over when they arrived. Lieutenant Pamala-Plum Martin and her ex-LRDG navigator were already in the cockpit, ready to take off.

The chase Anson also had its motor running. SOP on desert flights was to always have two planes fly together in the event one went down.

Ex-Lt. Jaxx and King were there. They loaded Lt. Col. Randal's equipment aboard. Both men had their weapons in the canvas carrying cases ex-Lt. Jaxx had made in Cairo.

"John," Lt. Mandy said, "do you know what MI-5 did with the enemy agent I shot?"

"Negative," Lt. Col. Randal said.

"Treated his wound and let the man go free," Lt. Mandy said. "Sammy said the idea was to allow him to describe your U.S. Paratrooper Wings to the other side.

"Sammy claimed it would give our opposite numbers trying to piece together Allied Order of Battle something to think about and said I should not worry . . . he shall come to a sticky end eventually."

"If Maj. Sansom said that," Lt. Col. Randal said, "your spy's a dead man."

Lt. Plum-Martin revved the Anson's engines. She was ready to taxi.

"See you by morning," Lt. Col. Randal said as Lady Jane kissed him on the cheek. He boarded the aircraft and did not look back.

Lt. Col. Randal hated good-byes.

It was a long flight to the landing ground Blue Patrol had marked with railroad flares. Lieutenant Westcott Huxley may have found an old abandoned/emergency landing ground built by the Italians or just marked a flat patch of ground. There was no way to tell from the air at night.

The strip was clearly outlined.

Lt. Col. Randal, ex-Lt. Jaxx and King were asleep in the back of the Anson. When Lt. Plum-Martin lined up on the landing ground, the pitch of the airplane's engine changed. Lt. Col. Randal's eyes came open.

"Blue Patrol in sight, John," Lt. Plum-Martin said over her shoulder. "Be on the ground in a minute."

Ex-Lt. Jaxx and King were unbuckling their seatbelts.

Lt. Col. Randal moved up to the cockpit and leaned between Lt. Plum-Martin and the ex-LRDG navigator. The burning flares marking the airstrip were up ahead. The time was 2235 hours.

The moon was not scheduled to rise until 0100 hours. There were two schools of thought on raiding at night. One is that you can raid only in the full moon so you can see the enemy. The other held that pitch dark prevents the enemy from seeing you.

Lt. Col. Randal did not buy into either one. Raiding Forces carried out raids when it had a target. They operated in all light and weather conditions – except excessive winds when jumping.

"Nice job," Lt. Col. Randal said to the ex-LRDG navigator.

The Anson lined up between the two rows of flares. Lt. Plum-Martin touched down as light as a feather. The chase plane circled and came in to land right behind her.

Lt. Huxley was standing by the door when King popped it open.

While ex-Lt. Jaxx and King were unloading their gear, Lt. Col. Randal and Lt. Huxley had a short conversation.

Lt. Col. Randal said. "I want two jeeps to drive us to within a mile of the airfield. They'll wait until we carry out the raid then bring us back here.

"As soon as we get back, we'll take off immediately. Then, Westcott, you get Blue Patrol as far away from here as possible before daylight.

"Did you prepare the explosives I requested?

"Wilco," Lt. Huxley said.

"Let's do this," Lt. Col. Randal ordered.

He slipped his 9mm Beretta MAB-38 out of the canvas case and left his Brixia 45mm slung over his shoulder. King had his submachine gun out, but ex-Lt. Jaxx left his weapon in the case.

The objective was ten miles away. The ground was firm, so it only took a little over thirty minutes to arrive at the ORP one mile from the airfield.

The Blue Patrol Navigator, a former French Foreign Legionnaire, provided the azimuth. Lt. Col. Randal dialed it in on the bezel of the compass he wore on a cord around his neck and carried in his left front pocket.

"Good luck, Colonel."

Slipping the brass wire thumb ring of the compass over his thumb, Lt. Col. Randal glanced at it to check the reading and said, "Move out, King."

They patrolled to the airfield in the dark. And it was really dark, absolutely black. King moved fast followed by Lt. Col. Randal who watched the compass and called corrections softly when he strayed off azimuth. Ex-Lt. Jaxx brought up the rear.

Lt. Col. Randal was clicked on, very aware but relaxed.

OOOOF!

King had walked straight into a concrete post that marked one of the corners of the airfield. It was that dark.

A single strand of barbed wire ran behind the post. And that was it for defenses. There were several flak towers on each side of the landing strip, but Lt. Col. Randal knew from Lt. Huxley's quick briefing that they were not manned at night.

A short, whispered confab was held. Lt. Col. Randal asked for suggestions on the best approach to the built-up area at the far end of the airstrip. The night was so dark they could not see it from where they were.

The buildings were blacked out. That was the sole concession that there was a war on by whoever was in charge of airfield security. Why bother? The field was over a thousand miles from the fighting at Tobruk.

"Let's walk straight down the center of the tarmac," ex-Lt. Jaxx said. "No one would ever expect us to do that.

"King, you speak Italian. Stay on point. If anyone challenges you, tell 'em we've been lost in the desert ever since our truck broke down yesterday."

"Roger, Chief."

The three Raiders moved out, single file, strolling down the middle of the landing strip. The night was so dark they could not see the edges of the tarmac. The trip to the end of the airfield was a spooky experience. Nothing was stirring except for a lone hyena that drifted away when they approached.

Finally King walked straight into the side of a building. Since the Merc could see like a cat at night, it was beyond totally dark. Visibility was zero.

This was a problem.

"There's such a thing as carrying 'under cover of darkness' too far," ex-Lt. Jaxx whispered. "How are we going to find the officer's mess, sir?"

"I have no idea," Lt. Col. Randal whispered back.

"Keep going, King."

Tonight was nothing at all like the Blue Duck. Then all he had to do was walk down the sidewalk to the bar. Easy to find that place – there were cars parked in front with drivers standing outside smoking cigarettes. There had even been a sign hanging over the door with a blue duck painted on it.

Moving slowly, the three slipped between the dark buildings. The prefabricated wooden structures were spaced out approximately ten yards apart and may have been barracks, but no one was stirring. Normally, a concentration of enemy personnel in their quarters would have been a worthy target . . . but not tonight.

They were there to kill pilots.

King halted, sticking his hand back to stop Lt. Col. Randal who froze in mid-step. Ex-Lt. Jaxx almost bumped into him.

"Three men walked past," King whispered.

"Follow 'em."

The Merc drifted into the dark like a phantom. He could move without making a sound. Shortly a light flared ahead as the men they were tailing opened a door and pushed through a blackout curtain.

Inside what sounded like a crowd of drunk Germans could be heard singing loudly.

"There it is," ex-Lt. Jaxx whispered. "Want to go order a Blackjack, Colonel?"

"How do you know about that?"

"Lady Jane told me."

"I'm not thirsty," Lt. Col. Randal said, slipping the gun case containing the Brixia 45mm mortar off his shoulder.

"King, when I give the word," Lt. Col. Randal said, slipping a round into the chamber of the stubby shoulder-fired mortar, "step over there, open the door, then get back here fast."

"On your command, Chief."

Ex-Lt. Jaxx slipped his gun case off his shoulder, pulled out a bizarre-looking weapon and started loading it."

"What is that?"

"9mm Italian Villar Perosa, sir," ex-Lt. Jaxx whispered. "Double-barreled submachine gun – sixty rounds quick.

"Perfect for sweeping out a bar room."

"Stand easy," Lt. Col. Randal whispered. "You wait till I say 'go,' Jack."

"Roger."

"I'm first, you're second, then King – you take out anybody left.

"Everyone set?"

"Affirmative," King whispered.

"I'm up," ex-Lt. Jaxx whispered.

"Move out, King," Lt. Col. said through clenched teeth.

The Merc stood up and walked over, opened the door, propped it against the outside wall with no wasted motion, then stepped back to where Lt. Col. Randal and ex-Lt. Jaxx were crouching.

Someone inside shouted something unintelligible in German – "shut the door"?

Lt. Col. Randal fired the 45 mm mortar through the opening. It punched through the flaps of the blackout curtain into the bar and detonated.

FLASH! BOOOOM! Glass tinkled, but the blackout curtains muffled the light and the walls dampened the explosion somewhat.

Men were screaming.

At the sound of the explosion, the airbase went crazy, machine guns blazing in every direction – some straight up. The Italians had other MGs firing on fixed lines so that they could be triggered by remote control – meaning unmanned.

The guns were putting out impressive firepower along likely avenues of approach.

Fortunately, the tracers indicated the machine guns were mounted to fire about three feet high making it possible to low-crawl under them. However, that was not necessary. The airfield defense plan did not allow for the fixed guns to shoot through the built-up area.

And they could not be sighted to fire toward any of the Luftwaffe airplanes or in the direction of the aviation fuel storage tanks.

Basically, the fixed guns on the airfield were useless. In fact, they were worse than useless. The machine gun fire pinned down any Italian reaction force by preventing them from maneuvering, in the unlikely event they chose to. It did not hinder the Raider's attack on the pilot's lounge.

"I'm in," Lt. Col. Randal said.

He jumped to his feet and ran to the door while unslinging his submachine gun, bringing it to his shoulder as he pushed his way through the shredded blackout curtains.

Inside in the harsh white light the bar was a scene of mass destruction – virtually all of the three squadrons of pilots were present. Dead, wounded and stunned Nazis littered the room. Some were sprawled on the floor, others flung on tables or hanging off chairs. A row of pilots were in a line lying on the ground – mowed down by the 45mm mortar round where they had been standing at the bar.

Several were staggering around in shock.

Ever since the bridge at Pas-de-Calais, where hundreds of women and children were slaughtered by Ju-87s indiscriminately attacking a trapped and helpless civilian traffic jam, Lt. Col. Randal had hated Stuka pilots. He did not like Me-109 pilots much better.

He opened immediately, firing short, crisp, deadly three-round bursts at anyone not on the ground. His magazine was loaded all tracers for maximum shock effect. No one even attempted to fight back.

He knocked down every Nazi still standing.

Killing Nazi pilots was personal with him.

When his 9mm Beretta MAB-38 ran dry, Lt. Col. Randal stepped back outside, reloading automatically without even looking down at his weapon. Jack Cool sailed past and through the door, double-barreled submachine gun at the high port.

Originally designed as an aircraft-mounted anti-aircraft weapon in the last war, after the Armistice, the Regia Aeronautica converted some of the Villar Perosas to be shoulder-fired. The weapon's main virtue was that it had a high cyclic rate.

Ex-Lt. Jaxx's twin top-mounted thirty-round magazines emptied fast, extremely fast… spewing rounds. It was impossible to distinguish individual rounds. The 9mm submachine gun made a high-pitched whine that had no resemblance to gunshots.

When ex-Lt. Jaxx came out, King charged past him and emptied his 9mm Beretta MAB-38 submachine gun into the room.

As the Merc emerged changing magazines, Lt. Col. Randal pitched in a No. 36 Mills bomb.

He said, "Let's get the hell out of Dodge."

15

SYMPATHETIC DETONATION

LIEUTENANT COLONEL JOHN RANDAL, EX-LIEUTENANT BILLY Jack Jaxx and King exfiltrated the enemy airbase by going out the same way they came in – straight back up the runway. The Italian security force machine guns were silent. That was another problem with fixed guns – someone had to reload them. The Blackshirts were not about to venture out to go around and do it right now.

Not with an enemy on the loose.

The night was beginning to lighten as the moon started to come up. As the three men patrolled up the strip, they could see the dim shadows of airplanes parked in the grass along the edges of the runway. They passed what appeared to be an isolated built-up area but it was most likely the aviation fuel storage tank farm – it was still too dark to make an accurate assessment.

The march to the ORP was uneventful.

Sheltering on the far side of the gun jeeps, Lt. Col. Randal passed out cigarettes to ex-Lt. Jaxx and King, then lit them with his old U.S. 26th Cavalry Regiment Zippo.

"Sheriffs have nights like this in Texas," King asked, "arresting crooks?"

"We have to be a little more discreet," ex-Lt. Jaxx said. "Can't blow up a house with a 45mm round before we make entry – at least not in town."

The night was quiet. There was only silence from the direction of the airfield. There were no signs of any attempt to locate the intruders.

After thirty minutes, Lt. Col. Randal said, "Let's go get those airplanes."

"Are you kidding, sir?" ex-Lt. Jaxx asked.

"Send one jeep back to Lieutenant Huxley," Lt. Col. Randal ordered the Blue Patrol assistant patrol leader, a former French Foreign Legion sergeant who had deserted to join Raiding Forces.

"Tell Lt. Huxley to leave one gun jeep with Lieutenant Plum-Martin to provide security for the two Ansons. Take the rest of the patrol and move as far away as possible."

"Yes, sir," the sergeant said. "I will personally command the stay-behind jeep guarding Lieutenant Plum-Martin, Colonel."

"You can take off and try to catch up with Blue Patrol when we get back," Lt. Col. Randal said. "Under no circumstances are you to continue to travel after daylight. Enemy air will be out in force at first light looking for payback.

"Is that clear, Sergeant?"

"Sir!"

"Put the three packs Lt. Huxley assembled for me in the jeep staying here," Lt. Col. Randal ordered. "Then move out."

"Yes, sir. Good hunting, Colonel."

Lt. Col. Randal, ex-Lt. Jaxx and King climbed in the back of the jeep staying behind. The AVG driver cranked the motor, and they rolled out on an azimuth taking them straight to the Nazi landing ground.

"What is in these packs, Chief?" King asked.

"Each one contains twenty half-pound prepared demolition charges with one-hour time pencils," Lt. Col. Randal said. "Once we get started we're going to have to work fast."

"I've done a lot of crazy stuff, sir," ex-Lt. Jaxx said. "Going back to hit the same airfield twice in one night – definitely tops on the list.

"You sure about this, Colonel?"

"'The first rule is,'" Lt. Col. Randal said, "'There ain't no rules.'"

Ex-Lt. Jaxx said, "I didn't think you were serious about that one, sir."

"'Plan raids backward – know how to get home,' Chief," King said. "You take that rule into consideration?"

The Merc had an ancillary contract with Captain the Lady Jane Seaborn to "bring Lt. Col. Randall back alive." Not an easy task. He always felt guilty collecting the money.

"Well, that's why we have these packs full of explosives," Lt. Col. Randal said.

"What I thought," King said.

The jeep arrived at the wire marking the boundary of the airbase.

"Be ready, Jones," Lt. Col. Randal ordered the AVG driver. "We'll be coming out hot."

"Yes, sir."

The three Raiders left their submachine guns in the jeep. For this phase of the operation, stealth was paramount. If forced to fight they would resort to their sidearms, but flight into the night was the best defense.

The men shouldered their packs.

"Let's go," Lt. Col. Randal said.

King held up the limp strand of rusty barbed wire and they walked under it onto the runway. The plan was to swing off to the left behind the aircraft parked on that side of the strip, move all the way down the runway and place explosives on the aviation fuel storage tanks first. King would cross over and take one side of the tarmac while Lt. Col. Randal and ex-Lt. Jaxx took the other. Then they would work their way back to the jeep, placing charges on the parked planes as they went.

The airfield was perfectly still. Everyone had gone back to bed. Hard to imagine on a base where thirty to forty pilots had been killed or wounded less than an hour before. Clearly, no one expected Raiding Forces to come calling again.

The Raiders patrolled to the storage tanks staying well clear of the airplanes parked along the airstrip. On the way they stumbled across the underground bomb storage bunkers. There were five of them. Three concrete steps led down to where the bombs were stockpiled.

"Let's lay the charges on the fuel tanks first," Lt. Col. Randal whispered. "Jack and I'll come back and get these bunkers. King, you cross the strip like we planned. Start working your way along the other side back to the jeep."

"Roger."

They slipped into the fuel tank area. No one was on guard. There were six giant aviation gas storage tanks about twenty feet tall. Each man placed a pair of demolition charges against two tanks, squeezing the time pencils which activated the acid contained inside. The liquid would eat its way down to the blasting cap and set the explosives off in one hour.

Unfortunately, the fuses were not precise.

After redistributing the prepared charges they had left in their packs, King slipped across the runway while Lt. Col. Randal and ex-Lt. Jaxx went back to the five bomb storage bunkers.

"Unscrew the fuse on the nose of one of the bombs and attach your charge," Lt. Col. Randal whispered. "I'll get the first bunker. You get the second. We'll leapfrog each other down the line."

"Roger that."

Lt. Col. Randal tiptoed down the concrete steps. The bunker was open-air, like the entrance to a cave. He stepped inside and, closing one eye to protect his night vision, flashed his hand-held torch on and off. Rows and rows of aerial bombs were stacked to the ceiling so far back he could not see the end of the cave-like facility.

Inching his way sideways between the stacks until he reached what he estimated was approximately the center of the bunker, very, very carefully Lt. Col. Randal unscrewed the fuse on one of the bombs, attached the prepared charge over the end by taping it down and squeezed the time pencil.

Then for redundancy, he set a second charge on another bomb in case the first one failed to blow for any reason.

Back outside, Lt. Col. Randal encountered ex-Lt. Jaxx coming out of the second bunker. White teeth flashed in the dark, "Going to make a big-time boom, Colonel."

"Get moving, Jack," Lt. Col. Randal whispered, "clock's ticking."

After setting the explosives in his second bunker, Lt. Col. Randal leapfrogged ex-Lt. Jaxx again, putting a pair of demolition charges in the last one.

"Follow me," Lt. Col. Randal whispered as he came back up the concrete steps.

"Have to be careful from here on, Jack. The Italians have a bad habit of stationing sentries on their airplanes at night."

"I'm right behind you, Colonel."

Moving up the edge of the runway, the shadow of an airplane appeared. Lt. Col. Randal edged toward it, moving silently like a hunting cat. Sure enough, there was a dark form on the ground under one wing of the Ju-87.

The sentry was sound asleep – snoring.

WHIIICH, WHIIICH. Lt. Col. Randal shot him in the head from point-blank range with his silenced .22 High Standard Military Model D.

Ex-Lt. Jaxx moved up and placed a charge on the wing at the point where it joined the fuselage.

In less than a minute, the two were moving on to the shadow of the next airplane. Ex-Lt. Jaxx took the lead. There was a sentry asleep under the wing of the second one. He sat up.

WHIIICH, WHIIICH.

"Bad dream," ex-Lt. Jaxx whispered as Lt. Col. Randall placed a charge on the plane.

The two continued leapfrogging each other down the line of airplanes. There were two squadrons of planes – all Ju-87s. They lost count, but believed it was around thirty airplanes. Each plane had a sentry.

Each one of them was asleep.

By the time the last plane was reached, they had used up all their prepared demolition charges and were nearly out of .22 caliber ammunition. After Lt. Col. Randal silently eliminated the sentry, ex-Lt. Jaxx climbed up into the dive-bomber's cockpit and smashed the instrument panel with the steel butt of his High Standard Military Model D. Then he emptied the remainder of the silenced pistol's bullets into it – best he could do.

The hour on the first time pencil was nearly up.

They made a beeline for the Blue Patrol gun jeep waiting at the end of the runway.

King was at the jeep when they arrived.

BOOOOOM!

A charge on one of the airplanes went off prematurely. The Ju-87 exploded in a violent flash. The airbase erupted in gunfire once again.

"Someone must have gotten up the nerve to reload the fixed machine guns, sir," ex-Lt. Jaxx said.

"Looks like," Lt. Col. Randal said.

The fuel farm went up in an amazing series of explosions, each tank sending a flaming mushroom-shaped ball 200 feet into the sky. Aviation gas makes a flash fire. There was a lot of it in the storage tanks.

Night turned into day.

In the confusion, the Italians and the Germans stationed on different parts of the airbase started firing at each other.

Then the ground underneath the Blue Patrol jeep gave a sharp violent shake. It felt like an earthquake. One after the other the underground bunkers cooked off. The earth on top dampened the shrapnel effect as it was designed to, but it could not contain the massive explosions.

Smoke billowed out.

"Can we get the hell out of Dodge for real this time?" ex-Lt. Jaxx said as he watched the fantastic pyrotechnic display. Tracers flashed back and forth. Individual airplanes were blowing up like a string of giant firecrackers. The flaming fuel tanks and thick columns of smoke pouring out of the bomb storage bunkers was an incredible sight.

The Germans and Italians continued to do battle with each other.

"I've had about enough excitement for one night, sir."

Lt. Col. Randal said. "We got what we came for."

0200 HOURS, THE NEXT NIGHT.

The Dodge 30-cwt truck with the British roundels painted over and replaced with an Afrika Korps palm tree indicating it had been captured and pressed into service by the Nazis was rolling down a dirt track headed toward a massive Regia Aeronautica aviation fuel storage installation. King was at the wheel with GG sitting in the passenger seat. The Merc spoke fluent Italian. GG was Italian.

Riding in the back of the truck under the tarp on a bench seat, Lieutenant Colonel John Randal (who was in the process of standing up Lady Jane) was sitting next to Captain "Pyro" Percy Stirling across from ex-Lieutenant Billy Jack Jaxx. The Dodge was packed with explosives. The fuse was in place.

All that was needed to set it off was to initiate the time pencil by squeezing it. The demolitions were designed to have a thirty-minute burn with a safety delay of twenty seconds. When the acid ate its way down to the twenty-second mark before the explosives detonated, there would be a loud distinctive warning "click."

No one was planning on being anywhere in the vicinity to hear the click. The idea was to drive into the base masquerading as Italians, park the truck in the center of a sprawling 500-acre fuel tank farm then force march due south as hard and fast as they could go. Lt. Stirling's Railroad Wrecking Crew II patrol would be waiting to pick them up three miles out.

After rendezvousing with Lt. Stirling's patrol, it would drive twenty-five miles into the desert where Lieutenant Pamala Plum-Martin and the chase plane would be waiting. Then Lt. Col. Randal, ex-Lt. Jaxx and King would board the lead Anson and be flown back to Oasis X. From there they would transfer to the Hudson and fly on to Cairo.

Lt. Col. Randal was supposed to be in the city right now having dinner with Lady Jane, but there had been a change of mission. This target was too juicy to pass up.

No one had ever seen a tank farm as big before.

Field Marshal Erwin Rommel was pre-positioning the petroleum, oil and lubrication (POL) he needed for his upcoming winter offensive. Afrika Korps was going to require massive amounts of fuel. In desert warfare, POL was the lifeblood of a panzer army.

"How many pounds of explosives do we have on board, sir?" ex-Lt. Jaxx asked.

"Four hundred," Capt. Stirling said.

"That's a lot, right?"

"Enough to turn Mt. Everest into a volcano," Capt. Stirling said cheerfully. "P-for Plenty – the basic Raiding Forces' formula for explosives when in doubt.

"I have no idea how to take out a target this vast."

Ex-Lt. Jaxx was aware of Capt. Stirling's reputation as a demolitions man. The word was when he blew something up, it stayed blown up.

King was driving with his lights on. This was fairly common practice for the Germans and Italians traveling after the hours of darkness due to the fact the Royal Air Force had an extremely limited night-fighter capability in the Middle East. A truck with its lights on would not raise any eyebrows.

"Percy, are you related to a lieutenant named David Stirling?" Lt. Col. Randal inquired.

"My first cousin," Capt. Stirling said. "Why do you ask, sir?"

"He's been given command of a new outfit," Lt. Col. Randal said. "L-Detachment, Special Air Service. Mad Dog's instructing Stirling's boys on the finer points of jumping out of airplanes. They'd been trying to teach themselves with predictable results."

"I thought *we* were the Special Air Service, sir," Capt. Stirling said.

"Sometimes we have been," Lt. Col. Randal said.

"David would be the last person I would have ever expected to be given command of anything, sir," Capt. Stirling said. "Not known to be much of a thinker. Can be impulsive. And, his nickname is 'Big Sloth.'

"On the plus side, he is ambitious and courageous to the point of being foolhardy."

"Anyone who would try to teach themselves how to jump out of an airplane," Lt. Jaxx said, "has to be crazy brave."

"Un-oh!" King said from the driver's seat, loud enough to be heard in the back of the truck. "Red light dead ahead, Chief."

Lt. Col. Randal knelt down from his bench seat in the rear of the truck and peered through the open back window out the front of the Dodge's dusty windows. Up ahead was an Italian soldier waving a red-lensed flashlight. He was standing in the beams of the truck's headlight in front of what looked like a five-bar gate. Coils of concertina wire were strung out on both sides of the gate.

The razor-sharp tangles ran out of sight into the dark. There was no way around and no way to turn around.

GG started shouting out the window at the sentry.

"What's he saying?" Lt. Col. Randal asked King through the window.

"GG is telling them we are Italian soldiers who were lost in the desert when our truck was strafed and caught fire. We walked for three days before we captured this truck from the British," King said, "We have no idea what the password is or have any identification cards because they were burned up."

"How's he doing? That story won't fly – we're in an Afrika Korps' marked truck."

"The sergeant in charge of the guard at the gate is not having any part of it. He has ordered up a squad of Germans to come check us out."

"Not good," ex-Lt. Jaxx said.

"Think we should rush the gate?" Capt. Stirling asked.

"Way it's looking, Chief," King said over his shoulder in a relaxed tone as GG continued yelling.

"This is an ambush. The opposition probably has armored cars, tanks, maybe even airplanes waiting for us to make one false move."

"Definitely not good," ex-Lt. Jaxx said, slipping his silenced .22 High Standard Military Model D out of his holster.

Lt. Col. Randal already had his in hand. The advantage of this particular model pistol was that it had an exposed hammer. His was cocked and unlocked because he pulled back the hammer automatically when he drew it.

Ex-Lt. Jaxx's weapon was not.

A German Feldwebel pulled back the flap and shined a light into the bed of the truck. Ex-Lt. Jaxx made direct eye contact with him. Then he cocked the hammer on his pistol.

It made four unmistakable clicks.

Jack Cool.

Things were about to go very wrong for the Afrika Korps NCO very quickly. Being a seasoned veteran of Poland, France, Crete and now Africa, he knew to a certainty what was about to happen.

The German switched off his torch. He carefully lowered the tarp, shouting for the Italian guards to open the gate. Then the Feldwebel walked around to the front of the cab and waved them through.

Maybe these people in the Dodge were who they said they were . . . maybe not. Someone else could sort it out. Why be a hero?

The Merc put the pedal to the metal. The Dodge shot through the gate, spewing gravel.

"Must have been a married man," ex-Lt. Jaxx said.

Not wanting to run the chance of a repeat encounter, King swung off road, going cross-country. He switched off his lights. Intelligence supplied by one of Mr. Zargo's Arab operatives placed the fuel tanks approximately a mile inside the installation.

The Senussi informant claimed the tanks were "too numerous to count." While that sounded like a lot, no one knew exactly how good the Arab's math skills were.

The Dodge bounced along. The moon was out, giving King enough visibility to drive by. Any time now they should be approaching their objective.

Capt. Stirling sat up straight. He sniffed the air. He screamed, "BAIL OUT! THE FUSE IS BURNING!"

King grabbed his Beretta MAB-38, pulled the throttle out all the way, twisted it left to lock it in place and exited the door with the truck rolling at speed. GG jumped from the other side. Ex-Lt. Jaxx rolled over the back gate. Lt. Col. Randal dived after him. Out of his peripheral vision he saw Capt. Stirling, looking like Superman – arms outstretched, sailing over the top of his back.

"What the hell?" Lt. Col. Randal said, limping to his feet.

"Bloody fuse must have activated from all the bouncing," Capt. Stirling said, brushing off from the fall. "Maybe a faulty time pencil."

"Never smelled anything," GG said.

"Neither did I," King said.

"Almost had a heart attack," ex-Lt. Jaxx said.

"Next time," the Merc said, "the better idea would be *not* to insert the fuse into the demolitions before we are ready to ignite it."

"Roger that," Lt. Col. Randal said.

No one was seriously injured, but they had all taken a hard fall. Everyone on the team was dinged up to some degree. The truck had been traveling at close to thirty miles per hour.

The unspoken question was, "How long had the fuse been burning?"

"Let's get the hell out of Dodge," Lt. Col. Randal said in disgust.

"Ex-Lt. Jaxx said, "How do we live this down?"

The runaway truck disappeared into the night with the throttle locked, driving on its own like a ghost ship doomed to travel the perfectly flat desert forever . . . or at least until it ran out of gas.

KABOOOOOOOOM!

Clearly, the time pencil had been burning for a while before Capt. Stirling noticed the odor. The truck had only been out of sight for a minute or so when it blew.

As explosions went, this was one of the sharpest Lt. Col. Randal had ever heard – "P for Plenty."

The skyline went white. Fuel storage tanks began cooking off: one, two, three or more at a time. Mr. Zargo's Senussi had not been exaggerating.

There were too many to count.

Capt. Stirling jabbed his fist, "YES!"

The horizon was on fire as far as the eye could see. New explosions continued in the distance. Flames shot hundreds of feet in the air.

The pyrotechnic display was of such incredible magnitude it was hard to imagine they had been the cause. Millions of gallons of fuel were on fire. The conflagration made the tank farm they had blown the night before seem Lilliputian by comparison.

As far as the eye could see there were burning fuel tanks dotting the desert.

"What happened?"

"Sympathetic detonation, Colonel," Capt. Stirling said, "resulting from the shock wave created by the explosives in the truck, shrapnel, flaming fuel, heat in conjunction with atmospheric conditions or most likely all the above."

Anyone who had ever been present when Capt. Stirling was blowing things up had witnessed amazing explosions. He was a big bang artist without peer. The Raiders did not call him "Pyro" without justification.

"On a scale of one to ten," King said, "this is a fifteen."

"Overachieved again," Lt. Col. Randal said. "That's just not possible."

Ex-Lt. Jaxx said, "Scratch one tank farm."

LIEUTENANT COLONEL JOHN RANDAL WAS SITTING IN ONE OF THE theatre seats bolted against the bulkhead of the Hudson. Lieutenant Pamala Plum-Martin was sitting on one side of him with her head on his shoulder, sound asleep. She had been up the better part of two days, made two landings on improvised airstrips behind enemy lines, and was exhausted.

Ex-Lieutenant Billy Jack Jaxx was stretched out on a canvas bench seat with his head on his bag and his cut-down Australian bush hat over his face sound asleep against the far bulkhead.

King was asleep in the tail of the plane.

Rita was up in the cockpit watching Squadron Leader Paddy Wilcox fly the Hudson.

Captain the Lady Jane Seaborn was sitting on Lt. Col. Randal's other side reading a letter from "The Great Teddy."

"Teddy says to tell you he is a cadet at Sandhurst enrolled in an accelerated officer's training course conducted on weekends with summer camps," Lady Jane said. "The OTC course runs concurrently with his classes at Eton."

"Good for him," Lt. Col. Randal said.

"During inspection the sergeant major found a dead fly in his locker."

Lt. Col. Randal said, "That's a grievous offense."

"Teddy was written up for two infractions," Lady Jane giggled. "Unauthorized pet and failure to feed it properly."

Lt. Col. Randal took out one of Waldo Treywick's thin cigars and stuck it between his teeth, unlit.

"Lucky he didn't get gigged for cruelty to insects."

"During the rest of the school year," Lady Jane read from the letter, "his three sports are boxing, rowing and gymnastics. Teddy believes they will be useful for his career as a magician someday.

"He also wants you to know Captain McKoy advised him to join the pistol team. While it is not considered a sport at Eton, they do have one. Teddy says the Captain invited him to travel with his Wild West Show performing magic illusions and doing shooting tricks after the war if he can master the pistol."

Lady Jane became tickled again as she read aloud, "Captain McKoy has recruited Rita and Lana to be 'hoochy-koochy' dancers in a side tent at the show."

"The captain," Lt. Plum-Martin said waking up, "offered me the role of 'starring' in the dunking booth."

"Dunking booth?" Lady Jane asked.

"I am supposed to wear my swimsuit and sit on a plank suspended over a tank of water," the Vargas Girl look-alike Royal Marine said.

"Men pay money to throw baseballs at a small bull's-eye. If they hit the target, I fall into the water.

"Could be fun."

"Can I come with you, Pam?" Lady Jane said. "What about you, John? Want to run off and join the Wild West Show with us?"

Lt. Col. Randal said, "Sounds like a plan."

A giant wearing a pair of pointy-toed cowboy boots and the largest Hawaiian shirt Lt. Col. Randal had ever seen came out of the cockpit. He must have weighed over 300 pounds but moved with the ease of a professional dancer.

"James B. McGovern," he introduced himself. "Friends call me 'Earthquake McGoon.'

"Paddy's giving me a check ride. I'm Warthog's new Kingfisher pilot on the *King Duck*.

"Wanted to let you know, Colonel, our flight's been diverted to Alexandria," Earthquake McGoon said. "A gentleman named Jim and a Major Sansom will meet you at the airport. ETA is approximately ninety minutes.

"The Anson chase plane will be continuing on to Cairo."

Ex-Lt. Jaxx slid the bush hat back from where it had been covering his face. "Wonder what that's about?"

"We'll find out," Lt. Col. Randal said.

JAMES "BALDIE" TAYLOR AND MAJOR A.W. "SAMMY" SANSOM were waiting on the tarmac when the Hudson rolled to a stop. The two men were strictly business. Lieutenant Colonel John Randal clicked on immediately,

"Colonel," Jim said, "we require a few hours of your time. Major Sansom and I would like for you and King to accompany the two of us on a short road trip. After that you can fly on to Cairo.

"Field Marshal Auchinleck is expecting you this evening."

"Road trip?"

"I will explain on the way," Jim said. "Arrangements have been made for Lady Jane and Lt. Plum-Martin to have a car and driver to take them shopping in town.

"Lt. Jaxx, you can spend the time at the bar in the airport, bearing in mind you are having dinner with the Field Marshal tonight."

"Understood, sir."

"Colonel," Jim said, "bring your field glasses."

There were two tan Chevrolet staff cars in addition to the one for the shopping expedition. Jim and Lt. Col. Randal climbed into one, and Maj. Sansom and King got in the other.

Maj. Sansom had a quiet word with King as they walked over to their car. The Merc sat in the back seat behind a colonel he did not know in the passenger seat.

Jim took the wheel, and the two cars drove off the airfield through town and headed out into the countryside.

As they drove, Jim explained what was taking place, ticking off points in staccato. "You saw the colonel. He's the Army of the Nile's transportation officer.

"Frequents the Kit-Kat Club. Sleeps with one of the dancers. She is an enemy agent. He does not know that.

"The colonel likes to brag about how important his work is. Takes his briefcase home with him at night. The dancer rifles it while he is asleep. The case contained our complete Order of Battle. Now the opposition has a copy."

"Why not just shut down the Kit-Kat?" Lt. Col. Randal said. "It's a hotbed of spies."

"Exactly why we allow places like it to stay in business," Jim said. "Makes it easy for us to know where to find enemy agents."

"I see."

"Maj. Sansom is explaining to the Colonel that he has been compromised by his mistress. He is married with three children. The man is ruined."

"That's a fact," Lt. Col. Randal said.

Jim asked, "Have you ever heard of the 'Haversack Ruse'?"

"Negative."

"In the last war in the Middle East there was an intelligence officer named Colonel Richard Meinertzhagen. He came up with a plan to mislead our enemy the Turks by planting a false map on them containing what appeared to be the battle plan for our upcoming offensive.

"As the story goes, he saddled up and rode alone toward the Turkish lines until he ran into an enemy cavalry patrol. Meinertzhagen then stabbed his horse with the small blade of his pocket knife, smeared blood on the map, fired a few shots with his pistol to draw the enemy's attention and then somehow managed to escape on foot, leaving the horse and a bloody map behind."

"The Turks took the bait, we attacked somewhere else, and the battle was won."

"You believe that story?" Lt. Col. Randal asked.

"Maybe, maybe not," Jim said. "History is replete with battles won or lost because one side or the other came into possession of their opponent's plan."

"Maj. Samson is giving the Colonel two options as we speak.

"Death by firing squad for espionage or he can drive down this road into no man's land until he comes to the portion that has been mined by the Germans."

"Then what?"

"His car blows up," Jim said. "There is a map in a briefcase in the trunk with the entire battle plan for OPERATION CRUSADER – the code name of our upcoming offensive."

"We're giving Rommel our plan?"

"No," Jim said. "This is a modern-day version of the Haversack Ruse – plan's false."

"So why am I here, General?"

"Raiding Forces is going to be asked to carry out a series of high-risk missions in support of CRUSADER," Jim said. "We believe it useful for you to witness how far our side is willing to go to ensure OPERATION CRUSADER is a success. The idea is for you to be convinced how important your role in CRUSADER is."

The car drove around a curve in the road. A Medford truck with a squad of engineers sitting in the back was parked to the side. Jim pulled in behind it.

He got out and walked over to have a word with the lieutenant in command of the detail. The young officer climbed back in the truck. It turned around and drove back the way they had come.

"From this point on, German armored cars patrol the road," Jim said.

"The colonel was briefed about the mines?"

"Oh, yes," Jim said.

Maj. Sansom pulled past and stopped. Then he and King stepped out of their car.

The colonel exited. No words were exchanged. He did not make eye contact with anyone. Pale as a sheet, hands shaking, he walked around to the driver's side and climbed in behind the wheel.

His world had turned upside down.

The colonel put the car in gear and drove slowly away. The road made a lazy turn about a half a mile ahead. There was nothing in sight but dirty brown desert.

Lt. Col. Randal leaned against the hood of the parked staff car watching the scene unfold. He stuck a cigar between his teeth. Through his Zeiss binoculars he followed the colonel's progress.

"How do you know that stretch of the road is mined, General?"

"We planted the mines."

BOOOOOM!

16

CONFUSION TO THE ENEMY

LIEUTENANT COLONEL JOHN RANDAL AND CAPTAIN THE LADY Jane Seaborn were sitting behind a palm in the back of the Gezira Club. King and GG were at the table next to them. Lieutenant Pamala Plum-Martin was at another table having a drink with a group of fighter pilots. Major Sir Terry "Zorro" Stone and ex-Lieutenant Billy Jack Jaxx were at the bar chatting up a pair of Flying Clipper stewardesses.

Plans had changed. Dinner with Field Marshal Claude Auchinleck had been canceled. Now they were expected at his residence at twenty hundred hours for cocktails. James "Baldie" Taylor had said he would meet them there.

As usual, Lady Jane was entertaining Lt. Col. Randal with a story. He was addicted to her stories but somewhat distracted tonight.

Lt. Col. Randal was wondering what role Raiding Forces was slated to play in OPERATION CRUSADER that could be so important that it had been deemed necessary for him to be physically present to observe a British officer knowingly drive to his death.

"There's Lady Hermione Ranfurly with Peter Fleming and Bill Stirling – David's brother," Lady Jane said. "The three of them have shaken up Special Operations Executive. Remember, she was smuggling out incriminating evidence against SOE's management in her bra?"

"How could I forget?"

"Colossal scandal," Lady Jane said. "People fired from top to bottom. But Lady Hermione paid a price.

"She's out too."

"Why?"

"People say she is a troublemaker and that Peter Fleming is only mad because SOE appropriated a vessel he was planning to use. The firm needed it to rescue Greek civilians. Peter wanted the ship to transport the swim teams he brought out to the Middle East to attack enemy shipping with limpet mines.

"By the way," Lady Jane said, "Ranfurly's husband's uncle was at the country house in Kenya when the Earl of Errol dropped his fiancée off the night he was murdered."

"Really?"

"As you may recall, it was a wife-swapping debauch of the type Joss Hay found irresistible. Only, on that occasion he had to return to town."

"Small world," Lt. Col. Randal said. "She know the man was at a sex orgy?"

"We did not touch on that subject," Lady Jane laughed. "He was a suspect in the murder case for a while. Half the husbands in Kenya were.

"Joss had slept with their wives . . . or they suspected he had."

Lt. Col. Randal said, "Man had a reputation."

"Lady Hermione believes she knows who killed the Earl," Lady Jane said.

"Who might that be?"

"Why me, of course," Lady Jane said. "She was raised around horses and guns before her father squandered the family fortune.

"Hermione was admiring the 'Raiding Forces' carved on my ivory grips...."

"*My* ivory grips," Lt. Col. Randal said.

"Grips formerly carried by you – mine now," Lady Jane said, bombarding him with her patented heart attack smile.

"Upon discovering my Colt was a .38 Super, she informed me a single shell casing of that caliber was found at the scene of the murder.

"SOE confiscated the brass, never to be seen again."

"As I recall," Lt. Col. Randal said, "you were carrying your Walther PPK – 7.65mm."

"The night *you* shot the 'World's Greatest Pouncer,'" Lady Jane said, "I was deeply regretting not bringing a Thompson submachine gun and a purse full of hand grenades."

"Hay was the Italian's man in Kenya," Lt. Col. Randal said. "Should've picked another line of work if he didn't want to get shot."

"That," Lady Jane said, "has never been confirmed."

Now she had his full attention.

UNDER FIELD MARSHALL SIR ARCHIBALD WAVELL, THE Commander-in-Chief's residence had been a vibrant household. He had brought his entire family out to Egypt. Now that Field Marshal Claude Auchinleck had arrived to assume command, leaving his wife back in India, the place had turned into a high-toned army barracks.

FM Auchinleck was a soldier's soldier. Most of his troops could not bring their wives to Egypt, so he did not bring his. Rumor was that decision had turned out to be a mistake – his wife was openly having an affair with a senior RAF officer back in Cawnpore.

While FM Auchinleck had a stellar career steadily climbing up the ranks to high command, his critics did not rate it a spectacular career. The wags at Grey Pillars claimed he lacked vision, imagination and original thought. Also, they said he placed far too much confidence in his generals.

That FM Auchinleck was leading by example and that he had inherited the generals with the job was lost on the GHQ armchair Commando set, who had a high opinion of their own military skills even though most had never heard a shot fired in anger.

FM Auchinleck did have bad luck with generals. They were being knocked over like tenpins. Car wrecks, plane crashes and the odd enemy action – killed, captured, or wounded so seriously they could not continue on active service. Likely, no CinC had ever lost more general officers in such a short period of sustained inaction as Auchinleck had.

On the credit side of the ledger, FM Auchinleck loved being a soldier. He loved being in the Army. And he could make the hard decision when it needed to be made.

More important for Raiding Forces, FM Auchinleck was an advocate of irregular operations.

The cocktail party was a ruse.

Lieutenant Colonel John Randal, Major Sir Terry "Zorro" Stone, Lieutenant Pamala Plum-Martin, ex-Lieutenant Billy Jack Jaxx, King and GG were surprised when they arrived and discovered they were attending a private investiture instead of a cocktail party. Only Captain the Lady Jane Seaborn was not surprised – she had known the drill all along.

James "Baldie" Taylor was present along with Brigadier Raymond J. "R.J." Maunsell, Brigadier George Davy and Vice Admiral Sir Randolph "Razor" Ransom.

Because the medals were immediate awards and the actions for which they were presented were classified, the citations were brief. They all read simply, "For service to the Crown."

The ceremony was as short as the citations. Those to be decorated lined up in a single rank, shoulder to shoulder. The Field Marshal started with Lt. Col. Randal. Then he worked his way down the line, speaking briefly with each recipient as he pinned on his medal.

"Colonel," FM Auchinleck said, "congratulations on your recent raids. I understand patrols under your personal command have surpassed the century mark in Axis aircraft destroyed. Y-Service has intercepted enemy radio traffic that the Germans and Italians are hysterical over their losses and our ability to strike when and where we choose – Rommel's convinced Raiding Forces is vastly larger than it is.

"This bar to your DSO, your fourth, is a token of Great Britain's appreciation for your gallant battlefield performance."

"Thank you, sir."

"Lieutenant Plum-Martin," FM Auchinleck said, replacing her Distinguished Flying Cross with one displaying two bars. "For reasons known only to themselves, the RAF does not accord women the privilege to wear standard-issue pilot's wings. You have proved them to be very wrong-headed. Not many fliers have earned three DFCs – you are without doubt the most decorated woman in the Air Transport Auxiliary Service.

"Good show!"

When he came to ex-Lt. Jaxx, FM Auchinleck said, "Nice to see you again, Texas.

"Racking up decorations at a fast clip. Keep up this pace and we shall soon have to indent for more medals.

"I want to thank you personally for stepping forward to fight for the Empire."

"My pleasure, sir."

GG was next in line. He was wearing a borrowed Lancelot Lancers Yeomanry uniform sporting the insignia of a lieutenant. The Field Marshal pinned on his Military Cross.

"Quite a mystery to me how the Raiding Forces' chef managed to be deep behind enemy lines blowing up an enemy POL installation, but do accept my compliments on your heroic actions."

Not trusting his English and scared to death, GG simply nodded while standing at a rigid position of attention.

"Mr. King," FM Auchinleck said, slipping a fat envelope into the inside pocket of the Merc's dinner jacket, "I hope we can continue to count on your services."

"Affirmative, sir."

"Now," FM Auchinleck said, "R.J., you and your crowd are free to retire to the library to conduct business in private.

"Ladies, if you will accompany me, we shall have those cocktails now."

"Colonel," R.J. said, "you and Major Stone come with us."

Lt. Col. Randal knew what was coming next.

Ex-Lt. Jaxx, King and GG went outside to the car.

One of FM Auchinleck's aides followed the party into the library carrying a covered map with a stand. He set it up, then immediately departed the room.

R.J. went first. "Everything we say here tonight is classified. No one not in this room has the 'Need to Know' all of what we discuss in total, though each of us shall be briefing elements under our individual commands on certain aspects of it.

"Brigadier Davy, if you will do the honors."

Brig. Davy, the Army of the Nile's Operations Officer, had briefed Raiding Forces on its mission to attack enemy transports on the Via Balbia when Desert Patrol was first being organized. He had made a favorable impression at the time and continued to maintain a close working relationship with the unit ever since.

"Gentlemen," Brig. Davy said, whipping the cover off the map, "I give you OPERATION CRUSADER."

The map showed a long rectangular AO running from Tobruk to Tripoli. Essentially it was the same area that Raiding Forces considered its private hunting preserve. That was the problem with the war in the Middle East – while the AO was 1,200-plus miles long, modern armies could only operate on the narrow strip of hard ground along the coast known as "good going" and the "good going" was only approximately fifty miles wide.

Eighth Army's maneuver area was tightly restricted, bordered on one side by the Mediterranean and the other by the Great Sand Sea. The terrain restraints cut both ways – FM Rommel faced the same problem.

"Eighth Army will attack, relieve Tobruk, then drive on Tripoli. You may notice those movements are not indicated on this map. Our actual scheme of maneuver is classified and no one present tonight other than R.J. and myself have the requisite 'Need to Know.'

"I keep a copy of 'Raiding Forces' Rules' on my desk. In the spirit of those missives, I shall 'Keep It Short and Simple' tonight.

"Colonel, are you prepared to receive a Warning Order?"

It was not a question.

"Yes, sir."

"Raiding Forces will have four primary objectives in CRUSADER. One: Raid enemy airfields with an eye to keeping as many Luftwaffe attack aircraft out of the fight as possible.

"However, highest priority is to Ju-52 tri-motors," Brig. Davy said. "Afrika Korps is known to be short air transports. MEHQ Intelligence in conjunction with RAF Intelligence will provide Intel on which landing grounds host Ju-52s for you to target.

"Two: Destroy enemy fuel dumps, installations and supply points. Rommel uses up half his POL allocation hauling supplies to the front – Raiding Forces' mission is to blow up the other half.

"Three: Interdict the secondary tracks that parallel the Via Balbia.

"Four: Demonstrate in the Tripoli area. This will be by way of carrying out reconnaissance of the beaches where British Forces can conduct an amphibious tank landing. The idea is to tie down as many of Rommel's troops as possible defending against an amphibious attack that may never come – or possibly it will.

"CRUSADER will begin with a Commando raid to assassinate Field Marshal Rommel by a team selected out of the remnants of 8 Commando from the recently disbanded Layforce – led by Lieutenant Colonel Geoffrey Keyes, the son of Admiral Sir Roger Keyes, Commander of Combined Operations.

"Simultaneously, in its combat debut, L-Detachment, Special Air Service, recently expanded by fifty men, will conduct a night parachute drop, raid five enemy airfields then march to a rally point where a patrol of the Long Range Desert Service will be waiting to pick them up.

"Questions?"

"When do I need to have my squadrons ready to take the field, sir?" Lt. Col. Randal asked.

"The exact start date of CRUSADER has not been determined," Brig. Davy lied.

"By the beginning of the second week in November, Desert Patrol must be ensconced in laying-up positions, ready to launch raids against targets of your choosing as specified in the Warning Order.

"Sea Squadron can delay the start of their beach reconnaissance missions until CRUSADER is underway.

"Any other questions… no? Then R.J., if you will wrap up."

"The normal chain of command for Raiding Forces is from Brigadier Davy to A-Force to Jim to you, Colonel Randal – at least on paper," Brig. Maunsell said. "Our problem is Colonel Clarke has not arrived back in Cairo from his travels as of yet and is not expected until around the time CRUSADER is to commence.

"Dudley has been away nearly three months – he was only expecting to be gone two weeks. I have been filling in for him at A-Force, but he kept his cards close to his vest. I was not privy to everything he had in his bag of tricks and do not have the foggiest idea what other tasks he might have had in mind for Raiding Forces.

"My idea is to allow you to craft your own plans in accordance with Brigadier Davy's four-point Warning Order," Brig. Maunsell said.

"Which means Raiding Forces will be operating independently but conforming to the CRUSADER scheme. That stipulated, all battles are fluid and, as you know, once the first shot is fired the best of plans goes up in smoke.

"Be prepared to take on new missions that conform to the exigencies of the situation or that Colonel Clarke may require of you once he returns."

"Raiding Forces is capable of changing missions on short notice," Lt. Col. Randal said. "We train for that.

"Try not to assign us any task we're not geared to accomplish, sir – all we ask."

"Noted," Brig. Maunsell said. "Jim shall be working with you as usual. Know he will have signed off on any mission we ask you to perform."

"Colonel," Jim said, "if there is even the slightest possibility Raiding Forces is being asked to carry out an operation outside the usual scope of the missions we normally perform, I will personally accompany the element designated to carry it out."

"Fair enough," Lt. Col. Randal said.

Immediately after the briefing, Lt. Col. Randal's party departed.

Standing outside on the steps of his residence as they watched Lady Jane's Rolls-Royce drive away, FM Auchinleck said to Jim, "An eclectic collection of individuals serving in Randal's band of cutthroats.

"That fellow GG never uttered one single word all night. What is his story?"

"GG's an Italian captured in Abyssinia. He claimed he could cook, so Randal signed him on with Force N," Jim said.

"My God!" FM Auchinleck said. "You mean I decorated an enemy combatant?"

"GG is an excellent cook," Jim said.

VICE ADMIRAL SIR "RAZOR" RANSOM RODE WITH LIEUTENANT Colonel John Randal, Lt. Pamala Plum-Martin and Captain the Lady Jane Seaborn in her Rolls-Royce chauffeured by Flanigan. Major Sir Terry "Zorro" Stone, ex-Lieutenant Billy Jack Jaxx, King and GG followed in the Admiral's staff car. They were all en route to Mena House Hotel.

"Admiral," Lt. Col. Randal said, "would you consider taking command of the seagoing elements of Raiding Forces for the duration of CRUSADER?"

"Duck Patrol," VAdm. Ransom said, "The *King Duck*, Sea Squadron, Randy's two MAS boats and the trawler we have in dry dock refitting. Sounds like an irregular outfit to me.

"Nothing I would rather do, Colonel.

"By the way, Mud Cat Ray is out of jail. We waived training and commissioned him directly into the Royal Navy Patrol Service. Skipper of our Sea Squadron trawler."

"Glad to hear he met with your approval, sir," Lt. Col. Randal said. "Mud Cat runs a tight ship."

"You know any more like Skipper Ray," VAdm. Ransom said, "I shall find him a command no matter who he killed."

When they arrived at the suite that Lady Jane maintained at Mena House, Lt. Col. Randal called a meeting in the living room.

"Give me a status report on Desert Patrol, Terry."

"We have eight patrols, four each in the Wing and the Regiment. Roy Kidd's new Scout Patrol, Percy's Railroad Wrecking Crew II and your Ranger Patrol are independent.

"Normally Desert Patrol keeps two patrols in the field on operations, two traveling to their AO, two returning from patrol and two pulling maintenance on their vehicles and equipment or on a week's leave following their patrols.

"Patrols traveling out to their AOs are cleared to hit targets on the way, as are patrols returning," Maj. Stone said.

"One of Mr. Zargo's men links up with each patrol as it passes through his sector going and coming. He provides the patrol leader with current intelligence and guides the patrol to targets that lie on their line of march.

"When the patrol crosses over into the next sector, another of Mr. Zargo's people is waiting at the boundary to escort it across his territory. That relay keeps up from zone to zone until the patrol reaches the AO where it's going to spend the next two weeks or arrives back at X.

"The tight control exercised by Mr. Zargo's people ensures the patrols going out do not interfere with the patrol assigned to that sector or those returning home.

"While it's a big desert," Maj. Stone said, "things might become crowded if we do not coordinate our activities.

"You've had about twenty minutes to think about CRUSADER, " Lt. Col. Randal said. "What's your plan, Terry?"

"I can put all eight of my patrols in the field for the first three weeks," Maj. Stone said. "After that, expect mechanical failure; men sick, killed or wounded; and lack of ammunition, water and fuel to degrade our ability to stay in the field.

"As you and I discussed, if we lose patrol leaders there is no pool of qualified replacements."

Lt. Col. Randal said, "Not sure how I let that happen."

"Three weeks of maximum effort," Maj. Stone said. "After that, Desert Patrol's combat power will begin to degrade."

"Call in all your patrols," Lt. Col. Randal ordered. "Cancel all leave. Put Desert Patrol on alert."

"I shall send out the recall tonight," Maj. Stone said. "May take a week or more for all the patrols to rally at X."

"We're short on time," Lt. Col. Randal said, "Patrols that come in late will have to do a crash refit, turn around and take the field again immediately."

"I can shuffle the patrol's AOs," Maj. Stone said. "Late arrivers can take the sectors closest to X. That will get them in the fight faster."

"Pam," Lt. Col. Randal asked, "can we resupply our patrols by air?"

"In Abyssinia we had a major air base at Camp Croc dedicated to supplying Force N," Lt. Plum-Martin said.

"Things are different now. All we have is our Hudson, four obsolete Ansons, a pair of antique Walruses and the Italian IMAM Ro.63.

"Only the Hudson is a transport.

"The Luftwaffe and the Regia Aeronautica will be out in force during the day which limits our flying to the hours of darkness.

"Difficult, John."

"Any chance," Lt. Col. Randal asked, "of borrowing a couple of transports from the RAF?"

"I would say no," Lt. Plum-Martin said. "The air force would like to take away the planes we have. If you recall, they refused to even authorize us to paint RAF identification roundels on them when we first arrived."

"Forgot about that," Lt. Col. Randal said.

"The RAF will not be helpful," Lady Jane said. "The fools are still refusing to fly close air support missions for CRUSADER. I overheard a terrible row between Brigadier Davy and one of the air marshals about their lack of cooperation."

"Admiral," Lt. Col. Randal said, "you've had about as long as Terry to make a plan for our seagoing assets. What's your initial thought, sir?"

"The primary mission of Sea Squadron is to conduct beach reconnaissance in the vicinity of Tripoli," VAdm. Ransom said.

"The difficulty with that assignment is we do not have the capability to steam to the target area, land a shore party, allow it to carry out its mission, recover it and return to the safety of the RAF air umbrella under cover of darkness.

"Like Pam said, enemy air shall be out in strength from sunrise to sunset. Enemy air poses the most serious threat to the *King Duck* and Randy's two motor gunboats. We do not want to risk being caught underway after first light."

"Mud Cat Ray's trawler can alleviate the problem, but it will not solve it entirely. The ship does not have the speed to reach a target that far up the coast and return to safe harbor in a single night. What I have in mind for it is to sail as far away from Tripoli as possible, then to disguise itself as a wreck – hide in plain sight. Before the sun comes up."

"Need to be careful, sir," Lt. Col. Randal said. "Sounds like a high-risk proposition."

"It will be."

"Consider limiting the number of Sea Squadron troops stationed on board ship for any single mission like we discussed, sir," Lt. Col. Randal said.

"We can do that, Colonel," VAdm. Ransom said. "Our immediate problem is that Skipper Ray's trawler may not complete its refit in time for CRUSADER."

"I know you have a plan, Admiral," Lt. Col. Randal said.

"Tomorrow morning will find me at the dry dock when the workers arrive. My *forte* is infusing a sense of urgency where it has not previously existed. If the workers are not fired with enthusiasm, they will be," VAdm. Ransom said.

"At the same time I will be in contact with the First Submarine Flotilla based out of Alexandria. It has old China Fleet submarines that were recalled to the Mediterranean in 1940. The flotilla is dedicated to clandestinely transporting small parties on long distance missions – called 'The Magic Carpet Service.' By definition that falls under Irregular Operations – meaning me.

"Right now I would hazard Sea Squadron will end up using the Magic Carpet Service to transport them to the Tripoli area for the majority of their beach reconnaissance missions."

"Impressive report, Admiral," Lt. Col. Randal said. "I'm not going to waste any time worrying about Sea Squadron."

"I shall keep you informed of developments," VAdm. Ransom said. "While not much was said on the subject, my takeaway from tonight's briefing is the beach reconnaissance mission is of vital importance. Germans guarding beaches we do not land on are Germans our Eighth Army does not have to engage."

"Lt. Jaxx," Lt. Col. Randal said, "anything you want to add?"

"Taking out enemy pilots seems to make even more sense now," ex-Lt. Jaxx said, "than when Pam first suggested it, sir."

"Sure does," Lt. Col. Randal said. "We'll use Ranger Patrol personnel if the right target presents itself.

"Pam, you're going to be overtasked with Squadron Leader Wilcox away," Lt. Col. Randal said. "But, you'll have to come up with a way to fly in a Ranger team if the opportunity develops to take down a group of enemy pilots."

"I will, John."

"Sir," ex-Lt. Jaxx said, "we need a code word identifier for the mission – we never got around to picking one."

Lt. Col. Randal asked, "Any suggestions?"

"Name it after Pam, sir," ex-Lt. Jaxx said. "*Bombshell.*"

"I like it." Lt. Col. Randal said.

"King?"

"Has my vote, Chief."

"Pam?"

"Now I understand," Lt. Plum-Martin said, "why those Texas sorority girls refused to testify at your trial, Billy Jack."

Ex-Lt. Jaxx said, "Is that a good thing?"

AFTER EVERYONE HAD DEPARTED EXCEPT FOR LIEUTENANT Pamala Plum-Martin, who was spending the night in the guest bedroom, Lieutenant Colonel John Randal and Captain the Lady Jane Seaborn put on swimsuits and went out to the private pool.

Under a black sky salted with a million glittering stars, they sat in the water on the steps at the shallow end of the pool looking at the shadows of the Great Pyramids. Lady Jane had her arm over his shoulder with her scarlet-tipped nails splayed on his chest.

"You are quiet," Lady Jane said. "Anything bothering you, John?"

"I've done everything possible to motivate my patrol leaders to concentrate on attacking truck transport on the Via Balbia," Lt. Col. Randal said. "Not go cowboying airfields."

"Yes, you have."

"Tonight Brigadier Davy informed me enemy airbases, specifically those hosting Ju-52s, are our top priority."

"Change two. Duty calls," Lady Jane laughed. "You are in the Army now, John."

"The boys have been killing a lot of trucks," Lt. Col. Randal said. "They're going to think I'm an idiot when I order them to go back to raiding airfields."

Lady Jane said, "You gave it the All-American try."

LIEUTENANT MANDY PAIGE WAS AT RAIDING FORCES' Headquarters when ex-Lieutenant Billy Jack Jaxx and King arrived from Mena House.

"Billy Jack," she said, seeing the medal dangling from his blouse, "were you awarded another Military Cross tonight?"

"That's a Rodge."

"You are turning into *such* a Christmas tree," Lt. Mandy said. "What is it for?"

King said, "That's classified."

"No it's not," ex-Lt. Jaxx said. "I got this one for falling out of a truck."

Jack Cool.

BRIGADIER RAYMOND J. "R.J." MAUNSELL AND JAMES "BALDIE" Taylor arrived at Raiding Forces' Headquarters. One of Jim's operatives was with them. He was carrying a heavy leather suitcase.

Jim and the agent with the suitcase went to one of the empty bedrooms on the second floor. Brig. Maunsell proceeded to Rikke Runborg's room. She answered the door on the first knock.

By the time Brig. Maunsell and Rocky arrived at the second-floor bedroom, Jim's operative had opened the suitcase and was setting up the radio delivered to her by Amal Atrash for the German Secret Intelligence Service, the Abwehr.

Jim's operative went out into the hall and took up position in front of the door.

Rocky sat at the table where the radio had been placed. Brig. Maunsell handed her a piece of paper with a short message on it. She glanced at the note then began tapping the key.

The ice-blond spy was a skilled teletypist.

```
3 NOVEMBER 41
TONIGHT AUCHINLECK ALERTED HIS SPECIAL FORCES
COMMANDER THE EARLIEST DATE THE BRITISH
OFFENSIVE CAN COMMENCE IS 25 NOVEMBER 41.
GAULITIER
```

The Abwehr radio operator in Tripoli who received the message recognized the hand of the sender. Each teletypist has a unique signature that is as identifiable as a fingerprint. He authenticated the signal with a notation in black ink then initialed it. The message was on Field Marshal Erwin Rommel's desk within the hour.

FM Rommel read it as soon as it arrived. He immediately set the date of *his* offensive for 23 November 41 – two days before CRUSADER.

Then he made arrangements to fly to Rome to celebrate his birthday with his wife. The Desert Fox planned to return to Tripoli two days prior to his attack.

The best-kept secret at MEHQ – known only to five senior officers – was the actual date OPERATION CRUSADER would commence – 13 November 41.

The British and the Germans were building up their armies to launch offensives. Both adversaries hoped the campaign would be the decisive battle in the Middle East. The side that got off first would achieve the element of surprise.

Misleading the Afrika Korps about the actual date of the British attack, tricking FM Rommel into being out of the country away from his command post on the day the battle began, gave Empire Forces an advantage.

Rocky, known to the Abwehr by the codename GAULITIER, was Rommel's most trusted agent in Egypt. The two officers in the room knew that if Rocky's message worked as planned, she would have accomplished a misinformation coup of unparalleled magnitude so far in this war.

The misinformation might decide the outcome of OPERATION CRUSADER and the war in the Middle East.

And, if FM Rommel did go to Rome to celebrate his birthday, it would confirm that Rocky was working for British Intelligence against the Germans, not the other way around. Brig. Maunsell, the senior counterintelligence officer in the Middle East Command, was very interested in establishing that fact for certain.

It would not settle the question of whether or not she was Marina Lee – the Russian spy who was known to have infiltrated the Abwehr prior to the Germans invading Russia and then sent by the Nazis to spy on the British.

Only three people in MEHQ possessed the Need to Know the complete details of tonight's ploy: Field Marshal Claude Auchinleck, Brigadier George Davy and Brig. Maunsell. Jim was cleared to know everything except the CRUSADER start date.

That is how compartmentalization works. People involved in an intelligence operation only know what is necessary for them to carry out their individual part of the plan.

Rocky only knew what she transmitted.

On the way back to their quarters in Cairo, the three intelligence officers stopped by the Long Bar at Shepard's Hotel.

Brig. Maunsell proposed a toast, "Confusion to the enemy."

They drank to that.

17

DOUBLE FROGSPAWN

LIEUTENANT COLONEL JOHN RANDAL WAS IN THE SMALL MAP room/briefing area of the third-floor suite he shared with Captain the Lady Jane Seaborn at Raiding Forces' Headquarters. He was studying the map of the Mediterranean coastline from Tobruk to Tripoli. Specifically, he was looking at the Via Balbia. One of Raiding Forces' objectives in OPERATION CRUSADER was to attack the series of secondary roads that paralleled the hardball that ran along the coast.

No one had said so, but he guessed the reason he had not been ordered to attack the enemy's primary high-speed axis of approach was because it would be clogged with enemy traffic once the offensive started. Rommel would be rushing reinforcements to the front, which would cause enemy convoys to divert to the secondary roads. Since the secondary dirt tracts ran up to fifty miles inland in some cases, so much traffic on them would make it extremely hazardous and time-consuming for a jeep patrol to infiltrate across the dirt roads undetected to the Via Balbia.

Raiding Forces had developed simple doctrine based on experience for setting up a clandestine desert Laying Up Position (LUP): Never set up in the only patch of brush in the area. Never set up near a road/high-speed avenue of approach.

Violating the second policy would be a given if there were heavy enemy traffic on the secondary tracts. Once inside the road network, a patrol would be near a road anywhere it stopped to set up.

Exfiltrating back to the protection of the Great Sand Sea undetected after carrying out an attack on the main supply route or raiding one of the roadhouses along it would be problematic, particularly if the patrol were being pursued.

One of Raiding Forces' Rules was: Plan raids backward – know how to get home.

Lt. Col. Randal was not going to put the Via Balbia off limits to Desert Patrol for CRUSADER, preferring to give his patrol leaders the freedom to choose their own targets. But he intended to make his feelings known that they should not strike for the hardball unless it was absolutely necessary or unless some special circumstance offered an unusual opportunity worth the risk.

With Desert Patrol out of the picture, Sea Squadron could assume primary responsibility to land ashore and mine Afrika Korps' only black-topped road paralleling the coastline. It could raid truck parks, ambush convoys traveling at night, and attack roadhouses then retreat back into the Mediterranean to sail away under cover of darkness. Lt. Col. Randal had no intention of letting FM Rommel have the free use of his main supply route – invasion or no invasion.

Lady Jane walked in the front door of the suite in her black French-cut swimsuit; she was drying her mahogany hair with a towel. She and her Royal Marines had finished their morning PT. They always ended with a swim.

"You might want to check on Billy Jack," Lady Jane said. "Downstairs around back."

Lt. Col. Randal jumped up, dashed down the stairs and out the front door of RFHQ. He went around to the back of the building.

Ex-Lieutenant Billy Jack Jaxx was lying on the ground clad in his swim trunks in the throes of an attack of the dry heaves. He looked like he might die.

"What the hell, Jack?"

"Nazi bitch," ex-Lt. Jaxx groaned, "nearly killed me."

"Who are you talking about?"

"Rocky had us do some kind of ballet torture exercises. Those were bad enough. Then the refugee from Poland who had coached the women's Olympic gymnastics team put us through the entire routine – you wouldn't believe how tough that is, Colonel.

"After that, Lady Jane led a mile swim which turned out to be a full-on race. I'm from Texas – all we ever had to swim in was a cattle tank."

King had followed Lt. Col. Randal when he ran down the stairs.

"I warned you not to do it."

"Yeah," ex-Lt. Jaxx said, "but you weren't half as convincing as Rocky in her swimsuit and legwarmers."

Lt. Col. Randal said, "I can see how that might be."

King asked, "Which one are you calling a Nazi?"

"CAPTAIN PELHAM-DAVIES, HORNBLOWER AND HEADHUNTER Hoolihan, Chief," King said.

"Eighth Army is launching its offensive sometime in the next few weeks," Lieutenant Colonel John Randal said. "Sea Squadron is slated to play a starring role."

"So we heard, sir," Captain Jeb Pelham-Davies said. "Admiral Ransom alerted us."

"Jeb, I've asked the Admiral to take command of all of our seagoing assets for the duration of the operation. He's agreed. You report to him."

"Yes, sir."

"There's three reasons to do it that way," Lt. Col. Randal said.

"I'm taking the field with Ranger Patrol, so you need someone who can run interference for you at MEHQ.

"The Admiral can manage the trawler being refitted, he can guarantee the *King Duck* gets priority dock and oiling service, plus he says he can line up submarines out of Alexandria to carry your raiding parties on long-range missions.

"And I want you free from administrative duties to concentrate on planning and executing the continuous string of raids I'll explain in a minute."

"I enjoy working with the 'Razor'," Capt. Pelham-Davies said.

"Admiral Ransom has already arranged the submarines, sir," Lieutenant Butch "Headhunter" Hoolihan said. "My troop is being trucked to Alexandria this afternoon to begin DSEA training with the First Submarine Flotilla."

"What's that?"

"Davis Submerged Escape Apparatus, sir," Lt. Hoolihan said, "in case the submarine sinks."

"Oh, that sounds great," Lt. Col. Randal said, feeling claustrophobic. "Try not to ever have to use it, Butch."

"Roger, sir."

"Desert Patrol," Lt. Col. Randal said leading the two officers over to the map, "has been assigned missions that do not include attacking the main supply route down the coast of the Via Balbia. I want Sea Squadron to take over that responsibility.

"Sergeant Major Mikkalis' Duck Patrol will mine the hardball, carry out raids on roadhouses, attack targets of opportunity and conduct ambushes of enemy convoys traveling at night. Duck Patrol's only limitation is they have to be back on board the LCT in time for it to reach the safety of the RAF umbrella before sunrise.

"Randy, I want your two MAS boats with one of the Commando platoons operating further up the coast mining the highway. They can take on roadhouses if the opportunity presents itself. However, their primary mission is to interdict the hardball.

"Hammer the Via Balbia somewhere, anywhere, every night if you can, Jeb."

"Roger, sir," Capt. Pelham-Davies said.

"Now listen up," Lt. Col. Randal said. "Sea Squadron's *priority* mission is to perform beach reconnaissance surveys in the Tripoli area.

"That'll be you, Butch, since you've apparently been tapped to be the submarine troop commander."

"Sir!"

"Continue the recon missions until Admiral Ransom tells you to stand down," Lt. Col. Randal said.

"The main thing is – and we are not having this conversation – Butch, you need to make sure the bad guys know what you're doing. Your beach surveys are what might be described as *semi*-clandestine.

"Is that clear?"

"Not exactly, sir," Lt. Hoolihan said.

"This does not leave the room," Lt. Col. Randal said. "The idea is to tie down the maximum number of enemy troops defending beaches in the Tripoli area against an amphibious landing."

"Will there be a seaborne assault, sir?" Capt. Pelham-Davies asked.

"I have no idea," Lt. Col. Randal said. "You are to proceed as if there will be. Either way, this portion of Sea Squadron's mission has strategic implications."

"Understood, sir," Capt. Pelham-Davies said, "loud and clear."

"You might have a conversation with Captain Merryweather," Lt. Col. Randal said.

"He's a master at mind games. Beach surveys we want the bad guys to know we're carrying out seem like the perfect opportunity for his brand of psychological warfare."

"Too bad, sir," Capt. Pelham-Davies said, "the Germans would not be intimidated by orange squirrels."

"Italians might," Lt. Hoolihan said.

"MAJOR STONE AND RED TO SEE YOU, CHIEF," FLANIGAN SAID.

Major Sir Terry "Zorro" Stone and the stunning red-headed Clipper Girl walked in. It was no secret that Red had a major-league crush on Sir Terry Stone or that Zorro was still playing the field. Less well-known was that both Red and Zorro were in the employ of the British Secret Intelligence Service, MI-6.

"You wished to see me, John?" Red asked.

"What's your schedule look like for the next month or so, Red?"

"Depends," Red said. "I can rearrange my calendar if necessary."

Red had been Lt. Col. Randal's assistant during part of the siege at RAF Habbaniya. She was very capable. You had to be to earn a BOAC slot as a Clipper Girl – the most prestigious flying job in the world.

"It's no secret Field Marshall Auchinleck is building up for an offensive," Lt. Col. Randal said. "When it kicks off I've got a problem. Maybe you can help."

"You know I shall be happy to if possible."

"When Raiding Forces goes into action," Lt. Col. Randal said, "I want armed female bodyguards assigned to Jane, Brandy and Mandy. Parker will have to stay here at RFHQ to supervise the Royal Marine staff. Normally she and Brandy are always together – that leaves me one bodyguard short.

"Jane and Brandy are flying out to Oasis X tomorrow. Rita and Lana can protect them. Mandy is there now.

"Any chance you could be available?"

"Absolutely," Red said, "provided you do a favor for me in return."

"Like what?"

"Allow me to keep a room here at RFHQ to use when I am on layover in Cairo," Red said. Maj. Stone, standing behind Red, was vigorously shaking his head and mouthing, "NO!"

The last thing Sir Terry wanted was the Clipper Girl keeping an eye on him full-time when he was in from the field.

Lt. Col. Randal said, "My pleasure."

RED LEFT TO NOTIFY BOAC TO TAKE HER OFF THE ROSTER indefinitely. Since she stood down from flying status from time to time, the airline was used to finding a replacement for her – no questions asked. The Cairo staff had their marching orders about her from the corporate headquarters in London, which had theirs from MI-6.

"Thanks, old stick," Major Sir Terry "Zorro" Stone said. "Cooked my goose."

"What can you tell me about Lieutenant Stirling and L-Detachment, SAS?" Lieutenant Colonel John Randal said.

"Why do you ask, John?"

"Mad Dog has been working with 'em. He says the men have been trying to teach themselves how to jump out of airplanes. Two were killed because they didn't know to put the safety pin in the snap hook when they hooked up.

"No one told Stirling they needed a steel cable to attach their static lines to, so the jumpers hooked up to the legs of the seats in the airplane."

"Taught themselves how to parachute?" Maj. Stone asked. "Insane."

Lt. Col Randal said. "As you heard last night, MEHQ assigned L-Detachment a raid at the beginning of CRUSADER."

"They've been ordered to break down into five teams of ten men, board five Bombay aircraft, fly to five different drop zones under cover of darkness, jump in, reassemble, then raid five separate airfields before marching thirty miles through the desert to a RV with the LRDG – all before sunrise."

"Dreamed up by gabardine swine at Grey Pillars, no doubt," Major Stone said. "We would never attempt anything as complex – that plan is insane."

"Mad Dog," Lt. Col. Randal said, "tells me the SAS men are more afraid of jumping out of the airplanes than attacking the targets."

"Will they be dropping to reception parties at each DZ?" Maj. Stone asked.

"Jumping blind."

"Not going to end well," Maj. Stone said.

"Back to your original question – David Stirling is from an aristocratic Scottish family. I believe 'Pyro' Percy is a cousin. His father is General Sir Archibald Stirling.

"I know David from his days in the Scots Guards.

"My recollection, he was a so-so subaltern. His nickname is the 'Big Sloth.' "Lord Shimi Lovat, who I know much better, is also related to David and detests him."

"The Lovat Scouts Lovat?" Lt. Col. Randal asked.

"His grandfather formed the regiment," Maj. Stone said.

"As we know, Dudley Clarke has been obsessed with having a Special Air Service unit in the Middle East for ages to mislead and mystify the enemy. Dudley cut a deal with David. He would secure permission from Auchinleck to raise a parachute raiding unit provided David would promise to name it 'L-Detachment, SAS,'" Maj. Stone said.

"Let's face it, Dudley is something of a social lion hunter. He wanted a parachute demonstration team for his deceptions and he wanted to ingratiate himself with the Stirling family. Kill two birds with one stone."

"Colonel Clarke's a social climber?"

"Afraid so," Maj. Stone said.

"Dudley was under no illusions about creating an operational unit. L-Detachment was intended to be like those dummy plywood tank regiments that consist of 'sunshields' that fit over the body of a truck but look real enough from an airplane."

"That raid is no illusion," Lt. Col. Randal said.

"Dudley has been away for three months now, leaving L-Detachment twisting in the breeze," Maj. Stone said

"David demonstrated initiative no one suspected him of possessing by attempting to learn how to parachute on his own – having a hard time believing that story."

"It's true all right."

"My guess," Maj. Stone said, "the operations staff at MEHQ, who have never been near a parachute, saw what appeared to be an airborne qualified unit on paper and developed a plan they hoped would be useful as part of CRUSADER.

"Besides, from the staff's perspective, should L-Detachment fail, no great loss – the unit is obscure enough to be expendable, and in the larger scheme of CRUSADER, no one would even notice if a platoon-sized raiding party was wiped out.

"Most likely not knowing the first thing about planning parachute drops, David agreed to carry out GHQ's scheme without realizing the operation is flawed to the point of being suicidal."

Lt. Col. Randal said, "Waste of good men."

"SERGEANT RAWLSTON, CHIEF."

Ex-Sergeant Hank Rawlston came in, chewing on the stub of an unlit cigar, "You wanted to see me, Colonel?"

Lieutenant Colonel John Randal said, "Raiding Forces has been alerted to take part in the offensive that's about to start.

"How many new jeeps have you got ready to go?"

"A dozen right now, Colonel," ex-Sergeant Rawlston said. "We can get us six or eight more in a week to ten days."

"Once the Eighth Army launches," Lt. Col. Randal said. "Raiding Forces is going to be operating around the clock. I need a fast turnaround for our broken-down jeeps and a lot of spares.

"I want you to relocate your workshop to Oasis X. Leave a couple mechanics here to handle any vehicles Duck Patrol might bring in and to continue desertizing the last consignment of jeeps Lady Jane secured for us."

"When you need me in place, sir?"

"If you could have your men ready to roll out tomorrow that would be good."

"I ain't never led no desert convoy, Colonel," ex-Sgt. Rawlston said.

"No problem," Lt. Col. Randal said. "Lieutenant Jaxx will escort you out. Take everything you think you might possibly need. There's no telling how long this operation is going to last.

"Can do, sir."

"Once this show gets started your team may be working night and day," Lt. Col. Randal said. "You're key man – pace yourself. That's an order."

"Yes, sir."

"Lady Jane will be keeping her eye on you to make sure you comply. I can't replace you, Sergeant."

"Rest easy, Colonel," Sgt. Rawlston said. "We'll keep your jeeps runnin' – you keep killin' Nazis."

"CAPTAIN MAD DOG, CHIEF."

Captain Roy "Mad Dog" Reupart entered, followed by ex-Lieutenant Billy Jack Jaxx. Jack Cool was looking much better than when Lieutenant Colonel John Randal had last seen him.

"Colonel," Capt. Reupart said. "Request permission to accompany L-Detachment on their combat mission."

"Denied."

"Sir," Capt. Reupart said, "those SAS men are not fully qualified parachutists. The troops are excellent material, but they have want of experienced men as stiffeners."

"Colonel," ex-Lt. Jaxx said. "Before Capt. Reupart got there the trainees built ten-foot high platforms in the beds of trucks. Jumped off the back while going about fifteen miles per hour thinking they would learn how to make parachute landing falls that way. They've had a crazy stupid training casualty rate.

"I'd like to jump in with 'em too, sir," ex-Lt. Jaxx said. "L-Detachment needs the help."

"Negative."

"When the LRDG picks the SAS up after hitting the airfields, they could drop me off at X. Pam said she'd fly me out to Ranger Patrol, sir."

"Not happening, Jack."

"Brandy, Chief," King said from the door.

"Send her in."

"Roy," Lt. Col. Randal said. "I have you penciled in to be first in line to take over a patrol leader slot in the event one goes down.

"On the other hand, if you happened to cobble together a patrol out of the volunteers you've been training for Raiding Forces, you can take the field with Desert Patrol when we move out."

"Request withdrawn, sir," Capt. Reupart said.

He had been Raiding Forces' training NCO when they went through No. 1 British Parachute School. He had volunteered to join them when they graduated provided he could see active service. In Kenya, given a direct commission, he had set up and run a primitive jump school to train the new non-jump-qualified members of Force N and Special Operations Executive.

Later, Capt. Reupart had commanded a troop 1 Guerrilla Corps (Parachute), Force N Abyssinian mule cavalry. He got his wish to see action.

"I select the men, sir?"

"Except for the navigator," Lt. Col. Randal said. "I'll make sure you get an experienced ex-LRDG man. If he doesn't measure up you can RTU him, and I'll find you another one."

"My patrol will be organized by the noon meal, sir," Capt. Reupart said. "I can pull out for X in twenty-four hours."

"Thought you might," Lt. Col. said.

Brandy came in as Capt. Reupart was rushing out the door.

"Billy Jack," Brandy said, flashing a dazzling smile, "enjoy our morning workout?"

The golden girl was beginning to recover her sense of humor.

Lt. Jaxx said, "It was just swell."

"Jack," Lt. Col. Randal said, "Sergeant Rawlston is relocating his workshop to X. You're going to lead the convoy. His men are not trained for desert driving. You may want to consider skirting wide around the end of the Sand Sea toward the Suez.

"Your call – be there three days from tomorrow."

"Yes, sir."

Lt. Col. Randal said, "Volunteering to help L-Detachment was a good thing. But I'm not about to let one of my people anywhere near that operation – poor prior planning produces poor results. That's the worst plan I've ever heard."

"That's a definite Rodge, sir."

CAPTAIN THE LADY JANE SEABORN HEARD BRANDY'S VOICE AND walked out of the master bedroom.

"Pack your bags, ladies," Lieutenant Colonel John Randal said. "I want you at Oasis X for the duration of CRUSADER. You're flying out this afternoon."

"Fun," Lady Jane said.

"Aye aye, sir," Brandy said. "But why?"

"The last time British Forces attacked," Lt. Col. Randal said, "Rommel counterattacked and nearly drove our Army back into the Suez Canal."

"Do you feel that is a possibility with CRUSADER?" Lady Jane asked.

"Don't know," Lt. Col. Randal said, "but I'm not taking any chances – not with you two."

Brandy said, "I shall be on the plane."

"Me too," Lady Jane said. "I love it at X."

"I've asked Red to fly out," Lt. Col. Randal said. "Mandy's already there.

"From the minute the plane lands, I want Rita, Lana, or Red with you and Mandy at all times. Always travel in pairs. Wear your service automatics. Carry your small pistols in your purse.

"That's an order."

"You really are concerned, John," Lady Jane said.

"Just be careful," Lt. Col. Randal said.

"If things do go south – the Desert Fox somehow manages to turn things around and drives on Cairo, I want you where you can travel with Desert Patrol when it strikes deep into the desert. We'll find a distant place far away to set up a remote base and hold out until the situation stabilizes."

"Gives me a nice feeling," Brandy said, "knowing you are trying to protect me."

"Agreed," Lady Jane said.

"Don't worry," Lt. Col. Randal said. "Never going to happen."

LIEUTENANT COLONEL JOHN RANDAL WAS TALKING TO CAPTAIN the Lady Jane Seaborn, running down a list of things that needed to be done before she and Brandy flew out.

Brandy was in her room packing.

"Tell Karen Montgomery to round up as many of the obsolete parachutes stored at RAF Habbaniya as possible and have them flown to Oasis X. She can use 'em when we need to airdrop supplies to patrols in the field."

"Captain Merryweather, Chief," King said from the door.

"I shall go start packing," Lady Jane said as Captain Hawthorne Merryweather strolled in. He was Raiding Forces' happy psychological warrior, and today the look on his face was what you might expect to see on a cat that was getting ready to eat the canary.

"Stick around a second," Lt. Col. Randal said to Lady Jane.

Capt. Merryweather said, "Double FROGSPAWN."

"Double *FROGSPAWN*?"

"Two high-priority missions, sir," Capt. Merryweather said. "I need fifty jeeps we can mount 'sunshields' on, and A-Force wants one of Raiding Forces' Desert Patrol elements to plant a false map on the enemy at a time and location to be determined later."

"You can't have fifty jeeps," Lt. Col. Randal said. "That's the second time today I've heard the term 'sunshields' – what's it mean?"

"'Sunshield' is the codename for dummy tanks. We construct a plywood and canvas frame to fit over a thin-skinned vehicle. From a distance or from the air it looks like a tank. The idea is for General Cunningham's Eighth Army to suddenly have tanks appear where Rommel never expected us to have any.

"Smoke and mirrors, sir."

"You have fifty jeeps, Jane?"

"I did," Lady Jane said. "Half of them are preparing to make the trip to X for the offensive."

"Out of luck on the jeeps, Hawthorne," Lt. Col. Randal said. "We'll plant your map for you."

"Ford has a Model F-60," Lady Jane said. "When I was shopping trucks for Raiding Forces – before we discovered how wonderful jeeps are – I had settled on the Ford because it had four-wheel drive. They may work for you, Hawthorne."

"Where do I find them?"

"Go see Major Sansom," Lt. Col. Randal said. "He might have an idea how to resolve your truck problem.

"Tell him I sent you."

CAPTAIN THE LADY JANE SEABORN WAS PACKING. SHE WAS AS excited as if they were going to a five-star resort. Lieutenant Colonel John Randal thought she was the most unspoiled woman he had ever met.

It did not take much to make her happy.

He was standing in front of the map of the AO, staring at it, but not seeing anything. Desert Patrol was going to be attacking enemy airbases. The idea was to ground as many German and Italian airplanes as possible during the initial phase of CRUSADER.

The plan was to raid the Axis airfields closest to the places Eighth Army was going to attack and then fall back deeper across Egypt into Libya toward Tripoli as the offensive advanced.

There were two reasons Lt. Col. Randal liked the plan. First, the best place to knock out enemy airplanes is on the ground. Damaging or destroying Axis aircraft would allow the maneuver elements of Eighth Army to advance free –

or at least freer – from air attack. The reason that was vital was because enemy air had proven an even bigger threat to British tank formations than Panzers or German 88 antitank guns.

Second, and this was of great personal interest to Lt. Col. Randal and the men of Desert Patrol, every German or Italian airplane damaged or destroyed while it was parked at a target they raided prevented enemy pilots from flying out on those planes at sunrise to search for them as they were "getting the hell out of Dodge."

The problem was that there were a lot of Axis airfields – big and small – in Egypt and Libya. Desert Patrol would be attacking somewhere almost every night. It was inevitable the patrols were going to suffer casualties.

There was a critical shortage of qualified officers to replace those killed, wounded or sidelined due to sickness. Replacing the other ranks was almost as difficult. A handful of new volunteers were ready for assignment to a patrol when needed, but after that, there was no pool of desert-qualified operators for Desert Patrol to draw from.

Like Major Sir Terry "Zorro" Stone had said, the longer Desert Patrol was in action, the more degraded it was going to become.

"King," Lt. Col. Randal ordered, "get Jack up here."

Ex-Lieutenant Billy Jack Jaxx arrived to find Lt. Col. Randal studying the map of Egypt and Libya. There were a lot of red pins stuck in it.

"You wanted to see me, sir?"

"Jack, you see those pins?"

"Yes, sir."

"Every one of 'em represents an enemy airfield," Lt. Col. Randal said. "There's over a hundred."

"That's a lot of airfields, sir."

"These are just the ones we know about.

"The plan is to hit the bases closest to the Eighth Army's point of attack and fall back, staying out front of the main line of resistance fifty to a hundred miles behind the enemy lines – taking out airfields as we go."

"Sounds pretty ambitious, Colonel."

"True," Lt. Col. Randal said. "Counting Ranger Patrol and Scout Patrol we can put ten patrols in the field – less than one hundred eighty men all up to cover the entire desert.

Ex-Lt. Jaxx said, "We're going to be stretched to the max, sir."

"If you were me," Lt. Col. Randal said, "how would you go about it?"

"Some of the bases are bound to be more heavily guarded than others," ex-Lt. Jaxx said. "Those are the ones that pose the problem, sir."

"We can infiltrate the lightly guarded airstrips and place demolitions on the airplanes. We've proven that.

"If conditions are right, we can drive down the tarmac in our gun jeeps shooting up the parked planes with our machine guns.

"But the ones heavily guarded, well, it'll take a long time to sneak in undetected past the bad guys, place the bombs and exfiltrate back to the RV. Won't give us much margin to hightail it out of there before first light, sir."

"So what's the plan, Lieutenant?"

"Colonel," ex-Lt. Jaxx said, "there's another thing to consider. Carrying out the kind of raids we've been doing, the way we've been doing 'em, we're going to take casualties, sir."

"Why do you think we're having this conversation, Jack? What's the plan?"

"Hit and run," ex-Lt. Jaxx said, "just like you taught me, sir. What we need is stand-off capability. Strike from long range and be gone. Limit our exposure."

"How do you propose we do that?"

"Mortars," ex-Lt. Jaxx said. "Set up at maximum effective range, have a forward observer survey the airfield from concealment and plan the fire mission so we can execute it under cover of darkness. Fire the concentration, roll out, go somewhere else and do it again the next night."

"You know much about mortars, Jack?"

"Not a thing, sir."

"Neither do I," Lt. Col. Randal said. "We quit carrying the mortars we have because no one could hit anything with 'em."

"When I was in Officers Candidate School at Ft. Benning, sir, there was an infantry mortar committee. The instructors put on a demonstration for my class where they hit a fifty-five-gallon drum full of explosives with an 81mm mortar at three thousand yards on the first shot. Very impressive – big boom."

"So?"

"MEHQ not only organized an Officer Training Unit, but there's an NCO Academy as well," ex-Lt. Jaxx said.

"I'm aware of the schools," Lt. Col. Randal said.

"I bet they both have mortar committees, sir."

"Most likely," Lt. Col. Randal said.

"All we have to do is hijack those instructors, Colonel," ex-Lt. Jaxx said. "Shanghai 'em into Desert Patrol. We'll have the best mortar men in the Army."

Jack Cool.

"SIR," EX-LIEUTENANT BILLY JACK JAXX ASKED, "WHAT WAS your plan?"

Lieutenant Colonel John Randal said, "I didn't have a plan."

18

MÉNAGE À TROIS

OASIS X WAS A SCENE OF INTENSE ACTIVITY. MOST OF THE PATROLS were already in. As they arrived, the patrol leaders were alerted to prepare for a rapid turnaround and immediate redeployment. Feverish preparations were underway to make sure each patrol had everything it needed for an extended time in the field: food, water, ammunition, spare tires, explosives, camouflage netting, etc. The list went on and on. Armorers checked weapons; mechanics tuned engines.

It had been six months or more since this many of Desert Patrol's personnel had been at the Oasis at the same time. There had never been as many gun jeeps on site.

The Raiders were working with a sense of urgency, aware that Desert Patrol was going to be a part of something big. And time was short.

Normally patrol prep was a laid-back affair. It being important to make sure each jeep was combat loaded exactly the way the crew wanted it, no one got in a hurry.

Patrols were particular. They liked to do things their own way. No two were configured exactly alike. Each one was like a tiny, exclusive military club.

Raiding Forces was easier to get into than to stay in. Any member who did not pull his own weight or "mesh" was out – RTU'd. There was no appeal.

That applied to officers as well as other ranks and made for a tight-knit unit.

Ex-Lieutenant Billy Jack Jaxx arrived from RFHQ with his convoy consisting of new desert-ready jeeps, ex-Sergeant Hank Rawlston, his mechanics and all the equipment they could pile aboard five three-ton trucks, all the unassigned volunteers for Raiding Forces who had completed the selection program, and two ten-man teams of mortar instructors who had been unceremoniously drafted into Desert Patrol – the only non-volunteers in Raiding Forces.

He also had one of James "Baldie" Taylor's men attached, driving a captured German staff car. Ex-Lt. Jaxx had some thoughts on how he could put it to use. He had no idea what to make of the Nazi SS captain riding in the back seat in handcuffs and leg manacles.

Jim flew in on one of the regular flights out of Raiding Forces' Headquarters. He was there to confer with Lieutenant Colonel John Randal prior to Desert Patrol taking the field.

He was in possession of information obtained from a recent ULTRA intercept confirming Field Marshal Erwin Rommel intended to be out of the country in Italy when OPERATION CRUSADER launched. He was not going to provide that piece of intelligence to Lt. Col. Randal. In fact, he was not authorized to share it with anyone.

ULTRA was the MOST SECRET of all secrets in the United Kingdom – "ULTRA SECRET." Fewer than a half dozen people in the military or government combined knew all the details of how the German code had been cracked and what it took to keep it cracked. Jim was not one of them, and he was the highest-ranking MI-6, British Secret Intelligence Service (Special Operations) officer in Middle East Command.

However, and this was significant, Rikke Runborg had apparently accomplished her mission.

If in fact Rommel was in Italy when CRUSADER started, Rocky would no longer be under a cloud of suspicion that she was a German plant.

And that would make her the single most valuable asset in the MI-6 stable of spies worldwide – the most important person in Middle East Command, including Field Marshal Claude Auchinleck.

A Field Marshal can be replaced.

Rommel's most trusted spy, personally vouched for by Admiral William Canaris, the chief of the German Intelligence Service (OKW) – impossible to replicate.

The "Need to Know" list on that MOST SECRET information was seven people long.

Jim found Lt. Col. Randal in his apartment carved out of snow-white stone at the top of the escarpment. He was in conference with Desert Patrol Commander

Major Sir Terry "Zorro" Stone, the Wing Commanding Officer Captain Taylor Corrigan, DSO, MC, and the Regiment Commander, Major Jack Black.

When the meeting broke up, Jim and Lt. Col. Randal walked out on the deck alone. Down below the river plunged. Everywhere they looked, men were on the move. Desert patrol was preparing to move out. The first patrols would be departing X tonight.

"Colonel," Jim said, "you ordered Lady Seaborn and Brandy to ride out CRUSADER at X. Was that because you thought it would be safer here at the Oasis?"

"It was."

"Would it be an imposition," Jim asked, "if Rocky were to fly out to stay here as well?"

Lt. Col. Randal knew Jim never asked for anything without a reason.

"No, but there is a problem, General. I have Jane, Brandy and Mandy paired up with Red, Rita and Lana to provide security for each other. Always travel in pairs, armed – watch each other's back.

"We're one woman short to cover Rocky."

"R.J. and I need her to be secure," Jim said.

"You got it, sir," Lt. Col. Randal said. "I'll work something out."

CAPTAIN "GERONIMO" JOE MCKOY REPORTED TO LIEUTENANT Colonel John Randal.

"You wanted to see me, John?"

Capt. McKoy was in his element. The ex-Arizona Ranger was the picture of calm in the eye of a storm as Desert Patrol scrambled to be ready to roll out for who knew how long.

As usual, Capt. McKoy was armed to the teeth. He wore a Single Action Colt .45 on one hip, a Colt .38 Super automatic in a chest holster high on the right side almost to his shoulder for a high, quick draw with his right hand, plus a High Standard .22 w/silencer in a cross-draw holster, butt first on his left hip.

A big pair of Zeiss binoculars was dangling from his neck. The field glasses were an item of military equipment he had lusted after ever since he first saw the pair Lt. Col. Randal brought back from Pas-de-Calais.

Capt. McKoy's had been captured from a recently deceased German colonel of the 90th Light Division who, when in the middle of nowhere traveling between his regiment's battalions on inspection, had the misfortune to drive by White Patrol in his command car.

"I'm thinking about expanding your patrol into a squadron," Lt. Col. Randal said. "You've got three experienced officers commanding jeeps. Be easy to build patrols around 'em."

"You want me to be squadron commander?"

"I do."

"Naw," Capt. McKoy said. "I don't want the job, John. You can have the officers. Good men, been with me all the way through Abyssinia and six months out here in the desert.

"I ain't interested in handlin' all the administration that'd go with being a squadron commander. Patrol's all I want."

"Let me know if you change your mind," Lt. Col. Randal said. "I'll probably have to take you up on the offer of your lieutenants. We don't have backups in case a patrol leader goes down for any reason."

"Been meanin' to talk to you 'bout that, John," Capt. McKoy said, sticking a big unlit cigar in his jaw. "My boys deserve their own patrols. Have for some time. Recommend you give 'em one first chance you get."

"They can have patrols right now," Lt. Col. Randal said, "if you'd turn White Patrol into White Squadron."

"Thanks but no thanks," Capt. McKoy said. "Patrol Leader's the best job I ever had in the Army. Ain't lookin' to get promoted out of it."

"For a captain who doesn't care for advancement," Lt. Col. Randal said, "the President of the United States and the King of England have both referred to you as 'Colonel' in my presence.

"Would you like to explain that?"

WALDO TREYWICK PULLED IN WITH RANGER PATROL. HE HAD been a reluctant patrol leader. However, under his command the patrol had been extraordinarily successful. It had shot up over seventy trucks of various makes and models along the Via Balbia.

Waldo was used to slipping in and out of places where getting caught had bad consequences – a skill learned as a teenager when he had started a long career of poaching ivory in Portuguese territory.

Ranger Patrol had carefully scouted its targets in advance along the Axis' main supply route. Then they waited until the time was right, went back late at night and shot up the trucks laagered beside the highway when the drivers were sound asleep.

On Waldo's watch, there was none of the cruising down the Via Balbia looking for targets of opportunity with guns blazing like Lieutenant Colonel John Randal specialized in.

He reported in at the condominium that served as Lt. Col. Randal's unofficial HQ.

"Nice job, Mr. Treywick."

"We done alright," Waldo said, "but it's time for you to get back in charge, Colonel. I'm used to workin' alone or with one or two picked men. Ain't to my likin' bein' accountable for all those men, got wives and family – don't want 'em on my conscience."

"You inflicted a lot of damage," Lt. Col. Randal said. "Brought everyone back. That's what counts.

"Shoot up another thirty trucks, Mr. Treywick, and we'll get you decorated."

"You know I ain't no medal hound."

"Maybe not," Lt. Col. Randal said, "but I'm going to make sure you collect one more when you hit the magic number.

"Hook up with Jack. He's got a mortar specialist who will be traveling with Ranger Patrol when we roll out.

"He'll be riding with you," Lt. Col. Randal said. "Keep your eye on him. This will be his first time in the desert."

"Just make sure you're in the command jeep leadin' the patrol while I'm babysittin' him," Waldo said.

"Word is he can hit a fifty-five-gallon drum with a mortar out to three thousand yards," Lt. Col. Randal said.

"That's real good," Waldo said, "in case we ever need to kill a can."

Lt. Col. Randal said, "Allows us to stand off two miles and let the mortar do the work instead of having to sneak in to place bombs on the target or do a gun jeep beat up."

"In that case, he's gonna be my new best friend," Waldo said. "Count on me to take real good care a' the man, Colonel."

"Thought you might see it that way."

MR. ZARGO CAME IN AS WALDO WAS LEAVING. "WE HAVE identified *Red Indian* target, Colonel."

"This is not the time," Lieutenant Colonel John Randal said.

"One of my operatives located an isolated weather station," Mr. Zargo said, "deep in the Sand Sea, five men living in tents collecting data. Germans."

"King," Lt. Col. Randal ordered, "have Jack report up here."

Captain the Lady Jane Seaborn came out of the bedroom.

"Jane," Lt. Col. Randal said, "Jim is flying Rocky out on Auchinleck's plane. He wants us to keep her here at X for the Duration of CRUSADER. Can you find a place for her?"

"Absolutely, there are several rooms available."

"Good," Lt. Col. Randal said. "Here's how I want to work security – you and Brandy team up, stick together. Mandy and Red do the same. Rita and Lana guard Rocky."

"Quit worrying, John," Lady Jane laughed. "We shall carry knives and grenades in addition to our pistols if it will make you feel better."

"Just do it."

Ex-Lieutenant Billy Jack Jaxx arrived.

"Jack," Lt. Col. Randal said, "Mr. Zargo is going to brief you on a *Red Indian* target. Check with the LRDG to see if they have a patrol anywhere near it we can use to support a raid.

"Alert Ranger Patrol it will be traveling light. Some of the patrol are needed for the *Red Indian* mission – you plan it. Pick the men you need."

"Roger that, sir."

"I want to take down the target fast. Get Ranger Patrol's personnel back here as soon as possible," Lt. Col. Randal said.

"Can do, sir."

James "Baldie" Taylor came in as Lt. Col. Randal was saying, "I want to hear your concept of the operation the minute you have one, Jack."

"You got it, sir."

"Colonel," Jim said, "I understand Captain Merryweather briefed you on the A-Force intention to plant a map on the opposition."

"He did."

"Who do you rate as your best patrol leader?" Jim asked, already knowing the answer.

"They're all good," Lt. Col. Randal said. "Captain McKoy's the most successful."

"I need to borrow him for a couple of days," Jim said. "Phantom received the execute signal from R.J. Time to put the game in play."

"Do you need all of White Patrol, General?"

"No, I only require Captain McKoy and two gun jeeps as an escort," Jim said.

"King," Lt. Col. Randal ordered, "have Captain McKoy report here. We have an immediate priority mission for him."

"On the way, Chief."

When he arrived, Captain "Geronimo" Joe McKoy listened to Jim's briefing. When it was finished he said, "The ole' Haversack Ruse."

"You've heard of the Haversack Ruse?" Lt. Col. Randal asked.

"Oh yeah," Capt. McKoy said. "I knowed Meinertzhagen. To hear him tell it, he's the world's best military strategist, intelligence operative and ornithologist – a *birdwatcher*. You can make them kinda claims when you write your own books about yourself. "He didn't invent plantin' fake maps on the opposition, John."

Lt. Col. Randal said, "Makes a good story."

Jim took Capt. McKoy outside. "You still have that sap you twirl on your finger from time to time?"

"I do," Capt. McKoy said. "Custom-made – No. 8 birdshot covered in a double layer of saddle leather, triple stitched."

"Make sure you have it in your pocket when we depart," Jim said. "There are a couple of things I left out."

Capt. McKoy said, "Figured there might be."

LIEUTENANT COLONEL JOHN RANDAL, ACCOMPANIED BY CAPTAIN the Lady Jane Seaborn, went down and made their way from patrol to patrol. The bearded operators gathered around. Everyone was glad to take a short break and interested in hearing their commander's view on the upcoming operation.

The Raiders liked Lady Jane.

Desert Patrol had never been involved in something as big as OPERATION CRUSADER, though several of the Raiders had as members of other regiments in other campaigns before they volunteered for Special Service. Anticipation was running high.

Lt. Col. Randal said the same thing to each patrol.

"Expendable is not a term we use in Raiding Forces. You men are irreplaceable. Make sure I don't have to replace any of you.

"Fight smart. Or better yet, don't fight at all. If you do, never fight fair.

"Remember our Raiding Forces' Rule: It never hurts to cheat. If an installation is heavily guarded, move on to another one . . . there's no shortage of targets.

"Strike hard under cover of darkness, concentrate your firepower, then be gone fast – on to another objective.

"Hit and run, utilize surprise, speed, violence-of-action and – *brains.*

"Good luck and good hunting."

"One last thing, men. When you're going after airplanes, place your demolitions on the *left* wing. Rommel will be forced to bring in more left wings from Italy because there won't be enough warehoused in Libya to replace all those you're blowing off.

"Then we'll switch to right wings."

The result was always the same. When Lt. Randal and Lady Jane departed the area, the troops – hard, tough combat veterans – were laughing. Desert Patrol was being given license to carry out the kind of free-ranging guerrilla war they were trained, equipped and mentally prepared to fight.

The Wrecking Crew II Patrol arrived as the last patrol in. Captain "Pyro" Percy Stirling was waiting when Lt. Col. Randal and Lady Jane returned. He and his men had been in the field longer than any other element in Desert Patrol. They had been on continuous operations hammering away at the only two railroads the Axis had.

One glance was all Lt. Col. Randal needed. "Have your men fly out on the first available aircraft. Two weeks leave in Cairo."

"Sir," Capt. Stirling said, "that means we miss the offensive."

"Look in the mirror, Percy," Lt. Col. Randal said. "Two weeks on the town then you and your boys can come back here. Pick up where you left off.

"There'll be plenty of war left."

"Yes, sir."

"Y-Service intercepts indicate the Wrecking Crew has virtually eliminated Rommel's rail capability," Lt. Col. Randal said.

"Good job, stud."

"Squadron and Patrol Leaders briefing on the roof in one zero, old stick," Major Sir Terry "Zorro" Stone said, poking his head in the door.

"Care to address the group before I issue the Operations Order?"

Lt. Col. Randal said, "I do."

Men could be heard climbing up the outside steps to the roof as the Squadron and Patrol Leaders assembled for the Operations Order.

When Lt. Col. Randal arrived, everyone was seated in folding chairs. There was a large map of the AO propped up in front of the group. Nothing new there – they had all seen it before.

Someone called, "ATTENTION!"

Lt. Col. Randal immediately ordered, "As you were."

As the officers took their seats, Maj. Stone said, "The Colonel would like to say a few words."

"This is the biggest offensive since we arrived in the desert," Lt. Col. Randal said. "In support of it, Raiding Forces' mission is to conduct a series of raids from land and sea.

"While Desert Patrol is striking out of the desert, Sea Squadron will be conducting amphibious operations all the way up the coast to Tripoli.

"Desert Patrol's mission is to strike the enemy where he's weak. The idea is to cause strategic material damage and to force Rommel to divert troops away from the battlefield to guard his fixed installations. First we take on his air force with raids targeted against airfields. Second, we shift to destroying fuel storage depots. After that we switch to ambushing the secondary roads paralleling the Via Balbia.

"Then we do it all over again.

"Three things – keep them in mind at all times. Economy of Force: Small parties have proven to be just as – or in some cases more – effective than a full patrol. Patrol Leaders, break your patrols down into elements in order to take on multiple targets simultaneously when the opportunity presents itself.

"Hard intelligence, soft targets: Never attack any target unless you have eyes-on intelligence provided by Mr. Zargo's men or you have personally conducted your own reconnaissance.

"Shoot, move and communicate: Each patrol has been provided at least one 81mm mortar expert. When the opportunity presents itself, fire from standoff range then move out to another target. Try not to travel in daylight. Make your prescheduled radio checks. Major Stone will likely order a change of mission at some point.

"Hit hard, move fast, keep the tempo up."

Lady Jane came up on the roof and made eye contact with Lt. Col. Randal.

"Take it to 'em, gentlemen," Lt. Col. Randal said.

WHEN LIEUTENANT COLONEL JOHN RANDAL AND CAPTAIN THE Lady Jane Seaborn arrived in their private suite, a handsome RAF officer, prematurely graying at the temples, was chatting with Lieutenant Pamala Plum-Martin out on the deck. He had a silver-headed cane on his lap.

"Colonel," Lt. Plum-Martin said, "this is Wing Commander Ronald Gordon. He flew in to be our liaison officer with the RAF."

Wg. Cdr. Gordon struggled to his feet, "Nice to finally meet you, Colonel. Pam has told me quite a lot about your exploits."

"Ronnie is recovering from an injury received when his plane was shot down," Lt. Plum-Martin said. "How many does the last crash make?"

"Five," Wg. Cdr. Gordon said, "if you count the time the Home Guard mistook me for a Jerry. Makes me an ace for the other side, what!"

"I wasn't expecting an RAF liaison officer," Lt. Col. Randal said. "Haven't much wanted to cooperate with us in the past."

"RAF has had a modest change of heart about supporting the Army," Wg. Cdr. Gordon said. "At least as far as Raiding Forces is concerned. Since I was dead weight, the Vice Air Marshal sent me here to explore our common interests."

"Like what?"

"For example, if we could persuade you to concentrate more on ambushing the vehicles traveling the Via Balbia at night it might cause the Afrika Korps to run all their convoys during the daylight hours. Makes them rather easy prey for our fighter bombers," Wg. Cdr. Gordon said.

"Talk to Major Stone," Lt. Col. Randal said. "I think we can accommodate you on that one."

"Your *Bombshell* missions have attracted the particular interest of the RAF High Command," Wg. Cdr. Gordon said.

"How exactly," Lt. Col. Randal said, "did you hear about them?"

"I briefed Ronnie," Lt. Plum-Martin said. "We were having drinks at Shepard's with the commander of the Desert Air Force. Ronnie is serving as his senior aide until he returns to flying status."

"Based on Pam's story, the Air Vice Marshal concluded the RAF and Raiding Forces could possibly both profit if we provided you at least a modicum of air support," Wg. Cdr. Gordon said.

"The idea of killing drunken German pilots on the ground is, in a word, brilliant."

"What kind of support?"

"Not all that much actually," Wg. Cdr. Gordon said. "RAF is willing to lend you nonessential flying craft that Raiding Forces may find to be useful. We will agree to service your gypsy air fleet at any of our bases in Middle East Command starting immediately.

"And, the Air Vice Marshal desires to station a liaison officer, hopefully not me for long, with Raiding Forces to facilitate communications. He is even contemplating the possibility of having junior RAF officers ride with your patrols to evaluate other joint opportunities."

"Sounds good," Lt. Col. Randal said. "Now if you'll excuse me, Wing Commander, I'm really pressed for time."

"Tell him, Ronnie," Lt. Plum-Martin said.

Lt. Col. Randal clicked on hard.

"Yeah . . . let's hear it Ronnie."

"*Bombshell*!"

"You have got to be kidding me," Lt. Col. Randal said.

"Afraid not," Wg. Cdr. Gordon said. "Air Intelligence in Alexandria has identified a splendid target. The Luftwaffe is bulking up air assets for their offensive. The Germans are flying in squadrons daily from Italy. Using surplus Regia Aeronautica bases to operate from – there are quite a number of them.

"Intelligence located a bordello strategically situated where it can service three of the landing grounds recently taken over by the Luftwaffe. Remote setting, bored pilots, hookers, booze – it's the quintessential *Bombshell* target.

"I have the map coordinates."

"Pam," Lt. Col. Randal said, "go pull King out of the briefing."

As they waited, Wg. Cdr. Gordon said, "Sorry old chap. Appears our timing is less than ideal."

"You have no idea."

"Always the case, what!" Wg. Cdr. Gordon said. "Strictly between us, pulling this *Bombshell* mission off would go a long way toward cementing relations between our two organizations."

"Why don't you," Lt. Col. Randal asked, "just bomb it?"

"The Nazi pilots do not frequent the place during the day," Wg. Cdr. Gordon said. "Afraid we do not have pinpoint night flying capability for a target that tiny."

"You wanted to see me, Chief?"

"King, this is Wing Commander Gordon," Lt. Col Randal said. "He has a *Bombshell* target."

"Joke," the Merc said, "right?"

"Negative – you and Pam coordinate with the Wing Commander. Bring me a plan.

"Make it fast."

"JANE," LIEUTENANT COLONEL JOHN RANDAL SAID, "WOULD YOU go up and tell Mr. Treywick to see me as soon as Terry's Op Order's over?"

Lady Jane laughed, "Surely you are not planning to tell him what I think you are."

"I am."

Red and Brandy arrived with their luggage.

Newly promoted Captain Penelope "Legs" Honeycutt-Parker was in command of the RFHQ complex. She was shuttling people out to Oasis X for CRUSADER as fast as the Ansons and the Hudson could complete a circuit.

Ex-Lieutenant Billy Jack Jaxx came in.

"Sir, there's no LRDG patrol anywhere near the Nazi weather station."

"What's the plan, Lieutenant?"

"We're going to have to jump in, sir," ex-Lt. Jaxx said.

"How do we get home?"

"There's an airstrip scraped out next to the target," ex-Lt. Jaxx said. "That's how the Germans set these weather stations up, sir. They use the strip to fly in supplies and rotate personnel.

"We'll have Pam pick us up, sir."

"Could be a problem," Lt. Col. Randal said. "She and King are in the Operations Room right this minute discussing a high-priority *Bombshell* mission."

Ex-Lt. Jaxx said, "Wow!"

Maj. Stone's Operations Order concluded. He turned the group over to the Wing and Regiment commanders who would in turn conduct their own briefings at their squadron HQs. Then the Patrol Leaders would return to their patrols and give individual patrol briefings to the troops.

Waldo arrived.

"You wanted to see me, Colonel?"

"Ranger Patrol's line of departure time is zero six hundred hours, Mr. Treywick," Lt. Col. Randal said, lighting a cigarette with his old U.S. 26th Cavalry Regiment Zippo.

"Jim and Captain McKoy are off carrying out a Haversack Ruse. Lieutenant Jaxx is planning a *Red Indian* raid. And I have just been alerted for a *Bombshell* mission which King and Pam are evaluating as we speak.

"That means, Mr. Treywick, you are the acting commander of Ranger Patrol."

"Not again!"

"Lt. Jaxx is going to require four or five of your men. When King and Pam complete their plans shortly, they may need a couple more. Ranger Patrol will be taking the field light."

"Don't do this to me, Colonel."

"I'll link up with you as soon as possible," Lt. Col. Randal said. "You have my word on that."

Mr. Treywick said, "I ain't cut out to be a troop commander."

"You're underestimating your capabilities, Mr. Treywick," Lt. Col. Randal said.

"Pretend you're sneaking over the border to poach Portuguese ivory – like the old days."

"Some of them good ole days wasn't so good," Waldo said. "You ain't never seen the inside of a Portuguese prison."

"Move out at sunrise."

Maj. Stone walked in, "Not like you to skip a briefing, old stick."

"Raiding Forces was just alerted for a *Red Indian*," Lt. Col. Randal said, "and a *Bombshell* mission."

"Typical," Maj. Stone said. "Anything you require of me?"

"Just keep doing what you're doing," Lt. Col. Randal said.

"Jack's on the *Red Indian*, and King's the on the *Bombshell*. It's not clear what my role will be, so Waldo's taking out Ranger – White is under Capt. McKoy's second-in-command while he's away with Jim carrying out a special operation."

"Hold Scout Patrol back when your patrols move out," Lt. Col. Randal said. "I may need Roy Kidd."

"Roger," Maj. Stone said. "Let me know if I can be of assistance."

Lieutenant Pamala Plum-Martin leaned in the door, "John, would you come down to the Operations Room for a moment? You as well, Jack."

Desert Patrol's Operations Room aka Tactical Operations Center (TOC) was located on the floor directly below. It was a spacious room, with a lot of people working in it performing a wide-ranging number of tasks – operations, intelligence, logistics and supply, communications, etc. The TOC ran twenty-four hours a day.

Something was always going on.

Banks of radios were manned by Phantom operators, and maps covered the walls. There were a lot of pins stuck in the maps indicating any number of things. From time to time one of Captain the Lady Jane Seaborn's Royal Marines would move a pin.

King, Mr. Zargo, and Wing Commander Ronald Gordon were huddled around one of the maps.

"Here are the three airfields the Luftwaffe has appropriated approximately fifty miles outside Tripoli," King said. "This is the target, located about three miles equidistant from each of the bases. Notice anything, Chief?"

"What's that long rectangle in the middle represent?"

King looked at Wg. Cdr. Gordon, "Told you he would go straight to it."

The RAF officer said, "That's an auxiliary emergency airstrip. Services all three airbases – shot-up planes returning from combat missions needing to crash land divert to it so they will not interfere with flight operations on the active airfields.

"The only troops stationed on it are emergency firefighting and medical personnel during the day. The field is abandoned at night."

"We need confirmation to be certain, Colonel," Mr. Zargo said. "Major Peniakoff is in the area. I should be able to have you an answer when Popski makes his nightly radio check tonight."

"That strip runs right by the target," Lt. Col. Randal said. "Within five feet."

"The house of ill repute," Wg. Cdr. Gordon said, "is located in the old abandoned Regia Aeronautica Operations Building which was situated on the edge of the runway. Some enterprising party saw an opportunity and converted it to its current commercial use."

"Pam, can you land on the emergency strip," Lt. Col. Randal asked, "about zero one hundred hours some night?"

"Yes," Lt. Plum-Martin said. "It would be helpful if Popski would be able to place a few flares on a small section of the strip to guide on."

"For maximum effect," Lt. Col. Randal said, "we need to raid the place the night before CRUSADER starts."

"Makes perfect sense," Wg. Cdr. Gordon said.

"My problem is, I don't know when that is," Lt. Col. Randal said. "Since our patrols are subject to being captured, we don't have the 'Need to Know.'

"Provide me the date of CRUSADER twenty-four hours in advance," Lt. Col. Randal said. "You can tell your boss Raiding Forces will take out his *Bombshell* target the night before the invasion starts, weather permitting."

"I shall contact the Vice Air Marshal straight away," Wg. Cdr. Gordon said. "Since all our subordinate commanders will be in possession of the date by that time, I cannot fathom any reason you should not be privy to the same information.

Lt. Col. Randal said, "Now, if you will excuse me, I really am pressed for time."

"DID YOU NEED ME, JOHN?" LIEUTENANT MANDY PAIGE ASKED when he returned to the suite.

"Step out on the deck, Mandy."

When they were alone, Lieutenant Colonel John Randal said, "We're not having this conversation."

"Love it when you say that," Lt. Mandy said.

"Rocky is flying in," Lt. Col. Randal said. "Rita and Lana are going to be her bodyguards for the duration of her stay at X.

"You keep your eye on Rocky too – be discrete. Don't let any of the locals approach her."

"Absolutely," Lt. Mandy said. "Why?"

"We don't know who Rocky is exactly," Lt. Col. Randal said, "and that's all you get to know."

"In that case," Lt. Mandy said, "we *are* having this next conversation."

"Don't do it, Mandy," Lt. Col. Randal said when he saw the look in her eye.

"One of the citizenry has come into possession of a stash of gold coins," Lt. Mandy said.

"That's not good," Lt. Col Randal said. "How'd you find out?"

"He showed a few to Rita and Lana," Mandy said.

"And why would he do that?"

"Pervert offered to pay them to perform a *ménage à trois*."

"A what?"

"I believe you Californians call it a threesome," Lt. Mandy said.

"The girls made a date with Romeo for later tonight at one of the ancient Roman baths.

"Will you loan me your quiet pistol, John?"

"Negative," Lt. Col. Randal said. "We need to take him alive."

"I want to liquidate the sex maniac," Lt. Mandy said.

"You don't get to shoot him tonight," Lt. Col. Randal said. "Maybe later.

"Come get me an hour before lover boy's supposed to meet Rita and Lana."

"See you here at twenty-two hundred," Lt. Mandy said. "Let's not step in too quickly, John. I want to watch."

"I'm going to tell your mother you said that," Lt. Col. Randal said.

Drop-dead gorgeous Captain the Lady Jane Seaborn was reclining on the bed reading a magazine when Lt. Col. Randal walked in the bedroom. She looked up inquisitively when he took his pistols out of their holsters, tossed them on the side of the bed then began inspecting them.

"Going somewhere, John?"

"Mandy and I are heading to a *ménage à trois*," Lt. Col. Randal said.

Lady Jane said, "How nice for you."

19

THAT'S WHAT I CALL A
HAVERSACK RUSE

LIEUTENANT COLONEL JOHN RANDAL, LIEUTENANT COMMANDER Ian Fleming, Wing Commander Ronald Gordon, Ex-Lieutenant Billy Jack Jaxx and King were en route to Cairo in Field Marshal Claude Auchinleck's personal Hudson.

Lieutenant Pamala Plum-Martin was in the cockpit chatting with the pilot.

Ex-Lt. Jaxx asked, "Who was that local you and Mandy brought in last night, sir?"

"Mandy found a man in possession of gold coins," Lt. Col. Randal said. "We need to know who gave them to him."

"No one at X has any gold," ex-Lt. Jaxx said. "Except maybe the emir, and I bet he doesn't have much."

"Mr. Zargo and Mandy are conducting the interrogation. They'll sort it out," Lt. Col. Randal said.

Ex-Lt. Jaxx said, "Mandy's turning into a pretty good spy catcher."

"Yes she is."

"Colonel," Lt. Cdr. Fleming said, "would you step in the back for a word?"

As Lt. Col. Randal was making his way to the rear of the airplane, Wg. Cdr. Gordon said, "I presume we do not have the requisite 'Need to Know'?"

Ignoring the comment, ex-Lt. Jaxx said, "Does anyone ever call you 'Flash' Gordon sir?"

"No," Wg. Cdr. Gordon said. "They call me 'Flash Bang' Gordon."

"Really?"

"*Flash*, my aircraft is hit," Wg. Cdr. Gordon said. "I bail out, the plane slams into the ground – *bang*."

"Giving you a hard time, huh, sir?"

"Never live down all those crashes," Wg. Cdr. Gordon said, "no matter how many bandits I flame."

When they were seated in the tail of the Hudson all alone, Lt. Cdr. Fleming said, "I realize there could not be a worse time, Colonel but a *Golden Fleece* presented itself out of the blue.

Lt. Col. Randal asked, "What's the target?"

"A Vorpostenboot experienced engine trouble off a remote part of Crete and is anchored in a rocky inlet awaiting assistance from a support ship.

"By mere chance I was in Alexandria conferring with the Chief of Naval Intelligence Middle East when we learned what had transpired.

"There is reason to believe secret intelligence communications equipment is on the ship," Lt. Cdr. Fleming lied. He knew *for a fact* there was an Enigma encoding device onboard.

Lt. Col. Randal was not authorized to know an Enigma machine existed, much less how Lt. Cdr. Fleming knew one was on the disabled ship or even that he did know.

In fact, Lt. Col. Randal had never heard the word "Enigma" used in any other context than a mystery or a puzzle.

"I need you to board the Vorpostenboot, seize the crew and secure them so a naval intelligence team can remove the communications equipment, codes, technical manuals, etc.

"Extremely important," Lt. Cdr. Fleming said. "No fingerprints – no one can ever know this operation ever took place.

"Questions?"

"When?"

"Tonight," Lt. Cdr. Fleming said, tapping a Player's cigarette on his engraved case. "We have to strike before help arrives or the crew manages to effect repairs on their own."

"What's a Vorpostenboot and how many sailors are on board?"

"The Royal Navy would call it a trawler," Lt. Cdr. Fleming said. "Crew is generally fifty to sixty men."

"Why Raiding Forces? You could use the Eleventh Royal Marine Battalion stationed in Alexandria. The Marines would jump at the chance for a boarding operation like this."

"Simple answer, Colonel," Lt. Cdr. Fleming said, flicking his monogrammed cigarette lighter."

"When we approach the Navy with a mission, they inquire about moon and tide data, study all manner of charts, consult meteorologists, gaze into crystal balls.

"You simply go do it."

"Have a plan, Commander?"

Lt. Cdr. Fleming said, "Admiral Ransom and Captain Pelham-Davies are at RFHQ working one up as we speak."

"With a crew of fifty to sixty sailors onboard, how do we carry this off without any 'fingerprints'?" Lt. Col. Randal asked.

"Leave that problem to me," Lt. Cdr. Fleming said. "Your assignment is to take down the ship, lock the crew in the hold, then disembark. At that point, your part in the operation will be concluded."

"Sounds easy," Lt. Col. Randal said. "Think it will be?"

Lt. Cdr. Fleming said, "Never has been in the past."

"Glad you understand that," Lt. Col. Randal said.

"Colonel, this is a 'Pinch Operation'," Lt. Cdr. Fleming said. "My nonclassified description for what we are doing tonight – *Golden Fleece* targets – which once identified we also call *Red Indians* because the code word identifier *Golden Fleece* is so highly restricted.

"I am personally responsible for ensuring 'Pinches' are successfully carried out worldwide. The Germans have a code we can spend an enormous amount of man hours trying to break or you can go steal it for us."

"In the future, Raiding Forces shall function as the action arm for executing all Royal Navy Intelligence 'Pinch Operations' in the Middle East Command Area of Operations," Lt. Cdr. Fleming said.

"There are three types of Pinches–Chance, Opportunity and Design."

"When Lieutenant Jaxx captured the German weather station and their code books, that would be an example of a Chance Pinch."

"OPERATION RUTHLESS when we took down the German E-Boat was a Design Pinch . . . splendidly executed by your lads, I might add.

"Tonight is an Opportunity Pinch – the Vorpostenboot broke down. We found out about it and intend to exploit the situation."

Lt. Col. Randal said, "What exactly are we pinching – a code book?"

"If you should ever discover the answer to that question," Lt. Cdr. Fleming said, "then you shall never be allowed to participate in any more Pinch Operations or in fact, continue to serve in any capacity which might place you in a position where you run the risk of being captured and interrogated."

"Like I said before, make sure you don't ever let me find out," Lt. Col. Randal said.

He stood up and walked to the front of the Hudson.

"What 'nonessential' aircraft with the heaviest forward-firing armament do you have available to loan Raiding Forces, Wing Commander?" Lt. Colonel Randal asked.

Looking slightly embarrassed, Wg. Cdr. Gordon said, "There are no nonessential aircraft in the Desert Air Force. RAF was not playing cricket with you when they made that offer."

Lt. Col. Randal said, "That's what I thought."

"In answer to the firepower part of the question," Wg. Cdr. Gordon said, "Lend-Lease has recently delivered a squadron of twin-engine A-20 Havocs – RAF calls them the 'Boston.' By all reports, the plane is a very forgiving aircraft to fly. Four 20mm Hispano Mk III cannons are mounted in the nose. We have a couple modified by adding six Browning .50 caliber machine guns in pods on the sides and under the chin of the fuselage to make them more effective ship strafers. We could probably arrange the use of one for a single mission provided the target is worthy.

"The aircraft with the heaviest standard forward-firing armament in our inventory is the Bristol Beaufighter. It is also a twin-engine with the same four Hispano 20mm cannons in the nose as the Boston. RAF has a model that sports an additional six Browning .30 caliber machine guns.

"Most likely I could obtain a Beaufighter with the .30 caliber wing-mounted guns with the same proviso – a worthwhile mission."

"I'll get back to you."

Lt. Col. Randal walked up to the cockpit and leaned in, "Pam, which aircraft do you like best – Boston or Beaufighter?"

The Vargas Girl look-alike Royal Marine turned to look at him with a glossy-magazine toothpaste-advertisement smile, "Paddy checked me out in both of them when I was going through my twin-engine transition. I prefer the Havoc A-20. Fabulous airplane John, a dream to fly."

"Good."

Lt. Col. Randal walked back to Wg. Cdr. Gordon, "I need a Havoc. The model with the extra .50s."

"Am I permitted to inquire whatever for?"

"Negative," Lt. Col. Randal said. "Better make that two. Raiding Forces' policy is for our planes to fly in pairs. That way if one goes down in the desert we know where to send a patrol to pick up the crew."

"Sound logic," Wg. Cdr. Gordon said. "Run your own air rescue service."

"Raiding Forces has a pilot qualified to fly a Havoc," Lt. Col. Randal said. "We need another for the chase plane."

"Could be problematical," Wg. Cdr. Gordon said. "Desert Air Force is dreadfully short attack aircraft aviators."

"I don't have any rule," Lt. Col. Randal said, sticking one of Waldo's long, thin, custom-rolled cigars between his front teeth, "prohibiting an experienced pilot walking with the aid of a cane from flying special operations missions."

"In that case," Wg. Cdr. Gordon said, "I can virtually guarantee you two modified Havoc A-20 ship strafers."

Lt. Col. Randal said, "Glad we could get that worked out."

LIEUTENANT COLONEL JOHN RANDAL, VICE ADMIRAL SIR Randolph "Razor" Ransom, Brigadier Raymond J. "R.J." Maunsell, Lieutenant Commander Ian Fleming, Captain Jeb Pelham-Davies, Lieutenant Randy "Hornblower" Seaborn, Acting Provisional Sub-Lieutenant Skipper Mud Cat Ray, RNPS, Lieutenant Butch "Headhunter" Hoolihan, ex-Lieutenant Billy Jack Jaxx and King were in the Tactical Operations Center at Raiding Forces' Headquarters.

VAdm. Ransom had a series of 8x10 aerial photos pinned to one wall. They showed a ship at anchor in a tiny inlet off a rugged mountainous section of Crete.

"SOE's operative in the area has the Vorpostenboot under surveillance," VAdm. Ransom said. "There is no beach. A sheer cliff runs straight up for approximately a hundred feet. The ship is anchored and there is a cable lashed to a rock landward.

"Tonight at zero one hundred hours the submarine *Perch* will surface one mile offshore and shine a navigational beacon seaward of the Vorpostenboot. Upon identifying the light, Skipper Ray in command of the trawler *Pirate's Dream* will hove to.

"Capt. Pelham-Davies, Lt. Hoolihan and his Sea Squadron troop, traveling aboard the *Perch,* will launch a boarding party in rubber rafts. The Raiders will paddle to the Vorpostenboot, board her, round up the crew and lock them below deck in one of the holds.

"At that point, on signal from Captain Pelham-Davies, Commander Fleming's intel team consisting of three intelligence officers shall disembark from the *Pirate's Dream* and board the enemy ship. The RN intel team will secure the desired signals equipment, radio frequencies, code books and anything else of intelligence value, then immediately disembark and return.

"Upon recovering the Royal Navy team with its booty, Skipper Ray will steam into the inlet and take the Vorpostenboot under tow, a job for which he is an acknowledged professional.

"The enemy sailors will be transferred to the *Pirate's Dream.*

From that point on, the prisoners will be kept in total isolation until such time as they can be placed on a special prison ship assigned to a convoy routed for Canada. Once there they will go into a POW camp in the most remote, uninhabited part of the country for the duration of the war.

"Approximately a mile offshore, the Vorpostenboot will be cut free. The *Pirate's Dream* will continue on to Alexandria to dispose of the prisoners.

"At sunrise when there is full visibility from Crete, the *Perch* will torpedo the Vorpostenboot. The ship will sink in deep water where there is no chance of it ever being recovered. By all outward appearances there will be no survivors.

"This operation never happened – does not even have a name."

"Questions?"

Lt. Hoolihan asked, "Where do the crew sleep, Admiral?"

"It's cold nights," Admiral Ransom said. "The crew will be in their hammocks below deck."

Capt. Pelham-Davies asked, "Any information on where the watches will be stationed onboard, sir?"

"A Vorpostenboot is not a regular Kriegsmarine ship-of-the-line," VAdm. Ransom said. "They are civilian craft pressed in to service – mostly serving as coastal steamers between the islands. It is not unknown for a German Wehrmacht sergeant to command one.

"Which means discipline may be lax.

"My guess is there will be one sailor stationed on the bridge with another standing radio watch. Possibly a seaman on the bow to keep an eye on the anchor chain and one on the stern cable. The crew has no reason to be expecting trouble at night – hidden the way they are," VAdm. Ransom said.

"From their standpoint, there would not be much anyone onboard could do about it if the ship were attacked. Other than a few light antiaircraft weapons, it's virtually unarmed."

"What's the chance," Lt. Col. Randal asked, "a couple of sailors might be stationed on land to keep their eye on the cable where it's tied off to make sure it doesn't slip?"

"A possibility," VAdm. Ransom said. "As I said, there is no beach. The cliff face is quite jagged but a small party conceivably could be ashore."

"So if everything goes like clockwork," Lt. Col. Randal said, "after the boarding party cuts the cable, Skipper Ray takes the ship under tow."

"That is the plan," VAdm. Ransom said.

"In the event there's a detail on shore when Mud Cat hauls the Vorpostenboot out to sea," Lt. Col. Randal said, "we'll be leaving witnesses behind."

Cdr. Fleming said, "That would be a problem."

"I do not recommend, Colonel," Lt. Hoolihan said, "sending a boat team past the Vorpostenboot to verify if anyone is ashore. We might compromise the element of surprise… plus the surge of the ocean against a cliff face always makes for a risky landing.

"Good point, Butch," Lt. Col. Randal said. "Someone has to go down that cliff before the Vorpostenboot is boarded and make sure there isn't anyone there. Is communications with your SOE operative capable of having his people pull that off?"

"We can only contact him at prearranged times," Lt. Cdr. Fleming said. "The next scheduled radio contact is twenty-two hundred tonight, but that might not give our man time to organize a team of guerrillas for the job."

"Typically there will not be any sailors ashore," VAdm. Ransom said, "but we have to make absolutely sure. Problem is, if we attempt to land from the Vorpostenboot after we capture it we run the risk of being discovered by any Germans ashore and risking them dispersing among the rocks to evade us."

"Tell your SOE man to mark a Drop Zone near the top of the cliff at twenty-four hundred hours," Lt. Col. Randal said.

"King and I'll do the rest."

"Not without me, sir," ex-Lt. Jaxx said. "I've been eliminating sentries serving warrants in Texas since I was a teenager."

Lt. Col. Randal said, "You're still a teenager, Jack."

JAMES "BALDIE" TAYLOR AND CAPTAIN "GERONIMO" JOE MCKOY were in Capt. McKoy's command jeep. They were making their way through the desert, having crossed the Great Sand Sea at its narrowest point the morning before. Now at 2400 hours they were approximately a mile from a known Italian roadhouse – one of the few built on an auxiliary dirt road that paralleled the Via Balbia.

The captured German staff car with Nazi SD prisoner shackled in the back seat was following the gun jeep being driven by one of Jim's operatives. It was followed by the second of White Patrol's gun jeeps that had been detached for the specific purpose of escorting the MI-6 Chief of Special Operations, Middle East Command on a clandestine mission.

There was a full moon out and visibility was as good as it gets in the desert at night. The vehicles were not running with their cat's eye headlights on. Without warning, Capt. McKoy drove up on the dirt road they were attempting to intersect.

The road confirmed where they were, almost. Capt. McKoy pulled over and stopped. When he did, the vehicle commander of the second jeep pulled in behind the German staff car and stopped. He hopped out and walked up to the command jeep.

"We're gonna' run up the road here a bit," Capt. McKoy said. "You keep your eye on the staff car till we get back."

"Roger."

Capt. McKoy turned on the cat's eye blackout lights and, driving very slowly, proceeded in the direction of the hostel they hoped was not far away. If they did not find the rest stop within two miles then their navigation had been slightly off and he would turn around and drive back the other direction until he found it.

The jeep came over a slight rise, and in the distance a glow was visible as a door was opened and shut at the roadhouse they were searching for.

"Bingo," Capt. McKoy said.

He turned the jeep around and drove back to the other two vehicles.

"Take the wheel, Johnson," Capt. McKoy said to his AVG volunteer driver who was riding in the back of the jeep tonight because Jim was along.

"Keep your lights off."

Then Capt. McKoy and Jim climbed into the back seat of the German staff car with the Nazi prisoner. The man, a captain in the SD, gave them a surly look. He was not happy that he had been hauled around the desert for the last four days.

Capt. McKoy grabbed the German and manhandled him out of the car. He pulled the prisoner to the front door on the passenger side, opened it and shoved him in. Then he got back in the car and sat directly behind the SD officer.

As soon as he was on board, Jim's operative pulled around the command jeep and took the lead of the small convoy.

"Hit the lights," Capt. McKoy said. Now the residents of the roadhouse could see them coming if they happened to be looking. No one would be alarmed. Vehicles driving with cat's eye blackout lights came and went at all hours.

When the car came to the slight rise there was no glow, but Jim and Captain McKoy knew where they were.

"Pull over," Jim said.

The instant the car stopped, Capt. McKoy hit the Nazi SD officer on the back of his head as hard as he could with the sap he had been twirling on his finger.

Everyone got out of the car except the unconscious Nazi. Jim's operative unlocked the handcuffs and leg shackles restraining the prisoner.

He took them to the gun jeep parked behind the car and tossed them in the back.

Capt. McKoy dragged the SD man over behind the steering wheel. Then he sprinkled several of the Great Teddy's camel chip mines on the road in front of the car. Jim wedged one directly under the front of the wheel on the driver's side.

They walked back to the command jeep and Capt. McKoy took the wheel. He carefully edged forward until his bumper touched the back bumper of the German car and gave it a nudge.

KAAAAAAABOOOOOOOM!

The force of the explosion stunned everyone in the jeep. The mine was so small that they had expected nothing more than a loud pop. The camel chip delivered a bigger bang than expected.

The front end of the staff car bounced up in the air and landed with its wheel blown off. Jim got out of the jeep, walked up to the driver's side and tossed a grenade in between the Nazi's legs.

When it went off with a muffled WHUUUUUMP, Jim opened the back door and placed a briefcase on the floor of the car. Then he got back in the command jeep.

Capt. McKoy turned the jeep around pulled off the road and drove back across the desert in the direction of Oasis X.

He said, "Now that's what I call a Haversack Ruse."

THE ANSON SKIMMED ACROSS. THE WAVES. THE ISLAND OF CRETE came into view. Lieutenant Pamala Plum-Martin was at the stick with Wing Commander Ronald Gordon along as her co-pilot. The Vargas Girl look-alike Royal Marine did not need her ex-LRDG navigator tonight. She could fly this mission with her eyes closed.

The passenger seats had been removed from the aircraft. On the floor in the back, Lieutenant Colonel John Randal, ex-Lieutenant Billy Jack Jaxx and King were resting on their X-type parachutes. All three were asleep.

In the Army the rule is never run when you can walk, never walk when you can stand still, never stand still when you can sit and never sit when you can lay down and sleep – every chance you get.

That rule did not generally apply when flying in an airplane strapped into a parachute, getting ready to drop on an enemy-held island in the dark of night.

"Red light, John," Lt. Plum-Martin said over her shoulder.

All three Raiders' eyes opened.

There was no light system on the Anson. They would go on the pilot's and then the jumpmaster's orders.

"Hook up," Lt. Col. Randal said in a conversational tone.

The Anson was small. The three jumpers struggled to their feet and attached the snap links on their static lines to the steel cable that ran the length of the cabin in the sequence they would jump: Lt. Col. Randal, ex-Lt. Jaxx and King.

The jump commands were highly modified for tonight's jump.

"Check static line."

"Here we go," Lt. Plum-Martin said.

The Anson swooped up over the cliff to 500 feet, banked right and leveled off. The three jumpers had to hang on hard to keep from being thrown off their feet.

When the aircraft leveled off, Lt. Col. Randal braced his canvas-topped raiding boots on both sides of the door, stood spread-eagled gripping the rim that ran around it with his fingertips, and arched his body outside the aircraft. The wind whipped his sand green Denison parachute smock, distorted his face and nearly blinded him at first.

Up ahead he could see the letter T burning on the ground.

Lt. Plum-Martin throttled back, flying not much faster than stall speed to reduce the opening shock, which was negligible with the X-type parachute. She was a professional and wanted to give her jumpers every possible advantage tonight.

"Close on the door."

Ex-Lt. Jaxx and King inched forward until all three Raiders were physically touching.

When the bottom of the letter T was about an inch from the tip of the toe of his right boot, Lt. Col. Randal shouted, "Let's go" and exited the aircraft, followed instantly by ex-Lt. Jaxx with King almost on top of him.

Before the static line deployed his parachute, Lt. Col. Randal saw the Anson fly out of sight, banking back out to sea. The chute cracked open, took two swings, then he felt the familiar rushing sensation as he came in for a right front parachute landing fall.

He made the classic school solution PLF where the jumper hits all five points of contact in sequence – almost never happens in real live jumps but it did tonight. Lt. Col. Randal popped the quick release on his parachute as he sprang to his feet.

Ex-Lieutenant Jaxx was down with King silently coming in behind him.

Captain Patrick "Paddy" Leigh-Fermor was there almost immediately.

"Nice to see you again, sir," the SOE operative said. "Appears you have recovered fully from your wound. No need for a permission slip from your doctor this trip."

"I'm good," Lt. Col. Randal said. "You ready to go?"

"Yes, sir," Capt. Leigh-Fermor said. "We're a half mile from the top of the cliff over the German ship. My men have your rope in place.

"Will you require any additional assistance, Colonel?"

"Negative," Lt. Col. Randal said. "Send down the parachutes, haul up the rope after the trawler departs, then disappear. We were never here."

"Simple enough, sir."

Ex-Lt. Jaxx and King had their chutes in their bags ready to travel. Lieutenant Karen Montgomery, the Raiding Forces' Chief Rigger, had issued strict instructions for them to bring the chutes back at the end of the mission. Parachutes were not plentiful in Middle East Command.

"OK," Lt. Col. Randal ordered, "move out."

The terrain to the cliff was as flat as a pool table. The march was a stroll in the park. Two of Capt. Leigh-Fermor's men were waiting when they arrived seaside.

The first fifty feet down the incline were easy enough to negotiate. The rest of the way was a sheer precipice requiring the use of a rope.

The three would utilize the technique known as the "Commando rappel," which meant no rappel seat and no snap link to use as a brake. The rope went over the left shoulder and up under the right arm. To go, the person on rappel pointed his right gloved hand straight down and let the rope play out freely through the fingers of his right hand. To stop, the rope was brought up sharply to the chest with the right hand, squeezed tight and pressed into the body hard.

The Commando rappel worked better when the rope went over a rifle or submachine gun slung across the back. Especially when it was time to brake. However, tonight the Raiders were carrying only their sidearms.

King went first. When he reached the bottom he shook the rope vigorously twice to signal for the next man to come down. Ex-Lt. Jaxx had insisted on being second down the rope. In an instant he was away and gone.

"Good luck, sir," Capt. Leigh-Fermor said.

It really hurt when Lt. Col. Randal brought the rope into his chest with his gloved hand to stop – burned all the way across his back and along his ribs. He dangled up and down a lot like he had when jumping out of the thirty-four-foot tower at Ft. Benning.

Except for ex-Lt. Jaxx and King, there was no one on the shore. The steel cable was lashed to a rock with waves lapping against it. The Vorpostenboot was on the other end of the cable resting at anchor in the inlet.

There did not appear to be anyone on watch on the stern quarter of the ship.

"What do we do now, Chief?" King asked.

"In about thirty minutes Butch is going to come storming on board that Vorpostenboot," Lt. Col. Randal said. "I'd hate for any of his Commandos to get hurt if there's an armed sentry on the bow or the upper deck."

"That'd be too bad," ex-Lt. Jaxx said. "We wouldn't want that to happen, sir."

"How do you want to play it, King?"

"Jack and I'll take the upper deck," King said. "Most likely someone's on watch in the wheelhouse or the radio shack – probably both.

"You take the bow, Chief."

"Think you can shinny up that cable, Jack?" Lt. Col. Randal said.

"Give me a break, sir."

"That's right," Lt. Col. Randal said. "You scaled those vines at the Tri-Delt House like Tarzan."

He took off his right-hand glove and cut the trigger finger off with his Fairbairn Fighting Knife while ex-Lt. Jaxx and King watched. The cable was braided steel wire and might have splinters. Gloves were a must, but his were too thick to allow him to fire his silenced .22 High Standard in an emergency.

"Same order we came down the cliff," Lt. Col. Randal said. "Move out, King."

The Merc grabbed the cable and pulling with both hands and one of his boots locked over the cable and the other dangling down for balance, hand-over-handed his way up the incline toward the Vorpostenboot. He was moving fast.

Ex-Lt. Jaxx followed as soon as there were six feet separating the two.

Watching King, Lt. Col. Randal waited before getting on the cable. As the Merc was about to reach out and grab the rail of the ship, a man stood up. The German sailor must have been sleeping on deck.

The silenced .22 High Standard appeared in Lt. Col. Randal's hand. *WHIIICH, WHIIICH, WHIIICH.*

The distance was long for a .22, but there were three distinct *WHAP, WHAP, WHAP* sounds as the bullets struck home.

The German did not go down, but King was over the rail in an instant, driving the blade of his Fairbairn Fighting Knife into the sailor's neck.

Ex-Lt. Jaxx reached the rail as Lt. Col. Randal holstered his pistol and started shinnying up the cable. It was a lot harder work than the other two made it appear. They had disappeared by the time he swung aboard.

Lt. Col. Randal stepped over the dead sailor. He made his way toward the bow of the trawler. There was no reason to crouch or try to sneak. That would have been a dead giveaway. The idea was to try to look like one of the crew coming up for a breath of fresh air.

Up ahead he could see the red tip of a cigarette glowing. There was someone on the bow. Either a sailor pulling his watch or one of the crew who had come up on deck for a smoke.

When Lt. Col. Randal got close, the smoker called out in German.

Not speaking one word of German, Lt. Col. Randal shot him five times in the chest with the silenced .22 High Standard. The man went down. Most likely the sailor never understood what had happened.

Lt. Col. Randal put one more round in the Nazi's head to be absolutely sure.

With his hook-nosed flashlight he started flashing the letters *R* and *F* in Morse out to sea. He did not want Lieutenant Butch "Headhunter" Hoolihan's men mistaking him for one of the bad guys when they came aboard.

Finally . . . *dot, dot, dot – dot, dot, dot* blinked back – the letters SS.

Sea Squadron was coming in hot.

Lt. Col. Randal retreated to the upper deck. It would not be a good idea to be standing there when the Headhunter's boys came over the side.

King had the radio room secured. The radio operator was tied up with an electrical cord. That should make Lieutenant Commander Ian Fleming happy.

Lt. Col. Randal said, "Good work."

In the wheelhouse he found ex-Lt. Jaxx had shot two men who had been engaged in a game of cards. Double taps to the head. They were stone dead.

"Should have been standing watch, not playing on the job," ex-Lt. Jaxx said. "Tried to rush me when I came in, sir."

"Clearly a mistake," Lt. Col. Randal said taking one of Waldo's custom-rolled cigars out of the inside pocket of his Denison parachute smock and sticking it between his teeth.

"Nice job, stud."

Down on the deck the sound of metal clinks was heard as grappling hooks flew over the rails on both sides of the ship. Then Lt. Hoolihan's men began swarming aboard.

"Topside's secure," Lt. Col. Randal called. "Go below."

Lt. Cdr. Fleming and his three-man team of Naval Intelligence operatives came on board. They made their way to the upper deck and went straight to the radio room. King joined Lt. Col. Randal and ex-Lt. Jaxx out on the walkway in front of the wheelhouse.

Two muffled gunshots came from below deck. Then Lt. Hoolihan arrived on the upper deck. He was cool as ice.

"Minor resistance encountered," Lt. Hoolihan reported. "Overcome – the ship is secure, sir."

"Looked good, Butch," Lt. Col. Randal said, "coming over that rail."

Lt. Cdr. Fleming joined them.

"Find what you were searching for?" Lt. Col. Randal asked, lighting his cigar with his old Zippo.

"Mission accomplished," Lt. Cdr. Fleming said.

"By the way," Lt. Col. Randal said, "did I mention a *Red Indian* target we plan to take down, Commander?"

"No, you absolutely did not reference any *Red Indian*," Lt. Cdr. Fleming said. "An oversight on your part, Colonel, no doubt.

"When?"

"We're headed there now," Lt. Col. Randal said. "Care to tag along?"

THE RED LIGHT WAS ON IN THE CABIN OF THE HUDSON. THAT meant the aircraft was ten minutes out from the drop zone. The jump door was open in the tail of the airplane. The wind was howling.

"Six minutes, John," Lieutenant Pamala Plum-Martin announced over the intercom.

"Stand up and hook up," Lieutenant Colonel John Randal ordered. He was not shouting the jump commands in the approved Airborne manner – everyone was an experienced jumper and there were only five: ex-Lieutenant Billy Jack Jaxx, King and the Lovat Scouts, Lionel Fenwick and Munro Ferguson.

It was thirty minutes before Beginning Morning Nautical Twilight, which is what the military likes to call sunrise, on the morning following the takedown of the Vorpostenboot. They had been flying for nearly thirty hours.

First, Earthquake McGoon had flown them back to RFHQ in the Kingfisher that had been borrowed from the *King Duck* and carried aboard Acting Provisional Sub-Lieutenant Skipper Mud Cat Ray's trawler *Pirate's Dream* specifically for that task. Immediately upon arriving, they boarded the Hudson and flew to Oasis X where the airplane was refueled and Scouts Fenwick and Ferguson came on board.

From X the Hudson had continued on for 400 miles into the heart of the Great Sand Sea to the German weather station targeted by one of Mr. Zargo's operatives.

The plan, designed by ex-Lt. Jaxx and Lt. Plum-Martin, was to jump into the desert two miles away from the weather station a half hour before first light, move overland to the objective while the Hudson racetracked, take down the target then signal the airplane to land on the airstrip once the objective was secure.

Lieutenant Commander Ian Fleming would deplane with his three-man team of Naval Intelligence operatives to conduct the search.

Then everyone would reboard the Hudson and return to X.

Wing Commander Ronald Gordon, who had done much of the flying – trading off with Lt. Plum-Martin – was in the back observing the jump. He found watching men calmly preparing to jump out of an aircraft in flight strangely disconcerting.

He had made five jumps himself but all had come when he was saving himself after his airplane had been shot up – which was a different matter entirely.

"Check your static line."

The metal-on-metal rasping of the steel snap hooks filled the compartment.

"Check your equipment."

Everyone was jumping heavily armed. While the plan called for capturing the "weathermen," anything could happen.

"Sound off for equipment check."

"OK, OK, OK – all OK," ex-Lt. Jaxx said to Lt. Col. Randal.

There was not much point in making a jumpmaster check outside the airplane. It was still dark and they were jumping blind. There was no one to mark the DZ. Lt. Col. Randal checked anyway.

He did not see anything.

Tonight they were trusting the accuracy of Lt. Plum-Martin's ex-LRDG navigator.

"Close on the door."

Lt. Col. Randal had no idea how long before the green light. As if reading his mind, Lt. Plum-Martin announced over the intercom, "One minute."

When the green light flashed, Lt. Col. Randal shouted, "GO!" He was away before the word was completely out of his mouth.

There was no reason to drop low. No one was going to see them unless it was some Arab nomad, and they were not going to tell anyone in the middle of nowhere. Tonight the jump was from 1,000 feet.

Lt. Col. Randal enjoyed the ride down. The trick to a good PLF, whether you hit your points of contact or not, was to keep your elbows in, touching on your chest with your head down – then keeping your feet and knees together, slightly touching but completely *unlocked.* So loose there was no way possible to make a stand-up landing even if you landed as light as a feather.

He always rocked his just to make sure.

WHAAAM! Lt. Col. Randal was down. That hurt. Oh well, any PLF you can walk away from is a good one.

By the time he had his parachute in its bag, the other four Raiders were there ready to go. Lt. Col. Randal took out his compass. The azimuth was preset on the luminous bezel. He checked it, stuck his thumb in the brass wire carrying ring and started off at a fast trot.

Twenty minutes later as the sky lightened, the sun coming up scorching hot, the Raiders came over a sand dune immediately behind the large pyramid tent that the Germans used for their weather station and caught the five weathermen outside doing their morning PT.

Not a shot was fired.

20

BEST LITTLE WHOREHOUSE IN LIBYA

LIEUTENANT COLONEL JOHN RANDAL WAS STRETCHED OUT ON A canvas bench seat with his cut-down bush hat over his eyes, asleep in the Hudson winging its way back across the Great Sand Sea to Oasis X. Ex-Lieutenant Billy Jack Jaxx was asleep on the other side of the aisle. King was in the back guarding the prisoners who were handcuffed to their seats.

The German weathermen were also blindfolded.

Lieutenant Commander Ian Fleming and his team of naval intelligence specialists were combing through the pile of material captured at the weather station.

Wing Commander Ronald Gordon came out of the cockpit and walked down the aisle to where Lt. Col. Randal was sleeping.

Lt. Col. Randal pushed back the bush hat – wide awake before Wg. Cdr. Gordon could reach down to shake his shoulder.

"A coded message from the Air Marshal," Wg. Cdr. Gordon said. "The CRUSADER twenty-four-hour clock starts ticking at zero six hundred in the morning."

"What's our ETA at the Oasis?"

"Approximately an hour."

"Send a message to Major Stone," Lt. Col. Randal said. "Instruct him to place any of the patrols still remaining at X on Red Alert. Ask Mr. Treywick to meet the plane when we land. "

"Anything else, Colonel?"

"That's it for now – did you have those two Havocs delivered to the Oasis?"

"Arrived this morning."

"You and Pam take thirty minutes to freshen up after we touch down," Lt. Col. Randal said. "Then report to my suite for a briefing on your *Bombshell* target."

"Will do."

When the Wing Commander started to make his way back to the cockpit, ex-Lt. Jaxx, who had been quietly listening to every word from under his bush hat, asked, "Are we going to jump in or airland on the auxiliary strip to take down that whorehouse, sir?"

"Neither one," Lt. Col. Randal said. "I've got other plans for us, Jack."

Waldo Treywick was waiting on the landing strip when the Hudson touched down at Oasis X. Ranger Patrol's departure had been delayed because Lt. Col. Randal had decided to return Lovat Scouts Fenwick and Ferguson before the patrol left Oasis X.

Lt. Col. Randal said, "Mr. Treywick, take charge of Ranger Patrol. Roll out right now. Drive as hard as you can to link up with Lt. Huxley's Blue Patrol.

"Jack and I will be there when you arrive."

"You want me to hit targets on the way, Colonel?"

"Negative," Lt. Col. Randal said. "I need you to get there as soon as possible – probably take a week."

"We'll try to make it a little faster 'en 'at," Waldo said.

"Be careful," Lt. Col. Randal said. "Enemy air's going to be very active – starting in about two days."

"Got it – loud and clear," Mr. Treywick said. "See you when I see you."

Lt. Cdr. Fleming came off the airplane. "I understand my group and the prisoners will be flying on to Cairo in one of your Walruses."

"Hope you got what you needed," Lt. Col. Randal said.

"We did well," Lt. Cdr. Fleming said, "Always a pleasure doing business with you, Colonel."

Ex-Lt. Jaxx and King came down the steps carrying their gear.

Lieutenant Mandy Paige was waiting with a jeep to drive them to their quarters.

Brandy Seaborn was in another jeep to pick up Wg. Cdr. Gordon and Lieutenant Pamala Plum-Martin.

"Hard day at the office, John?" Mandy asked.

"Not too bad," Lt. Col. Randal said. "Lot of flying – little tired.

"Jack, you and King hit the rack as soon as you get to your quarters," Lt. Col. Randal said over his shoulder to the two in the back. "The three of us will be taking off again as soon as Pam and the Wing Commander log eight hours sleep."

Captain the Lady Jane Seaborn was sunbathing topless on the deck of their snow-white condominium when he walked in.

Lt. Col. Randal decided he was not so tired after all.

WING COMMANDER RONALD GORDON AKA "FLASH BANG" Gordon and Lieutenant Pamala Plum-Martin rolled in on their target. The two were flying Havoc A-20s, each armed with four Hispano Mark III 20mm cannon and six Browning .50 caliber machine guns. The snow-blonde Vargas Girl look-alike Royal Marine pilot was flying lead with her ex-LRDG navigator sitting in the co-pilot's seat.

Wg. Cdr. Gordon had completed a tour flying Hurricanes during the Battle of Britain, then a tour commanding a squadron of night fighters during The Blitz, another tour flying Hurricanes again on Malta (possibly the most dangerous RAF duty in the war) and was currently in command of a wing of Spitfires in Egypt. At least he had been until his last shoot-down when he was injured bailing out of his burning fighter.

What he and Lt. Plum-Martin were about to do tonight was the most insane undertaking he had ever imagined could be attempted with an airplane. Wg. Cdr. Gordon decided that when he returned to his wing he was going to punch in the face the next pilot who made a snide comment about it "being easy for a female to be awarded the Distinguished Flying Cross in the Air Transport Command" in reference to Plum-Martin's three DFCs.

Because of his injury, Wg. Cdr. Gordon was off flying status, which is why he had been assigned to Raiding Forces as the RAF liaison officer for OPERATION CRUSADER. While officially on light duty, in the past 100 hours, Wg. Cdr. Gordon had flown more hazardous combat missions in a shorter period than at any other time in his entire career.

Tonight was a first, a RAF job planned by a ground officer – Lieutenant Colonel John Randal. The mission was crazy. No, it was insane.

Lt. Plum-Martin spotted six red railroad flares light up – three on each side of the auxiliary emergency airstrip. Two gun jeeps from Lieutenant Westcott Huxley's Blue Patrol had put the flares out to mark the far south end of the landing ground.

During the day, the Luftwaffe used the strip as an emergency field to divert battle-damaged aircraft; if the planes crash-landed they would not interrupt flight operations.

By night a wildly popular bordello described by ex-Lt. Billy Jack Jaxx as the "best little whorehouse in Libya" was open for business in the abandoned Regia Aeronautica Operations Building located approximately halfway down the runway.

Raiding Forces was about to come calling.

"Spot on," Lt. Plum-Martin said to her navigator, "as usual."

THREE MILES EAST OF THE AUXILIARY AIRSTRIP, TWO MORE GUN jeeps from Blue Patrol were outside another Luftwaffe landing ground parked in defilade a mile from the Nazi airfield. The detachment had a Lend-Lease 81mm mortar set up under the command of Corporal Boyce Malcom a former mortar instructor at the Middle East Command's Non-Commissioned Officers Academy. At zero one hundred hours, the instructor corporal was going to drop a preplanned concentration of HE on the thirty-five Me-109s parked at the airfield. It was said that Cpl. Malcom was one of the best mortar men in the British Army.

Blue Patrol was about to find out.

THREE MILES SOUTH OF THE AUXILIARY LANDING GROUND, Lieutenant Westcott Huxley was on station at the second of the three Luftwaffe air bases that used the abandoned airstrip as an auxiliary landing ground. He had the remaining two Blue Patrol gun jeeps, one of which carried the patrol's twin 20mm Oerlikon cannon. At H-hour – zero one hundred hours – the 10th Lancer officer intended to make a single pass straight down the landing ground blasting the twenty-nine Stuka JU-87s parked along both edges of the strip and be gone into the night.

The two gun jeeps were also planning to strafe the aviation fuel storage tanks.

Hit and run.

THREE MILES NORTH OF THE AUXILIARY LANDING GROUND AT the third Luftwaffe airbase that used the abandoned Regia Aeronautica strip to land their battle-damaged aircraft, Lieutenant Colonel John Randal, ex-Lieutenant Billy Jack Jaxx and King were silently infiltrating the base. They were carrying packs full of prepared explosive devices.

The team had jumped into Blue Patrol the night previous.

The Raiders intended to place the explosives on the left wings of the twenty-three Ju-52 transports parked along the east side of the tarmac. The explosive charges did not have any incendiary properties. The trick was to place them just so near the fuel tank.

Since the German transports were the highest priority airplane on the target list, Lt. Col. Randal had decided to make sure of their destruction. He planned to go in and do it by hand.

H-hour was zero one hundred.

The team had to execute. The fuses on the explosives were set for sixty minutes. However, the time pencils were not always precise. If they averaged three minutes to attach one of the incendiary devices to each plane, the first charge would go off before they exited the airfield.

The reason Lt. Col. Randal elected to cut it so close was because he believed the longer the fuse, the greater the chance of an explosive charge being detected and removed. He was taking a calculated risk tonight because of the strategic value of the JU 52s.

Right about now Lt. Col. Randal was regretting not adding Lieutenant Roy Kidd to the team. After thinking it over, he had decided to have Lt. Kidd take the field with his Scout Patrol.

That might have been a mistake.

Another potential problem Lt. Col. Randal's party faced tonight was although the Germans flew off the airfield, Italians defended it. They had the nasty habit of placing a sentry on each airplane. Although the plane guards were usually to be found asleep, it would take time to eliminate them without sounding the alarm.

The concept of the operation called for Lt. Col. Randal's team to slip in, place the explosives, then slip out and head for an RV with Lieutenant Westcott Huxley who would then drive them to another rendezvous with Blue Patrol's other two detachments. It was a good plan – short and simple.

What could possibly go wrong? Just about everything.

The night was dark as pitch. There were clouds in the sky, and a storm was clearly brewing though there was no rain as of yet, but it was coming – they could smell it. The wind was blowing, which was good because it dispersed sound, making sneaking and creeping easier.

King led the way. Although the team had not had the opportunity to recon the objective, Major Vladimir Peniakoff aka "Popski" had surveyed the airfield extensively. The tubby Russian briefed them in detail on the layout.

Tonight, in the interest of saving time, the three Raiders were not going to go after the fuel storage tanks or other targets of opportunity. The Ju-52s were the only target. Getting in, placing the explosives, and egressing fast being the main considerations.

Lt. Col. Randal's team infiltrated the wire easily enough, which, as usual, was only a single strand of rusted barbed wire that was lying on the ground in places. Their route took them close to the built up area. They wanted to work their way away from it so they could escape into the desert at the far end of the airfield.

King turned right the minute he hit the edge of the tarmac.

At this point Lt. Col. Randal took the lead. The party was armed only with sidearms. He held his High Standard Military Model D .22 with silencer affixed in both hands as he carefully approached the first JU-52.

Sure enough, the form of a man sleeping under the left wing swam into view.

Lt. Col. Randal took three careful steps forward to close the distance. He shot the guard three times. *WHIIICH, WHIIICH, WHIIICH.*

King moved up to place the explosive charge on the wing. Ex-Lt. Jaxx moved into the lead. As the Merc worked, he and Lt. Col. Randal advanced on the next airplane.

It was so dark they could not see the big JU-52 transport even though it was only ten yards away. Ex-Lt. Jaxx moved under the wing and shot the guard three times as he lay sound asleep on the ground. The Blackshirt never made a sound.

Having learned from experience on their last airfield raid, when they ran out of ammunition conducting sentry elimination, tonight both Lt. Col. Randal and ex-Lt. Jaxx were carrying several spare magazines for their High Standard .22s.

King drifted past and placed a charge on the left wing.

Lt. Col. Randal retook the lead.

The three continued working their way up the line of JU-52 transports with Lt. Col. Randal and ex-Lt. Jaxx leapfrogging each other. From time to time they replenished King's supply of demolitions from their packs.

Lt. Col. Randal glanced at the lime green hands on his Rolex. They were making good progress. Right about now the length of the Great Sand Sea elements of Desert Patrol were in the process of attacking twenty-nine German and Italian airfields.

OPERATION CRUSADER was set to kick off at dawn.

THE FIRST SHOTS OF THE CAMPAIGN (NOT COUNTING THE silenced High Standard .22s) fell to the pair of modified Havoc A-20 gunships loaned to Raiding Forces.

Lieutenant Pamala Plum-Martin, closely followed by Wing Commander Ronald Gordon, lined up on the Blue Patrol flares marking the sides of the south end of the runway, then came in for a landing – Wg. Cdr. Gordon was wondering how he had managed to get himself into this madness. The two heavily armed attack aircraft touched down and taxied down the strip in trail. The Havoc's rolled past a parking lot that must have contained thirty or forty cars and military vehicles of assorted models.

The planes rolled up to the two-story frame building that had served as the Operations/Air Traffic Control building in years past and was now a brothel, came to a stop and swung left facing the building. A thin outline of yellow light was visible around the edges of the blackout curtains covering the windows.

Airplanes did not normally land on the auxiliary strip at night. Several curious German pilots strolled out, drinks in hand, to investigate. That was a mistake.

Wingtip to wingtip at a range measured in feet, both A-20s commenced firing. The concentrated cannons and heavy machine guns opening all at once made an explosion of sound. The roar was staggering.

The Nazi pilots were vaporized.

Instantly, the wooden structure was reduced to matchsticks

Eight 20mm cannons and twelve .50 caliber machine guns at point-blank range are devastating. A hurricane of monster-sized shells tore into the building, ripping through it from top to bottom and shattering everything inside. Every inch of the front of the bordello seemed to have a bullet hole through it. The ceiling on the first floor fell down.

Then the place caught fire.

In lockstep, the two A-20 Havocs turned as one, ran back up the airstrip and took off, leaving death and destruction in their wake. Lt. Plum-Martin immediately made a hard bank as soon as she had altitude, came around and made a low-level gun run on the building and the parking lot. Her wingman, Wg. Cdr. Gordon, was tucked in right behind – hammer down on the trigger.

Ammunition expended, the two Havocs zoomed up into the night, turning into a heading that would take them back to Oasis X. Within seconds the planes were gone from sight.

As for OPERATION CRUSADER – the balloon had just gone up.

THE BLUE PATROL DETACHMENT WITH THE 81MM MORTAR heard the sound of gunfire in the distance. Their orders were to commence fire at "zero one hundred hours or in the event they heard gunfire" from one of the other airfields.

Corporal Boyce Malcom had drilled two Blue Patrolmen to be his assistants. No. 1 man loaded the tube. No. 2 man handed the loader the next mortar round from the pile stacked up with charges attached.

Lying under a camouflage net spread out on the ground before the sun had gone down, the instructor corporal had employed the patrol's range finder to establish the exact distance to each airplane and the aviation fuel tank storage area. Then he methodically dialed in his target data so he could fire mission in the dark.

On command, No. 1 dropped the first three 81mm mortar rounds down the tube – one right after the other as fast as the rounds fired – just the way they had practiced. The rounds were aimed at the aviation fuel storage tanks.

Before the first round landed, the instructor corporal was making adjustments.

"Hang it."

The next round went down the tube and was sailing skyward in an instant. More twiddling of knobs.

"Hang it."

The Corporal walked the rounds down the line of parked ME-109s. The mortar team was on their fifth adjustment when the first three rounds slammed into the fuel storage tanks, creating a massive fireball. A mile away the airfield turned from night into day.

The base Air Raid siren wailed.

Searchlights beamed skyward, sweeping the sky for an intruder. Every automatic weapon on the airfield commenced firing straight up. The Italian defenders believed they were under air attack.

The Corporal was not distracted. He stayed at his eyepiece, twisting the elevating/traversing knobs, making the adjustments he had worked out in advance, ordering, "Hang it." He was as calm as if he were putting on a 81mm mortar demonstration for a bleacher full of students and visiting dignitaries the way he had done a hundred times before.

Cpl. Malcolm lived up to his advanced billing. Peering through the night from a vantage point, the Blue Patrol detachment commander could make out the rounds impacting through his field glasses. Me-109s were being tossed about like toy model airplanes.

No one needed binoculars to see the landing ground was in flames.

In less than five minutes from start to finish, the last round was on the way. The 81mm mortar was broken down, loaded in one of the jeeps, and the Blue Patrol detachment was moving to the RV.

Mission accomplished.

LIEUTENANT WESTCOTT HUXLEY HAD HIS TWO GUN JEEPS parked on the end of the runway, sitting on the landing ground he intended to raid. Their engines were switched off to conserve fuel. Since the wind was blowing in the opposite direction, he did not hear the two Havoc A-20s firing or the mortar rounds detonating, but he could see a glow on the horizon from the direction of his Blue Patrol detachment armed with the 81mm mortar.

Lt. Huxley was watching the luminous dial on his elegant Audemars Piguet wristwatch. When the hands reached straight up zero one hundred hours, he ordered his AVG driver, a lanky Louisiana Cajun who liked to be called Jake, "Cwank it up!"

Both gun jeeps roared to life.

"Woll out, Jake."

Jake drove straight down the center of the tarmac. By now the wind was so stiff that the sound of the jeeps was almost entirely muffled. Anyone who heard them would most likely not be alarmed – other than to fear it might be one of the officers coming around to make a snap inspection.

There was a storm brewing.

Lt. Huxley made a mental note not to drive into any wadis or dry riverbeds when they egressed the landing ground on the way to the RV to pick up Lieutenant Colonel John Randal's party. During a rainstorm, intermittent streams could turn into raging rivers in the desert in a heartbeat. The young 10th Lancer was a peerless patrol leader, born to command, always thinking ahead.

He simply could not pronounce the letter *R*.

Blue Patrol knew exactly where the enemy airplanes were parked. They had arrived at their ORP an hour before sundown three miles out from the landing ground. Each man in the patrol had been allowed a chance to study the target through Lt. Huxley's binoculars.

There were three groups of JU-87 Stukas parked by squadrons along both sides of the tarmac. Blue Patrol had to get them all or the surviving planes would be out at dawn looking for revenge. Nothing was more dangerous to a jeep patrol than a dive bomber flown by a skilled pilot.

German Stuka pilots are highly skilled.

Up ahead through the dark the first JU-87 began to appear right where it was supposed to be.

"Commence fiwing!"

Jake had his pair of .303 Vickers K machine guns angled to the left. Lt. Huxley was already engaging with his pair before the lanky American could pull the trigger. The gunner in the back on the pair of pedestal-mounted Vickers K was leaning into his weapon firing short, crisp bursts.

The gunners on the second jeep opened as soon as they could identify the target. Everyone knew to make every shot count.

This was a death match. They had to get the Stukas or the Stukas would get them.

The 20mm Oerlikon was steadily going *Pokka, Pokka, Pokka.*

Lt. Huxley counted airplanes. When he reached nine he ordered, "Cease Fiwe – shift."

Everyone on board the jeeps knew the next group of ten aircraft was parked on the right side of the airfield.

The gunners were all locked in behind their machine guns ready when they saw the dim silhouette of the first Stuka appear on the opposite side of the runway. Blue Patrol engaged immediately. Ten .303 Vickers K machine guns and two 20mm Oerlikon fast-firing cannon vectored in on the JU-87. The airplane was instantly torn into scrap metal.

From behind the jeeps on the far side of the tarmac, one of the Stukas they had already shot up cooked off, *KABOOOOOM!*

The JU-87s were topped off with fuel and armed with their bombs ready to take off at first light. That practice allowed the dive bombers to get an early start each morning but also made them extremely vulnerable. A Stuka carried almost 4,000 pounds of externally mounted bombs.

The first blast caused the other airplanes to have sympathetic explosions. All nine went up with an earth-shattering blast – 36,000 pounds of bombs.

The boom startled Lt. Huxley's two gun jeep crews. None of the airplanes had appeared to be on fire when they drove past, even though all the planes had been shredded with machine gun and cannon fire. One must have been burning internally.

The shock wave from the massive explosion rattled the jeeps, but the gunners maintained their composure, stayed dialed in and kept relentlessly pouring fire into the parked JU-87s in the second group.

The number two plane in the line exploded immediately. The remaining Stukas detonated simultaneously. The detonation was so fast and in their face, Blue Patrol was momentarily stunned.

The Italian defenders guarding the airfield engaged, firing their weapons straight up in the misguided belief that the field was under air attack, strafed and then bombed.

Searchlights came on, and the beams of million-candlepower lights began swaying back and forth, probing the low-level storm clouds.

"Shift," Lt. Huxley commanded, loud enough for the men in the trailing jeep to hear even though their ears were ringing and their night vision destroyed by the last blast.

The remaining squadron of JU-87s were back on the left side of the airfield parked in a neat row about 200 yards from the aviation fuel storage tanks. Blue

Patrol could not see them yet because their night vision was impaired, but time spent on reconnaissance is rarely wasted – they knew the planes were there.

"Stay in the middle, Jake," Lt. Huxley ordered.

Blue Patrol was almost completely surrounded by machine guns firing at nonexistent aerial intruders. The Italians were putting up an impressive defense. Lesser men might have lost heart, but Lt. Huxley's Raiders ignored the fire and drove on.

Jake said, "I'd sure as hell hate to be a pilot attacking this place."

"Wojer that."

Then the last group of JU-87s came in view, and Blue Patrol opened as one. The first plane erupted like a volcano when the 20mm Oerlikon fired a three-round burst, *POKKA, POKKA, POKKA*, and struck one of the bombs mounted under its wing. The rest of the airplanes started cooking off in sequence – one right after the other.

"Shift fiwes to the fuel tanks," Lt. Huxley ordered.

A hailstorm of .303 machine gun and 20mm fire converged on the aviation fuel tank farm. The guns were loaded with tracer, incendiary and armor piercing, and the 20mm also had high explosive rounds. Within seconds the tanks were flaming.

"Hawd wight, Jake – time to go."

The two Blue Patrol jeeps bumped across the rough ground between the tarmac and the single strand of barbed wire around the perimeter of the airfield. Jake spotted a section that was lying on the ground and drove straight toward it. In minutes they were away and gone into the dark heading for the RV with Lt. Col. Randal's team.

As Blue Patrol was crossing over the wire, the Italian security personnel on the far side of the base finally realized they were under ground attack and started firing at imaginary infiltrators. Their machine gun rounds snapped by the Italians on the near side of the field, who rightly thought that they were being shot at and immediately returned fire.

Long after the two Blue Patrol gun jeeps had departed the area, the Italian's base security forces were still battling it out with each other. A lot of ammunition was expended. No casualties were inflicted.

Spray and pray.

KING WAS AFFIXING THE EXPLOSIVE CHARGE TO THE LAST JU-52 when a siren went off. There was the faint sound of a multiengine aircraft approaching the field. Search lights came on and pencil-like beams of light started sweeping the sky.

"What the hell?" Lieutenant Colonel John Randal said.

"Uh-oh that's one of ours," Ex-Lieutenant Billy Jack Jaxx said when the beams caught the intruder in the apex of a half dozen columns of silver light. "Air Raid!"

It was a Wellington bomber. The lights had the RAF plane pinned.

A furious barrage of anti-aircraft fire erupted. Tracers streaked skyward. There seemed to be millions of them. None of the gunners was firing short, crisp bursts. The Italians were running their guns.

Lt. Col. Randal had no idea there were that many anti-aircraft weapons positioned around the field.

The Wellington dipped. It banked. It slipped, but the lights had it trapped. The RAF crew seemed desperate to escape. The plane's engines raced.

There was no way for the British airplane to evade the lights. No way to get away. Why the bomber had not already been shot out of the sky seemed a miracle.

The three Raiders watched in horror.

The pyramid of searchlight beams moved directly overhead, following the course of the plane. The thunder of the anti-aircraft guns reached a crescendo.

The Wellington dropped its full 4,500-pound payload of bombs. There was a screaming sound.

Instinctively, Lt. Col. Randal ran toward a slit trench dug along the side of the tarmac and dove in headfirst. Ex-Lt. Jaxx and King were right behind him.

Two Italians were occupying the trench, their faces buried in the dirt. Neither one bothered to look up when the three Raiders arrived unannounced. One of the Blackshirts was praying hysterically, having problems making the sign of the cross while lying face down.

The Wellington's payload hit with a thundering rapid fire string of mind-numbing explosions. The ground shook like in an earthquake. The bombs landed on the far side of the landing strip.

The RAF did not hit a thing.

The plane zoomed off, leaving the lights to search an empty sky. Even with no target in sight, the antiaircraft gunners continued to fire.

"Let's get the hell out of Dodge," Lt. Col. Randal said through gritted teeth.

KABOOOOOOOM! The first of the JU 52 blew up right on time.

The two Italians sharing the slit trench were shaking in terror. They never looked up when the Raiders rolled out of the trench. Those two Blackshirts were not about to stick their noses above ground.

Not tonight.

"That was ugly," ex-Lt. Jaxx said as they headed toward the far end of the airfield. "Thought you coordinated tonight's targets with Flash Bang Gordon, sir."

"I did."

King said, "So much for inner-service cooperation."

CAPTAIN THE LADY JANE SEABORN TAPPED ON THE DOOR TO Rikke Runborg's room. Rocky opened it on the first knock. Lady Jane led her back to her suite.

Lieutenant Colonel Dudley Clarke, James "Baldie" Taylor and one of his operatives were in the living room. They had the suitcase radio set up. Lt. Col. Clarke handed Rocky a message for her to transmit.

```
13 November 41
URGENT! URGENT! URGENT!
CHURCHILL ORDERED
AUCHINLECK TO MOVE UP BRITISH
OFFENSIVE. ATTACK IMMINENT!
GAULITIE
    R
```

Rocky sat down at the key and began to tap out the message.

Lt. Col. Clarke, who had arrived back in Egypt from his adventures abroad only that morning and immediately flown straight to Oasis X, was attempting to rehabilitate his (and Great Britain's) most valuable Human Intelligence (HUMINT). The idea was for Rocky to inform the Abwehr that the date of the British attack had changed prior to it taking place – but too late for Afrika Korps to react to the new information.

Lt. Col. Clarke knew from an ULTRA intercept that Field Marshal Erwin Rommel had carried through on the decision to travel to Rome for his birthday based largely on Rocky's previous report.

It might work.

21

WE COULD LOSE THIS THING

BLUE PATROL HAD BEEN ABLE TO TRAVEL ONLY TWENTY MILES away from the four enemy airfields attacked – three active airfields and one cathouse on an abandoned airstrip – before they were forced into setting up a hasty laying-up position. The storm that had been threatening had finally broken. A monsoon-class rain came down in sheets, accompanied by near-hurricane force winds.

The desert turned into quicksand. All the gun jeeps were mired in mud. This was a problem. The plan had been to put as much distance between the patrol and the airfields as possible before setting up a LUP before sunrise.

To make things worse, there was no place to take cover in defilade. The wadis were raging rivers within minutes of the rain starting. The gun jeeps were under camouflage netting, but they were still vulnerable.

The good news was Blue Patrol had destroyed or damaged nearly all the enemy aircraft on the three active airfields, which cut down on the Luftwaffe's ability to conduct an air search. Fortunately any planes that had survived unscathed were grounded until the storm abated. Visibility was zero.

It stormed for two days.

On the third day the sun came out hot. The desert dried up in about ten minutes. The wadis ran dry. The wind continued to blow and the dried mud quickly turned into dust.

Blue Patrol moved to a better hide position, put up camouflage netting and set out its decoy LUP as per standard operating procedure. Enemy air was far and away the biggest threat Raiding Forces faced. With the change in weather it was a sure bet the Germans would be up combing the desert to find them.

Lieutenant Colonel John Randal called for a leader's conference. Lieutenant Westcott Huxley and ex-Lieutenant Billy Jack Jaxx came to his command jeep and huddled under the camouflage netting. King and Diamond, one of Mr. Zargo's men who was responsible for intelligence in Blue Patrol's area of operation, also sat in.

Lt. Col. Randal said, "We were supposed to be a hundred miles away from here by now."

"Lucky to make it this faw, Colonel," Lt. Huxley said. "That was a fewocious stowm."

"It wouldn't take much," ex-Lt. Jaxx said, "to really hate Libya."

Lt. Col. Randal said, "The original idea called for Ranger Patrol to link up with us as fast as possible. The storm disrupted our timetable. We need a new plan."

"Let's get Diamond to break out his target list," ex-Lt. Jaxx said. "Pick out a few of the juicy ones to take down while we're waiting for Ranger to arrive."

"Why go to the trouble?" Lt. Col. Randal said. "We can turn around, go back and hit those same three airfields again tonight."

"Saves on mission prep," ex-Lt. Jaxx said. "But I don't think Lady Jane would approve, sir."

"Affirmative," King said.

Major Vladimir Peniakoff aka Popski rode in alone on a depressed-looking camel. He and his Senussi spies had been monitoring the landing ground since the raids. Popski had intelligence to report.

"Two of the three air bases were back in operation within ten minutes after being attacked," Maj. Peniakoff said. "Runway lights came on and planes started landing as if nothing had happened. Amazing."

"How'd you know that was going to happen, Colonel?" ex-Lt. Jaxx asked.

"I didn't," Lt. Col. Randal said.

Then what made you want to go back and attack the same tawgets again, suw?" Lt. Huxley asked.

"They're close."

BLUE PATROL WAS NOW ONE HUNDRED MILES EAST OF THE THREE airfields they had raided for the second time in three nights. By their rough estimate, they had destroyed more than fifty-three more aircraft. The security at the bases was even more lax than the first time Blue Patrol hit them.

While it was an impressive tally, most likely the Luftwaffe would simply fly in replacement aircraft from Italy or Crete. The German war machine was extremely efficient.

"Hard to believe those airfields were back in operation so fast," Lieutenant Colonel John Randal said. "So much for killing airplanes. Rommel can't fly in a new truck, Jack."

"I'm beginning to see your point, sir," ex-Lieutenant Billy Jack Jaxx said. "Taking out pilots and wheeled transports – that's what hurts the bad guys. But I love blowing up those Nazi planes."

The two were standing on an abandoned Regia Aeronautica airstrip. It was twenty-two hundred hours, pitch dark. Blue Patrol had been notified to set up a landing ground. The word FROGS

PAWN had been used as the message prefix.

One minute there was dead silence, the next the sound of approaching aircraft could be heard in the distance.

"Do it, Jack," Lt. Col. Randal said.

Ex-Lt. Jaxx ignited a flare and tossed it on the ground. Flares lit up all down the length of the strip marking the sides of the runway. An Avro Anson piloted by Lieutenant Pamala Plum-Martin appeared and came in for a landing.

King walked up, followed by Lieutenant Westcott Huxley.

"I have no idea," Lt. Col. Randal said, "why I'm being pulled out of the field, Westcott. You have your orders. Start working through Diamond's target list. Concentrate on fuel storage depots first. They're at the top of our priority list and impossible to defend."

"Suw!"

"Stay loose," Lt. Col. Randal said. "A change of mission could be in our future."

"Hope not, suw," Lt. Huxley said. "We have the dweam guewwla cavalwy assignment."

"That's what bothers me," Lt. Col. Randal said. "Too good to be true.

"You stand ready, stud."

Three hours later the Anson landed back at Oasis X. Captain the Lady Jane Seaborn was at the airfield to meet the plane. She and Lieutenant Mandy Paige were sitting in a jeep.

Lt. Col. Randal, ex-Lt. Jaxx and King slung their gear in the back and climbed in.

Lady Jane drove them back to the Oasis. Then they trudged up the winding torch-lit path to the top of the escarpment to Desert Patrol headquarters.

Colonel Dudley Clarke and James "Baldie" Taylor were waiting in the Tactical Operations Center. If Col. Clarke was embarrassed about his misadventures in Spain, he did not show it. Normally the cherubic unconventional warrior was unflappable. He was not rattled now; however, the commander of A-Force was clearly tense.

Jim was wearing a serious expression.

Lt. Col. Randal clicked on instantly.

"You two hit the rack," he said to ex-Lt. Jaxx and King.

"If it's OK, sir," ex-Lt. Jaxx said, "I'd like to sit in."

King nodded in agreement.

"You got it," Lt. Col. Randal said.

Lady Jane and Lt. Mandy had no intention of leaving either.

"I shall make this as short as possible," Jim said. "OPERATION CRUSADER is a disaster. Everything that could go wrong has gone wrong.

"Commandos led by Colonel Laycock and Colonel Keys launched a raid to assassinate Rommel at what they believed was his residence. Unfortunately, they did not do their due diligence. Not only was the building they attacked not Rommel's quarters, the Desert Fox was not even in Libya. He was at a birthday party in Italy, which I could have told Laycock if he had only asked.

"Keys was killed. No one knows what happened to the rest of the Commandos – dead, captured or on the run. High seas due to the storm made it impossible for the submarine standing by offshore to extract the team to remain on station.

"Against advice to stand down Captain Stirling's L-Detachment, Special Air Service took off and jumped in excessive winds. The LRDG who was to pick them up after their raids has reported two thirds of L-Detachment have been killed or are missing in action. None of the airfields were raided.

"General Cunningham was supposed to attack, relieve Tobruk, force Rommel to concentrate his armor in order for the Seventh Armored Division to destroy it *en masse.*

"The relief of Tobruk was not accomplished. The Italian Ariete Panzer Division is fighting much harder than anticipated – virtually destroyed the Desert Rats.

"Rommel flew back to North Africa. Straightaway he concentrated his panzers, as hoped, but by then Cunningham had dispersed his tanks in penny packets on fool's errands, and now it's our armor that is in peril of being wiped out.

"Auchinleck has flown to Cunningham's headquarters. The rumor is the Field Marshal is there to relieve him and take personal command of the battle.

"We could lose this thing."

Lt. Col. Randal took out one of Waldo's cigars and stuck it between his teeth. "What's the good news?"

"The *King Duck* sank a U-boat," Jim said. "The Kriegsmarine sent a wolf pack into the Mediterranean to try to stop the Royal Navy from sinking their resupply convoys sailing out of Italy. Our LCT sailed right over one of the submarines.

"Warthog is a national hero."

"What do you want from me?"

"Two things," Col. Clarke said. "Brigadier Davies has requested you take over responsibility for attacking the five airfields L-Detachment was assigned.

"And he needs Raiding Forces to concentrate its efforts on ambushing road traffic on the Via Balbia west of El Aghelia."

Lady Jane was studying Lt. Col. Randal. She was not smiling. He had switched from his normal demeanor of laid-back awareness to dead quiet calm.

Lady Jane knew that meant he was angry – very angry.

Jim knew it too.

So did Lt. Mandy.

And King.

Ex-Lt. Jaxx knew something had happened, but he was not sure what.

Lt. Col. Randal glanced at King. The Merc stood up and left the room. He went to find Mr. Zargo – the Colonel did not trust tactical intelligence obtained from anyone else.

"Where's Terry?" Lt. Col. Randal asked.

"Riding with his cousin on his first patrol as a newly commissioned officer," Lady Jane said, cold as ice.

"I need him back here."

"We can arrange to extract Terry tomorrow night," Lady Jane said.

"Good."

"Colonel, what is your answer?" Col. Clarke asked. "The military situation is rapidly deteriorating."

"I'll raid the airfields," Lt. Col. Randal said. "Interdicting the Via Balbia during a German counterattack – Charge of the Light Brigade for my gun jeeps."

"You believe attacking Rommel's main supply route is the equivalent of riding into the Valley of Death?" Col. Clark asked.

"Negative," Lt. Col. Randal said. "Worse."

"What shall I tell the Brigadier?"

"Consider it done."

LIEUTENANT COLONEL JOHN RANDAL AND CAPTAIN THE LADY Jane Seaborn were sitting out on the deck of their private suite looking at a million sparkling stars and the mellow candles flickering in the houses on both sides of the river down the cliff face of the Oasis.

It was a beautiful night. They were enjoying each other's company, not saying much. The radio was playing.

The music stopped… *"We interrupt this broadcast to bring you an important bulletin . . . Flash. Washington. The White House announces Japanese attack on Pearl Harbor…"*

~ ~

THE MISSION CONTINUES IN

– The Sharp End –

BOOK X IN THE RAIDING FORCES SERIES

COMING SOON

~ ~

Be the first to get updates and know about upcoming releases.
To be on our notification list, scan the QR below and sign up.

The Raiding Forces series continues all the way to VE Day.
phil@philward.com

~ ~

ACRONYMS

1SAS Brigade – 1Special Air Service Brigade
AB 40 – Autoblinda
AO – Area of Operation
AP – Armor Piercing
APL – Assistant Patrol Leader
AT – Anti–Tank
AVG – American Volunteer Group
BOAC – British Overseas Airways Corporation
COW – Coventry Ordnance Works
DSEA – Davis Submerged Escape Apparatus
DUKW – A two and a half–ton swimming tank
DZ – Drop Zone
ERP – Extraction Rally Point
FANY – Field Auxiliary Nursing Yeomanry
GHQ – General Headquarters
GHQME – General Headquarters Middle East
GP – General Purpose
HE – High Explosive
HUMINT – Human Intelligence
KDS – Khaki Drill Service (uniform)
LAF – Libyan Arab Force
LCT – Landing Craft Tank
LCVP – Landing Craft Vehicle Personnel
LRDG – Long Range Desert Group
LUP – Laying Up Position
MAS boat – Torpedo armed motorboat
MCF – Mobile Coastal Force
MEHQ – Middle East Command Headquarters
OCI – Office for Coordination of Information
ORP – Objective Rally Point
PLF – Parachute Landing Fall
POL – Petroleum, Oil and Lubrication (facilities)

ACRONYMS

PWE   – Political Warfare Executive
RAF   – Royal Air Force
RFHQ – Raiding Forces Headquarters
RNPS – Royal Navy Patrol Service
RTU   – Returned to Unit
SO   – Special Operations
SOE   – Special Operations Executive
SOP   – Standard Operating Procedure
TO&E –Table of Organization and Equipment
TOC   – Tactical Operations Center

AFRICA 1941
LIST OF CHARACTERS

Acting Provisional Sub-Lt. Skipper "Mud Cat" Ray, RNPS
Acting Provisional Sub-Lt. Skipper Warthog Finley, OBE, RNPS
Adm. William Canaris
Adm. of the Fleet Sir Roger Keyes
Air Chief Marshall Sir Richard Peirce
Amal Atrash
Bill Stirling
Brig. George Davy
Brig. Raymond J. "R.J." Maunsell
Capt. "Geronimo" Joe McKoy, OBE
Capt. "Pyro" Percy Stirling, DSO, MC
Capt. A.W. "Sammy" Sansom
Capt. Hawthorne Merryweather
Capt. James J. (Jimmy) Roosevelt
Capt. James M. Gavin
Capt. Jeb Pelham-Davies, DSO, MC
Capt. Lionel Chatterhorn, MC
Capt. Patrick Leigh Fermor
Capt. Penelope "Legs" Honeycutt-Parker, OBE, RM
Capt. Peter Fleming
Capt. Roy "Mad Dog" Reupart
Capt. Taylor Corrigan, DSO, MC Horse Guards
Capt. the Lady Jane Seaborn, OBE, RM
Capt. William P. Yarbrough
Cdr. David 'Big Sloth' Stirling
Cdr. Mallory Seaborn, RN
Cdre. Richard "Dickie the Pirate" Seaborn, VC, OBE
Col. Hugh Boustead, MC
Col. Stewart Menzies, DSO
Col. William 'Bill' Lee
Col. William "Wild Bill" Donovan
Count Laszlo Almásy
Cpl. Basil Bunfried
Cpl. Boyce Malcom
Diamond
Ex-Capt. Travis McCloud
Ex-Tech.Sgt. Hank W. Rawlston
Flanigan

Cont....

CHARACTERS Cont.

FM Claude Auchinleck
FM Erwin Rommel
FM Sir Archibald Wavell
Frank Polanski
Gen. Sir Archibald Stirling
Guns
James B. "Earthquake McGoon" McGovern
Jones
King
Lady Hermione Ranfurly
Lana Turner
2nd Lt. Billy Jack "Cool" Jaxx, MC
Lt. Alexandra (Mandy) Paige, RM
Lt. Butch "Headhunter" Hoolihan, DSO, MC, MM, RM
Lt. Fraser Llewellyn
Lt. Karen Montgomery
Lt. Jock Lewis
Lt. Pamala Plum-Martin, OBE, DFC w/2bar, RM
Lt. Randy "Hornblower" Seaborn, OBE, DSC, RM
Lt. Roy Kidd
Lt. Westcott Huxley, MC (Bar)
Lt. Cdr. Ian Fleming, RN
Lt. Cd. Milner-Gibson
Lt. Col. Dudley Clarke
Lt. Col. Geoffrey Keyes
Lt. Col. John Randal, DSO (4Bar), MC
Lovat Scout Lionel Fenwick
Lovat Scout Munro Ferguson
Maj. Clive Adair
Maj. Edwin Chapman-Andrews
Maj. Jack Black
Maj. Orde Wingate
Maj. Sir Terry "Zorro" Stone, KBE, DSO, MC
Maj. Vladimir "Popski" Peniakoff
Maj. Gen. James "Baldie"
Taylor, OBE
Mr. Z argo
Rikke (Rocky) Runborg

Cont....

CHARACTERS Cont.

Rita Hayworth
Sgt. Ned Pompedous
Sgt. Maj. Mike "March or Die" Mikkalis, DSM, MM
Sqn. Ldr. Paddy Wilcox, DSO, OBE, MC, DFC
The Great Teddy
VAdm. Sir Randolph "Razor" Ransom, VC, KCB, DSO, OBE, DSC
Veronica Paige
Waldo Treywick, OBE
Wg. Cdr. Ronald Gordon

ABOUT THE AUTHOR

Phil Ward is a highly decorated combat veteran commissioned when he was nineteen. He served as an instructor at the Army Ranger School. Now days Phil lives on a mountain overlooking Lake Austin.

<u>OTHER BOOKS IN THE RAIDING FORCES SERIES</u>:

Those Who Dare

Dead Eagles

Blood Wings

Roman Candle

Guerrilla Command

Necessary Force

Desert Patrol

Private Army

Africa 1941